THE ORIGINS OF EVERYTHING

OF

EVERYTHING

DIGGING INTO THE BEGINNINGS OF THINGS

WEST
SIDE
PUBLISHING

Contributing Writers: Jeff Bahr, Patricia Barnes-Svarney, Ellen Cutler, Susan Doll, Katherine Don, James Duplacey, Dave Gerardi, J. K. Kelley, Yi Shun Lai, Bill Martin, David Morrow, David A. Murray, Ken Sheldon, Peter Suciu, Donald Vaughan, and Jennifer Plattner Wilkinson

Factual Verification: Leigh Smith, Marci McGrath, and Chris Smith

Cover Illustration: Adrian Chesterman

Louis Weber, CEO
Publications International, Ltd.
7373 North Cicero Avenue
Lincolnwood, Illinois 60712

ISBN-13: 978-1-4127-1652-9
ISBN-10: 1-4127-1652-7

Manufactured in U.S.A.

8 7 6 5 4 3 2 1

Contents

❖ ❖ ❖ ❖

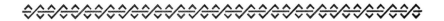

What Came First?

✦ ✦ ✦ ✦

On the face of it, it's the proverbial chicken-or-egg question. But as we developed the concept for our new *Armchair Reader™: The Origins of Everything,* we thought we might take a look at the idea from a different perspective. To start, we decided to research some synonyms for the word *origins.* Here's what we came up with: *source, provenance, root, derivation, base, basis, foundation, genesis, dawn, beginning, start, inception, outset, conception,* and *birth.* Of course, there are many others, but this list seemed like a good way to *begin* to create some sort of *foundation* for this book.

We know our readers appreciate trivia, so we hope your interests also extend to the origins, beginnings, and sources of all things—trivial or not. May you find this book as fascinating and enjoyable to read as we did while researching and compiling it for you.

As anthropologist George Dorsey said, "Play is the beginning of knowledge." In that spirit, please join us on an intellectual treasure hunt as we uncover the origins of topics that run the gamut from historically tantalizing to downright wild and wooly, including:

- The madman who made significant contributions to the *Oxford English Dictionary*
- The startling story behind the United States' role in the attack on Pearl Harbor
- The shocking truth about the inspiration for the Taser

As usual, please feel free to flop into your favorite armchair, kick back, and enjoy at your leisure the factual feast we've prepared.

Allen Orso
Publisher

P.S. If you have any questions, concerns, or ideas pertaining to this book, or you would like more information about other West Side titles, please contact us at: **www.armchairreader.com**

Language
The Vandals' Bad Rap

❖ ❖ ❖ ❖

It is generally believed that the word vandalism *derives from the barbarian Vandals who sacked Rome in* A.D. *455. In reality, the word has a more civilized origin.*

The Vandals were a Germanic barbarian tribe that made quite a name for themselves in the Mediterranean during the fifth century. Over 30 years, the Vandals romped from Poland westward through Europe, the Iberian peninsula, and North Africa, eventually establishing the Kingdom of the Vandals in modern-day Tunisia and Algeria after vanquishing Carthage in A.D. 439.

Have Pity for the Vandals
Why? Because their reputation as conquering warriors is not the one they have today. Instead, thanks to their plundering of Rome in A.D. 455, the Vandals are credited with inspiring the term that describes an act of malicious destruction.

The Vandals were only one of many barbarian hordes during the Dark Ages that ravaged the Western Roman Empire until its fall in A.D. 476. But they weren't any more barbaric than others, nor were they even the first to pillage Rome. Their German cousins, the Visigoths, had turned that trick 45 years earlier.

After a diplomatic falling-out between the two Mediterranean powers, the Vandals headed to Rome, where they plundered the city for two weeks. But even that was considered to be a relatively civilized affair, because the Vandals graciously refrained from wanton burning and violence.

So if the Vandals weren't all that vandalistic, where did the word *vandalism* originate? The answer is France, during the French Revolution. As that great experiment in civil liberty and equality began to descend into chaos, the bishop of Blois, Henri Grégoire, denounced what he termed the *vandalisme* of unruly mobs that went around destroying churches and private property.

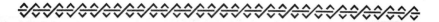

Inventions
The Cat Who Came in from the Cold
❖ ❖ ❖ ❖

Ed Lowe's innovation led to a new kind of pet—the indoor *cat.*

Cats have been beloved pets for thousands of years. For much of that time, though, felines were considered outdoor animals. They would often spend time in the house, but owners usually put them out at night. Staunch cat lovers who kept their pets indoors paid a rather smelly price, as commonly used cat box fillers such as sand, sawdust, or ashes did little to combat the notoriously rank odors that little Fluffy left behind.

In 1947, Kay Draper of Cassopolis, Michigan, found herself short of cat box filler and went to a neighbor's to see if he might have something she could use. Lucky for Kay and for cat lovers everywhere, her neighbor Ed Lowe was in the business of selling industrial absorbents, and he suggested she try some Fuller's earth—small granules of dried clay used for soaking up oil spills and such. After trying the clay, Draper raved that it was not only cleaner than other fillers she had used, but it also helped keep odors down, thanks to its tendency to chemically bind with the offending ammonia.

Smelling an opportunity, Lowe filled several paper bags with the stuff, scrawled the name "Kitty Litter" on the side, and headed to a local pet store. The owner was skeptical of the idea. Who would pay 65 cents for a bag of dirt when sand and sawdust were virtually free? Undaunted, Lowe told him to give the bags away to any customer willing to try it. Within a short time, those customers came back saying they would gladly pay for more.

Lowe spent the next few years driving around to pet stores and cat shows to promote his new product, and his diligence paid off. Today, Americans spend nearly $800 million a year on clay cat box filler—much of which goes to Lowe's company—and millions of pampered felines enjoy the luxury of indoor living.

Holidays & Traditions
An Eggscellent Easter Tradition

❖ ❖ ❖ ❖

Ancient confusion about animals in springtime led to a holiday icon.

Easter is both the most solemn and the most joyous event on the Christian calendar. But the history of this celebration is complicated, and modern Easter traditions include elements from a variety of spiritual practices. For instance, the term *paschal* describes the Christian season but also refers to *Pesach,* the Jewish Passover.

Decorated eggs have long been a part of Easter observances. In the 13th century, the church didn't allow eggs to be eaten during Holy Week, the week prior to Easter Sunday. Eggs reappeared on the dinner table on Easter Day as part of the celebration. These eggs were often colored red to symbolize joy. Hunting for eggs and giving decorated eggs as gifts came later.

Why, though, does the Easter Bunny deliver the eggs? When did this tradition begin? The link between Easter and rabbits is ancient. The word *Easter* is likely derived from the name of the mother goddess *Eostre,* who was worshipped by the ancient Saxons of northern Europe. Her festival coincided with the lengthening days that marked the arrival of spring and the return of life after a barren winter. Eostre's emblem was the hare; rabbits and hares have often been regarded as symbols of fertility. In one legend, Eostre magically changed a beautiful bird into a hare that built a nest and laid eggs.

Myths and folk traditions frequently offer explanations for natural events. Hares raise their babies, which are called *leverets,* in "forms." A form is a hollow in the ground of a field or meadow. Female hares, or does, often divide a litter among two or three forms for safety. Abandoned and empty forms attract plovers, a kind of wading bird, which occasionally move in and use the form as a nest for their own eggs. People saw hares in fields—seemingly hopping away from forms full of eggs—and concluded that the hares had laid the eggs.

As Christianity spread throughout the known world, it absorbed pagan beliefs and practices, endowing them with Christian meaning. Church officials placed observances of the events surrounding the crucifixion of Jesus in the early spring. Eggs, the source of new life, came to stand for Christ's resurrection from the tomb. The celebration of spring and the worship of the goddess Eostre became Christian Easter. In time, as distinctions between hares and rabbits were blurred, Eostre's hare became the Easter Rabbit.

The link between rabbits and Easter emerged most strongly in Protestant Europe during the 17th century, particularly in Germany. Boys and girls built "nests" with their caps and bonnets, and good children were rewarded with a "nest" full of colored eggs brought to them by the *Osterhas,* or Easter Rabbit. Variations of this practice came to America in the 18th century, especially with immigrants from Germany. A hunt for decorated Easter eggs left by the Easter Bunny became common in the 19th century.

One of the most charming and original takes on the Easter Bunny is *The Country Bunny and the Little Golden Shoes,* written by Dubose Heyward and illustrated by Marjorie Flack in 1939. Happily for devotees of Easter and rabbits, it is still in print.

Speaking of holiday icons, Rudolph the Red-nosed Reindeer was born 100 years later than the rest of his reindeer pals. This shiny-nosed hero of Christmas was created in 1939 by Robert L. May, a copywriter for Montgomery Ward, as an advertising gimmick.

Health & Medicine
Birth of the Magic Pill

❖ ❖ ❖ ❖

*Before 1960, activist Margaret Sanger dreamt of a
"magic pill" for birth control that women could take
as easily as an aspirin. This dream became a reality,
thanks to Sanger and a few well-placed friends.*

In the 1950s, as American women were having babies in unprecedented numbers, a big family was the perceived ideal. However,
many women longed for an inexpensive, reliable, and simple form of
contraception. Diaphragms were costly. Condoms and other contraceptives were unreliable. None were easy to use.

Fortunately, history brought together Margaret Sanger, Katharine McCormick, Gregory Pincus, and John Rock.

The Players

Born in 1879, Margaret Sanger was 19 when her mother, who
had given birth to 11 children and suffered 7 miscarriages, died
from tuberculosis. In 1916, as a nurse in New York treating poor
women recovering from botched illegal abortions, Sanger began
defying the law by distributing contraceptives. In 1921, she founded
the American Birth Control League, a precursor to the Planned
Parenthood Federation, and in 1923 opened the first legal birth
control clinic in the United States. For the next 30 years, Sanger
advocated for safe and effective birth control while dreaming of
a "magic pill" that would usher in an era of female-controlled
contraception.

Katharine Dexter McCormick was born into a prominent Chicago family in 1875. In 1904, she married Stanley McCormick, heir
to the International Harvester Corporation fortune. McCormick's
life changed when her husband developed schizophrenia. Believing
the condition to be hereditary, McCormick vowed to remain childless. In 1917, she met Sanger at a suffragette rally and took up her
cause. Following her husband's death in 1947, McCormick dedicated
his $15 million estate to the discovery of Sanger's "magic pill."

In January 1951, Sanger met Dr. Gregory Pincus, a once-heralded biologist at Harvard University who was vilified as "Dr. Frankenstein" after developing in-vitro fertilization in rabbits in 1934. Booted from Harvard, Pincus was working in obscurity at a Clark University lab when he met Sanger. He told Sanger her "magic pill" was possible by using hormones as a contraceptive. Sanger quickly arranged a grant from Planned Parenthood for Pincus to research the use of progesterone in inhibiting ovulation and preventing pregnancy. Within a year, Pincus confirmed that the drug was effective in lab animals.

A Bitter Pill

Pincus next set out to invent a progesterone pill, unaware that both Syntex and G.D. Searle pharmaceutical companies had already achieved it. (Neither company pursued its use as an oral contraceptive for fear of a public backlash.) Worse for Pincus, Planned Parenthood halted its funding, saying his research was too risky.

Things turned for Pincus in late 1952 following a chance encounter with Dr. John Rock, a renowned fertility expert and birth control advocate from Harvard. Rock was a devout Catholic who reconciled the Vatican's rigid stance against artificial birth control with his personal conviction that planned parenting and contraception promoted healthy marriages. Rock floored Pincus when he explained that his tests using progesterone injections on female patients (ironically, he was attempting to stimulate pregnancy) worked as a contraceptive.

A New Era

Then in June 1953, Sanger introduced Pincus to McCormick. Sold on Pincus's research, McCormick cut him a check for $40,000 to restart the pill project. Pincus recruited Rock, and in 1954, using progesterone pills provided by Searle, they conducted the first human trials of the drug with 50 women, successfully establishing the 21-day administering cycle still used today.

In May 1960, Searle received FDA approval to sell the progesterone pill, Enovid, for birth control purposes. Within five years, six million American women were using Sanger's "magic pill."

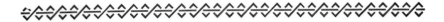

Household Items
A Perfect Container...But How Do You Open It?

❖ ❖ ❖ ❖

The can opener was certainly a sharp invention,
but it was also long overdue.

Before the can opener, there was a revolutionary (albeit somewhat half-baked) invention called the can. The process for canning food-stuffs was patented by Peter Durand of Britain in 1810, and the first commercial canning factory opened three years later. The British Army quickly became a leading customer for the innovative product. After all, the can greatly simplified the logistics of keeping the nation's soldiers fed. In 1846, a new machine that could produce 60 cans per hour increased the rate of production for tinned food tenfold. Life made easier through the wonders of technology, right?

Well, not exactly. In all that time, no one came up with a way to address the most serious drawback of this perfectly sealed, air-tight, solid-iron container: It was incredibly difficult to open! In fact, some cans actually came with instructions that read, "Cut 'round the top near the outer edge with a chisel and hammer."

It wasn't until the middle of the century—when manufacturers devised methods for producing thinner cans made of steel—that there was any hope of creating a simple and safe way to open them. In 1858, Ezra Warner of Connecticut patented the first functional can opener, a bulky thing resembling a bent bayonet that you shoved through the top of the can and then carefully forced around the lid. It was an improvement, no doubt, but still a tiresome and potentially dangerous way to get at your potted meat.

Then, in 1870, a full 60 years after the canning process was perfected, William Lyman designed an easy-to-use wheeled blade that could cut a can open as it rolled around the edge of the lid—essentially the same function as that of the can openers we use today. The next two big inventions in can-opening technology were a long time coming: The electric can opener appeared in the 1930s, and pull-open cans arrived in 1966.

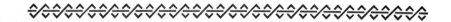

BIRTHDAYS OF THE RICH AND FAMOUS

Who can resist poking around to discover whether they share a birthday with a famous leader, legendary movie star, talented musician, or notorious celebrity?

January 31 is a great day to celebrate baseball birthdays. Jackie Robinson, the first African American to play major league baseball, was born on that day in 1919, as were Nolan Ryan (1947) and Mr. Cub himself, Ernie Banks (1931).

Now we're wondering whether Justin Timberlake likes to play baseball—he was born on January 31, 1981.

Rock legends Elvis Presley and David Bowie were born on January 8. Elvis was welcomed into the world by parents Vernon and Gladys in 1935, while Bowie, a.k.a. Ziggy Stardust, crash-landed in 1947.

Though we don't celebrate Martin Luther King Jr.'s birthday on the same day each year, his birth date is January 15, 1929.

Let's go down the rabbit hole. Lewis Carroll, author of *Alice's Adventures in Wonderland*, was born on January 27, 1832.

Remember to look up in the skies on February 4, because that is the birthday of aviator Charles "Lucky Lindy" Lindbergh (1902) and astronomer Clyde Tombaugh (1906), who discovered Pluto.

February 5 is National Weatherman's Day because that is the birthday of the first official weatherman, John Jeffries, born in 1744. Jeffries kept weather records from 1774 to 1816.

Famous athletes Jim Brown and Michael Jordan were both born on February 17—Brown in 1936 and Jordan in 1963. They are in the unlikely company of the infamous Paris Hilton, who was born on that day in 1981.

Beware the Ides of March, which is the 15th. On that day in 1961, model and I Can't Believe It's Not Butter! spokesperson Fabio was born.

Language
"Keeping up with the Joneses"

❖ ❖ ❖ ❖

*On the surface, keeping up with the Joneses may seem
to be a cultural cliché about competing with one's
neighbors, but its origin is far more literal.*

"Keeping up with the Joneses" refers to the need to be considered
as good as one's neighbors, contemporaries, or coworkers, using the
accumulation of material goods as a measuring stick.

Although the popularity of the phrase is usually credited to a
popular comic strip of the same name that was created by cartoonist
Arthur R. "Pop" Momand, its origin can be traced to a column in the
February 15, 1894, edition of a New Philadelphia, Ohio, newspaper
called *Ohio Democrat.* In a report on common surnames in the area,
the paper reported "The New Philadelphia Directory shows the
names of 30 Smiths, 30 Millers, 29 Joneses, and 28 Kniselys. This is
a pretty good showing for the Millers and the Kniselys, when they
can keep up with the Smiths and the Joneses."

The *Keeping Up With the Joneses* comic strip created by
Momand ran in *The New York World* newspaper from 1913 until
the early 1940s. Mr. Momand said the strip was based on his obser-
vations of life in Cedarhurst, New York, where he and his wife had
lived "far beyond their means" in a vain effort to keep pace with "the
well-to-do class." The main characters in the strip were the McGinis
family—dad Aloysius, mom Clarice, daughter Julie, and housemaid
Belladonna. Interestingly, the Joneses of the title were often mentioned in the strip but never seen, which added to their allure.

In the 1950s, *The Daily Mirror* newspaper, the British daily that
spawned the popular *Andy Capp* cartoon, also ran a strip called
Keeping Up with the Joneses, but it had no relation to Pop Momand's
creation beyond the title.

Inventions
An Indispensable Machine

❖ ❖ ❖ ❖

*Vending machines are a part of modern living, but
they've been around much longer than you think.*

Vending machines seem to be distinctly modern contraptions—steel automatons with complex inner workings that give up brightly packaged goods to anyone with a few coins to spare. The first modern versions were used in London in the 1880s to dispense postcards and books. A few years later, they were adopted in America by the Thomas Adams Gum Company for dispensing Tutti-Frutti-flavored gum on subway platforms in New York City. The idea of an automated sales force caught on quickly, and vending machines were soon found almost everywhere. The idea perhaps reached its peak in Philadelphia with the Automat, which opened in 1902. These "waiterless" restaurants allowed patrons to buy a wide variety of foods by plunking a few coins into a box.

Today, we think of vending machines as an everyday part of our lives. Americans drop more than $30 billion a year into them, and Japan has one vending machine for every 23 of its citizens. All kinds of products—from skin care items, pajamas, and umbrellas to DVDs, iPods, ring tones, and digital cameras—can be bought without ever interacting with a salesperson.

As high-tech as all that may be, the most remarkable thing about vending machines lies not in the modern era but in the distant past. A Greek mathematician and engineer named Hero of Alexander built the very first vending machine in 215 B.C.! Patrons at a temple in Egypt would drop a coin into his device. Landing on one end of a lever, the heavy coin would tilt the lever upward and open a stopper that released a set quantity of holy water. When the coin slid off, the lever would return to its original position, shutting off the flow of water.

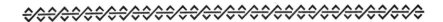

Places & Landmarks
State Capitals

The capitals of more than half of the 50 United States were once somewhere else. Some states moved their capitals for convenience or political gain. Others used to have co-capitals or rotating capitals. Match each state to its original capital.

State	Capital
Alabama	Bowling Green
Arkansas	Cahawba
California	Charleston
Connecticut	Chillicothe
Delaware	Corydon
Georgia	Detroit
Illinois	Donaldsonville
Indiana	Exeter
Iowa	Guthrie
Kentucky	Iowa City
Louisiana	Kaskaskia
Maine	Kingston
Michigan	Lancaster
Mississippi	Milledgeville
Missouri	Murfreesboro
New Hampshire	Natchez
New York	Neosho
North Carolina	New Bern

State	Capital
Ohio	New Castle
Oklahoma	New Haven
Pennsylvania	Newport
Rhode Island	Portland
South Carolina	Vallejo
Tennessee	Washington
Vermont	Wheeling
West Virginia	Windsor

Some Current States and Their Early Names

- *Delaware—Lower Counties on Delaware*
- *Connecticut—Connecticut Colony*
- *Rhode Island—Colony of Rhode Island and Providence Plantations*
- *Vermont—Province of New York and New Hampshire Grants*
- *Kentucky—Virginia (Kentucky County)*
- *Tennessee—Province of North Carolina, Southwest Territory*
- *Ohio—Northwest Territory*
- *Maine—Massachusetts*
- *Texas—Republic of Texas*
- *California—California Republic*
- *Oregon—Oregon Territory*
- *Hawaii—Kingdom of Hawaii, Republic of Hawaii*

Fads & Fashion
The Ears Have It

♦ ♦ ♦ ♦

An industrious boy earned a fortune by keeping his ears warm.

Chester Greenwood was a hard-working boy from Farmington, Maine, who endured a typical hardscrabble childhood in rural New England. Disciplined and diligent, he dropped out of school to help his large family by working on the farm and trekking eight miles to deliver eggs and fudge to his neighbors. This was one of the few occasions when he had the opportunity to indulge in the fun that led to his fortune.

A Cool Idea

In the winter of 1873, the 15-year-old headed to a nearby pond to try out a new pair of ice skates. Before he reached his destination, he had to turn back because the bitter cold was hurting his ears. Determined to go skating, Greenwood took a piece of baling wire he found around the farm and formed a loop at each end. He brought the wire and some beaver fur to his grandmother and asked her to sew the material onto the loops. Then he slipped the device over his head.

Getting Warmer

Young Chester never had to worry about cold ears—or making his first million—again. His "Greenwood Champion Ear Protector" eventually became the familiar winter item we call earmuffs—but only after a few more years of tinkering. Unsatisfied with the loose fit of the original design, Greenwood improved his invention by using a wide steel band instead of wire. This allowed him to add hinges where the band connected to the muff, so the fabric could fit snugly against the ears and the device could be folded when not in use.

Chester earned a patent for the revised design in 1877 at the age of 18 and then opened a factory near his hometown. His business became a central part of Farmington's economy, and it remains the largest producer of earmuffs in the world.

FOOD & DRINK

I Scream, You Scream, We All Scream for Ice-Cream... Cones!

Germs and sheer chance prompted an American classic.

The story of the first ice-cream cone has become part of American mythology. The stock story is that a young ice-cream vendor at the 1904 St. Louis World's Fair ran out of dishes. Next to him was waffle-maker Ernest Hamwi. Hamwi got the idea to roll his waffles into a cone, and now, more than a century later, we're reaping his legacy.

But the ice-cream cone wasn't just born of convenience or a vendor's poor planning. Germs played a role, too. Italian immigrants spearheaded the introduction of ice cream to the general public, first in Europe and then in the United States. Called *hokey pokey men* (a bastardization of an Italian phrase), these street vendors sold "penny licks," a small glass of ice cream that cost a single penny. The vendors wiped the glass with a rag after the customer was done and then served the next person. Forget the fact that people occasionally walked off with the glasses. Forget the fact that the glasses would sometimes break. This is about as sanitary as the space under your refrigerator. Unsurprisingly, people got sick. Ice-cream vendors needed a new serving method.

In the early 1900s, two people—Antonio Valvona and Italo Marchiony—independently invented an edible ice-cream cup. But this was just a cup; again, the cone did not appear until 1904.

Today, cones come in many varieties, but in 1904, Hamwi was making *zalabia*, a cross between a waffle and a wafer covered in sugar or syrup. He called his creation a *cornucopia* (a horn-of-plenty, a symbol of autumn harvest), and after the fair, he founded the Cornucopia Waffle Company with a business partner. A few years later, he started his own company, the Missouri Cone Co., and finally named his rolled-up waffles "ice-cream cones." How sweet it is!

Clubs & Organizations
Behind the Seal

❖ ❖ ❖ ❖

The secret's out: A legendary fraternal organization is not quite as mysterious as people have been led to believe.

Conspiracy theorists delight in telling how the Freemasons rose from the ashes of the Knights Templar (an earlier secret society that protected Christians on the road to Jerusalem and supposedly guarded the location of the Holy Grail), founded the United States of America, and continue to shape world politics under the guise of their sister organization, the Illuminati. The truth, however, is much more sedate and much less "Hollywood."

Freemasonry is a fraternal organization—originally comprised of stonemasons and craftsmen—that now admits anyone who believes in a Supreme Being, is invited by an existing member, and enacts several secretive rituals. Before it became a gentlemen's society in the 1600s, Freemasonry was a guild of stonemasons working in and around England and Scotland. The "free" part of the name refers to the fact that they were not tied to the land, unlike most European people of the 14th and 15th centuries.

Secretive or Just Undocumented?

Although Freemasonry practices secrecy, its murky origins are due more to the lack of reliable historical records than to outright conspiracy. Freemasons pass down a story called the "Key of Solomon" as an allegorical creation myth for their guild. This story describes Freemasonry as originating during the building of Solomon's Temple, which itself was a monumental work of stonecraft in the 10th century B.C. Sources point to meetings at Masonic lodges in England as early as 1390, but it wasn't until the 1800s that the group had a real lasting impact. The first Grand Master was elected in 1717 at London's Goose and Gridiron alehouse. This new Mother Grand Lodge of the World ushered in the founding of Grand Lodges around Europe and North America and began the society's most influential period.

The principles of Freemasonry echoed those of the Enlightenment, such as charity and religious and political tolerance. The symbols that make up the seal of the Freemasons—a crossed square and compasses—are an architect's tools and represent the Masonic belief in a "Great Architect"—God. The three central tenets of Freemasonry are brotherly love, relief (charity), and truth.

During the 18th century, the Age of Enlightenment ushered in reform throughout Europe and North America. Freemasonry subscribed to these principles and helped shape the American and French revolutions, although—contrary to conspiracy theorists' claims—it did not foment these events alone. Freemasonry should instead be seen as part of the intellectual framework that countered the tyranny and superstition still dominating Europe.

Because of their nondenominational religious beliefs and criticism of the role of the Church, Freemasons were first condemned by the 1738 Papal Bull, *In Eminenti,* which charged Church authorities to pursue and punish people involved in Freemasonry. Later pronouncements contained similar censure. During the mid-20th century, Nazi Germany and Stalinist Russia sent Freemasons to concentration camps.

The abject secrecy propagated by members has fostered numerous myths and legends about their origins. Some of these myths have become fodder for conspiracy novelists like Dan Brown and Umberto Eco. Still, links between the Freemasons and the Knights Templar (as their direct successor) or the Catholic Church (as their private group of church builders) or even the Illuminati (as proponents of a New World Order) are only speculative.

Fun and Fellowship

What *is* known is that the Freemasons act to help each other by providing business and political contacts and resources. Purported members include almost every British king, Voltaire, Mozart, Benjamin Franklin, and presidents George Washington and Franklin Delano Roosevelt—an impressive list. The Shriners (the guys with the red fez hats and tiny cars) are also Masons. Primarily a charitable organization, the Shriners, or Shrine Masons, began in 1872 to promote "fun and fellowship." Not so mysterious anymore, is it?

Television
The Origins of the Couch Potato
❖ ❖ ❖ ❖

We couldn't remotely *imagine watching TV without
our trusty remote controls, but believe it or not,
American families used to do just that.*

These days, remote controls are a key part of the television viewing experience. In fact, virtually 100 percent of the televisions sold
in this country come with a remote control. But when TVs started
cropping up in living rooms across the United States in the late
1940s, viewing programs required a lot of up and down activity. As
families gathered together to catch the latest variety shows, countless
children of that generation became begrudgingly accustomed to the
order to "get up and change the channel."

Taking Control
In 1950, Zenith became the first television manufacturer to offer
a remote control for its product. The Lazy Bones device allowed
viewers to turn the channel up or down and switch the TV on or
off, but it was a wired device and the 20-foot cable strung across the
living room floor was such a nuisance that few customers used it.
Seeking to eliminate the cord, Zenith engineers came up with the
Flashmatic, which was essentially a bulky flashlight that sent a signal
to light receptors in one of the four corners of the screen to control
the television. This system also had its shortcomings: The receptors
in the screen could also be activated accidentally by other light
sources.

Things Start to Click
Zenith engineer Robert Adler hit on the idea of using ultrasonic
sound for the control mechanism. He and his team developed a
system that used carefully tooled and cut aluminum rods inside the
remote. When someone pressed a button on the remote, a hammer
struck these rods. Each rod was cut to a slightly different length
and vibrated at a slightly different frequency, making each produce

a distinct ultrasonic sound. A complex array of receptors in the
set recognized the sounds, performing a different action for each
one. One remarkable aspect of Adler's device, which was called the
"Space Command," was that it was entirely mechanical. The remote
operated without batteries or any other power source. Some factions
at Zenith objected to the idea of a battery-powered remote because
they actually feared that if the batteries went dead, customers would
assume their television was broken. One serious shortcoming of the
Space Command, though, was that it increased the cost of a set by
30 percent, due largely to the expense of the receptors.

The company began manufacturing Adler's Space Command
remote in 1956, and the ultrasonic technology remained in use in
virtually all remotes for the next 25 years, though in the 1960s the
devices switched from the mechanical design to one that relied on
transistors. Today's models use infrared light rather than sound to
send their signals to the set.

The Mystery Control

*As an interesting aside, the Lazy Bones was not the first device used
in the home to control an entertainment system. Some radio and phonograph manufacturers also offered remotes for their products as
early as the 1930s. Philco, for example, sold one whose name speaks to
the novelty of the technology at that time—the Mystery Control. This
bulky contraption had a rotary dial much like a telephone. Each "number" on the dial controlled a different function by emitting radio waves
that were recognized by the radio or phonograph. Remarkably, the
very first remote control devices of any sort appeared at the end of the
19th century; one of the earliest patents was awarded to famous inventor Nikola Tesla. These remotes were intended to operate machinery or
even vehicles, but the applications never proved practical.*

*"Television is like the invention of indoor plumbing. It didn't change
people's habits. It just kept them inside the house."*
—Alfred Hitchcock

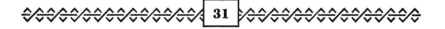

Prolific Producers

*These "movers and shakers" are responsible for more than
their fair share of the world's greatest accomplishments.*

With more than 570 million copies of her books in print, and each
one a best-seller, **Danielle Steel** is regarded as one of the most
popular current authors. Branching out from this wide-reaching
platform, 21 of the author's novels have been adapted for television. In a marketing coup staged during the 1980s, one or more
of Steel's books graced *The New York Times* best-seller list for a
period lasting more than 390 consecutive weeks. The amazing feat
earned Steel a spot in the 1989 edition of the *Guinness Book of
World Records.*

In addition to vast humanitarian contributions, famed educator
George Washington Carver left his prolific signature on the field
of agricultural research. Carver's work resulted in the creation of
some 325 peanut-based products, alongside hundreds of additional
products stemming from potatoes and plants. All added mightily to
the fiscal advancement of the American South—a cotton-centered
region sorely in need of economic stimuli.

When it comes to Olympic gold medals, American swimmer
Michael Phelps is without peer. Since the 2004 Summer Games
in Athens, Phelps has run roughshod over most of his challengers
and accumulated an astounding 14 gold medals. In 2008 at the
Beijing Games, Phelps won eight Olympic gold medals. The
improbable tally eclipsed the bounty of seven that had been
awarded to American swimmer Mark Spitz in 1972. Equally
astounding, Phelps set seven world records in the process. With
plans to compete in the 2012 Summer Olympics, Phelps's "hardware hunt" may yet bear more golden fruit.

ADVERTISING

Origins of 11 Modern Icons

Who knows what makes some characters endure while others slip through our consciousness quicker than 50 bucks in the gas tank? In any case, you'll be surprised to learn how some of our most endearing "friends" made their way into our lives.

1. The Aflac Duck
A duck pitching insurance? Art director Eric David stumbled upon the idea to use a web-footed mascot one day when he continuously uttered, "Aflac...Aflac...Aflac." It didn't take him long to realize how much the company's name sounded like a duck's quack. There are many fans of the campaign, but actor Ben Affleck is not one of them. Not surprisingly, he fields many comments that associate his name with the duck and is reportedly none too pleased.

2. Alfred E. Neuman, the face of *MAD* magazine
Chances are you're picturing a freckle-faced, jug-eared kid, right? The character's likeness, created by portrait artist Norman Mingo, was first adopted by *MAD* in 1954 as a border on the cover. Two years later, the humor magazine used a full-size version of the image as a write-in candidate for the 1956 presidential election. Since then, several *real* people have been said to be "separated at birth" from Mr. Neuman, namely Ted Koppel, Jimmy Carter, and George W. Bush.

3. Betty Crocker
Thousands of letters were sent to General Mills in the 1920s, all asking for answers to baking questions. Managers created a fictional character to give the responses a personal touch. The surname Crocker was chosen to honor a retired executive, and Betty was selected because it seemed "warm and friendly." In 1936, artist Neysa McMein blended the faces of several female employees to create a likeness. Crocker's face has changed many times over the years. She's been made to look younger, more professional, and now has a more multicultural look. At one point, a public opinion poll rating famous women placed Betty second to Eleanor Roosevelt.

4. Duke, the Bush's Baked Beans Dog

Who else to trust with a secret recipe but the faithful family pooch? Bush Brothers & Company was founded by A. J. Bush and his two sons in 1908. The company is currently headed by A. J.'s grandson, Condon. In 1995, the advertising agency working for Bush's Baked Beans decided that Jay Bush (Condon's son) and his golden retriever, Duke, were the perfect team to represent the brand. The only problem was that the real Duke is camera shy, so a stunt double was hired to portray him and handle all the gigs on the road with Jay. In any case, both dogs have been sworn to secrecy.

5. The California Raisins

Sometimes advertising concepts can lead to marketing delirium. In 1987, a frustrated copywriter at Foote, Cone & Belding was working on the California Raisin Advisory Board campaign and said, "We have tried everything but dancing raisins singing 'I Heard It Through the Grapevine.' " With vocals by Buddy Miles and design by Michael Brunsfeld, the idea was pitched to the client. The characters plumped up the sales of raisins by 20 percent, and the rest is Claymation history!

6. Joe Camel

Looking for a way to revamp Camel's image from an "old man's cigarette" in the late 1980s, the R.J. Reynolds marketing team uncovered illustrations of Old Joe in their archives. (He was originally conceived for an ad campaign in France in the 1950s.) In 1991, the new Joe Camel angered children's advocacy groups when a study revealed that more kids under the age of eight recognized Joe than Mickey Mouse or Fred Flintstone.

7. The Coppertone Girl

It was 1959 when an ad for Coppertone first showed a suntanned little girl's white buttocks being exposed by a puppy pulling on her bottoms. "Don't be a paleface!" was the slogan, and it reflected the common belief of the time that a suntan was healthy. Artist Joyce Ballantyne Brand created the pig-tailed little girl in the image of her three-year-old daughter, Cheri. When the campaign leapt off the printed page and into the world of television, it became Jodie Foster's acting debut. As the 21st century beckoned, and along with it changing views on sun exposure and nudity, Coppertone revised the drawing to reveal only the girl's lower back.

8. The Gerber Baby

Contrary to some popular beliefs, it's not Humphrey Bogart, Elizabeth Taylor, or Bob Dole who so sweetly looks up from the label of Gerber

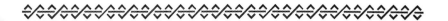

products. In fact, the face that appears on all Gerber baby packaging belongs to mystery novelist Ann Turner Cook. In 1928, when Gerber began its search for a baby face to help promote its new brand of baby food, Dorothy Hope Smith submitted a simple charcoal sketch of her four-month-old neighbor, Anne Cook—promising to complete the drawing if chosen. As it turned out, that wasn't necessary because the powers that be at Gerber liked it just the way it was. In 1996, Gerber updated its look, but the new label design still incorporates Cook's baby face.

9. Mr. Whipple
The expression "Do as I say, not as I do" took on a persona in the mid-1960s—Mr. Whipple, to be specific. This fussy supermarket manager (played by actor Dick Wilson) was famous for admonishing his shoppers by saying, "Ladies, *please* don't squeeze the Charmin!" The people at Benton & Bowles Advertising figured that if, on camera, Mr. Whipple was a habitual offender of his own rule, Charmin toilet paper would be considered the cushiest on the market. The campaign included a total of 504 ads and ran from 1965 until 1989, landing it a coveted spot in the *Guinness Book of World Records*. A 1979 poll listed Mr. Whipple as the third most recognized American behind Richard Nixon and Billy Graham.

10. The Pillsbury Doughboy
Who could resist poking the chubby belly of this giggling icon? This cheery little kitchen dweller was "born" in 1965 when the Leo Burnett advertising agency dreamt him up to help Pillsbury sell its refrigerated dinner rolls. The original vision was for an animated character, but instead, agency producers borrowed a unique stop-action technique used on *The Dinah Shore Show*. After beating out more than 50 other actors, Paul Frees lent his voice to the Doughboy. So, if you ever craved Pillsbury rolls while watching *The Rocky and Bullwinkle Show,* it's no wonder...Frees was also the voice for Boris Badenov and Dudley Do-Right.

11. Ronald McDonald
Perhaps the most recognizable advertising icon in the world, this beloved clown made his television debut in 1963, played by future *Today* weatherman Willard Scott. Nicknamed the "hamburger-happy clown," Ronald's look was a bit different back then: He had curly blond hair, a fast-food tray for a hat, a magic belt, and a paper cup for a nose. Today, McDonald's serves more than 52 million customers a day around the globe.

Fads & Fashion
Maybe She's Born with It...

❖ ❖ ❖ ❖

*T. L. Williams boosted his sister's love life and
revolutionized the cosmetics industry in the process.*

It was 1913, and as the story goes, Mabel Williams had man trouble:
Another woman had caught the eye of her beau, Chet, and poor
Mabel didn't know what to do. Her brother, T. L. Williams, a chem-
ist by trade, set his sights on a solution to the problem. The answer?
More dramatic eyelashes, of course! He came up with a concoc-
tion of Vaseline-brand petroleum jelly and coal dust to darken and
thicken Mabel's eyelashes. What man could resist? Apparently not
Chet—he and Mabel married the following year.

Mr. Williams realized that what worked for Mabel would work for
any woman. To market his new mascara, he formed a company called
Maybelline—named after his sister and Vaseline, one of the lash darkener's principal ingredients—and took the cosmetics industry by storm.

Of course, T. L. Williams was not the first person to come up
with this kind of beauty aid. The earliest known eye darkener, kohl,
was an ancient Egyptian mixture that came in a variety of formulas based on minerals such as malachite, lead, or manganese. The
upper classes of many later cultures also had their own methods of
accentuating eyelashes. But Williams's invention was both affordable
and convenient to use. He sold it via mail order in cake form, with a
small brush that would be wetted, rubbed in the mascara, and then
dabbed on the lashes. He also enjoyed the benefit of excellent timing, as prudish Victorian attitudes about "painted ladies" were fading
and the dark-eyed vamps of Hollywood silent films, such as Theda
Bera, were just coming onto the scene.

Soon Maybelline mascara was a must-have item on every woman's vanity, and by the 1930s, it was commonly available in retail drug
stores across the nation. And just in case you're wondering, Maybelline and all other cosmetics companies long ago abandoned the use
of coal-based ingredients in their products, having found safer and
more effective coloring agents.

Visual Art
A Portrait of Oils

✦ ✦ ✦ ✦

The unique characteristics of oil paint contributed to the accomplishments of the Renaissance—and still inspire artists today.

Paintings are among the most ancient of artworks. More than 30,000 years ago, Neolithic painters decorated caves with patterns and images of animals. All paints include two elements: pigment and a liquid binder. Pigments from charred wood and colored minerals are ground into a fine powder. Then they are mixed into the binder; linseed oil is the most popular, but other oils, including walnut oil, are common.

The idea of using oil as a binder for pigment is very old, but oil paints as we know them are relatively modern. In the 12th century, a German monk named Theophilus wrote about oil paint in his "Schoedula Diversarum Artium" and warned against paint recipes using olive oil because they required excessively long drying times. The Italian painter and writer Cennino Cennini described the technique of oil painting in his encyclopedic *Book of Art*. Oil paints came into general use in northern Europe, in the area of the Netherlands, by the 15th century and, from there, spread southward into Italy. Oils remained the medium of choice for most painters until the mid-20th century.

Oil paintings are usually done on wood panels or canvas, although paintings on stone and specialty paper are not uncommon. In any case, the support material is usually prepared with a ground to which oil paint easily adheres. Oil paints dry slowly, an advantage to artists, who adjust their compositions as they work. When the painting is done, a protective layer of varnish is often applied. In the 19th century, oil paint in tubes simplified the painter's work. A rainbow of innovative, synthetic colors contributed to the emergence of new approaches to art and, in particular, modern abstract painting.

Clubs & Organizations
Doomed Cults and Social Experiments

❖ ❖ ❖ ❖

On the upside, cults have the possibility of offering people acceptance and a sense of community when they would not otherwise have it. On the downside, if you join a cult, you could die.

The People's Temple

The Leader: Jim Jones started his People's Temple with the idea that social justice should be available to all—even the marginalized, the poor, and minorities. He established a commune outside San Francisco in 1965 with about 80 people. Jones capitalized on the rising tide of activism in the 1960s, recruiting affluent, Northern California hippies to help the working-class families who were already members of the People's Temple. The People's Temple helped the poorer members of its group navigate the confusing social welfare system. The Temple opened a church in an impoverished section of San Francisco that provided a number of social services, such as free blood pressure testing, free sickle-cell anemia testing, and free child care for working families.

The Turning Point: Not all was as it appeared inside the People's Temple. A perfect storm of complaints from disaffected members, media reports that questioned the Temple's treatment of current members, and an IRS investigation led Jones to move the People's Temple to Guyana, on the northern tip of South America. In the summer and fall of 1977, the People's Temple started what was supposed to be a utopian agricultural society, which it called Jonestown.

The Demise: In November 1978, U.S. Representative Leo Ryan of San Francisco led a fact-finding mission in response to constituents' concerns that members of the Temple were being kept in Guyana against their will. He offered to help anyone who wanted to leave. A few members joined him, but as the congressional party was waiting

on a landing strip for transportation, attackers drove out of the jungle and shot at them. Ryan and four others were killed.

Apparently worried about the closer scrutiny all this could bring, Jones ordered his followers to commit "revolutionary suicide" by drinking FlavorAid laced with cyanide on November 18. More than 900 members of the People's Temple died.

The Family

The Leader: Charles Manson was worried about pollution and the damage it would do to the environment. Unfortunately, he manifested his concern by brainwashing teenagers and sending them on murder sprees. Manson had a hard life—spent mostly in juvenile halls, jail, and institutions. He eventually ended up in San Francisco, surrounded by young women, most of whom were emotionally unstable and in love with him. With a group of these girls, he headed south to Los Angeles.

The Turning Point: After moving into the Spahn Ranch north of Los Angeles, where Manson and his followers survived by scavenging food discarded from grocery stores, he started to polish what he considered his philosophy—an Armageddon in which race wars, what he called *Helter Skelter*, would break out. According to this philosophy, Manson would, coincidentally, be the one who would guide the war's aftermath and, therefore, rule the world.

Reportedly in an attempt to spark these race wars, the Manson Family staged a series of mass murders, most famously that of Sharon Tate and her houseguests on August 9, 1969. On orders from Manson, four members of the Family killed Tate and her three friends. They did it, according to Susan Atkins, one of the murderers, to shock the world.

The Demise: Bragging to others about their murder sprees ultimately undid the Family. Friends of Manson eventually told police details of the murders. But the problem wasn't exactly finding the culprits—the problem was proving that members of the Family were responsible for the murders Manson ordered them to perform. Ultimately, a grand jury took only 20 minutes to hand down indictments in the cases against members of the Family.

Branch Davidians

The Leader: David Koresh joined the Branch Davidians in 1981. The group had been in existence since 1955, having broken off from the Davidian Seventh-Day Adventists, which itself was a group that split with the Seventh-Day Adventist church more than 20 years before that. Koresh was amiable and flamboyant, easygoing and intelligent. After a face-off with the son of the leader of the Branch Davidians, Koresh ended up as the group's leader and spiritual guide. As all serious cult leaders know, it was important not only to establish himself as the lord, but also to impress upon his flock the impending apocalypse and the absolute necessity of following the rules he created.

The Turning Point: Koresh stockpiled weapons in anticipation of inevitable attacks. He taught his followers that they should prepare for the end. He questioned their loyalty and expected them to kill themselves for the cause. On February 28, 1993, the end began. Based on reports of illegal arms sales, child abuse, and polygamy, federal agents raided the Mount Carmel Center near Waco, Texas, setting off a gunfight that ultimately set up a 51-day siege of the Branch Davidian compound.

The Demise: On April 19, 1993, federal agents, in an attempt to force the Davidians out, launched tear gas into the compound. Koresh and the Davidians, none too happy about this, began shooting. The agents injected more gas, and the tug-of-war continued for several hours. About six hours after the gassing began, fires erupted inside the compound. Accusations were made as to which side was responsible for the fires, but later investigations concluded that they had been set by the Branch Davidians. The fires were followed by more gunfire in the compound, and agents on the scene reportedly believed the Davidians were either killing themselves or shooting one another. Firefighters came to the scene but were not allowed to combat the flames for some time out of fear of gunfire. After the smoke had cleared, 75 people within the compound were found dead. Koresh was identified by dental records; he had been killed by a gunshot to the head.

War & Military
Bomb in a Bottle

❖ ❖ ❖ ❖

You don't toast the bride with this cocktail.

The Molotov cocktail is a crude but effective hand-held weapon that can be put together as simply as a grade-school science experiment: Fill a slim, easily gripped bottle to about the three-quarter mark with gasoline or other flammable liquid (kerosene and even wood alcohol will do); push a wicklike shred of oily rag snugly into the neck of the bottle; and wait for the perfect moment. Then light the rag, fling the bottle, and watch for the red-orange explosion of fire. The ideal outcome is a panicked scramble of enemy troops, some of them ablaze and many out in the open, where they can be picked off by gunfire.

Originally known as the petrol or gasoline bomb, this simple but intimidating weapon took its most enduring name from Soviet Foreign Minister Vyacheslav Molotov, who claimed on radio broadcasts during his nation's brutal 1939–40 Winter War against Finland that the USSR wasn't dropping bombs on the Finns, despite all evidence to the contrary. The Finnish Army jokingly responded to the foreign minister's lie by calling the Soviet air bombs "Molotov breadbaskets." Finnish troops had already been using petrol bombs against the invading Soviets (the devices had been widely used in the Spanish Civil War of 1936–39) and soon dubbed them "Molotov cocktails."

During the Winter War, Finland's national alcohol retailing monopoly, Alko, manufactured 450,000 bottle bombs made from a mix of ethanol, tar, and gasoline—perhaps the only time the weapon has been professionally produced on a mass scale.

That winter, the Finns bloodied the Soviets far more seriously than the world anticipated, and although they ultimately lost the brutish little war, "Molotov cocktail" would shortly enter the popular lexicon.

Cheers.

Places & Landmarks
From Desert Watering Hole to Sin City

❖ ❖ ❖ ❖

Two events and three men combined to create Las Vegas and its glittering strip of fantasy-themed casino resorts. Now it's one of the world's top gambling and tourist destinations.

There's really no place in the world like Las Vegas. It's a world-renowned mecca for gaming, entertainment, and shopping. Once a mobster paradise, the city now bills itself as the Entertainment Capital of the World, and it's still a place where one can get into trouble without actually getting into *trouble*.

Before all the lights and splendor, however, Las Vegas wasn't much of anything. It began as a 19th-century pioneer trail outpost where desert-weary California-bound settlers drew fresh water from the artesian wells in the surrounding Las Vegas Valley.

No Gambling? No Dice!

In 1905, Las Vegas became a railroad town (incorporated as the City of Las Vegas in 1911) with service facilities, supply stores, and saloons. But Vegas's growth was stunted for the next two decades when in 1909, the Nevada legislature killed the best thing the town had going for it: legalized gambling.

The Appeal of the Gambling Repeal

In 1931, Nevada repealed the ban on gambling, ostensibly to raise tax money to fund its public school system but also to undermine the state's thriving illegal gambling industry. Soon downtown Las Vegas became host to a slew of roughneck casinos sporting a few slot machines, gaming tables, and—in some cases—sawdust floors.

That same year, construction began on the Hoover Dam 34 miles south of Las Vegas, bringing an unprecedented influx of workers and tourists to southern Nevada. But with nothing to do in nearby Boulder City (the town built by the federal government for dam workers where alcohol and gaming remained illegal), workers and tourists

alike streamed north along Highway 91, heading to Vegas to find their fun.

The Strip Is Born

One man, Thomas Hull (owner of the California-based El Rancho motel chain), noticed the busy traffic—particularly the heavy flow of Vegas-bound travelers from Los Angeles. Seeking to attract their business, Hull opened the El Rancho Vegas in April 1941 on a stretch of Highway 91 just south of Vegas city limits. This area eventually morphed into the famous Las Vegas Strip.

The El Rancho wasn't your typical Vegas gaming joint. The sprawling Spanish mission–style complex featured a main casino building surrounded by such welcoming amenities as 65 guest cottages, a swimming pool, a nightclub, a steakhouse, retail shopping, and recreation areas. It had a casual "boots and jeans" ambience that placed an emphasis on comfort and pleasure. The El Rancho brought gambling and vacationing together in Vegas's first casino resort and became the model for future casino development.

Observing the success of the El Rancho, movie theater mogul R. E. Griffith emulated Hull's model and added a new dimension. In October 1942, Griffith opened the Hotel Last Frontier on the site of the old Pair-O-Dice nightclub near the El Rancho. Aiming to trump the El Rancho, Griffith designed the Last Frontier around an authentic Old West theme, featuring frontier-style decor, genuine historical artifacts, and costumed employees. Griffith thus introduced the fantasy theme concept to Vegas.

Consequently, the stage was set for the notorious Benjamin "Bugsy" Siegel, who in 1946, with the opening of the Mafia-bankrolled Flamingo down the road from the Last Frontier, elevated Hull's and Griffith's prototypes to new heights. Siegel spared no expense in creating an ultra-glitzy, ultra-glamorous "carpet joint" (to use his words) designed to lure the wealthy Hollywood set. His loose spending of mob money—combined with his girlfriend's penchant for skimming Flamingo cash—eventually cost Siegel his life. But Siegel established the trend of over-the-top luxury casino resorts that define Vegas today, and he brought an alluring mob mystique to Vegas that put the city on the map for good.

Inventions
Shop 'Til You Drop

◆ ◆ ◆ ◆

*An Oklahoma entrepreneur used a simple folding
chair to change the way the world shopped.*

In the late 1930s, Sylvan Goldman, like any good businessman, was
trying to find a way to increase sales. At his two grocery store chains
in the Oklahoma City area, Standard and Humpty Dumpty, he
noticed that when the wire hand baskets his stores provided became
full or heavy, most of his customers headed for the checkout line. He
imagined this problem could be remedied if shoppers had a way to
conveniently carry more items as they wandered the aisles. Puzzling
over the problem in his office one evening, he was struck by inspiration when a simple wooden folding chair caught his eye. What if that
chair had wheels on the bottom and a basket attached to the seat?
Or better, why not *two* baskets?

Goldman explained his idea to Fred Young, a carpenter and
handyman who worked at the store, and Young began tinkering.
After many months and many prototypes, the two men hit on a
design they thought would work. Goldman's first carts used metal
frames that each held two enormous baskets—19 inches long,
13 inches wide, and 9 inches deep. When not in use, the baskets
could be removed and stacked together, and the frames folded up to
a depth of only five inches, thus preserving the most precious com-
modity of any retail store: floor space.

Nowadays, most of us couldn't imagine a grocery store without
shopping carts, but Goldman's customers were reluctant to use
the strange new contraptions at first. Ever the salesman, he hired
models of various ages to troll his stores and shop with his "folding carrier baskets." Eventually, the innovation caught on, not only
at Goldman's stores but also at retail outlets across the country. In
1937, Goldman founded the Folding Carrier Basket Company to
manufacture his carts for other stores. They became so popular that
by 1940 he was faced with a seven-year backlog of new orders.

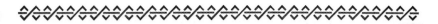

Film

From Comic Book to the Big Screen: 27 Movies That Were Originally Comic Books

❖ ❖ ❖ ❖

1. *Spider-Man*
2. *Batman*
3. *Superman*
4. *X-Men*
5. *Teenage Mutant Ninja Turtles*
6. *Richie Rich*
7. *Popeye*
8. *Men in Black*
9. *Josie and the Pussycats*
10. *The Incredible Hulk*
11. *Howard the Duck*
12. *Road to Perdition*
13. *The Fantastic Four*
14. *Dick Tracy*
15. *Casper*
16. *The Mask*
17. *Sabrina the Teenage Witch*
18. *The Rocketeer*
19. *Spawn*
20. *Judge Dredd*
21. *Sin City*
22. *The Crow*
23. *Swamp Thing*
24. *Timecop*
25. *Blade*
26. *Daredevil*
27. *Watchmen*

"Hollywood is a place where they'll pay you a thousand dollars for a kiss and fifty cents for your soul."

—Marilyn Monroe

"Hollywood is a place where a man can get stabbed in the back while climbing a ladder."

—William Faulkner

Health & Medicine
Calling for Help

◆ ◆ ◆ ◆

*The 911 emergency system was modeled
after the United Kingdom's 999.*

For Americans born after 1968, reaching emergency aid—whether police, fire department, or ambulance—has always been as simple as dialing 911. Before then, people in need had to dial the services directly or reach an operator who could place the call for them. The 911 system is a remarkable achievement in public safety and has saved countless lives—but it's not an American invention.

Some historians believe that the first telephone call ever made— by Alexander Graham Bell to his assistant, Thomas A. Watson, on March 10, 1876—was also the first emergency call. Bell and Watson were in separate rooms testing a new transmitter when Bell supposedly spilled battery acid on his clothing. Watson heard Bell say "Mr. Watson, come here. I want you!" over the transmitter and rushed to his aid.

999
Great Britain introduced the first universal emergency number in 1937. Citizens calling 999 reached a central operator who would dispatch the police, fire department, or ambulance, as needed. According to records, the wife of John Stanley Beard of 33 Elsworthy Road, London, made the first 999 call to report a burglar outside her home. The police arrived promptly, and the 24-year-old intruder was arrested. The British system proved so successful that other countries ultimately followed. Today, most industrialized nations now employ some sort of universal emergency number.

911
In the United States, the idea of a universal emergency number was introduced in 1967 at the urging of the Presidential Commission

on Law Enforcement. Congress quickly established a series of committees to determine how to make the system a reality. The committees had to work out several issues, foremost being the selection of a three-digit number that was not already a United States area code or an international prefix. Another consideration was ease of dialing on a rotary telephone. After much discussion, they finally decided on 911.

On January 12, 1968, AT&T, the nation's primary telephone carrier at the time, announced the designation of 911 as the universal emergency number during a press conference in the office of Indiana Representative Ed Roush, who had championed the cause before Congress. The AT&T plan initially involved only the Bell companies, not the small number of independent telephone companies across the country.

The first 911 call was placed on February 16, 1968, in Haleyville, Alabama. But it wasn't made through AT&T. Instead, the Alabama Telephone Company (a subsidiary of Continental Telephone) holds that honor, primarily because its president, Bob Gallagher, had read about AT&T's plan in *The Wall Street Journal* and decided to beat the telecommunications giant to the punch. Haleyville was determined to be the best place to roll out the program, and the company immediately set to work on the local circuitry system, with a scheduled activation date of February 16. Interestingly, that first call wasn't an emergency. It was a test call placed by Alabama Speaker of the House Rankin Fite from Haleyville City Hall to U.S. Representative Tom Bevill at the town's police station.

The first 911 systems sent callers to a predetermined emergency response agency, where an operator would dispatch the needed services based on what the caller reported. This occasionally proved problematic, especially when the caller was panicked, disoriented, or lacked the necessary information, such as an address.

A more sophisticated system, called "Enhanced 911," eliminated much of the confusion by providing an operator with a caller's location information and telephone number through special computers and display screens. Enhanced 911 also allows for selective routing and selective transfer of 911 calls to multiple emergency response jurisdictions.

Literature
The Vagabond Beat Generation

◆ ◆ ◆ ◆

A group of artists, poets, and writers became the first generation of postwar nonconformists to influence those that came after them.

The "Beat Generation" is the name given to a generation of poets, writers, artists, and activists during the '40s and '50s. The name originated in 1948 when Jack Kerouac, the most famous novelist among the Beats, told a magazine interviewer that his generation was "beat, man." Kerouac later said "beat" was short for "beatific."

Kerouac's novel *On the Road* (written in 1951 but published in 1957) became the Beat Generation's defining document. It was a thinly disguised autobiographical novel with many references to Kerouac's friends and fellow writers and poets Allen Ginsberg, William Burroughs, Gregory Corso, and Gary Snyder. According to some sources, Kerouac, to preserve his spontaneity, typed *On the Road* on a long roll of telegraph paper in one "take" with no corrections. His editor supposedly pleaded with him, "Jack, even Shakespeare made corrections—and Jack, you ain't Shakespeare!" The novel's central character, Dean Moriarty, was based on Neal Cassady, who didn't write much himself but became an avatar of the free life for his writer friends. Cassady wound up as the driver of author Ken Kesey's famous painted bus, "Further," during the 1960s.

The Beats' two other significant works were Ginsberg's long poem "Howl" (1956), which chronicled the adventures and misadventures of the same circle, and Burroughs's novel *Naked Lunch,* written in hallucinatory prose and banned for obscenity in several states for a time. Experiences chronicled by the Beats included drug use, free sex, homosexuality, crime, and stints in mental institutions and prison.

The Beats held San Francisco and New York in high regard. The Beat phenomenon coincided with the 1950's "San Francisco Renaissance" of poetry and art. San Francisco Beat poet Lawrence Ferlinghetti opened his famous bookstore and publishing company, City Lights, in 1953. Ferlinghetti was prosecuted for publishing

"Howl" in a landmark obscenity trial. Ferlinghetti's partner, Peter Martin (who left after two years), named the bookstore after Charlie Chaplin's film. It was the first all-paperback bookstore in the United States. Kenneth Rexroth, a slightly older San Francisco poet and cultural critic, was close to many Beats. He lived a similarly unconventional life, wrote about the Beats, and promoted them on a radio show he hosted in San Francisco.

Despite its nonconformity, the Beat Generation became a cultural phenomenon. By the late 1950s, the stereotype of the bearded, turtlenecked, beret-wearing, "beatnik" (and the black-leotard-and-sandal-wearing, unsmiling "beat chick") became ensconced in popular culture. In a letter to *The New York Times,* Ginsberg complained, "If beatniks and not illuminated Beat poets overrun this country, they will have been created not by Kerouac but by industries of mass communication which continue to brainwash man." Hollywood producer Albert Zugsmith actually copyrighted the term "Beat Generation" in order to make his 1959 film *The Beat Generation,* which was derided by many as a campy exploitation flick.

Strange Book Titles

- *How to Avoid Huge Ships* by John W. Trimmer
- *Be Bold with Bananas* by Crescent Books
- *Fancy Coffins to Make Yourself* by Dale L. Power
- *Across Europe by Kangaroo* by Joseph R. Barry
- *101 Super Uses for Tampon Applicators* by Lori Katz and Barbara Meyer
- *Suture Self* by Mary Daheim
- *The Making of a Moron* by Niall Brennan
- *How to Make Love While Conscious* by Guy Kettelhack
- *How to Be a Pope: What to Do and Where to Go Once You're in the Vatican* by Piers Marchant
- *How to Read a Book* by Mortimer J. Adler and Charles Van Doren

ADVERTISING

Moo Magic

Long dismissed as the beverage of the bland, milk got a boost from an astute ad agency that combined pop culture sensibility and a hip Hollywood director with a sexy stream of A-list celebrities to make sure everybody "got" milk.

It's nearly impossible to browse through a popular magazine or drive down a busy boulevard without seeing an ad or billboard of a Hollywood hotshot or superstar sports icon advocating the benefits of milk with a wink in their eye and a milk mustache on their lips. The Got Milk? advertising campaign revitalized the dairy industry and made cold milk cool.

The Got Milk? campaign was the brainchild of Goodby, Silverstein & Partners, a San Francisco ad agency that was just starting to compile a credible clientele. In 1993, the company was commissioned by the California Milk Processor Board to create an innovative and intriguing campaign that would encourage consumers to drink cow's milk.

The initial Got Milk? commercial, which was broadcast on TV for the first time in October 1993, featured a trivia buff who was given the opportunity to win a $10,000 prize if he knew who shot Alexander Hamilton in the famous duel. Although the knowledgeable nerd was an expert on the topic, his answer was unintelligible. He was marble-mouthed and crumb-clotted after eating a peanut butter sandwich because he didn't have any milk to wet his whistle. The ad's creative and comic approach, plus the high-style direction of Michael Bay—an MTV graduate who went on to helm a number of Hollywood blockbusters, including *Armageddon* and *Pearl Harbor*—helped put milk on the same playing field as soft drinks and other beverages. The "milk mustache" campaign, which began in 1995, is now seen as a gauge for measuring celebrity status.

SPORTS

Defining Moments in Sports Terminology, Part One

Bullpen: In the early days of baseball, relief pitchers warmed up behind the outfield fence because the fence and the signs above and around it provided shade from the afternoon sun. The outfield fences in those days often featured advertisements for Bull Durham chewing tobacco. The area became known as the bullpen.

Southpaw: A southpaw is a left-handed pitcher. In the early days of the game, baseball diamonds were designed so that the batters were facing east to prevent the late-afternoon sun from shining in their eyes. This meant that left-handed pitchers were throwing from the south.

Hat Trick: This hockey term was borrowed from cricket. The *Oxford English Dictionary* explains that a hat trick is "the feat of a bowler who takes three wickets by three successive balls: originally considered to entitle him to be presented by his club with a new hat or some equivalent." In the 1940s, a Toronto haberdasher would award a free hat to Maple Leaf hockey players who connected for three goals in a game. Today, any player who scores three goals in a game is credited with a hat trick, and his reward is the parade of hats that cascade down to the ice surface.

Dump and Chase: The "art" of shooting the puck into the corner and sending in a group of skaters to fight for and ultimately gain possession of the disc was originated by Detroit Red Wings coach Jack Adams during the 1942 Stanley Cup finals. The strategic ploy was meant to take advantage of the slow-footed (and skated) Toronto Maple Leaf defensemen.

Hail Mary: Dallas Cowboys quarterback Roger Staubach—a devout Catholic—coined the term when his desperation "wing and a prayer" pass in the waning moments of the Cowboys-Vikings 1975 playoff game was caught by receiver Drew Pearson for the winning touchdown. Staubach told reporters after the game that he "closed his eyes, threw the ball as hard as he could, and said a Hail Mary prayer."

Language

Without Question, A Useful Punctuation Mark

❖ ❖ ❖ ❖

What goes at the end of this sentence, and where would we be without it?

Punctuation is the bane of many an elementary school student, but reading printed text without it would be a terrible chore. Here, give it a try:

forcenturiesmostwrittenlanguagesusedneitherpunctuationmarksnorspacesbetweenwordsreadingwasatediousinterpretiveaffairleftlargelytospecialists

The text above isn't very easy to read without punctuation, is it? Here it is again: For centuries, most written languages used neither punctuation marks nor spaces between words. Reading was a tedious, interpretive affair left largely to specialists. And that was just fine, until Latin was adopted as a common language for scholars and clerics throughout Europe in the first century. The practice of reading and writing boomed, as intellectuals from different countries who spoke different languages could now communicate with each other in written text.

Even then, authors and scribes did not use punctuation of any kind, but people who did public readings of texts began marking them up to indicate pauses, bringing rhythm to their presentations and giving themselves a chance to catch their breath. Readers relied on a variety of marks but generally used them to indicate three things—a brief pause, like the modern comma; a middle pause, like the modern semicolon; and a full pause, like the modern period. In the seventh century, Isidore of Seville expanded on this practice by creating a formal punctuation system that not only indicated pauses but also helped clarify meaning. It was only then that authors began to use punctuation as they wrote.

And what about the question mark? Some say ancient Egyptians created it and that they patterned it after the shape a cat's tail made when the feline was perplexed. It's a cute story, but there's absolutely no truth to it. The question mark debuted in Europe in the ninth century; back then, it took the shape of a dot followed by a squiggly line. The modern version—a sickle shape resting atop a dot—was adopted after the invention of the printing press for the convenience of typesetters.

What Do You Mean by That?

Down in the Dumps

The word *dump* calls to mind nasty stuff, but this phrase has nothing to do with garbage or bodily functions. The origins of this expression are from the German word *dumpf*, which means "oppressive" or "heavy." To be "down in the dumps" means to feel weighted down by worry.

On the Nose

This term, which means to be "precisely on," comes from the early days of radio broadcasting. Producers would use hand signals to let their announcers (isolated in soundproof booths) know if the program was running on schedule. If it was, they'd touch their finger to their nose.

Armed to the Teeth

This phrase is said to be pirate terminology that means "to be well equipped with weaponry." In the late 1600s, Jamaica was a British colony surrounded by Spanish and Portuguese property, and the harbor town of Port Royal was a popular center for buccaneers engaged in constant, heavy attacks against the Spanish. To boost their efficiency, pirates would carry many weapons at once, including a knife held in their teeth for maximum arms capability.

Museums
The Mütter Museum: Abra-Cadaver

✦ ✦ ✦ ✦

*Sometimes mislabeled as a gallery of the gruesome
and a mausoleum of the macabre, the Mütter Museum
is much more than just skin and bones.*

It is, beyond any doubt, the oddest accumulation of artifacts on this planet, and that's including the National Museum of Scotland, which features more than a few anatomical anomalies preserved in jars of formaldehyde. The Mütter Museum, located at the College of Physicians in Philadelphia, is home to the world's most extensive collection of medical marvels, anatomical oddities, and biological enigmas. Among the items one may view at the Mütter are the conjoined livers of the world-famous Siamese twins, Chang and Eng; a selection of 139 Central and Eastern European skulls from the collection of world-renowned anatomist Joseph Hyrtl; and the preserved body of the "Soap Lady." Also on display are an assortment of objects that have been extracted from people's throats; a bevy of brains, bones, and gallstones; and a cancerous growth that was removed from President Grover Cleveland. There are also pathological models molded in plaster, wax, papier-mâché, and plastic; memorabilia contributed by famous scientists and physicians, plus a medley of medical illustrations, photographs, prints, and portraits.

Dr. Thomas Dent Mütter, a flamboyant and slightly fanatical physician obsessed with devising new and improved surgical techniques to cure diseases and deformities, donated the collection to the College in 1858. The professor of surgery at Jefferson Medical College in Philadelphia until his retirement, Mütter was ostracized by the medical community for both his methods and his predilection to preserve the remains of some of his more peculiar patients. The Mütter Museum officially opened its doors in 1863, and it has intrigued curious visitors ever since.

Music
All That Jazz

❖ ❖ ❖ ❖

Bebop expanded musical boundaries, invited
improvisation, and transformed jazz.

Bebop is a style of jazz that encourages improvisation and rapid
time signature changes while constantly varying the main theme
and melody of the performance piece. Its creative zenith was from
1939 to 1959, when luminaries such as saxophone specialists Cole-
man Hawkins and Charlie Parker, pianist Thelonious Monk, and
trumpeters Dizzy Gillespie and Miles Davis perfected the genre and
propelled it to its musical heights. Bebop encourages the performers
to solo at will, while the rhythm section of bass and drums lays down
the harmony and melody of the tune.

The classic bebop quintet consisted of a saxophone, a trumpet, a
bass, drums, and a piano. The 1939 recording of "Body and Soul" by
Hawkins is regarded as the standard bearer that introduced bebop to
the masses and influenced a whole generation of performers. Modern jazz performers such as Wynton Marsalis and Monty Alexander
have revisited the genre, but few of bebop's original practitioners are
alive today.

The genesis of the term *bebop* is uncertain, though it's rooted
in scat singing—the melodious mingling of nonsense syllables, all
in rhythm and time—which was popularized by jazz vocalists such
as Cab Calloway and, later, Ella Fitzgerald. Some jazz historians
speculate that Charlie Christian (1916–1942), who introduced the
electric guitar to the standard jazz quartet, helped coin the phrase
because that seemed to be the word he was constantly humming as
he vocalized the notes he was playing. It's also been suggested that
the repeated alliteration of "Arriba! Arriba!" used by Latin American bandleaders to rev the motors of their instrumentalists while on
stage contributed to the genesis of the word *bebop*.

Education
Making the Grade

❖ ❖ ❖ ❖

Methods of evaluating student work have changed with the times, and the A–F grading system in the United States is a recent phenomenon.

Grading Before Grades

Before the era of standardized tests, report cards, and voluminous grade books, most schools in the United States were rural one-room schoolhouses. Student evaluation consisted of qualitative descriptions of the student's progress and was the prerogative of the individual schoolmaster. The earliest schools to establish a consistent grading system were the first universities, including Harvard, Yale, and the College of William and Mary. Before grading systems became standardized, entrance to these colleges was based mostly on social class, reputation, social networking, and the scattered reports of childhood tutors.

As the American population grew, it became difficult for college professors to send detailed descriptions of each student's work to so many parents. In the late 1700s, Yale began to evaluate its students by four discrete categories, marked by Latin adjectives: Optimi, second Optimi, Inferiores, and Pejores. The four-point system—still in use today as the basis of GPA calculations—can also be traced to Yale: The four descriptive adjectives were matched up with the numbers 1–4.

The first numerical system at Harvard was based on a 20-point format, which is popular today in many countries. This was eventually replaced by a 100-point system, which was then adopted by other universities. The point system was often criticized as being too specific, so sometimes a range of points would be matched up with words or divisions. For example, in 1877, Harvard divided its students into six divisions, with Division One receiving between 90–100 points, and so on.

The first time that a modern letter grade was correlated with a range of numbers was at Harvard in 1883, when one report card

referenced a "B" grade. The first all-out A–F grading system—implemented at Mount Holyoke College in Massachusetts in 1897—was based on a 100-point system that would strike fear in the hearts of modern students: An A was 95–100, and anything below a 75 meant failure, which at that time was denoted by the now not-so-dreaded "E."

Grading the Grading System

It wasn't until the rapid urbanization of the mid-19th century that a consistent grading system became necessary outside of the university environment. Education came under the auspices of public funding; education bureaucrats experimented with different systems and tried to make schools in the same city practice the same system.

These early systems borrowed from the various conventions that were already popular at the major universities. The trendy letter system of this time period was quite different than the one that is in use today. The letters were based on descriptive adjectives rather than numeric ranges: E for Excellent, S for Satisfactory, N for Needs Improvement, and U for Unsatisfactory. This system is still used in primary education. It is likely that the disappearance of the "E" as a failing grade resulted from confusion with the "E" for Excellent.

The current A–F method became popular in the mid-20th century and is based on the "tens" system: 90–100 is an A, 80–89 is a B, and so on. A survey conducted by Georgia State University found it is practiced by 90 percent of colleges nationwide. The system is often criticized, as an "A" can mean different things to different schools and different teachers. A handful of universities have replaced grades with the qualitative descriptions of yore, but it seems the current system is in for the long haul.

"Education is what remains after one has forgotten everything he learned in school."

—Albert Einstein

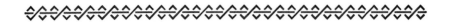

Saving Face: The Hockey Goalie Mask

❖ ❖ ❖ ❖

Gruesome facial injuries to two legendary hockey goalies spurred the invention and acceptance of the goalie mask. Yet despite the hazards posed by playing without a mask, the face-saving innovation took a long time to catch on.

On April 7, 1974, the Pittsburgh Penguins faced off against the Atlanta Flames as the 1973–74 National Hockey League regular season drew to a close. Playing in goal for the Penguins was a 30-year-old journeyman named Andy Brown.

Brown turned in a sievelike performance, and the sad-sack Penguins were thrashed 6–3. Worse yet, the loss turned out to be the last game of Brown's NHL career. But as he braved pucks whizzing past his head, Brown staked his place in hockey history: He would be the last goalie to play in an NHL game without a goalie mask.

Today, it's hard to fathom a hockey goalie playing without a mask. Indeed, all pro and amateur hockey leagues now require the mask to be part of a goalie's equipment. But for the first nine decades of hockey's existence, the goalie mask was an object as odd and rare as the U.S. two-dollar bill.

As crazy as it sounds, goalies actually chose not to wear masks despite obvious occupational hazards. Not surprisingly, then, the introduction and popularization of the goalie mask only came about after a near-tragedy involving two of the game's greatest netminders.

Clint Benedict played 18 pro seasons with the Ottawa Senators and Montreal Maroons, backstopping the Senators to Stanley Cup titles in 1920, 1921, and 1923, as well as helping lead the Maroons to their first Cup win in 1926. Arguably the best goalie of his era, Benedict revolutionized how the position was played. He earned the nickname "Praying Benny" due to his habit of falling to his knees in the era of the stand-up goaltender. As a result, the NHL eventually abandoned its rule prohibiting goalies to leave their feet.

In 1930, Benedict inadvertently led to yet another innovation to the goal-tending profession. That year, in a game between the Maroons and the Montreal Canadiens, the Canadiens' Howie Morenz nailed Benedict in the face with a shot that knocked him unconscious, shattered his cheekbone and nose, and hospitalized him for a month. When Benedict returned to the ice to face the New York Americans, he surprised the crowd by sporting a leather mask, making history as the first goalie to wear face protection in an NHL game.

After five games, Benedict fatefully discarded the mask, saying its oversize nosepiece hindered his vision. Shortly after, another Morenz shot struck Benedict in the throat and ended his NHL career. Amazingly, for the next 29 years, the first man to wear a mask in a game would also be the last.

The mask finally reappeared in 1959—albeit unexpectedly—in a game between the Montreal Canadiens and the New York Rangers. Three minutes into the game, Rangers star Andy Bathgate drilled the Canadiens' all-star goalie Jacques Plante in the nose and cheek with a hard shot, sending a badly bleeding Plante to the dressing room. Plante had been wearing a fiberglass mask in practices since the mid-1950s, but Montreal coach Toe Blake forbade him to don it in a game. Now, as Plante was being stitched up, he told the coach he wouldn't go back on the ice without his mask. An irate Blake, faced with no suitable backup goalie, was forced to relent.

Plante returned to the game wearing his mask and led the Canadiens to a 3–1 victory. Montreal subsequently reeled off an 18-game unbeaten streak, with a masked Plante in net for every game. The goalie mask was here to stay.

Within a decade, the mask became commonplace throughout hockey. By 1974, all NHL goalies wore a mask. Except, of course, for Andy Brown.

Personal Hygiene
On a Roll

❖ ❖ ❖ ❖

*Toilet paper is one invention that has been flushed
with success since its 14th-century origins.*

Like pasta and gunpowder, toilet paper was invented in China.
Paper—made from pulped bamboo and cotton rags—was also
invented by the Chinese, although Egyptians had already been using
papyrus plants for thousands of years to make writing surfaces. Still,
it wasn't until 1391, almost 1,600 years after the invention of paper,
that the Ming Dynasty Emperor first used toilet paper. The government made 2 × 3 foot sheets, which either says something about the
manufacturing limitations of the day or the Emperor's diet!

Toilet paper didn't reach the United States until 1857 when the
Gayetty Firm introduced "Medicated Paper." Prior to the industrial
revolution later that century, many amenities were available only
to the wealthy. But in 1890, Scott Paper Company brought toilet
paper to the masses. The company employed new manufacturing
techniques to introduce perforated sheets. In 1942, Britain's St.
Andrew's Paper Mill invented two-ply sheets (the civilized world
owes a great debt to the Royal Air Force for protecting this London
factory during The Blitz!). Two-ply sheets are not just two single-ply
sheets stuck together; each ply in a two-ply sheet is thinner than a
single-ply sheet. The first "moist" toilet paper—Cottonelle Fresh
Rollwipes—appeared in 2001.

What was the rest of the world doing? Some pretty creative stuff!
Romans soaked sponges in saltwater and attached them to the end
of sticks. There is little information about what happened when
the stick poked through the sponge, but the Romans were a hearty,
expansionist people and probably conquered another country for
spite. Medieval farmers used balls of hay. American pioneers used
corncobs. Leaves have always been a popular alternative to toilet
paper but are rare in certain climates, so Inuit people favor Tundra
moss. Of all people, the Vikings seemed the most sensible, using
wool. It's not easy being a sheep.

Law & Politics
One List You Don't Want to Be On

❖ ❖ ❖ ❖

With the Most Wanted List, the FBI came to rely on the
vigilance of good citizens for its most dangerous work.

During the middle part of the 20th century, nothing was cooler than
a G-man. Tough, dogged, honest, and dedicated to rounding up
America's most dastardly criminals, agents of the FBI enjoyed wide
and largely unwavering public support. This approval stemmed as
much from the agents' heroic efforts as from the notorious reputa-
tions of the outlaws they hunted: criminals such as Pretty Boy Floyd,
John Dillinger, and Bonnie and Clyde.

In 1949, a reporter for the International News Service capitalized
on the public's interest in the agency's work by writing a wire story
on the "toughest guys" the FBI was pursuing at the time. The article
became wildly popular, and Bureau Director J. Edgar Hoover, a
master of public relations, created the Ten Most Wanted Fugitives
List in response. When the list first appeared in 1950, it included
bank robbers and car thieves, but over time, the nature of the criminals who made the list changed. The 1970s saw a focus on organized
crime figures; more recently, emphasis has shifted to terrorists and
drug dealers.

Criminals must meet two criteria in order to become candidates
for the world's most famous rogues gallery. First, they must have
an extensive record of serious criminal activity or a recent criminal
history that poses a particular threat to public safety. Second, there
must be a reasonable likelihood that publicity from their presence
on the list will aid in their capture. Criminals are only removed from
the list for three reasons: They are captured, the charges against
them are dropped, or they no longer fit the criteria for the list.

Over the years, the program has proved remarkably effective.
Nearly 500 criminals have appeared on the list, and more than
90 percent of them have been captured. About a third of these former fugitives were caught as a direct result of tips from the public.

Household Items

The Diabolical Fork

✦ ✦ ✦ ✦

Using a fork was not always a demonstration of good manners. In fact, according to an anonymous writer, "It is coarse and ungraceful to throw food into the mouth as you would toss hay into a barn with a pitchfork."

In the case of the fork, the tool preceded the utensil. The English word *fork* comes from the Latin *furca,* which means "pitchfork." Thousands of years ago, large bronze forks were part of Egyptian sacrificial rituals. By the seventh century A.D., members of Middle Eastern royal courts were using small forks to eat.

Venice and the Fork

Table forks appeared in noble Italian homes in the 11th century, and over the next 500 years, they slowly made their way onto tables throughout Europe. The first forks arrived in Venice at the outset of the 11th century, when a Doge—the head of the government—wed a Byzantine princess. Her forks, however, were despised as an affectation and an example of oriental decadence. According to John Julius Norwich, "Such was the luxury of her habits that she scorned even to wash herself in common water, obliging her servants instead to collect the dew that fell from the heavens for her to bathe in. Nor did she deign to touch her food with her fingers, but would command her eunuchs to cut it up into small pieces, which she would impale on a certain golden instrument with two prongs and thus carry to her mouth." People in the West associated forks with the devil, and it was considered an affront to God to eat with something other than the hands and fingers he had designed for the job. When the princess died young, it was widely regarded as Divine retribution.

Exotic Object to Mainstream Convenience

Stories describing forks and their use appear in documents from the 13th century onward. Cookbooks and household inventories,

however, suggest that forks remained rare, valuable, and esoteric items. When the Italian aristocrat Catherine de Medici married the future Henry II of France in 1533, her dowry included several dozen table forks wrought by famous goldsmith Benvenuto Cellini. In 1588, forks were removed from La Girona, a boat in the Spanish Armada that wrecked off the coast of Ireland. During the 17th century, forks became more common in England, although numerous writers from the period scoffed at the utensil and the class of people who routinely used it.

During the reign of Charles I of England, the fork was relatively common among the upper classes; King Charles himself declared in 1633, "It is decent to use a fork." Soon, sets of forks and knives were sold with a carrying case, as only very wealthy households could provide eating utensils for everyone at the table. Travelers also had to provide their own knives and forks during stopovers at inns. Governor John Winthrop of the Massachusetts Bay Colony owned the first fork—and for some time, the only fork—in colonial America. George Washington was inordinately proud of his set of 12 forks.

Forks, Forms, and Fashion

The first dinner forks had two tines, which were often quite long and sharp. Eventually three- and four-pronged forks were made, with wider, blunted tines arranged in a flattened, curved shape. During the 19th century, forks became commonplace in the United States and were sometimes referred to as "split spoons."

Silver from the Comstock Lode flooded the market after 1859, and the electro-plating process made silverware affordable to nearly all people. Middle-class families subsequently claimed social refinement by acquiring complicated table settings featuring a unique utensil for every food. These place settings expanded from a few pieces to hundreds. Finally, in 1926, then Secretary of Commerce Herbert Hoover decreed that there could be no more than 55 pieces in a silver service, reducing, among other things, the number of forks dedicated to a single purpose. Indeed, it was time to put a fork in it.

War & Military
Thumbs-up: A Sign of Life or Death

❖ ❖ ❖ ❖

*An ancient hand gesture earned new meaning
during an era of strife and confrontation.*

The thumbs-up gesture supposedly originated in the arenas of
ancient Rome, where spectators would use it to signal whether they
wanted a vanquished opponent to be spared or put to death. The
Latin term for the gesture—*pollice verso*—means "with a turned
thumb." But when a gladiator found himself looking up at the
business end of a foe's sword, a sea of spectators' thumbs pointing
upward was the last thing he wanted. In the Coliseum, thumbs-up
was a signal to the victorious warrior that he should put the other
combatant to death, whereas a raised fist with the thumb concealed
was an indication to show mercy.

The gesture was resurrected and given an entirely opposite
connotation by American pilots during World War II. The flyboys
adopted the signal because they needed a nonverbal cue to indicate
to ground crews that they were ready to take off. But it was the
media that established it among the civilian population back home.
Photos of daring young flyers—grinning confidently from their cock-
pits before takeoff, their thumbs held high— saturated American
newspapers, magazines, and newsreels during the war. As a result,
the public, eager for good news and encouragement during those
dark days, heartily embraced the gesture. The thumbs-up sign fell
from favor with the youth generation of the 1960s, who disdained
its militaristic origins and preferred the peace sign instead. But the
wildly popular television show *Happy Days* brought it back in the
1970s; it was the signature gesture of the sitcom's iconic character,
The Fonz. Be careful where you use it, however; in countries such as
Iran and Greece, a thumbs-up is considered extremely rude.

Sports
Field of Dreams

❖ ❖ ❖ ❖

*Dubbed the eighth wonder of the world, the Houston
Astrodome was renowned not only for its innovative design and
remarkable roof but also for the artificial grass that covered
its playing surface and forever changed the face of sports.*

The synthetic substance that eventually became known as Astro-
Turf was originally designed as an urban playing surface meant to
replace the concrete and brick that covered the recreation areas in
city schoolyards. It was developed by employees of the Chemstrand
Company, a subsidiary of Monsanto Industries, leading innovators
in the development of synthetic fibers for use in carpeting. In 1962,
Dr. Harold Gores, the first president of Ford Foundation's Educational Facilities Laboratories, commissioned Monsanto to create an
artificial playing surface that was wear-resistant, cost-efficient, comfortably cushioned, and traction tested. Two years later, the company
introduced a synthetic surface called ChemGrass and installed it
at the Moses Brown School, a private educational facility in Providence, Rhode Island. The new product met each of Dr. Gores's
criteria except one: It was expensive to produce and wasn't a viable
substitute for cement on playgrounds. However, it soon found a new
home and a new name.

In 1965, the Astrodome, the world's first domed stadium, opened
in Houston, Texas, featuring a glass-covered roof that allowed real
grass to grow inside the dome. However, the athletes that used the
facility complained they couldn't follow the path of the ball because
of the glare caused by the glass. Painting the glass killed both the
glare and the grass, so the lifeless lawn was replaced in 1966 with the
revolutionary ChemGrass, which was quickly dubbed AstroTurf. The
new turf was a resounding success, and it soon became the desired
surface for both indoor and outdoor stadiums. Dozens of high
schools in the United States now have artificial playing surfaces.

Sports
America's Game:
32 Teams, 1 Trophy

❖ ❖ ❖ ❖

A fierce rivalry spawned the American sports world's biggest game.

Today, Super Bowl Sunday is practically a national holiday. Fans and nonfans alike gather for huge meals and expensive commercial breaks. The championship game, which began in 1967, helped boost the popularity of American football.

Throughout its history, the National Football League (NFL) faced rival competing leagues. Each time, the NFL would emerge the victor. But that all changed with the creation of the American Football League (AFL). The upstart AFL successfully wooed players from the NFL and helped lay the foundation for modern American football.

The AFL got its start when the NFL rebuffed Lamar Hunt, the son of an oilman, in his bid for an expansion team. In response, Hunt went on to found the AFL and the Dallas Texans in 1960. The league consisted of eight teams and was bankrolled by other would-be owners who had been unable to procure expansion franchises in the NFL.

While the NFL tacitly enforced unwritten quotas for African American players, the AFL actively recruited them. The younger league also competed for top college talent, nabbing Heisman-winner Billy Cannon in 1959 and Joe Namath in 1964. In 1966, new

AFL commissioner Al Davis actively wooed players from the NFL. This practice promoted bidding wars for players between teams in the two leagues.

Hunt and Dallas Cowboys President Texas "Tex" Schramm Jr. met privately to discuss the possibility of merging the two

leagues. On January 15, 1967, the champion team of each league met in the AFL–NFL Championship Game to determine an all-around winner. Suggesting some consistency with the college "bowl" games (e.g., the Rose Bowl, the Orange Bowl) used to crown regional champions, Hunt recommended "Super Bowl," a reference to the Super Ball toy his kids enjoyed. The name stuck but was not officially used until Super Bowl III in 1969. (The 1967 and '68 championship games are only called Super Bowl I and II retroactively; at the time, they were called the AFL–NFL Championship Games). The Super Bowl trophy was named the Vince Lombardi Trophy following the legendary coach's death in 1970.

Gridiron Grammar

Football has always had a language all its own, and it has adopted many terms and truisms from commonplace sources outside of sports.

Considering that the quarterback is often referred to as the "general" and his players are known as "troops," it's not surprising that many football terms, such as "blitz," "bomb," "trenches," and "gunners," have been borrowed from the military. In football, the blitz, like its wartime connotation, is a bombardment, but not from the air. It is an all-out frontal attack bolstered by 300-pound behemoths intent on planting the quarterback face-first into the turf. The football bomb is an aerial assault, but instead of an explosive-laden shell, this weapon is a perfectly delivered spiral carried triumphantly into the opposition's end zone. The trenches, much like their World War I counterparts, are pungent places, replete with sweat, spit, mud, and blood. Football's trenches are found along the line of scrimmage, where hand-to-hand combat determines who wins the day. Like their combative comrades, gridiron gunners are responsible for neutralizing the enemy and thwarting its attack. On the battle lines that are drawn between the boundaries, these gunners set their sights on the kickoff and punt-return specialists.

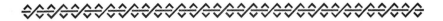

Visual Art
Something Old, Something New

❖ ❖ ❖ ❖

*The Art Deco style perfectly captured the
excitement and energy of a new century.*

The period between the two world wars was one of dramatic social,
political, and technological change throughout the Western world.
The old empires and aristocracies of the preceding five centuries
had all but fallen away, replaced by democratic governments and a
much looser, more egalitarian social order. The chasm between rich
and poor narrowed dramatically, as the middle class grew and as
entry to the wealthiest upper circles became easier through success
in business and industry. New inventions allowed more leisure time
for everyone; population centers shifted rapidly from rural areas to
fast-paced urban settings; and prudish Victorian notions of morality
were replaced by the fast and easy lifestyle of the Jazz Age. It was
almost as if the entire world had been completely reinvented in a
radical and exciting new way.

A Breath of Fresh Air

Inspired by this dizzying, liberating change, artists and designers
attempted to reflect and represent their new, distinctly modern
world while retaining what they found of value from the past. They
embraced sleek, clean designs that combined geometric patterns
and machine-tooled lines with traditional motifs, such as the female
form and floral patterns. Artists combined natural materials such
as jade, ivory, and chrome with new materials such as plastic,
ferroconcrete, and vita glass. They merged elements of cutting-edge
art movements such as Cubism and Bauhaus with traditional Greek,
Roman, Egyptian, and Native American styles. And they applied
their creation to all areas of this new modern world: buildings,
fashion, posters, advertising, appliances, and furniture. The result
was a sleek, elegant, sophisticated, and luxurious style now known as
Art Deco.

Exposition Internationale des Arts Décoratifs

The trend toward this modern new world—and the graphic style that so perfectly represented it—developed gradually in the first two decades of the 20th century. Art Deco saw its formal debut in 1925 at an exhibit held in Paris called the *Exposition Internationale des Arts Décoratifs et Industriels Moderne*. Designers and crafters from 23 countries displayed a breathtaking array of artifacts that together captured all that was innovative and exciting about the 20th century. At the time, the movement was generally referred to as *style moderne*; it wasn't until decades later that the term "Art Deco"—derived from the name of the Paris exhibition—came into use.

The Movement Hits the States

Though the United States did not participate in the 1925 show, the country quickly became an influential force in the Art Deco movement. The style swept across America and figured prominently in Hollywood movies. Studios were quick to see that Art Deco offered an ideal visual shorthand for conveying sophistication, wealth, and elegance. Through the efforts of costumers, set designers, and prop masters, the movement soon became a familiar backdrop against which Greta Garbo, Bette Davis, William Powell, and Fred Astaire played out the fantasies of the nation on the silver screen. Even the grand movie palaces built in the 1920s and '30s fully embraced the style, and the few that remain today offer excellent examples of the movement's influence on interior design. While Hollywood stars did little to define and shape the Art Deco style, they probably did more than anyone to popularize it, not only in the United States but also in Europe, where American films were screened regularly.

Art Deco has had a lasting influence on architecture. Most major urban areas in the United States and Europe still have buildings constructed in this style, though the most famous and representative examples can be found in these New York City landmarks: the Chrysler Building, the Empire State Building, Rockefeller Center, and the interior of Radio City Music Hall.

Education

A Clean Slate: The Cutting Edge in Classroom Technology

✦ ✦ ✦ ✦

The introduction of the blackboard revolutionized teaching practices. Chalk it up to a Scottish teacher's desire to get the word out.

Few things seem as mundane or uninspiring as a classroom blackboard: a slate surface covered in dusty, white text detailing tonight's reading assignment or the date of next week's test. What could be less revolutionary?

But when James Pillans, headmaster of the Old High School of Edinburgh, Scotland, began using one in his classroom in 1801, he sent ripples of excitement throughout the educational world.

Before that time, teachers had no way of displaying written material to an entire class; they also had no way of mechanically reproducing copies of material written on paper. Consequently, teachers spent a considerable amount of time writing out assignments, dictating them to the class, or painstakingly copying them down on each student's small slate.

The Writing Is on the Wall

Pillans's innovation was considered a revolutionary piece of technology that would—and did—transform the educational experience. In fact, in 1841, Josiah F. Bumstead, a writer and educator, said that the inventor of the blackboard "deserves to be ranked among the best contributors to learning and science, if not among the greatest benefactors of mankind." Teachers could now work out equations, diagram sentences,

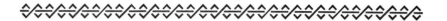

and write out the week's new spelling words for the entire class at one time. And students could now experience the dread of going up to the board to work out those impossible math problems while the whole class watched!

The first recorded use of the blackboard in the United States was likely by George Baron at the United States Military Academy at West Point in 1801. By the mid-1800s, a blackboard could be found in virtually every schoolroom in America—even the isolated one-room schoolhouses that dotted the Western frontier.

New Changes Afoot

Of course, many of today's classrooms have since replaced their chalkboards with whiteboards. Teachers are also increasingly relying on digital technologies that enable them to pass out and collect assignments electronically. Pillans's innovation may be on its way out, but there is no denying that it served teachers and students well for more than 200 years. Its impact won't be erased anytime soon.

"The true creator is necessity, who is the mother of our invention."
—PLATO

"In the modern world we have invented ways of speeding up invention, and people's lives change so fast that a person is born into one kind of world, grows up in another, and by the time his children are growing up, lives in still a different world."
—MARGARET MEAD

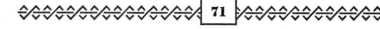

Where Did That Name Come From?

❖ ❖ ❖ ❖

WD-40: In 1953, the Rocket Chemical Company began developing a rust-prevention solvent for the aerospace industry. The name WD-40 indicates what the product does (water displacement) and how many attempts it took to perfect it.

Starbucks: *Moby Dick* was the favorite book of one of the three founders of this coffee empire. He wanted to name the company after the story's fabled ship *Pequod,* but he and his partners reconsidered and settled instead on the name of the first mate, Starbuck.

Google: In the 1930s, mathematician Edwin Kasner asked his young nephew to think of a word that could mean a very large number (1 followed by 100 zeros). The boy, Milton Sirotta, came up with *Googol.* The creators of the world's most popular search engine varied the spelling and adopted the word to represent an infinite amount of information.

M&Ms: Chocolate pellets coated in sugar were popular in Britain for decades under the brand name Smarties. When Forrest Mars (son of the founder of the Mars candy company) saw soldiers eating them during the Spanish Civil War, he and his partner, R. Bruce Murrie, bought the U.S. rights. But there was already an American candy product called Smarties, so Mars and Murrie used their initials to form a new brand name.

GAP: Don and Doris Fisher opened their first store in 1969 to meet the unique clothing demands of customers between childhood and adulthood, identified and popularized as "the generation gap."

Adidas: This sportswear giant's name derives from the name of its founder, Adolf "Adi" Dassler.

Shell Oil: The name was appropriated by Marcus Samuel, one of the company's founders. His father ran a London retail outlet called the Shell Shop, where he sold bags decorated with seashells. This grew into an import-export business, which diversified into a business that imported oil and kerosene.

Aspirin: In 1899, the German company Bayer trademarked the word *aspirin* as a composite of the scientific name of the drug. "A" indicates that it comes from the acetyl group, "spir" represents its derivation from the plant genus *spiraea,* and "-in" was a common ending for drug names in the 19th century.

Nike: In 1971, the founders of a small sports shoe business in Beaverton, Oregon, were searching for a catchy, energetic company name. Designer Jeff Johnson suggested Nike, the name of the Greek goddess of victory. Nike is now the largest sportswear manufacturer in the world.

Jeep: Eugene the Jeep, a character in a 1936 Popeye comic strip, was actually a dog that could walk through walls, climb trees, and fly. When U.S. soldiers were given a new all-terrain vehicle in the early 1940s, they were so impressed that they may have named it after the superdog. The Jeep trademark is now owned by DaimlerChrysler.

Scotch Tape: When the purportedly penny-pinching executives, or "Scotch bosses," at the Minnesota Mining and Manufacturing Company (3M) didn't put enough adhesive on their tape, people complained. The company responded by putting better adhesive on their new product. The tape stuck—and so did the name.

Rubik's Cube: This brain-teasing toy is named after its creator, Hungarian architecht Erno Rubik. First introduced in 1977, the perplexing puzzle was popular in the 1980s, with more than 100 million of the cubes sold. It sparked a trend, and similar puzzles were created in various shapes. The Rubik's Cube has seen a recent resurgence in popularity and retains a place of honor on many desktops.

Toys & Games
Toy Story

❖ ❖ ❖ ❖

For almost 150 years, FAO Schwarz has been the first name in fun.

No name is as synonymous with toys as FAO Schwarz. This paragon of playtime may be a New York institution, but it actually got its start in Baltimore.

The four Schwarz brothers left Germany for America in the mid-1800s. They settled in Baltimore, where they worked for Theodore Schwerdtmann, owner of a retail store for imported goods. Henry and younger brother Frederick August Otto (the "F.A.O." in FAO Schwarz) imported toys from other countries, including Germany, France, and Switzerland, for Schwerdtmann & Co, which became Schwerdtmann & Schwarz in 1871. In 1870, Frederick left to open another branch, the Schwarz Toy Bazaar, in New York. Henry took over Schwerdtmann & Schwarz in 1872, and brothers Gustave and Richard ran their own toy stores in Philadelphia and Boston.

The brothers pooled their purchasing power to bring a wide variety of European toys and trinkets to American stores. At the time, stores that sold only toys were all but nonexistent. Most Americans gave their children handmade toys rather than store-bought playthings. There was no Toys"R"Us; instead, toys cropped up on a shelf or two at local general stores. Baltimore, however, was another story. A disproportionately large population of German immigrants lived in the shipping center. As the Schwarz clan tapped directly into that market, demand spread.

Frederick would often request specific changes from European manufacturers, making many of the toys on FAO's shelves Schwarz exclusives. This practice became a tradition, as evidenced by the unique and lavish displays in the stores, particularly the giant keyboard made famous by Tom Hanks in the 1988 movie *Big*.

The venerable American toy icon experienced financial woes at the turn of the 21st century and changed ownership several times, but its flagship New York store continues to be a must-see attraction for tourists and toy enthusiasts alike.

ACCIDENTAL INVENTIONS

Chew, Chew, Pop!

A bad batch of chewing gum led to an iconic childhood treat.

If you've always assumed that chewing gum and bubble gum were invented around the same time, well—sorry to burst your bubble! Chewing gum has been around for more than 800 years, but bubble gum is a relatively recent discovery—and an accidental one. In the 1920s, the Fleer Company, purveyors of fine candy and gum, bought gum base from a supplier and added their own sweeteners and flavorings to create a distinctive brand. With the company facing financial problems, Fleer President Gilbert Mustin began looking for creative ways to cut costs and hit upon the idea of having Fleer manufacture its own gum base rather than purchasing it.

Mustin set up a workroom near the accounting department, just down the hall from his office, and began tinkering with different formulas. In the end, he didn't have much of a knack for it and lost interest fairly quickly. Fortunately for Fleer and for gum lovers around the world, Mustin had enlisted the help of 23-year-old accountant Walter Diemer, and Diemer pressed on with the experiments, willingly chewing over the possibilities.

One day, Diemer made a batch of gum with an entirely wrong consistency. It was thinner, gooier, and much less sticky than traditional chewing gum, but it also had a tendency to form bubbles. Eager to try out the new product, Diemer mixed up a large batch and tossed in pink food coloring because it was the only color he could find. In December 1928, he took 100 pieces down to a nearby candy store; it sold out that same afternoon. And the interest stuck: Over the next year, the company earned more than $1.5 million from Diemer's Dubble Bubble. Although he never earned any royalties from the invention, Diemer went on to become a member of Fleer's board of directors and also took on the responsibility of training the company's sales staff in the art of blowing bubbles so they could demonstrate the product.

Household Items
Garden Gnomes: Here (or There) to Stay

❖ ❖ ❖ ❖

*By mass-producing garden gnomes, German
statue makers became the kings of kitsch.*

Gnomes have appeared in folktales and mythology for hundreds of years, and they've been showing up in people's gardens for almost as long. Traditionally, these short, gnarled, ageless creatures were said to dwell underground, where they served as protectors of the earth's many treasures. So it's fitting that they now adorn backyard gardens that draw bounty from the soil.

A Gnome by Any Other Name...
The first garden gnomes were likely produced as early as the 1800s by the world-renowned statue makers of the German town of Gräfenroda. Similar to the gnomes we see today, these terra-cotta *gartenzwerge* (garden dwarves) were adorned with bright red caps, probably modeled after the head gear favored by the region's miners. Sir Charles Edmund Isham of Britain became enchanted with the little fellows while visiting Germany and brought about 20 of them back to his estate in Northamptonshire in 1847, beginning a gnome migration that would eventually spread across most of the globe. One of Isham's statues has survived to this day: Six inches tall and jauntily leaning on a shovel, he's known as Lampy, and he occasionally leaves the grounds of the estate to make appearances at conventions.

Gnome Sweet Gnome
After Isham helped popularize the little figures, two German ceramic artists, Phillip Griebel and August Heissner, began mass-producing them for the world. By 1900, more than a dozen companies in and around Gräfenroda were churning them out. The industry saw its ups and downs during the first half of the 20th century but came back strong in the 1960s. Griebel's company is still

in business and actually produces some models from its founder's original patterns and molds.

Roaming Gnomes

Today, there are as many people who love and collect gnomes as there are those who deride them. The latter group includes a tongue-in-cheek organization known as the *Front de Libération des Nains de Jardins* (the Garden Gnome Liberation Front), which first appeared in France in the 1990s and has local chapters in several countries. The stated goals of these pranksters are to end the evil of "gnome trafficking" and to free gnomes from "garden servitude," which they do by occasionally stealing large numbers of the statues from neighborhood gardens and "releasing" them in the woods. One year, they deposited stolen statues in the middle of a busy traffic circle with some of them arranged to spell out "Free the gnomes." Another year they hung about a dozen of them from a bridge in a "mass suicide," complete with notes lamenting their tortured existence as yard adornments. The organization was started as a protest against kitsch by a group of art students who deemed the figurines to be the epitome of poor taste. Though credited with pilfering some 6,000 statues (they're nothing if not dedicated), the group's plan backfired badly. Publicity over their stunts doubled the sale of garden gnomes throughout France.

Another common trick played on gnome owners has more uncertain origins but a decidedly more playful motive. Gnome-napping victims are whisked to various locations around the world and photographed in front of famous landmarks. The owners regularly receive pictures in the mail along with brief notes from their former yard residents detailing their travels. The practice was famously documented in the 2001 French film *Amelie*, when the main character enlists a stewardess friend to play a prank on her father as a way to bring him out of his shell. But the roaming gnome phenomenon predates the film by at least 15 years. The earliest known incident involves a missing gnome from Sydney, Australia, who sent his owners a postcard claiming he was vacationing in Queensland. The gnome reappeared in the yard two weeks later sporting a light coating of brown shoe polish—apparently, he'd gotten a suntan at the beach.

Holidays & Traditions
Watching Through the Night

✦ ✦ ✦ ✦

*Watch Night introduced a different way
to celebrate a familiar holiday.*

In one sense, New Year's Eve may be the most universal of holidays, as virtually every culture on the planet has some way of marking the passing of one era and the start of another. Of course, each culture celebrates at its own time of year and with its own set of traditions. For most Americans, December 31 is a time for counting down and drinking up, and January 1 is a time of empty resolutions and epic hangovers. But even in America there are alternative ways to mark the passing of an old year and the coming of a new one.

For many black Americans, the New Year's holiday centers around one of the most meaningful and popular religious services of the year: Watch Night. Throngs of people gather in churches on New Year's Eve for a long evening of song, reflection, celebration, and prayer in a ceremony that can fluctuate between pious and raucous.

Holy Origins
Watch Night originated with the Moravians, Christians whose roots trace back to the present-day Czech Republic. The first such services likely took place in Germany in 1733. In 1777, Methodism founder John Wesley brought the practice to the states, calling for his followers to renew their covenant with God in a monthly vigil that corresponded to the full moon.

Where Legend Meets Fact
It is commonly believed that the tradition of celebrating Watch Night on New Year's Eve dates to the American South during the days of slavery. This much is true. But why? Some sources claim that slave families gathered to pray together on New Year's Eve because they feared it would be their last night together. Many slaves saw their families broken up after New Year's when individuals were sold to raise funds to settle outstanding debts. But this explanation

falls short. The most significant evidence against this theory is that Southern businessmen were unlikely to conduct business on New Year's Day.

Let Freedom Ring!

What *is* known is that Watch Night became an important African American celebration during the Civil War, as slaves and free blacks across the country gathered in their churches on New Year's Eve 1862 to await a watershed moment in United States history. The next day, January 1, 1963, President Abraham Lincoln was scheduled to—and did—sign the Emancipation Proclamation. This simple but eloquent 725-word document freed everyone held in slavery in the Confederate States and declared all of them eligible for military service in the Union. Then and now, the document was criticized for having freed only those slaves residing in states that were in rebellion, but it irrevocably committed the federal government to abolishing slavery throughout the entire country.

The Watch Night tradition continued in black congregations for decades as a celebration of hard-won freedom and then waned in the early years of the 20th century. The practice was reinvigorated in the 1960s as part of the Civil Rights Movement and continues to this day, serving as a powerful reminder and celebration of one of the most pivotal moments in American history. Celebrations vary from church to church, but there are many commonalities. Services typically begin late, around 10 P.M., and continue until shortly after midnight, though some groups stay throughout the night and celebrate until dawn. One congregation will often host another, so that members of both churches can share the night together. There's usually a sermon, or the pastor may read the official church record from the year that's ending. Members of the church will often give spontaneous testimonials of the trials they've faced and the blessings they've received, putting the former behind them and expressing gratitude for the latter. The service sometimes includes a candlelight procession and is always interspersed with joyful singing. Just before midnight, worshippers crowd together around the altar and fall to their knees to pray in a moving scene that dedicates the start of the year to God. And so continues the Methodist notion of renewing one's covenant at New Year's.

Good Ol' Boys Make Good

✦ ✦ ✦ ✦

"Heck, I had faster bootleg cars than race cars."
—NASCAR pioneer Robert Glen Johnson Jr. (a.k.a. Junior Johnson)

The 1930s and 1940s saw a new breed of driver tearing up the back roads of the American South. Young, highly skilled, and full of brass, these road rebels spent their nights outwitting and outrunning federal agents as they hauled 60-gallon payloads of illegal moonshine liquor from the mountains to their eager customers in the cities below. In this dangerous game, speed and control made all the difference. The bootleggers spent as much time tinkering under their hoods as they did prowling the roads. A typical bootleg car might be a Ford Coupe with a 454 Cadillac engine, heavy-duty suspension, and any number of other modifications meant to keep the driver and his illicit cargo ahead of John Law.

And They're Off!

With all that testosterone and horsepower bundled together, it was inevitable that these wild hares would compete to see who had the fastest car and the steeliest nerve. A dozen or more of them would get together on weekends in an open field and spend the afternoon testing each other's skills, often passing a hat among the spectators who came to watch. Promoters saw the potential in these events, and before long organized races were being held all across the South. As often as not, though, the promoters lit out with the receipts halfway through the race, and the drivers saw nothing for their efforts.

Seeking to bring both legitimacy and profitability to the sport, driver and race promoter William "Bill" Henry Getty France Sr. organized a meeting of his colleagues at the Ebony Bar in Daytona Beach, Florida, on December 14, 1947. Four days of haggling and backslapping led to the formation of the National Association for Stock Car Auto Racing (NASCAR), with France named as its first president. The group held its inaugural race in 1948, on the well-known half-sand, half-asphalt track at Daytona. Over the next two

decades, the upstart organization built
a name for itself on the strength
of its daring and charismatic drivers. Junior Johnson, Red Byron,
Curtis Turner, Lee Petty, and the
Flock Brothers—Bob, Fonty, and
Tim—held regular jobs (some still
running moonshine) and raced the circuit in
their spare time. And these legendary pioneers
were some colorful characters: For example,
Tim Flock occasionally raced with a pet mon-
key named Jocko Flocko, who sported a crash helment and was
strapped into the passenger seat.

Dawn of a New Era

During these early years, NASCAR was viewed as a distinctly
Southern enterprise. In the early 1970s, however, Bill France Jr.
took control of the organization from his father, and things began
to change. The younger France negotiated network television deals
that brought the racetrack into the living rooms of Middle America.
In 1979, CBS presented the first flag-to-flag coverage of a NASCAR
event, and it was a doozy. Race leaders Cale Yarborough and Donnie
Allison entered a bumping duel on the last lap that ended with
both cars crashing on the third turn. As Richard Petty moved up
from third to take the checkered flag, a fight broke out between
Yarborough and Allison's brother Bobby. America was hooked.

France also expanded the sport's sponsorship beyond automak-
ers and parts manufacturers. Tobacco giant R. J. Reynolds bought
its way in, as did countless other purveyors of everyday household
items, including Tide, Lowe's Hardware, Kellogg's Cereal, the Cartoon Network, Nextel, and Coca-Cola. Today, NASCAR vehicles
and their beloved drivers are virtually moving billboards. Plastered
with the logos of their sponsors as they speed around the track, Jeff
Gordon, Dale Earnhardt Jr., Tony Stewart, Bobby Labonte, and
their fellow daredevils draw the eyes of some 75 million regular fans
and support a multibillion-dollar industry that outearns professional
baseball, basketball, and hockey combined.

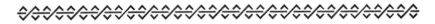

Literature
Too Big to Be True

❖ ❖ ❖ ❖

Made famous by French writer Francois Rabelais as a symbol of insatiable appetites, Gargantua was said to belong to a race of giants.

Gargantua is an icon of gluttonous hunger. According to myth, he was born from the ear of his mother, Gargamelle, and had a hunger so voracious that he consumed the milk of 17,813 cows every day. In a later adventure, he swallowed five people on religious pilgrimage, tossing these pilgrims and their staves into a salad. He was also the father of a lusty young giant named Pantagruel.

How did this myth spread? The son of a lord from Touraine, France, made this story famous. Francois Rabelais (c. 1494–1553) was educated in monasteries and at the universities at Paris and Lyon. He was trained as a physician and was a scholar of ancient Greek. Rabelais also published parodies of the predictions of astrology.

In 1532, Rabelais published the first of a series of books based on these characters, which he borrowed from an unknown author. *The Very Frightful Life of the Grand Gargantua* appeared in 1534. Thanks to the invention of movable type in 1450, Rabelais's books enjoyed wide readership and enormous popularity; among his greatest admirers was King Francis I of France. After the death of Francis I in 1547, however, literary praise for Rabelais's wit and satire turned to social condemnation. Rabelais left Paris for Metz and then went to Rome. He later became a curate in the town of Meudon, where he lived quietly and died in relative obscurity.

The name "Gargantua" comes from the word garganta, *meaning "gullet."*

Food & Drink
How Sweet It Is!

❖ ❖ ❖ ❖

In the early 1900s, American entrepreneurs brought an
exclusive treat of the wealthy to masses of children.

The origins of cotton candy appear a bit muddled, with most sources pointing to four different possible inventors. Just before 1900, John Wharton and William Morrison received a patent for a machine that melted sugar and then used centrifugal force to stretch it into thin strands. They sold almost 70,000 boxes of their "fairy floss" at the 1904 St. Louis World's Fair for 25 cents a pop—a hefty sum for a candy treat in those days. Meanwhile, Thomas Patton received a patent for a similar machine; he supposedly peddled his fluffy treats for the Barnum & Bailey Circus. To further complicate the story, a Louisiana dentist named Josef Delarose Lascaux is said to have had a homemade cotton candy machine in his office around the turn of the century.

So, who is the true inventor of the famous spun-sugar treat? Well, it's not Lascaux, Patton, or the team of Wharton and Morrison. They simply automated a process for spinning sugar that had been in use for at least 150 years. Recipes for creating wispy strands of solidified sugar by hand date to at least 1769. Around that time, confectioners provided meticulous instructions that detailed how to melt the sugar and then "take small portions and pass it quickly to and fro to form threads over an oiled rolling pin held in the left hand. A fork is best to use to take up the sugar." The process was labor-intensive and therefore expensive. But confectioners skilled in the art of hand-spinning sugar could create elaborate "nests" as Easter decorations or sparkling silvery-gold strands to top off desserts for their well-to-do clients.

Still, the accomplishments of these four early 20th-century inventors were significant. They took a decadent candy, typically sold to few in small quantities at high cost, and turned it into an iconic childhood treat enjoyed by millions of young people—eventually for nominally more than the cost of the sugar itself.

Inventions
The Firefighter's Best Friend
❖ ❖ ❖ ❖

*A device first conceived in the 1600s saves countless
lives and millions of dollars in property every year.*

Fire hydrants are one of the most ubiquitous fixtures in U.S. cities. Squat, brightly painted, and immediately recognizable, two or three of them adorn virtually every city block in the United States. New York City alone has more than 100,000 hydrants within city limits.

Fire hydrants as we know them today have been around for more than 200 years, but their predecessors first appeared in London in the 1600s. At that time, Britain's capital had an impressive municipal water system that consisted of networks of wooden pipes—essentially hollowed-out tree trunks—that snaked beneath the cobblestone streets. During large blazes, firefighters would dig through the street and cut into the pipe, allowing the hole they had dug to fill with water, creating an instant cistern that provided a supply of water for the bucket brigade. After extinguishing the blaze, they would drain the hole and plug the wooden pipe—which is the origin of the term *fireplug*—and then mark the spot for the next time a fire broke out in the vicinity.

Fanning the Flames of Invention
In 1666, a terrible fire raged through nearly three-quarters of London. As the city underwent rebuilding, the wooden pipes beneath the streets were redesigned to include predrilled plugs that rose to ground level. The following century, these crude fireplugs were improved with the addition of valves that allowed firefighters to insert portable standpipes that reached down to the mains. Many European countries use systems of a similar design today.

With the advent of metal piping, it became possible to install valve-controlled pipes that rose above street level. Frederick Graff Sr., the chief engineer of the Philadelphia Water Works department, is generally credited with designing the first hydrant of this type in 1801, as part of the city's effort to revamp its water system. A scant two years later, pumping systems became available, and Graff retro-fitted Philly's hydrants with nozzles to accommodate the new fire hoses, giving hydrants essentially the same appearance that they have today. By 1811, the city boasted 185 cast-iron hydrants along with 230 wooden ones.

Hydrants Spread Like Wildfire

Over the next 50 years, hydrants became commonplace in all major American cities. But many communities in the north faced a serious fire safety problem during the bitter winters. The mains were usually placed well below the frost line, allowing the free-flow of water year-round, but the aboveground hydrants were prone to freezing, rendering them useless. Some cities tried putting wooden casings filled with sawdust or other insulating material, such as manure, around the hydrants, but this wasn't enough to stave off the cold. Others sent out armies of workers on the worst winter nights to turn the hydrants on for a few minutes each hour and let the water flow.

The freezing problem wasn't fully solved until the 1850s, with the development of dry-barrel hydrants. These use a dual-valve system that keeps water out of the hydrant until it is needed. Firefighters turn a nut on the top of the hydrant that opens a valve where the hydrant meets the main, letting the water rise to street level. When this main valve is closed, a drainage valve automatically opens so that any water remaining in the hydrant can flow out. Very little else about the design of fire hydrants has changed since. In fact, some cities are still using hydrants that were installed in the early 1900s.

Fads & Fashion
A Brief History of Underwear

◆ ◆ ◆ ◆

From fig leaves to bloomers to thongs, people have covered themselves a little or a lot, depending on social preferences and mores. Here is a brief history of the undergarment.

- The earliest and most simple undergarment was the loincloth—a long strip of material worn between the legs and around the waist. King Tutankhamen was buried with 145 of them, but the style didn't go out with the Egyptians. Loincloths are still worn in many Asian and African cultures.

- Men in the Middle Ages wore loose, trouserlike undergarments called *braies,* which one stepped into and tied around the waist and legs about mid-calf. To facilitate urination, braies were fitted with a codpiece, a flap that buttoned or tied closed.

- Medieval women wore a close-fitting undergarment called a *chemise,* and corsets began to appear in the 18th century. Early versions of the corset were designed to flatten a woman's bustline, but by the late 1800s, corsets were reconstructed to give women an exaggerated hourglass shape.

- In the late 1800s and early 1900s, chastity was a big concern for married or committed couples. During that time, many inventors received patents for "security underwear" for men. These devices were meant to assure "masculine chastity." They ensured that men refrained from sexual relations with anyone other than the person with the key to open that particular device.

- Around 1920, as women became more involved in sports such as tennis and bicycling, loose, comfortable bloomers replaced corsets as the undergarment of choice. The constricting corset soon fell out of favor altogether.

- The thong made its first public U.S. appearance at the 1939 World's Fair, when New York Mayor Fiorello LaGuardia required nude dancers to cover themselves, if only barely.

Language
Pariahs: A People Apart

✦ ✦ ✦ ✦

A word that originally described the cultural function of a social group came to denote the most despised members of a society.

The word *pariah* (or a variation thereof) appears in a number of European languages, including English, French, and Portuguese, but it comes from the Tamil culture of southern India. Most Tamil people are Hindu, although some are Christians, Muslims, or Jains. It is within the Hindu caste system that the term acquired its most potent meaning of "outcast"—something or someone to be despised and shunned.

The word is derived from the Tamil *paraiyan,* or "drummer." In ancient times, members of this group were known as sorcerers and drummers who played at ritual occasions. However, pariahs also worked as laborers or menial servants. Eventually, the group was absorbed into the category known as "untouchables," the bottom tier of Hindu society.

Pariah appeared in Western languages in the 17th century. In 1498, the Portuguese were the first to trade in India, and other countries soon followed. The Dutch East India Company was formed in 1602 to protect Holland's trading rights in the east. England was an active presence in India by the end of the 17th century, and Queen Victoria was crowned empress of India in 1876. The word probably entered popular conversation through its frequent appearance in late 18th-century French novels.

In some contexts, the word *pariah* has become a gentler epithet. Formerly the pariah dog was any stray or undomesticated dog; now the term designates a primitive breed of dogs—but not a mixed breed or mongrel—that shares particular characteristics wherever it is found in the world.

Synonyms for *pariah* also include *leper* and *exile.* The word is most commonly used to describe people deliberately isolated from society—victims of antiquated social attitudes and prejudice.

Toys & Games
A "Fitting" Solution:
The Origin of Jigsaw Puzzles

♦ ♦ ♦ ♦

Puzzled over the origin of the jigsaw? We've put the pieces together!

In the 1760s, engraver and cartographer John Spilsbury cut a
wooden map of the British Empire into little pieces. Reassembling
the map from the parts, he believed, would teach aristocratic
schoolchildren the geographic location of imperial possessions and
prepare them for their eventual role as governors. Spilsbury called
his invention "Dissected Maps."

Spilsbury's "Dissected Maps" were soon popular among the
wealthy classes. By the end of the 19th century, however, these
"puzzles" functioned largely as an amusement. The early decades of
the 20th century were the heyday of the puzzle's popularity in the
United States. The first American business to produce jigsaw puzzles
was Parker Brothers; the company launched its hand-cut wooden
"Pastime Puzzles" in 1908. Milton Bradley followed suit with its
"Premier Jig Saw Puzzles," so named because the picture, attached
to a thin wooden board, was cut into curved and irregular pieces
with a jigsaw. As the Great Depression came to an end in the late
1930s, inexpensive cardboard puzzles were produced at prices nearly
anyone could afford.

The Big Picture

For more than a century, jigsaw puzzles have delighted people of
all ages; designers are constantly at work inventing new and more
difficult challenges. There are three-dimensional picture puzzles,
double-sided puzzles, and puzzles with curving and irregular
edges. A puzzle advertised as "the world's largest jigsaw puzzle"
has 24,000 pieces. Monochromatic puzzles include "Little Red
Riding Hood's Hood" (all red) and "Snow White Without the Seven
Dwarfs" (all white).

Sports
If You Build It, They Will Play

❖ ❖ ❖ ❖

It's safe to say that the inventor of miniature golf hit a hole in one!

Miniature golf has been described as a novelty game, but it requires the same steady hands, analytical observation, and maneuvering as regular golf.

In their infancy, miniature golf courses were designed the same as full-size courses but were built at one-tenth the size, much like the popular par-3 courses of today. In 1916, James Barber of Pinehurst, North Carolina, created a miniature golf course that resembles the game played today. He dubbed his design "Thistle Dhu," supposedly a twist on the phrase "This'll do." Barber's course was an intricate maze of geometric shapes coupled with symmetric walkways, fountains, and planters. Until 1922, mini-golf courses used live grass—just like the real game—and were subject to the same grooming needs and growing woes. That all changed when a man named Thomas McCulloch Fairbairn prepared a mixture of cottonseed hull—or mulch, sand, oil, and green dye—and used the concoction to resurface the miniature golf course he was designing. The first artificial putting green was born.

The game boomed for the next few years, with hundreds of miniature golf outlets opening around the country, including 150 rooftop courses in New York City alone. The arrival of the Great Depression severed the popularity of the pastime, and its growth remained stagnant until 1938 when brothers Joseph and Robert R. Taylor Sr. revitalized the game. The Taylors redesigned the sport by adding complicated obstacles such as windmills, castles, and wishing wells to increase the competitive enjoyment. Today, international miniature golf tournaments are held around the world.

Music
Hammond Organ: Tones of Endearment

❖ ❖ ❖ ❖

Long before keyboard wizards such as Patrick Moraz,
Keith Emerson, and Rick Wakeman made synthesizers and
mellotrons essential entries in the rock 'n' roll lexicon, the
Hammond organ was the straw that stirred the sound.

As essential to the sounds that shaped the '60s as feedback and the fuzz box, the Hammond B-3 organ provided a whirring cascade of effects that stirred soul, jolted jazz, and revolutionized rock.

The Hammond organ as we know it was designed and developed by Laurens Hammond in 1933. A graduate of Cornell University, Hammond had invented a soundless electric clock in 1928. He used a similar technology to construct his revolutionary keyboard, adapting the electric motor used in the manufacture of his clocks into a tonewheel generator, which artificially re-created or synthesized the notes generated by a pipe organ. By using drawbars to adjust volume and tone, Hammond was able to electronically simulate instruments such as the flute, oboe, clarinet, and recorder.

Thaddeus Cahill, who created an instrument dubbed the *telharmonium* in 1898, first formulated the concept of the tonewheel generator. While it was dynamic in design, it was cumbersome in concept, weighing seven tons and costing $200,000 to produce. Not exactly the potentially portable keyboard that Hammond was able to perfect 30 years later.

The effectiveness of Hammond's electric keyboard was greatly enhanced by the invention of the Leslie tone cabinet, a system that uses a rotating speaker to amplify, adjust, and enhance the intricacies of the Hammond sound. Invented by Donald Leslie in 1937, it proved to be a perfect partner to complement Hammond's keyboard, although there was bitterness between the two men, who thus never established a business partnership.

The Hammond B-3 was first manufactured in 1955. It remains a favorite among jazz musicians and rock groups.

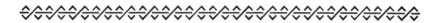

Film
Hooray for Bollywood

❖ ❖ ❖ ❖

Since the mid-20th century, the Mumbai-based industry
has made a "reel" mark on the world of film.

In American cinema, it is usually only musicals—or comedies satirizing musicals—that feature characters breaking out in grand song and dance numbers. Not so in Bollywood. In fact, these musical montages are a standard element of popular films from India, no matter the subject or story line.

Today, the Mumbai-based, Hindi-language film industry is one of the largest producers of movies in the entire world. But when and how did Bollywood originate? The name "Bollywood" is semiofficial and comes from the combination of Bombay (the former name for Mumbai) and Hollywood. But unlike its American cousin, there is no Bollywood sign and no epicenter of studios. And while the name "Bollywood" is often used (incorrectly) to identify all Indian-made films, it actually describes just one very popular subset.

The roots of the Indian movie industry date to 1913 with the release of *Raja Harishchandra,* but it was the 1931 release of *Alam Ara* that took Bollywood filmmakers in a new direction with the advent of talkies. Prior to independence from Great Britain in 1947, India produced films centered on social issues, including the Indian independence movement. By the 1960s, the films were lavish romantic musicals and melodramas that incorporated the epic musical numbers still popular to this day.

While many films became grittier, more violent, and less lavish throughout the 1970s and 1980s, the familiar song-and-dance sequences remained. By the 1990s, romantic love stories were back in vogue. Several actors and actresses from this period became very famous in India, even surpassing some of Hollywood's brightest stars.

Today, these films still feature catchy—albeit tangential—musical numbers, now a hallmark of Bollywood cinema.

Fads & Fashion
The Bikini: Scandal on the Beach

❖ ❖ ❖ ❖

Bikinis are such a common sight on public beaches that it's hard to believe the skimpy, two-piece bathing suits were considered scandalous when first introduced in France at the end of World War II. It's important to note, however, that French designers didn't actually invent the bikini; that honor goes to the ancient Romans.

Eons-old mosaics and murals suggest that a two-piece bathing suit—sort of a pre-bikini, if you will—was commonly worn by Roman women at the beach or poolside. Some historians believe two-piece swimwear may date back even further, as evidenced by recently discovered cave drawings that show Minoan women wearing primitive bikinis as far back as 1600 B.C.

The bikini as we know it today was developed by fashion designer Jacques Heim, who debuted his daring creation in a Cannes swim shop in 1946. He called the suit the "Atome" in honor of the tiny atom and christened it "the world's smallest bathing suit."

The Atome might have gone down in history as just another fad were it not for fellow designer Louis Reard, who unveiled his own two-piece suit on the fashionable French Riviera just three weeks after Heim. He called his suit the "bikini" after the Bikini Reef, upon whose atolls some of the first atomic bombs were tested.

The bikini arrived in the United States in 1947 to a lot of curiosity but few sales. Conservative Americans found the bathing suit a little too risqué, and some of the more staid communities even banned it. Two decades passed before American sexual attitudes loosened up enough for the average woman to feel comfortable baring her navel (and sometimes much more) at the beach.

The bikini has gone through some wild variations over the years, including the daring monokini of the freewheeling '60s, but today it is one of swimwear's most popular styles.

Clubs & Organizations
Down on the Farm

❖ ❖ ❖ ❖

A rural youth group helped to revolutionize agricultural practices.

In the United States, 4-H Clubs have been an inspirational and educational presence for more than a century. Ohio school superintendent A. B. Graham is generally credited with starting the first 4-H Club in the United States in 1902. The federal government even got involved, with Congress creating and funding the Cooperative Extension Service, of which 4-H remains a part.

In the early years, the organization had more on its mind than developing the skills of rural youth. The U.S. Department of Agriculture and other organizations faced difficulty getting many farmers to adopt the latest scientific advances in farming. They found that children, on the other hand, were eager to experiment with new ideas. The 4-H Clubs were intended, at least in part, to get the current generation of farmers to accept these new ideas by seeing their children succeed with them.

Over time, the organization grew in scope and redefined its focus. In the 1940s and 1950s, 4-H introduced international exchange programs, and clubs increasingly began to participate in scientific research. Local chapters carefully gathered and documented data on new kinds of livestock feed or planting practices, sharing the information with scientists. Clubs also spread to urban areas. Over the next several decades, emphasis gradually shifted to broader life skills, such as leadership, community involvement, reading, and math.

So, what does "4-H" stand for? Well, originally there were only three *H*'s—Head, Heart, and Hands. In 1911, one club organizer suggested adding a fourth *H* to represent "Hustle." But at some point, the last "H" came to stand for "Health" instead.

Holidays & Traditions
For the Love of Mom

❖ ❖ ❖ ❖

*Who doesn't love Mother's Day? As it turns out, the woman credited
with organizing the first "official" Mother's Day isn't a fan.*

The worship of motherhood goes back as far as ancient Greece. Rituals in honor of Rhea, the "mother of the gods," took place in spring
and were said to be wild ecstatic parties full of drumming, dancing,
and drinking. The Roman version of this festival—Matronalia, dedicated to Juno Lucina, the "goddess of childbirth"—was not the party
of Greek times, but a Roman mother could at least expect some
gifts. With the advent of Christianity, such festivals disappeared, but
eventually the church also provided a way to honor mothers.

In the 16th century, the fourth Sunday of Lent was set aside as
"Mothering Sunday," a time when people were expected to visit
the church where they were baptized (with some sort of offering,
of course!). This day ultimately became a family reunion of sorts.
Back then, many children were sent away from their parents to work
as apprentices or take jobs as servants. Their visits home for Lent
were known as "going a-mothering." The children would bring their
mothers wildflowers or small presents. "Mothering Sunday" is still
celebrated in Ireland and parts of the United Kingdom.

From Mothering Sunday to Mother's Day

Today, if you are anything like 96 percent of the American public,
you participate in Mother's Day by spending money. A lot of it.
Mother's Day is one of the biggest gift-giving holidays of the year.
In fact, we spend more only during Christmas. It is hard to believe
that early feminist activists gave this traditional (and commercial)
American holiday its start.

During the American Civil War, a woman by the name of Ann
Reeves Jarvis formed "Mother's Day Work Clubs" to help improve
living conditions (among other things) for soldiers on both sides of
the conflict. Her efforts inspired the suffragist Julia Ward Howe
(famous for writing "The Battle Hymn of the Republic") to call for

a "Mother's Day for Peace." Howe was convinced that if women had been running things, the horrors of the Civil War could have been prevented. In 1870, she wrote a "Mother's Day Proclamation" urging women to unite against all war. But neither woman's efforts amounted to any official recognition of Mother's Day.

The cause gained new life in 1905, after Ann Reeves Jarvis's death. Her daughter, Anna M. Jarvis, took up the "Mother's Day" mission—and it eventually took over her life.

This Wasn't What I Had in Mind...

It was Anna M. Jarvis's grief over her mother's death that most likely prompted her, on May 10, 1908, to stage what is considered to be the first "official" Mother's Day—a memorial to her mother. She gave white carnations to each of the mothers at her church and encouraged her fellow parishioners to set the day aside as one of commemoration and gratitude. The idea spread, and in the years that followed, she lobbied business leaders and politicians for a national mother's holiday. Finally, in 1914, Woodrow Wilson issued a proclamation setting aside the second Sunday in May to honor mothers. The country quickly embraced this idea in a distinctly American way—by shopping.

The commercialization of Mother's Day enraged its founder. Anna M. Jarvis saw what she'd envisioned as a holy day become another excuse to sell merchandise. In fact, when she saw "Mother's Day" carnations being sold to raise money for veterans, she tried to stop the sale and was arrested for disturbing the peace. She even filed a lawsuit to stop Mother's Day altogether. She died, childless, at the age of 84, regretting Mother's Day's existence. She never knew it, but her final medical bills were partly paid for by florists.

Anna Jarvis may have had a point. According to some estimates, more than 100 million Mother's Day cards are sold in the United States each year.

Inventions
Ant Farms

◆ ◆ ◆ ◆

They invade our homes, ruin our picnics, and make a general
nuisance of themselves. Ask most people what they think of
ants, and they'll tell you these insects are nothing but irritating
pests. But Milton Levine wouldn't agree. To him, ants are
amazingly industrious workers who are fascinating to watch.

In 1956, Levine was at a Fourth of July picnic when he was struck
with the idea for the ant farm. He reached for a sandwich and found
it covered with ants, but rather then being repulsed, Levine thought
back to his youthful fascination with insects. "I'd fill a jar with sand,
put in some ants and watch them cavort," he said in a 2002 interview. "So at the picnic I thought, why not make a toy that would let
kids watch the ants?"

The Ants Go Marching One by One...
Within a few months, Levine had designed the first plastic Ant
Farms, and a remarkable new toy was born.

Levine—known fondly to millions as Uncle Milton—fell into the
toy game after leaving the army in 1946. Along with his brother-in-
law, Joe Cossman, he formed a mail-order novelty company that sold
things such as plastic soldiers and circus animals for a dollar. The
company did well, and Levine eventually packed up his family and
moved to California, where he continued to sell children's novelties.
The ant farm, however, would ultimately prove to be his legacy.

A Few Bugs in the System
In the early days, the enterprise posed some unique challenges.
Levine had to develop and refine the two-step process in which
customers would first buy a farm and then mail in a certificate to get
the ants. But that's not all. Before he could send live ants through
the mail, Levine had to secure authorization on a state by state basis.
(If you live in Hawaii, you're out of luck—ants are labeled a nuisance
there, so the company can't ship its product to that state.) Another

issue was the sand. Levine first used beach sand, but it was the same color as the ants, so he switched to a whiter volcanic soil for better contrast.

Levine found that red harvester ants, which are found in the Mojave desert, worked best in his farms. Unlike other types of ants, red harvester ants work all the time. As a side benefit, their slippery feet made it impossible for them to crawl out of the plastic container.

Crawling with Success

Levine first advertised the ant farm in a small notice in the *Los Angeles Times* Sunday magazine and was soon overwhelmed with orders. This was good in that it proved he had hit on something big but bad in that he didn't have enough ants to fill the requests. He advertised for ant pickers, offering one cent per ant, but had trouble finding someone who was reliable.

Eventually, Levine signed a contract with the Gidney family, who created a special vacuum to gently collect the insects, delivering them to Levine on Sunday for Monday mailing to customers. The Gidneys provided Levine with ants for many years. When they were no longer able to do so, the job was given to another family, whose name is a company secret.

Levine bought out Cossman in 1965 and renamed the company Uncle Milton Industries. He kept the ant farm in the public eye through shrewd promotion, including appearances on *The Merv Griffin Show* and *The Shari Lewis Show.* Levine also planted his son, Steve, on children's television shows, where the host would inevitably notice him holding an ant farm and ask about the unusual toy.

The continued success of the ant farm never failed to amaze Levine. "I thought it would sell for maybe two years," he once said. But he couldn't have been more wrong. Uncle Milton Industries has sold more than 20 million Ant Farms over the decades and continues to sell approximately 30,000 a month.

Language
Dead as a Doornail?
Perish the Thought!

❖ ❖ ❖ ❖

Shakespeare scripted it and Dickens popularized it, but people
have been using the phrase "dead as a doornail" as a description
for demise for as long as words have been printed on paper.

Although the origin of the phrase "dead as a doornail" is not entirely
known, its meaning is certain. To be "dead as a doornail" is to be
truly and without question expired, passed on, totally bereft of life,
and pushing up daises. The phrase was used in the poem "The
Vision of Piers Plowman," which was written by William Langland
sometime in the late 1300s. And in Act IV, Scene X of his epic play
Henry VI, Part 2, William Shakespeare also scripted the slogan. The
character John Cade utters this threat, " . . . if I do not leave you all
as dead/as a door-nail, I pray God I may never eat grass more."

Okay, so the dead part is clear enough; it's the doornail part that
leaves most scholars scratching their heads. Charles Dickens popularized the parlance in the opening lines of his iconic novel *A Christmas Carol* when the narrator states emphatically that Old Marley is
dead as a door-nail, but just a few lines later, the narrator continues:
"Mind! I don't mean to say that I know, of my own knowledge, what
there is particularly dead about a door-nail."

Some astute authorities in the diction of demise have decided the
most logical conclusion relates to carpentry. If you hammer a nail
through a piece of timber, such as a door, and bend the end over
on the other side so it cannot be removed—a technique called
clinching—the nail is said to be *dead,* because it can't be used again.

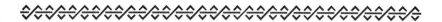

Fads & Fashion
Classy Chapeau

❖ ❖ ❖ ❖

The pillbox hat, like the container from which it
borrows its name, is compact, classy, and simple.

Historically, the pillbox hat was first worn as a ceremonial military
accessory, especially in Commonwealth countries. The Royal Canadian Military College, located in Kingston, Ontario, made the pillbox
hat and accompanying chinstrap an essential element of the institution's dress uniform in 1878.

But it wasn't until the early 1960s—when Jacqueline Kennedy,
the elegant wife of President John F. Kennedy, made it her chapeau
of choice—that the hat's popularity soared. When Mrs. Kennedy
wore a light-colored pillbox hat to her husband's inauguration ceremony in January 1961, American women flocked to the department
stores in search of similar styles. Bob Dylan, the generation's most
influential musician and spokesman of the street, heralded the hat
in his song "Leopard-Skin Pill-Box Hat," off his multimillion-selling
album *Blonde on Blonde.*

Much of the revival in pillbox popularity can be credited to
renowned stylist Oleg Cassini, the man Mrs. Kennedy selected to
design her extravagant gowns and complementary accessories. A
couture designer famous for his millinery style, Cassini created
the pillbox hats the First Lady wore so gracefully. Unfortunately,
Mrs. Kennedy was also wearing a pillbox hat on November 22,
1963, when her husband was assassinated and died in her arms. The
popularity of the pillbox hat declined sharply after that tragic day in
Dallas, and the fashion has never regained the status held during the
Kennedys' Camelot.

Law & Politics
The Coogan Bill: A Law Child Actors Can Trust

❖ ❖ ❖ ❖

Exploitation of a child star led to a protective law.

The Coogan Bill is an interesting piece of legislation, and it all began with a child actor by the name of Jackie Coogan, who later played the role of huggable Uncle Fester in the 1960s television series *The Addams Family*. Although the baby boomer generation associates Coogan with that memorable role, film buffs may recall a pint-size actor who equaled any in popularity. In fact, Jackie Coogan (née John Leslie Coogan Jr.) was the first major child star churned out by the Hollywood celebrity machine. With a breakthrough role in *The Kid* (1921) and subsequent roles in a score of silent films, the boy with the pageboy haircut became one of Hollywood's highest paid performers.

Despite his overwhelming success, Coogan's financial state was far from secure. From the very beginning of his career, his mother and stepfather had complete control of his holdings, and tragically for Coogan, they refused to part with any of it.

In 1935, Coogan was injured in an automobile crash that claimed the life of his father, Jack Coogan Sr., and child actor Trent Bernard "Junior" Durkin. In 1938, the former child star sued his parents' production company to reclaim his money. He would recoup just $126,000—exactly half the remaining value of the firm that his irresponsible parents had overseen and neglected. It was only a fraction of the estimated $4 million that Coogan had earned.

Coogan became a poster boy for exploited child actors. In 1939, the state of California enacted a preventative law to address the problem. The *California Child Actor's Bill* (Coogan Bill) stated that a portion of a young actor's earnings would be directly deposited into a trust fund. The law came a bit late to benefit Coogan—his financial problems had already "festered" for years—but at least the star's loss wasn't in vain.

Sports
Smooth Operator

✦ ✦ ✦ ✦

*Before Frank Joseph Zamboni Jr. invented his self-propelled
ice resurfacing machine, cleaning and clearing a sheet of
ice was laborious, time-consuming, and inefficient.*

Zamboni, an amateur inventor and the owner/operator of the Iceland Skating Rink in Paramount, California, needed a new method
for sweeping the ice surface of his rink. Artificial ice rinks were still a
novelty when Zamboni opened his facility in 1939, and it took a team
of three people to repair and resurface the ice after it was gouged
by hundreds of gliders, a procedure that took up to 90 minutes.
Zamboni came up with an idea for a motorized machine that could
do all the necessary work—sweep, scrape, and saturate—and could
be operated by one man. He stripped an old Jeep down to its nuts,
bolts, and bare underbody chassis and placed a blade on the under
train to shave the ice smooth. He devised a device to sweep up the
shavings and deposit the icy debris into a tank that melted the scrap-
ings and used the water to rinse the rink. After several attempts and
numerous prototypes, he perfected the "mechanical monster" and it
became a tourist attraction in its own right.

   In 1950, Sonja Henie, a three-time Olympic figure skating champion and one of Hollywood's top box-office attractions, was rehears-
ing her new Hollywood Ice Revue at the Iceland when she saw the
revolutionary resurfacer at work. She commissioned Zamboni to
build her a new model for her upcoming performances in Chicago.
That endorsement allowed Zamboni to mass-produce the machines
that now bear his name.

✧✧✧✧✧✧

*Zamboni does a slick business. In 2007, the company delivered its
8,500th machine.*

Inventions
The Sands of Time

❖ ❖ ❖ ❖

*A seemingly simple bit of technology has
a surprisingly complex history.*

Accurate timekeeping wasn't really possible until the Middle Ages
with the invention of the mechanical clock. But at least ancient
people had the hourglass to give them an approximate measure of
time passing, right? We've all seen these devices used in movies set
in ancient Egypt and Rome. Why, even the Wicked Witch of the
West had one in *The Wizard of Oz*.

A Grain of History

But actually, when sword-and-sandal flicks
incorporated hourglasses into their story lines,
they were indulging in a bit of cinematic
license. Though no one knows for sure when
the hourglass was invented, the first concrete
evidence of anyone using one didn't appear
until 1338, and even that evidence is indirect.
The Italian artist Ambrosio Lorenzetti
included an hourglass in a series of allegorical
frescoes he created for the Palazzo Pubblico
(Town Hall) in the city of Siena. The work
focused on the theme of good government
versus bad government, and a maiden holding
an hourglass represented the virtue of
Temperance. An earlier theory held that ancient Greeks used
them, based on a carving of an hourglass on an ancient coffin. It
was later discovered, however, that the carving had been added in
the early 1600s.

Of course, the hourglass in Lorenzetti's fresco still doesn't tell
us when these timekeepers first appeared, but it is clear that by the
end of the 14th century they were common household items. The
evidence this time—again indirect—comes from a handwritten

"household treatise" dated to the 1390s. Belonging to the household of a Frenchman, the book provides instructions for performing various household chores, among them recipes for making preserves, glue, ink, and the filler for an hourglass. Wait a minute—a recipe for sand? Well, that's another common misconception about these simple devices. Because grains of sand vary in size, they would flow through an hourglass at an irregular rate and thus make it unreliable. It was more common to use marble dust or ground eggshells that had been laboriously processed to create fine particles of even size. The Frenchman's recipe indicates just how involved the task was: "Take the grease which comes from the sawdust of marble when those great tombs of black marble be sawn, then boil it well in wine like a piece of meat and skim it, and then set it out to dry in the sun; and boil, skim, and dry nine times; and thus it will be good."

Out to Sea

One additional piece of information raises speculation as to when the hourglass was actually invented. The devices were often referred to as "sea clocks." For example, an inventory of the estate of King Charles V of France taken after his death in 1380 uses that term to describe a large hourglass he kept in a study at one of his chateaus. It's reasonable to infer from the term that the devices were commonly associated with sailing ships. A bit of further digging reveals that in the 11th and 12th centuries, new methods of navigation were developed in the Mediterranean region that made use of sophisticated sea charts and the newly discovered magnetic compass. The thing about this method of keeping a ship on course, however, is that it requires an accurate way to gauge the ship's speed, which in turn requires an accurate way to measure the passage of time. It's possible that the hourglass was invented around this time in order to meet this need for maritime vessels.

"Lives of great men all remind us we can make our lives sublime. And, departing, leave behind us footprints on the sands of time."
—Henry Wadsworth Longfellow

Clubs & Organizations
In Defense of Animal Rights

❖ ❖ ❖ ❖

For centuries, everyone from farmers to philosophers had
argued over the concept of cruelty toward animals. In 1824,
an Irish politician finally took steps to make it stop.

Today, the Society for the Prevention of Cruelty to Animals is an
international organization. It began, however, with a bill in the English Parliament in 1822. The sponsor of the bill was Colonel Richard
"Humanity Dick" Martin, scion of a prominent Irish family and a
member of Parliament from Galway. "Martin's Act," as it was known,
was intended to "Prevent the Cruel and Improper Treatment of Cattle" and applied to all livestock, including "Horses, Mares, Geldings,
Mules, Asses, Cows, Heifers, Steers, Oxen, Sheep, and other Cattle."
Individuals convicted of perpetrating such abuse were to pay a fine
"not exceeding Five Pounds, not less than Ten Shillings" or "be committed to the House of Correction or some other Prison . . . for any
Time not exceeding Three Months."

Early Efforts to Protect Animals
The earliest laws protecting animals date to the 17th century. A
1635 law in Ireland made it an offense to pull wool from a sheep
or to attach a plough to a horse's tail. In 1641, the Massachusetts
Bay Colony decreed "No man shall exercise any Tirrany or Crueltie
toward any bruite Creature which are usualie kept for man's use."
During the government of Oliver Cromwell in England, the Puritans
opposed blood sports like cockfighting and bull baiting. Citing the Old
Testament Book of Genesis, they argued that God made men responsible for the welfare of animals but did not make men their owners.

The SPCA in Great Britain and the United States
Martin convened a meeting with fellow animal rights activists and
in 1824 formed the Society for the Prevention of Cruelty to Animals
(SPCA). The SPCA sent inspectors to slaughterhouses to ensure that
animals were held and killed humanely. Inspectors also monitored

the treatment that carriage horses received from coachmen and cab drivers. In 1840, the organization was granted a royal charter by Queen Victoria and became the Royal Society for the Prevention of Cruelty to Animals (RSPCA).

In 1866, Henry Bergh founded the American Society for the Prevention of Cruelty to Animals (ASPCA). Bergh was incensed by the ill treatment of animals he witnessed while working as a diplomat in Russia. With the assistance of the RSPCA in London, he successfully lobbied for anticruelty laws in New York State and persuaded the state to give the ASPCA the authority to enforce the laws.

Bergh earned the moniker "The Great Meddler" for his efforts on behalf of what he called "these mute servants of mankind." As Bergh wrote in a letter to a reporter after the creation of the ASPCA, "Day after day I am in slaughterhouses, or lying in wait at midnight with a squad of police near some dog pit. Lifting a fallen horse to his feet, penetrating buildings where I inspect collars and saddles for raw flesh, then lecturing in public schools to children, and again to adult societies. Thus my whole life is spent."

The ASPCA did not ignore the welfare of cats and dogs. According to the information in its first annual report in 1867, one David Heath was sentenced to ten days in prison for beating a cat to death. When the judge read his verdict, Heath was reported as saying "the arresting officer ought to be disemboweled." For that remark, Heath received an additional penalty of $25.

Bergh's concern for helpless creatures did not stop with livestock and pets. In 1874, he and others from the ASPCA rescued a little girl named Mary Ellen, the victim of vicious abuse in the aptly named New York neighborhood, Hell's Kitchen. Bergh's efforts led to the founding of the New York Society for the Prevention of Cruelty to Children in 1875.

❖❖❖❖❖❖

One of the most famous animal rights groups, People for the Ethical Treatment of Animals (PETA), was founded in 1980. In 2008, PETA announced plans for a $1 million prize to the "first person to come up with a method to produce commercially viable quantities of in vitro meat at competitive prices by 2012."

Language
The Dumb Blonde Stereotype

❖ ❖ ❖ ❖

*How did a woman with blonde hair become
synonymous with "airhead"?*

If you were to do an informal survey of Caucasian American women,
you would find that one out of three has some shade of blonde
hair. Of these, only a small percentage are natural blondes. The
rest lighten their locks with the help of chemicals, partaking in a
ritual that goes back thousands of years. It turns out that in ancient
Greece, blonde hair was all the rage.

Dyeing to Be Blonde
The original blonde bombshell was Aphrodite, the Greek goddess
of love. Aphrodite embodied the erotic. She was said to have risen
out of the ocean in a wave of sea foam (which explains her white
skin and flowing blonde tresses). Aphrodite's paleness set her apart
from her dark-haired Mediterranean worshippers. What better way
to revere than to imitate? Hellenic women (and men) used saffron,
oils, lye, and even mud to yellow their hair. The demand for blonde
hair was so great that the Romans kidnapped fair-haired barbarians
just to keep their wigmakers well-supplied. Thus began one of the
longest lasting fashion trends in Western culture.

Since then, the only time that blonde has gone out of style was
during the Middle Ages. It was considered sinful for a woman to
show her hair in public, much less treat it with bleaches. The Catholic Church tried to make blondness a symbol of chastity and innocence. The Virgin Mary was depicted with golden hair (as was Jesus
at times). However, despite sermons and writings denouncing the
evil, carnal power of colored hair, it did not lose its allure. By the
time of Queen Elizabeth I, the use of hair dyes was in vogue again.

Playing the Part
In the 1700s, a Parisian courtesan by the name of Rosalie Duthe
became the first famously dumb blonde. It is said that she never

spoke but could seduce any man simply by looking at him and entrancing him with her elaborately styled golden hair. She was parodied in intellectual circles and was even featured in a comic play where she became the laughingstock of Paris. As women of "ill repute" increasingly colored their hair to boost business, the association between colored hair and cheap, wanton behavior deepened.

Hooray for Hollywood!

It took Hollywood to combine innocence and sexuality. Starlets like Jean Harlow and Marlene Dietrich paved the way for our own modern-day goddess—and ultimate blonde icon—Marilyn Monroe. Even today, decades after her death, she remains as alluring and enduring as Aphrodite herself. A succession of Tinseltown deities— including Brigitte Bardot, Farrah Fawcett, and Paris Hilton—all fit the "dumb blonde" stereotype placed on Monroe. There is, of course, no connection between a woman's hair color and her intelligence. Marilyn Monroe was, in fact, a woman of calculating intelligence. (For instance, she was known to relax between shoots by reading weighty authors such as Thomas Paine and Heinrich Heine.)

There is, however, a kernel of truth to the "dumb blonde" stereotype. A group of French academics conducted a study that proves blonde hair does influence intelligence—men's intelligence. It turns out that the sight of a blonde woman makes men dumber! Men were shown a series of photographs of women with various hair colors and then given a series of basic knowledge tests. Those who were shown blonde women scored the lowest. In the end, the joke seems to be on men!

"It takes a smart brunette to play a dumb blonde."

—Marilyn Monroe

Written Word
Origins of an Epitaph

❖ ❖ ❖ ❖

They might be six feet under, but a good epitaph means
they'll never been forgotten. Have you ever wondered about
the meaning behind particular gravestone inscriptions?
Here are the origins of some of our favorites.

1. Mel Blanc: "That's all folks!"
Arguably the world's most famous voice actor, Mel Blanc's characters included Bugs Bunny, Porky Pig, Yosemite Sam, and Sylvester the Cat. When he died of heart disease and emphysema in 1989 at age 81, his epitaph was based on his best-known line.

2. Spike Milligan: "Dúirt mé leat go raibh mé breoite."
The Gaelic epitaph for this Irish comedian translates as, "I told you I was ill." Milligan, who died of liver failure in 2002 at age 83, was famous for his irreverent humor, which was showcased on TV and in films such as *Monty Python's Life of Brian.*

3. Joan Hackett: "Go away—I'm asleep."
The actor, who was a regular on TV throughout the 1960s and 1970s, appearing on shows such as *The Twilight Zone* and *Bonanza*, died in 1983 of ovarian cancer at age 49. Her epitaph was copied from the note she hung on her dressing room door when she didn't want to be disturbed.

4. Ludolph van Ceulen: "3.14159265358979323846 264338327950288…"

The life's work of van Ceulen, who died from unknown causes in 1610 at age 70, was to calculate the value of the mathematical constant pi to 35 digits. He was so proud of this achievement that he asked that the number be engraved on his tombstone.

5. George Johnson: "Here lies George Johnson, hanged by mistake 1882. He was right, we was wrong, but we strung him up and now he's gone."

Johnson bought a stolen horse in good faith but the court didn't buy his story and sentenced him to hang. His final resting place is Boot Hill Cemetery, which is also "home" to many notorious characters of the Wild West, including Billy Clanton and the McLaury brothers, who died in the infamous gunfight at the O.K. Corral.

6. Lester Moore: "Here lies Lester Moore. Four slugs from a .44, no Les, no more."

The date of birth of this Wells Fargo agent is not recorded, but the cause of his death, in 1880, couldn't be clearer.

7. Hank Williams: "I'll never get out of this world alive."

The gravestone of the legendary country singer, who died of a heart attack in 1953 at age 29, is inscribed with several of his song titles, of which this is the most apt.

8. Dee Dee Ramone: "OK…I gotta go now."

The bassist from the punk rock band The Ramones died of a drug overdose in 2002, at age 49. His epitaph is a reference to one of the group's hits, "Let's Go."

Music

YOU USED TO BE CALLED WHAT?

Most famous bands had other names before they made it big.
See if you can match the former names to these famous bands.

1. Cheap Trick
2. U2
3. The Beatles
4. Styx
5. Queen
6. Led Zeppelin
7. The Beach Boys
8. Green Day
9. KISS
10. The Who
11. Def Leppard
12. Pink Floyd
13. Boyz II Men
14. Blondie
15. Simon and Garfunkel
16. Journey
17. Pearl Jam

a. Angel and the Snake
b. Atomic Mass
c. Tea Set
d. The Detours, The High Numbers
e. Tom and Jerry
f. Feedback, The Hype
g. Golden Gate Rhythm Section
h. Smile
i. Unique Attraction
j. Fuse
k. The Tradewinds
l. Sweet Children
m. Mookie Blaylock
n. The New Yardbirds
o. Wicked Lester
p. The Pendletones
q. The Quarrymen, Johnny and the Moondogs

Inventions
Holding It All Together

❖ ❖ ❖ ❖

*A few inches of wire twisted into a couple of
loops brought order to the office.*

You're sitting at your desk shuffling through a 12-page report; you've
spent four hours preparing it, and it's due in five minutes. One last
look reveals that everything is in order—but wait. It's not ready to go
yet. You can't just hand over a messy sheaf of papers. You have to put
it all together, neat and organized; without even thinking, you reach
for a paper clip.

Few things are as unappreciated yet so widely used as the lowly
paper clip. A few inches of wire twisted to form a loop within a
loop—what could be simpler? Believe it or not, this familiar office
product wasn't widely available until around 1900, when the Cush-
man and Denison manufacturing company began selling the Gem
paper clip that is so familiar today.

Why hadn't anyone come up with such a simple device before?
The first reason is that it wasn't until the mid-1800s that people
could produce malleable strands of thin wire in mass quantity. Why
did it take 50 years to come up with the paper clip? Well, it didn't.
The first wire clip for holding papers was patented by Samuel B. Fay
as early as 1867, and numerous other inventors around the world
very quickly produced their own versions in various shapes and
designs. In fact, at least 50 other paper clip patents were issued in
the latter half of the 19th century. But none of these inventors was
able to devise a machine that could cheaply manufacture their products. It wasn't until William Middlebrook of Connecticut patented
a machine for rapidly and economically producing the Gem design
that the paper clip could be made cheaply and in bulk. The only real
competition the Gem has seen in the last hundred years is from the
Gothic paper clip, which offers pointed rather than rounded loops
and extends the two ends of the wire all the way to the end, making
it less likely to tear paper.

Toys & Games
Without a Clue

❖ ❖ ❖ ❖

There's nothing puzzling about the origin of the crossword puzzle.

The first published crossword puzzle was created and constructed by an editor and journalist named Arthur Wynne, who was employed by *The New York World* newspaper, a daily rag that adorned doorsteps and magazine racks in the Big Apple from 1860 until 1931. Wynne was asked by his editors to create a new puzzle for the paper that would challenge, entertain, and educate. Wynne, who was originally from Liverpool, England, designed a format similar to Magic Squares, a popular word game he played as a child.

Wynne's puzzle, which was originally dubbed Word-Cross, first appeared in the Sunday, December 21, 1913, edition of *The World*. It was diamond-shape, contained no internal black squares, and provided one free solution (the word *fun*) to get the semantic search started. The clues were not separated into across and down divisions; a numbering system was used to guide the riddle researcher. The first clue to intrigue potential puzzlers was "what bargain hunters enjoy" which, of course, is "sales." Wynne also compiled the first book of crossword puzzles, hitting the bookshelves with his publication in 1924.

In February 1922, the first British crossword was printed in *Pearson's Magazine*, a monthly publication that specialized in essays on the arts and politics and helped spawn the careers of such notable authors as H. G. Wells and George Bernard Shaw. The first crossword to appear in *The Times*, England's national newspaper, was published on February 1, 1930.

The invention of cryptic crosswords, in which each clue is a puzzle in itself, is usually credited to Edward Powys Mathers, a brilliant English scholar, translator, poet, and linguist who compiled more than 650 puzzles for the *Observer* newspaper under the pseudonym Torquemada.

Science
The Ultimate Power Grab

❖ ❖ ❖ ❖

*One of the greatest U.S. inventors gets charged up
over some competition and tries to short-circuit
another promising innovator's career.*

Rivalry can bring out the best in people, but it can also bring out
the worst. Too often, it seems the latter is the case for otherwise
grounded individuals. Consider Thomas Alva Edison during the
famous "War of the Currents" waged over electricity during the
1890s. Edison put all his energy into discrediting the system discovered by Yugoslavia-born inventor Nikola Tesla even though Tesla's
was the superior setup.

By the late 19th century, the United States' ever-increasing
demands for energy required a revamped power-delivery system.
Edison's direct current (DC) method had worked up to this point,
but it suffered from inherent weaknesses: The system was cumbersome, could not easily be switched between high and low voltages,
and would suffer great power losses when transmitted over long
distances. It was then that Edison's former employee, Tesla, devised
a system for alternating current (AC). Point for point, it answered all
the problems that Edison's system presented and was more economical to boot. With the full financial backing of industrialist George
Westinghouse, Tesla quietly presented his system to the public.
Edison, however, was not so demure—the war was on.

In an effort to smear the science behind Tesla's invention, Edison
spread spurious information about fatal AC accidents and staged
public executions of animals using "dangerous" AC.

The smear campaign backfired on Edison. Alternating current
replaced direct current as the central station power choice across the
world, and Tesla's theories were proven correct. Years later, Edison
would admit that he should have listened to Tesla and embraced
alternating current. Amen to that.

Sports
Curious About Curling?

❖ ❖ ❖ ❖

If you've ever caught a curling match on TV, you
might have wondered: Who invented that?

History

Curling began in Scotland in the 1500s and was initially played
with river-worn stones. In the next century, enterprising curlers
began to fit the stones with handles. Curling was a perfect fit with
Canada's heavy Scottish influence and northerly climate. The Royal
Montreal Curling Club began in 1807, and in 1927, Canada held
its first national curling championship. Today, curling has millions
of enthusiasts around the world. Canadian curlers routinely beat
international competition, a source of national pride.

How to Curl

The standard curling rink measures 146 feet
by 15 feet. At each end are 12-foot-wide
concentric rings called *houses,* the center of
which is the *button.* There are four curlers
on a team. Each throws two rocks (shoves
them, rather; you don't really want to go
airborne with a 44-pound granite rock)
in an effort to get as close to the button
as possible. When all eight players have
thrown two rocks each, the *end* (analogous
to a baseball inning) is concluded. A game
consists of eight or ten ends.

Curling Strategy

You try to knock the other team's rocks out of the house—and thus
out of scoring position—while getting yours to hang around close
to the button. After all throws, the team with the rock closest to the
button scores a point for each rock that's closer to the button than
the opponent's nearest rock (and inside the house).

Proper Ice-keeping

The players with the brooms aren't trying to keep the ice clear of crud. The team *skip* (captain) determines strategy and advises the players using the brooms in the fine art of *sweeping*. Skips can guide the stone with surprising precision by skillfully sweeping in front of it with their brooms, but they can't touch (*burn*) that rock or any others in the process.

"Good curling!" "Thanks, you too."

Curling is a game that values good sportsmanship. Curlers even call themselves for burns. When a team is so far behind it cannot win, it is considered proper sportsmanship to concede by removing gloves and shaking hands.

Curling Jargon

Bonspiel: a curling tournament
Curler: curling player
Draw: shot thrown to score
Hack: foot brace curlers push off from, like track sprinters
Hammer: last rock of the end (advantageous)
Hog line: blue line in roughly the same place as a hockey blue line. One must let go of the rock before crossing the near hog line—and the rock must cross the far hog line—or it's hogged (removed from play)
Pebble: water drops sprayed on the ice between ends, making the game more interesting
Takeout: shot meant to knock a rock out of play
Up! Whoa! Off! Hurry! Hard!: examples of orders the skip might call to the sweepers
Weight: how hard one slides the rock

"Curling is not a sport. I called my grandmother and told her she could win a gold medal because they have dusting in the Olympics now."

—Basketball great Charles Barkley

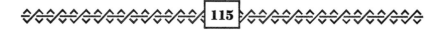

Health & Medicine
A Cure for Bedroom Blues

❖ ❖ ❖ ❖

Viagra began as a suprising breakthrough and ultimately became a genuine pharmaceutical phenomenon. Not since the birth control pill has a drug had such an astounding social impact.

Pfizer's "little blue pill" has brought relief to millions of men worldwide who suffer from erectile dysfunction, which is defined as an inability to maintain an erection. But that wasn't what its developers originally had in mind.

Sildenafil citrate, the active ingredient in Viagra, was originally designed as a heart drug. Because it acts as a *vasodilator* (a drug that helps blood vessels dilate), researchers thought it would be an effective treatment for high blood pressure and conditions such as angina.

However, sildenafil had an unusual side effect: The drug made it easier for men—especially those with erectile dysfunction—to get an erection. Pfizer, knowing a lucrative breakthrough when it saw one, changed direction and began studying sildenafil as a treatment for one of the most common sexual problems in the world. The rest, as they say, is history.

The response to Viagra has been phenomenal. Nearly 570,000 prescriptions were written during the drug's first month on the market in early 1998. Viagra remains one of the world's most frequently prescribed drugs and in recent years has been joined by competitors like Cialis (*tadalafil*) and Levitra (*vardenafil*).

Viagra works by boosting blood flow to the penis, blocking an enzyme known as *phosphodiesterase type 5* (PDE5). Approximately 70 percent of men who take Viagra for erection problems with a physical cause report success, noting that their erections develop faster, are harder, and last longer.

But Viagra is not perfect: Potential side effects include headache, a blue tint to vision, facial flushing, indigestion, and dizziness. Satisfied users say it's a small price to pay for a big boost in the bedroom.

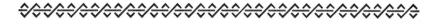

Famous Parents

The Apple Doesn't Fall Far from the Tree

The offspring of great achievers can sometimes equal or surpass their parents' success and popularity. Here's an eclectic grouping of families with that one-two generational punch.

It's probably safe to assume that when **John Adams** (1797–1801) was elected the second president of the United States in 1796, he would've been pleased to know that the torch would one day be passed to his son, **John Quincy Adams** (1825–1829). In 1824, just 16 months before the elder Adams's death, John Quincy was elected as the sixth president of the United States. They were the first father-and-son duo to be elected to the office.

Actress **Angelina Jolie Voight** has wowed audiences in such films as *Gia* and *Lara Croft: Tomb Raider*. Winning the Academy Award for Best Actress in a Supporting Role in 2000's *Girl, Interrupted*, Jolie was following a family path first blazed by actress mother **Marcheline Bertrand**, who operated as Jolie's manager until her death in 2007, and famous father **Jon Voight**, best known for his riveting performances in *Midnight Cowboy* and *Deliverance*. Voight won a Best Actor Oscar in 1979 for his performance in *Coming Home*.

When seven-time NASCAR Winston Cup champion **Dale Earnhardt** perished in a crash during his last lap of the 2001 Daytona 500, many thought it was the end of an era. In fact, it was only the beginning: **Dale Earnhardt Jr.** went on to become every bit as popular a driver as his "Intimidator" dad. "Junior's" wealth of "most popular" driver awards attests to his beloved status among race fans.

Immediately after **Evel Knievel** fearlessly—or foolishly, depending upon whom you ask—jumped his motorcycle a distance of 40 feet over a box of rattlesnakes, a mountain lion, and parked cars, an American icon was born. Knievel reportedly broke nearly 40 bones in his body during a lifetime of high-flying derring-do and suffered through an infamous 1967 crash (which left him comatose for 29 days) while attempting to jump the fountains at Caesar's Palace in Las Vegas. In 1989, son **Robbie Knievel** soared over the very fountains that had bettered his dad.

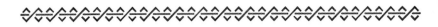

Sports
Creatures: A Sports Feature

❖ ❖ ❖ ❖

*Part cheerleader, part contortionist, and part comedian, the
mascot was inspired by the "fowl" play of a college student.*

The colorful and enthusiastic mascots that provide comic relief
and intermission entertainment at sporting events have become as
essential to the games as snacks and sodas. Most of these individuals
are talented athletes in their own rights, as dexterity in gymnastics,
dance, and occasional stunts are vital ingredients of their performances.

The first mascot to gain notoriety for his amusing antics was a
farcical fowl known as the San Diego Chicken. In 1974, a San Diego
State University student named Ted Giannoulas was hired by a local
radio station to dress like a chicken and hand out Easter eggs at the
San Diego Zoo. Giannoulas's shtick was so popular among the children that he decided to attend San Diego Padres baseball games and
act as the team's "unofficial" mascot. The Chicken attracted worldwide acclaim—in fact, the mascot was named one of the 100 most
powerful people in sports for the 20th century by *Sporting News*

Magazine. Soon, most professional
sports teams were using mascots to
entertain, amuse, and fire up the fans.

The first official sideline mascot
wasn't a gaily garbed goliath or dap-
perly draped demon, but it was definitely a beast. In 1889, Yale University
enlisted an English bulldog named
Handsome Dan to slobber along the
sidelines and support the college
football team, which became known
as the Bulldogs.

Some college mascots deserve high marks for originality. Here are some of our favorites:

Aggies (Texas A&M, New Mexico State, Utah State, and others): It's worth remembering that many land-grant schools initially taught mainly agriculture, so their students—and sometimes their teams— were called Farmers. "Aggies" grew as slang for this, and many of these schools now embrace the name proudly.

Banana Slugs (University of California–Santa Cruz): If a slug suggests a lethargic or reluctant team, that's just what students had in mind when they chose the image. The bright yellow banana slug lives amid the redwoods on campus and represents a mild protest of the highly competitive nature of most college sports.

Boll Weevils/Cotton Blossoms (University of Arkansas–Monticello, men/women): When cotton ruled Dixie, the boll weevil was more fearsome than any snake. Evidently, the women's teams didn't care to be named after an invasive insect, and who can blame them?

Cardinal (Stanford): It's the color, not the bird. That sounds odd until you consider the Harvard Crimson, Dartmouth Big Green, Syracuse Orange, and so forth. The university's overall symbol, however, is a redwood tree. A person actually dresses up as a redwood mascot, but the effect is more like a wilting Christmas tree than a regal conifer.

Crimson Tide (University of Alabama): The school's teams have always worn crimson, but the term "Crimson Tide" seems to have been popularized by sportswriters waxing poetic about epic struggles in mud and rain.

Eutectics (St. Louis College of Pharmacy, Missouri): *Eutectic* refers to the chemical process in which two solids become a liquid, representing the school's integration of competitive athletics and rigorous academic programs. ESPN recognized the Eutectic—a furry creature dressed in a lab coat—as one of the most esoteric mascots in the country.

Ichabods (Washburn University, Kansas, men): The university was established as Lincoln College, but it ran out of money. When philanthropist Ichabod Washburn bailed out Lincoln, the school renamed itself after Washburn.

Language
From Young Urban Professional to Yuppie

❖ ❖ ❖ ❖

Successful, materialistic, and self-indulgent *are three of the more polite words used to describe yuppies, the young, urban professionals who measured success by the price tag of their BMWs and the square footage of their condos.*

Depending on your source, the word *yuppie* was initially coined as a nickname for either "young, urban professional" or "young, upwardly mobile professional." One thing is clear: It refers to the generation of 20-somethings that regarded designer duds, chic coifs, expensive autos, and luxury pads as the gauges for social standing.

This materialist mob gained acclaim in 1984 when *Time* magazine printed an article called "Here Come the Yuppies!" discussing a new book called *The Yuppie Handbook: The State-of-the-Art Manual for Young Professionals,* which documented the dos and don'ts of the Yuppie kingdom. Thus, *Time* introduced this lifestyle to middle-class America and lent it cultural credence—but it didn't coin the term.

Joseph Epstein, an American editor and author best known for his book *Snobbery: The American Version,* is often credited with (or accused of, depending on your perspective) originating the term *yuppie* in 1982. But Epstein can't claim the glory (or blame) for coining the term either. The word first appeared—in a convoluted form at least—in a 1980 *Chicago* magazine article about urban renaissance written by Dan Rottenberg. But even that isn't the end of the story.

In 1983, the term *yuppie* vaulted to popularity when used by *Chicago Tribune* columnist Bob Greene in his article "From Yippie to Yuppie" about Jerry Rubin, a founder of the Youth International Party, and his conversion from radical activist to regular Joe.

❖❖❖❖❖❖

Newsweek magazine named 1984 "The Year of the Yuppie."

Inventions
The "Fax" Are In

❖ ❖ ❖ ❖

A quick scan of history reveals that the facsimile machine of the 1980s actually got its start in the 1840s.

Visit almost any office supply store, and you'll find that fax machines are in plentiful supply. Considered de rigueur in the workplace during the business boom of the 1980s, the fax or, more correctly, "facsimile" machine continues to hold its own in this day of lightning-quick e-mailing and dexterity-challenging text messaging. And why shouldn't it? The ability to "fax" a reproduced sheet of paper from here to virtually anywhere within a telephone's reach has changed the business landscape.

But this breakthrough invention doesn't actually hail from modern times. In fact, this gem came along when Abraham Lincoln was still an Illinois lawyer and the telephone—the yin to the fax machine's yang—had not yet been invented. But how was this possible?

Scottish mechanic and amateur clockmaker Alexander Bain used existing telegraph technology, paired with a stylus functioning as a pendulum, to work such magic. The stylus picked up images from a rotating metal surface (the crude precursor of modern-day scanning), then converted them to electrical impulses for transmission. This, in turn, was sent to chemically treated paper and *voilà*—the fax-transmitted image was born. Bain was granted a British patent for his groundbreaking invention on May 27, 1843, some 33 years before the telephone was patented.

The process underwent various upgrades and improvements over the years to reach its present form. By the 1920s, a new scanning system allowed the paper original to remain in a fixed position, precisely like many modern-day machines. During the same era, the American Telephone & Telegraph Company (AT&T) came on board, thus ushering the fax machine into modern times. On March 4, 1955, the very first fax transmission was sent via radio waves across the continent. Not bad for a pre–Civil War machine produced by an amateur.

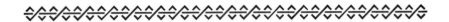

Language
Origins of Standard Symbols

❖ ❖ ❖ ❖

Removing a colon is pretty serious business—whether you're a surgeon or a copy editor. You use punctuation marks and other symbols on your computer keyboard every day, but have you ever considered their origins?

¶—The pilcrow is a typographical character used to indicate a new paragraph. The name may have come from *pylcraft,* a derivation of the word *paragraph,* and the symbol that resembles a backward *P* may have originated as a *C* for "chapter," or to represent a new train of thought.

!—Usually used to indicate strong feeling, the exclamation mark is a pictographic device believed to have originated in the Roman empire. Its resemblance to a pen over a dot was thought to represent a mark a writer might make when surprised or overjoyed at completing a long writing project.

*—The asterisk gets its name from *astrum,* the Latin word for *star,* which the asterisk is also called. It is not an "asterix"—that's the name of the star of a French cartoon. The asterisk was created in feudal times when the printers of family trees needed a symbol to indicate date of birth, which may explain why it's shaped like the branches of a tree.

;—The semicolon was invented by an Italian printer for two main purposes: to bind two sentences that run on in meaning and to act as a "super comma" in a sentence that already contains lots of commas. Excessive use of the semicolon is considered showy by many writers, especially when employed to create long, multisegmented sentences. Author Kurt Vonnegut once said, "Do not use semicolons. All they do is show you've been to college."

?—What is the origin of the question mark? The symbol is generally thought to originate from the Latin *quaestio,* meaning "question," which was abbreviated to *Qo,* with the uppercase *Q* written above the lowercase *o.* The question mark replaces the period at the end of an interrogative sentence. There's a superstition in Hollywood that movies or television shows with a question mark in the title do poorly at the box office. That may explain the mark's absence in the title of the game show *Who Wants to Be a Millionaire,* a program that would not exist without questions!

&—The ampersand, used to replace the word *and,* has been found on ancient Roman sources dating to the first century A.D. It was formed by joining the letters in *et,* which is Latin for *and.* Through the 19th century, the ampersand was actually considered the 27th letter of the English alphabet.

%—The percent sign is the symbol used to indicate a percentage, meaning that the number preceding it is divided by 100. The symbol appeared around 1425 as a representation of the abbreviation of *P cento,* meaning "for a hundred" in Italian.

=—The equal sign is a mathematical symbol used to indicate equality and was invented in 1557 by Welsh mathematician Robert Recorde. In his book *The Whetstone of Witte,* Recorde explains that he invented it "to avoid the tedious repetition of these words: 'is equal to.'" Recorde's invention is commemorated with a plaque in St. Mary's Church in his hometown of Tenby, Wales.

The word butterfly *is one of the most persistent and baffling mysteries of linguistics. All European languages, even such closely related ones as Spanish and Portuguese, have completely different words for* butterfly. *This is in stark contrast to just about all other words for everyday objects and animals.*

Fads & Fashion
With This Ring, I Thee Wed

✦ ✦ ✦ ✦

A wedding ring, traditionally a simple gold band, is a powerful symbol. The circle of the ring represents eternity and is an emblem of lasting love in many of the world's cultures. But the history of the wedding ring also includes less spiritual associations.

Historians suggest that wedding rings are a modern version of the ropes with which primitive men bound women they had captured. This suggests that the phrase "old ball and chain" may have referred more to the passage of a bride from person to prisoner than to the husband's matrimonial outlook.

Our current perceptions of the wedding ring evolved over time and are rooted in a variety of ancient practices. In Egypt, a man placed a piece of ring-money—metal rings used to purchase things—on his bride's hand to show that he had endowed her with his wealth. In ancient Rome, rings made of various metals communicated a variety of political and social messages. In marriage, the ring holding the household keys was presented to the wife after the ceremony when she crossed the threshold of her new home. Later, this key ring dwindled in size to a symbolic ring placed on the woman's finger during the wedding. Among Celtic tribes, a ring may have indicated sexual availability. A woman might have given a man a ring to show her desire; putting her finger through the ring may have symbolized the sexual act.

Wedding rings were not always made of gold. They could be made of any metal as well as leather or rushes. In fact, in the 13th century, a bishop of Salisbury in England warned young men against seducing gullible virgins by braiding rings out of rushes and placing them on their fingers. In the 17th century, Puritans decried the use of a wedding ring due to its pagan associations and ostentatious value, calling it "a relique of popery and a diabolical circle for the devil to dance in."

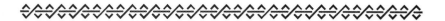

The Ring Finger of Choice

Why is the ring placed on the fourth finger of the left hand? According to fourth-century A.D. Roman grammarian and philosopher Ambrosius Theodosius Macrobius, the fourth finger is the one most appropriate to that function. Macrobius described the thumb as "too busy to be set apart" and said "the forefinger and little finger are only half-protected." The middle finger, or *medicusm,* is commonly used for offensive communications and so could not be used for this purpose. This leaves only the fourth finger for the wedding ring.

It was once believed that a vein ran directly from that finger to the heart, the so-called *vena amoris,* or vein of love. Since the right hand is commonly the dominant hand, some scholars suggest that wearing a ring on the left, or "submissive," hand symbolizes a wife's obedience to her husband. The importance of the Trinity in Christian theology provides another explanation for the identification of the fourth finger on the left hand as the "wedding ring finger." In the early Catholic Church, the groom touched the thumb and first two fingers of his bride as he said, "In the name of the Father, Son, and Holy Ghost." He then slipped the ring all the way onto the next, or fourth, finger as he said, "Amen." This four-step placement of the ring was a common custom in England until the end of the 16th century, and it remained a tradition among Roman Catholics for many more years.

"For years [my wedding ring] has done its job. It has led me not into temptation. It has reminded my husband numerous times at parties that it's time to go home. It has been a source of relief to a dinner companion. It has been a status symbol in the maternity ward."
—AMERICAN HUMORIST ERMA BOMBECK

Food & Drink
Corn Flakes

❖ ❖ ❖ ❖

*From the suppression of ardor comes a tasty breakfast
food—sprinkle that on your cereal in the morning.*

By their strictest definitions, corn flakes and potassium nitrate (ordinary saltpeter) should have little in common. Yet at some point,
these unrelated items were used to inhibit human sexual drive. Corn
Flakes, the innocuous breakfast cereal known and loved by all, was
devised as a sort of reverse Viagra, or *anaphrodisiac.* If the crispy
flakes did their intended job, consumers would be stripped of their
snap, crackle, and pop. (Oops, wrong cereal!)

John Harvey Kellogg (does the name sound familiar?) was born
in 1852 in Tyrone, Michigan. His family later moved to the village of
Battle Creek, Michigan. This anonymous hamlet would eventually
become world-famous as the home of breakfast cereals, but before
this could happen, Kellogg would need to grow up and assume a
more traditional, dignified stature.

In 1875, *Doctor* John Kellogg emerged from college and became
medical superintendent for the Western Health Reform Insitute.
There, the devout Seventh-Day Adventist advanced his religious
tenets by feeding patients a diet of bland foods. Kellogg believed
that sexual abstinence promoted good health and that bland foods
helped quell the libido. He and his brother, Will, a businessman,
invented many of the ardor-suppressing foods that he served to his
patients.

While cooking up a batch of wheat in 1894, the brothers stumbled upon a formula that produced crispy breakfast flakes. Will
wanted to add sugar to the new product and sell the tasty chips
outside the hospital. Ever-vigilant, John wasn't interested in such a
change, since it could cause sexual arousal. Eventually, Will Kellogg
would break free, change the wheat to corn and start a company that
marketed Kellogg's Corn Flakes. Despite its anaphrodisiac roots, the
cereal became one of the most successful in breakfast history. The
moral: Sugar is sweet, and sex sells. Sorry, Dr. John.

ACCIDENTAL INVENTIONS

Slippery Slopes

From our nation's first oil well came a clear slime with healing properties.

Some of the best inventions are the ones that come about accidentally. In 1859, while visiting the oil-boom town of Titusville, Pennsylvania, chemist Robert Chesebrough (1837–1933) literally stumbled upon petroleum jelly.

Chesebrough was in the Titusville region, home of the famous Drake Well, to strike crude oil deals with oil-drilling bigwigs. As the 22-year-old owner of an "illuminating oil" business, Chesebrough was one "slick" customer with his entrepreneurial eyes set firmly on future prizes. The young man wasn't aware of it yet, but he was about to realize success beyond his wildest dreams.

While touring Titusville's oil fields, Chesebrough noticed a worker scraping waxlike goo from a pump rod. Curious, he asked the man what he was doing. "Scraping off rod wax," came the reply. It turns out the substance was a pesky by-product of the drilling process that would cause the pumps to foul if allowed to accumulate.

Then the man told Chesebrough something that piqued his interest. When a worker would burn or cut himself, a dollop of this stuff applied to the wound would "fix it right up." Chesebrough was intrigued. *What magical healing ingredients might be in this oil?* he wondered. A new business venture was about to emerge.

Over the next decade, Chesebrough modified naturally occurring rod wax and used himself as a guinea pig to test its effectiveness. He became convinced of the product's curative properties and brought it to market. By 1875, the invention was selling at the rate of one jar per minute. By the 1880s, the substance was a staple in American homes. These days, people refer to it not as rod wax but as Vaseline. Chesebrough had found his success in the slimiest of places. We all share in his rewards.

Places & Landmarks
A Sign of the Times

❖ ❖ ❖ ❖

The famed Hollywood sign has had its ups and downs.

The massive Hollywood sign that overlooks America's movie-making mecca is one of the most famous landmarks in California. It has been featured in countless movies, television shows, and books and is instantly recognizable the world over.

Like the countless aspiring movie stars who arrive in Hollywood each day, the sign demands to be seen. Perched grandly atop the Hollywood Hills, it stands four stories high, with each letter measuring 30 feet across.

And yet, most people are unaware of its amazing origin—not to mention its intriguing history.

Hooray for Hollywood!

It was a unique combination of show business and real estate development that led to the sign's creation in 1923. Los Angeles was undergoing tremendous expansion, and the region around the Hollywood Hills was ripe for growth. *Los Angeles Times* publisher Harry Chandler saw opportunity there and joined forces with film producer Mack Sennett, who oversaw the investment company that sought to develop the region.

To promote the area, Chandler erected a huge sign in the Hollywood Hills reading "Hollywoodland." It was illuminated with 4,000 lightbulbs, and a cabin was erected nearby to house a maintenance man whose sole job was to change the bulbs when they burned out.

A Tragic Turn

The sign shone down from the hills without incident until 1932, when its image was tarnished by scandal. A young woman named Peg Entwistle had come to Hollywood in the late 1920s hoping to become a movie star. A stage actress in New York, Entwistle

believed motion pictures would be her key to fame and fortune, but things didn't work out as she had planned.

Though she managed to land some minor roles in a handful of movies, stardom eluded Entwistle. One day, she made her way up the hills to the Hollywoodland sign, found a maintenance ladder by the letter *H*, and climbed to the top. Then, with the city that had shattered her dreams laid out before her in the distance, she stepped off and plunged to her death.

Entwistle's suicide wasn't the only incident to take the shine off the Hollywoodland sign. The stock market crash of 1929 and the economic depression that followed took a heavy toll on the region's housing market. By the early 1940s, the developers were no longer able to pay for the sign's routine maintenance, so they sold it, along with the land it was on, to the city in 1944.

The Hollywoodland sign stood ignored and unattended until 1949, when a heavy wind knocked down the *H*. The Hollywood Chamber of Commerce, realizing the sign's promotional value, offered to remove the last four letters and restore the sign to its former glory.

But regular maintenance continued to prove difficult, and the sign eventually fell back into disrepair. By the late 1970s, it had become a termite-infested eyesore; an *O* had fallen down the hill, and arsonists set fire to the bottom of an *L*. Hollywood city officials determined that the sign would have to be completely rebuilt at a cost of $250,000.

Can I Buy a Vowel?

Playboy Magazine publisher Hugh Hefner immediately stepped in to help. He organized a fund-raising party at the Playboy Mansion, offering would-be donors the chance to "adopt" the letters of the new sign for $27,500 each. The campaign was a huge success, and people lined up for the opportunity to help bring the famous landmark back to its former glory. Hefner adopted the *Y,* cowboy actor Gene Autry bought an *L,* and rock star Alice Cooper kicked in to save an *O.* The new sign was unveiled in November 1978.

Today, the Hollywood sign stands proudly over the city it promotes, a constant reminder to all who view it that you can knock an icon down, but you can never knock it out.

Inventions
Sloshy Slumber

❖ ❖ ❖ ❖

*Nothing says the 1980s like a waterbed. But is it possible
the concept is much, much older than one would think?*

Although waterbeds were fixtures in university dorm rooms in the
1970s and 1980s, there is evidence to suggest that the Persians slept
on goat skins filled with water more than 3,600 years ago. However,
it's generally acknowledged that acclaimed Scottish physician Neil
Arnott invented the first official waterbed in the early 1800s. The
Hydrostatic Bed for Invalids—basically a trough of water covered
with a rubber cloth—was designed to prevent bedsores. Its therapeutic value was noted by author Elizabeth Gaskell, who references
a waterbed as a possible remedy for the character Mrs. Hale in her
1855 novel *North and South.* Mark Twain also mentions the waterbed in an 1871 article he wrote for *The New York Times.*

Curiously, Dr. Arnott did not patent his device, which allowed
other inventors to create their own designs. Dr. William Hooper of
Portsmouth, England, obtained the first waterbed patent in 1883.
Resembling a giant hot-water bottle, Hooper's invention was cold,
leaky, and thus a commercial flop, like all the other waterbeds that
followed it. It wasn't until the invention of durable, waterproof
fibers such as vinyl that the idea of a workable waterbed managed
to stay afloat. In 1968, three students at San Francisco State University attempted to make a new and innovative chair by filling a
large vinyl bag with cornstarch. Not surpris-
ingly, these experiments were
fraught with failure.
When they decided
to switch their focus
from sitting to sleeping
and substituted fluid for
cornstarch, the modern
waterbed was born.

Mythology & Folklore
Superstition: Three on a Match

❖ ❖ ❖ ❖

Almost everyone is superstitious in their own way, whether they knock on wood, refuse to walk under ladders, or steer clear of black cats. Many people, especially smokers, also consider it unlucky to light three cigarettes on a single match.

The origins of the "three on a match" superstition is thought to have its modern-day genesis in the military but could be rooted in older taboos regarding the use of one taper to light three candles or lamps. And like many superstitions, it is also based partially in reality: On a dark battlefield, a prolonged match flame can easily draw the attention of enemy snipers. Therefore, to light one cigarette is dangerous; to light three is to invite disaster.

Some historians believe this superstition started during the Boer War (1899–1902), when careless British soldiers became easy targets for Dutch sharpshooters by lighting up in the trenches. To be the third man in line for a light was extremely dangerous because you were likely already in the enemy's crosshairs by then.

Others believe that "three on a match" was started by Swedish match manufacturer Ivar Kreuger, who supposedly conceived the myth as a way of increasing sales during wartime. Kreuger certainly would have profited from this superstition, but there is very little evidence to suggest that the story is true.

What is true is that the history of superstition among soldiers dates back thousands of years, to the very first armed conflicts. "War is a situation in which you do everything possible to avoid being killed or your buddies being hurt, but so many things are out of your control," explains Dr. Stuart Vyse, author of *Believing in Magic: The Psychology of Superstition*. "Superstition gives servicemembers the feeling that they are doing something that might have an effect—that they are taking some action to control a situation that is by definition uncontrollable. And that gives them comfort."

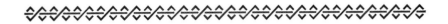

Religion
Wicca: That Good Ol' Time Religion?

❖ ❖ ❖ ❖

*Until Wicca grew more popular in the 1990s, many people
had never even heard of it. Even among Wiccans the
debate continues to percolate: How old is this, really?*

Definitions

To study the genesis of the religious and magical practice of Wicca,
one must be sure not to confuse "Wicca" with "witchcraft." Not all
witches are Wiccan; Wicca is a nature religion that can involve the
practice of witchcraft.

Antiquity

Throughout human existence, most cultures have had populations
that might be considered "witches": esoteric specialists, such
as midwives or herbalists, or people claiming spiritual contacts
or divinatory skill. To believe someone a witch is to believe that
person is able to foresee or change outcomes. Some cultures fear
and hate witches; others embrace them. We might call them folk
practitioners, shamans, or witch doctors. Wicca cannot demonstrate
descent from such folk practitioners, but it draws much inspiration
from old Celtic and English folk practice and religion.

During the worst medieval persecutions, Christian leaders slew
thousands of Europeans over witchcraft accusations. Many of that
era's popular definitions of witchcraft were hardly credible because
the persecutors themselves wrote them. They equated witchcraft
with diabolism simply because if it wasn't Christian, it had to be
Satanic.

Evidence suggests that the persecutions had little to do with witchcraft but much to do with vendettas, estate seizures (especially of
affluent widows), and the governmental need for a group enemy on
which to focus public anger. Some Wiccans claim that Wicca endured
in secret among the most skilled survivors of these persecutions.
Unfortunately, there's no evidence that recognizable Wicca existed
during "the Burning Times" in the first place, so survival is moot.

Victorian Renaissance

Interest in secret societies and the occult grew in Europe in the 19th century. With admiration of ancient Greco-Roman philosophy grew admiration of ancient divinity concepts—including a feminine divine presence or, more bluntly, the idea of God as a woman. While that notion revolted many Judeo-Christian traditionalists, others found it appealing.

By the early 1900s, several British occult organizations and movements drew upon and combined pre-Christian religious ideas and magical theory. Some groups were simply excuses to party, whereas others were stuffy study groups. Others blurred the distinctions or went back and forth. While none were visibly Wiccan, they would later help to inspire Wicca.

Gardner

During the 1930s, an English civil servant named Gerald B. Gardner developed a strong interest in the occult. Some sources claim that socialite Dorothy Clutterbuck had initiated him into a witches' coven, but that's doubtful because Mrs. Clutterbuck was widely known as a devout Anglican. More likely, his initiation came from a woman known only as "Dafo," who later distanced herself from occultism.

Wherever Gardner learned his witching, he definitely ran with it. In the early 1950s, Gardner began popularizing a duotheistic (the god/the goddess) synthesis of religion and magic that he inititally called "Wica." Why then? Well, in 1951, Parliament repealed the 1735 Witchcraft Act, so it was now legal. Wicca borrowed all over the place, creating a tradition of eclecticism that thrives today.

Buckland

When Wicca came to America with Gardner's student Raymond Buckland in 1964, its timing was impeccable. For Wicca, the 1960s counterculture was rich soil worthy of a fertility goddess. Today, self-described "eclectic Wiccans"—Wiccans who essentially define their own Wicca to suit themselves—probably outnumber Gardnerians, a group one might fairly call "orthodox Wiccans."

Rough estimates place the number of Wiccans in the United States today between 200,000 and 500,000.

Film
A Lion in Your Lap

❖ ❖ ❖ ❖

Hollywood embraced 3-D technology in the 1950s
to counter a decline at the box office.

Stereoscopic cinematography, or 3-D, is a process that emphasizes the illusion of depth by making the foreground, middle ground, and background of an image seem separate or spatially distinct.

Imagery in 3-D existed as far back as the late 19th century, when stereoscopic photographs were available as popular parlor items. Hollywood dabbled with 3-D movies as early as the 1920s. However, 3-D is most frequently associated with the 1950s, when Hollywood embraced this process to counter a loss of revenue due to competition from television and a change in the makeup of the moviegoing audience. Studios were determined to give audiences spectacle and novelty—to offer something they couldn't get from television. The history of 3-D in Hollywood is tied to its value as a novelty.

Studios exploited the 3-D technique by producing films that featured spears, rocks, animals, and human fists flying toward the audience. In 1953, during the publicity for *Bwana Devil*—the film that jump-started the 3-D craze—Gulu Productions promised viewers "A lion in your lap!" Unfortunately, audiences didn't necessarily want lions in their laps, and they grew weary of having projectiles tossed toward them. Exploitative rather than imaginative, the 3-D effects often got in the way of storytelling and character development.

The stereoscopic process of the 1950s used polarized lenses to create the 3-D effect, and audiences wore polarized eyepieces to experience the binocular vision. The glasses caused headaches and eye strain. Between these negative physical effects and the lackluster moviemaking, 3-D waned in popularity after a mere 18 months.

Periodically, the film industry introduces an improved 3-D process, generally at a time when box office revenues are in decline. Yet 3-D is a filmmaking technology rather than a filmmaking technique; its obviousness interferes with standard filmmaking practices such as editing and *mise-en-scene,* dooming it to the margins of the industry.

Inventions
Enlivening the Lunch Box

♦ ♦ ♦ ♦

*By adding Mickey Mouse, Hopalong Cassidy,
and other licensed characters, manufacturers of
school lunch pails thought outside the box.*

In the mid-1900s, many factory workers and laborers carried lunch
with them to work in a covered pail. Parents of that era often sent
their children off to school with a midday meal packed in an old
tobacco or cookie tin. That all changed shortly after the thermos
bottle appeared on the market in 1906—thanks to British inventor
James Dewar—but the story just begins there. A few years later, the
American Thermos Company started manufacturing and selling a
workman's lunch pail to hold its thermoses and the user's accompanying noontime repast.

By 1920, American Ther-
mos began offering a version for
schoolkids, but parents still tended to
rely on a paper sack or a reused tin.
Even after Mickey Mouse became the
first licensed character to appear on
a school lunch kit in 1935, most families weren't willing to spend the extra
money on a store-bought item, and most kids didn't seem to mind.

Then television entered the American home in the 1950s, and a
school lunch box suddenly became a must-have item. Chicago-based
Aladdin Industries secured licensing rights for the *Hopalong Cassidy
Show* in 1950 and sold 600,000 lunch boxes adorned with the famous
cowboy hero. American Thermos countered with Roy Rogers three
years later, and over the next two decades, every cartoon character, television star, sports hero, or other popular children's icon was
slapped onto a rectangular, latching steel box. The character lunch
box has become such a universally remembered piece of kitschy
Americana that the Smithsonian Institution created an exhibit in
its honor.

Sports
The Trampoline: A New Sport Springs to Life

❖ ❖ ❖ ❖

The trampoline has become a fixture in backyards and gymnasiums as a source of recreation. But can its origin really be traced to Alaska?

If postcards sold in the Anchorage, Alaska, airport are to be believed, the genesis of the trampoline can be traced all the way to the Arctic Circle. The tourist tokens show Eskimos stretching a piece of walrus skin and using the taut tarp to toss each other in the air. It's a good story, but it's not true.

It was actually an athlete and coach from the University of Iowa who created the first manufactured version of the rebounding rig known as the trampoline. During the winter of 1934, George Nissen, a tumbler on the college gymnastics team, and Larry Griswold, his assistant coach, were discussing ways to add some flair to their rather staid sport. The two men were intrigued by the possibilities presented by the buoyant nature of the safety nets used by trapeze artists. Griswold and Nissen constructed an iron frame and covered it with a large canvas, using springs to connect the cloth to the frame. The apparatus was an effective training device and a popular attraction among the kids who flocked to the local YMCA to watch Nissen perform his routines. The pair of cocreators eventually formed the Griswold-Nissen Trampoline & Tumbling Company and started producing the first commercially available and affordable trampolines.

Nissen can also claim fame for attaching a name to his pliant production. While on a tour of Mexico in the late 1930s, Nissen discovered the Spanish word for springboard was *el trampolin*. Intrigued by the sound of the word, he Anglicized the spelling, and the trampoline was born. In 2000, trampolining graduated from acrobatic activity to athletic achievement when it was officially recognized as a medal-worthy Olympic sport.

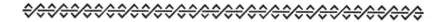

War & Military
Mystery Spot

❖ ❖ ❖ ❖

Area 51 is infamous for being the mystery spot to end all mystery spots. Speculation about its purpose runs the gamut from a top-secret test range to an alien research center. One thing is certain: The truth is out there somewhere.

Located near the southern shore of the dry lakebed known as Groom Lake is a large military airfield—one of the most secretive places in the country. It is fairly isolated from the outside world, and little official information has ever been published on it. The area is not included on any maps, yet nearby Nevada state route 375 is listed as "The Extraterrestrial Highway." Although referred to by a variety of names, including Dreamland, Paradise Ranch, Watertown Strip, and Homey Airport, this tract of mysterious land in southern Nevada is most commonly known as "Area 51."

Conspiracy theorists and UFO aficionados speculate that Area 51 is everything from the storage location of the rumored crashed Roswell, New Mexico, spacecraft to a secret lab where experiments are conducted on matter transportation and time travel.

The truth is probably far less fantastic and probably far more scientific. Used as a bomb range during World War II, the site was abandoned as a military base at the end of the war. So much for being home to that alien spacecraft from Roswell (it "crashed" in 1947). The land wasn't used again until 1955, when the site became a test range for the Lockheed U-2 spy plane and, later, the USAF SR-71 Blackbird.

Whether Area 51 was ever used to house UFOs isn't known for certain, but experts believe that the site at Groom Lake was probably a test and study center for captured Soviet aircraft during the Cold War. In 2003, the federal government actually admitted the facility exists as an Air Force "operating location," but no further information was released. Today, the area, including the various runways, is officially designated as "Homey Airport."

Language
"Kick the Bucket"

❖ ❖ ❖ ❖

*We bet you're just dying to know how the
phrase "kick the bucket" originated.*

While the meaning of "kick the bucket" has always been clear, the relationship between death and kicking the old kettle or booting the big bucket is murky at best.

The first known reference to the phrase can be found in the 1785 edition of Captain Francis Grose's *Dictionary of the Vulgar Tongue,* described by *Encyclopaedia Britannica* as "reflecting well the low life of the 18th century." Grose's entry—fittingly placed below "kicks" (breeches) and before "kickerapoo" (interestingly, another slang term for *death*)—reads: "To Kick the Bucket: to die. *He kicked the bucket one day; he died one day.*" Mr. Grose fails to make any connection between croaking and kicking, a mistake that was corrected in the 1811 edition of his classic tome—without Mr. Grose's knowledge, one assumes, seeing as how the old captain went to meet his own maker in 1791. In the updated publication, an important clarification was added. The refined entry reads: "To KICK THE BUCKET. To die. *He kicked the bucket one day: he died one day. To kick the clouds before the hotel door; i.e. to be hanged.*"

From this entry, one might conclude that the phrase means putting noose to neck, standing on a bucket and kicking the bucket away, thereby reaching out to the great beyond by one's own hand. Still, there is room for debate. *Cassell's Dictionary of Slang*, published in 2006, claims that the expression comes from an old method of slaughtering a pig by hanging the animal on a "bucket" or beam by its hind legs. As it dies, the pierced porker literally kicks the bucket.

Fads & Fashion
Brassieres: A *Bust*-ling Business

❖ ❖ ❖ ❖

A simple strap of linen led to the padded, wired
contraption that is the modern bra.

In Roman times, women who had active jobs often wore straps of fabric around their busts to keep things stable. Thereafter, women vacillated wildly between incredibly restricting corsets and less restrictive support. In 1889, French *couturier* Herminie Cadolle created a two-piece undergarment that began to topple the reign of the corset. Cadolle's *soutien-gorge*, or "breast supporter" (the top half of the two-piecer), was an instant hit at the Great Exposition of 1900. Alas, it was still expensive to purchase, since it was made primarily of the same materials as the traditional corset.

In 1913, socialite Mary Phelps Jacob was dressing for her New York debut when she realized that the light, gauzy dress she'd selected would never go with her heavy corset. She enlisted the help of her maid, and the two of them stitched together two handkerchiefs with some ribbon. Jacob called her invention the "backless brassiere," and the name stuck, both with her friends and the unknown person who sent Jacob a dollar to create one for her. (So *that's* what girls gossip about at those debutante balls!)

Jacob was a society girl, not a businesswoman, and though she had the wherewithal to apply for a patent in 1914 for her new undergarment, she either didn't enjoy running the business or couldn't keep up with the demand. She eventually sold her patent to the Warner Brothers Corset Company for $1,500.

Perhaps if she'd been as creative with her product name as she had with the name she'd created to run the business—Caresse Crosby—she might have had better luck with the item. As it was, Jacob ended up becoming a fairly major literary influence, establishing two publishing imprints, and also founded the organization Women Against War.

Written Word
The Secret Origin of Comic Books

❖ ❖ ❖ ❖

*Today's graphic novels have a long history that
stretches back to newspaper comic strips.*

In the 1920s and '30s, comic strips were among the most popular
sections of newspapers and were often reprinted later in book form.
Generally, these were inexpensive publications that looked like
newspaper supplements, though other formats were tried (including
"big little books" in which the comic panels were adapted and text
was added opposite each panel).

These so-called "funny books" were often given away as premi-
ums for products such as cereal, shoes, and even gasoline. Then,
in 1933, a sales manager at the Eastern Color Printing Company
in Waterbury, Connecticut, hit on a winning format: 36 pages of
color comics in a size similar to modern comics. *Famous Funnies:
A Carnival of Comics*, considered the first true comic book, featured
reprinted strips with such cartoon characters as Mutt and Jeff. It was
still a giveaway, but it was a hit. The next year, Eastern Color published *Famous Funnies #1* and distributed the 68-page comic book
to newsstands nationwide with a cover price of 10 cents.

As the demand for reprinted strips outpaced supply, publishers
began introducing original material into comic books. One publisher,
searching for features to fill the pages of a new book, approached
a young creative team made up of writer Jerry Siegel and artist Joe
Shuster, who had been trying for years to sell a newspaper strip
about an invincible hero from another planet. Siegel and Shuster
reformatted the strips into comic book form, and Superman debuted
in *Action Comics #1*. It was an instant smash hit. The "Golden Age"
of comics followed, introducing many of the popular heroes who
are still with us today, including Batman, Wonder Woman, Captain
America, and The Flash. In the 1960s, the "Silver Age" introduced
new, more emotionally flawed heroes such as Spider-Man, Iron Man,
and the Hulk. The comic book has certainly come a long way since
Mutt and Jeff.

Superman: The definitive superhero debuted in *Action Comics #1*, published in 1938. Kal-El, the only survivor of the planet Krypton, escapes its explosion after his father, Jor-El, puts him in a spaceship that crash-lands near Smallville, U.S.A. Kal-El, renamed Clark Kent by his adoptive parents, has superpowers of all kinds on Earth. Cocreator Jerry Siegel said he came up with Superman on a sleepless night in the early 1930s, but it took him several years to actually sell the pitch.

Batman: The alter ego of millionaire socialite Bruce Wayne first appeared in *Detective Comics #27* in 1939. In response to his parents' murder at the hands of a thief, Wayne pushes his body and mind to their limits and becomes a mysterious vigilante. Batman was actually born in 1938, after Bob Kane created a birdlike prototype for a superhero of the night. Comic-book writer Bill Finger collaborated with Kane and decided that a "Bat-Man" would be more sinister.

Spider-Man: Premiering in *Amazing Fantasy #15* in 1962, Spider-Man was teenager Peter Parker, who'd been bitten by a radioactive spider at a demonstration of a particle accelerator. The incident gave Parker spiderlike characteristics, such as the ability to cling to walls, as well as superhuman agility and speed. Marvel Comics' Stan Lee and Steve Ditko created Spider-Man as the first superhero with real-life problems, such as dating and paying rent.

Wonder Woman: The first major superheroine, Wonder Woman made her comic-book debut in 1941 in *All-Star Comics #8*. One of a race of warrior women called Amazons, Wonder Woman was given mega-strength and otherworldly powers by a cadre of Greek goddesses and gods. She was created by psychologist William Marston, who criticized comics for their "bloodcurdling masculinity." Marston used Wonder Woman's golden manacles (a symbol of female subjugation in a patriarchal society) to convey the idea that war could be eliminated if women took control.

The Hulk: In *The Incredible Hulk #1* (1962), Dr. Bruce Banner saves teenager Rick Jones from rays emanating from a gamma-bomb test, but in the process, Banner is irradiated. After that, whenever he becomes angry, he transforms into the green-skinned, seven-foot, 1,000-pound Hulk. Drawing on the Atomic Age for the Hulk's origin, cocreator Jack Kirby said he was also inspired by a news account of a woman lifting a car to save her child.

Television
The Truth About Telethons

✦ ✦ ✦ ✦

You turn on the television, hoping to tune in to your favorite sitcom—only to find that a telethon is airing in its place. And you wonder: How did the telethon get its start? And how long has it been around?

Q: How long have telethons been confounding viewers who had hoped to tune in to their regularly scheduled television show?
A: Telethons aren't a recent development; they have been a part of television since the 1940s. The first recognized telethon was a 1949 fundraiser for New York's Damon Runyon Cancer Memorial Fund and was hosted by comedian Milton Berle, who had become one of the biggest names in television as the host of the wildly popular *Texaco Star Theater.*

For an incredible 16 straight hours, Berle—fueled by black coffee and cold sandwiches—stood before the television camera performing his shtick and imploring viewers to donate. By the telethon's end, he had raised more than a million dollars.

Q: What does *telethon* mean, anyway?
A: The word *telethon* is a hybrid of "television" and "marathon" and very accurately describes these events, which can last from a few hours to a full week. They're a grueling way to raise money, but they keep airing because they work.

Q: When did Jerry Lewis become a name in telethons?
A: In 1950, Dean Martin and Jerry Lewis went before the cameras as the hosts of a telethon for the New York Cardiac Hospital and managed to raise a whopping $1 million. Two years later, singer Bing Crosby teamed with comedian Bob Hope to raise money to send the United States Olympic Team to the Helsinki Games. (This was long before deep-pocketed commercial sponsors came along.)

By the mid-1950s, telethons had become the fund-raiser of choice for a wide variety of charities and organizations. In 1955, Dean Martin and Jerry Lewis announced the biggest telethon yet, a massive appeal for the

Muscular Dystrophy Association (MDA). The event, broadcast from WABD in New York, was scheduled to run from 10:00 A.M. on Friday, June 29, to 7:00 P.M. Saturday night. The undertaking was so large that Martin and Lewis brought in a complete television production team from Hollywood at their own expense.

Q: So, what happened to Dean Martin?

A: Dean Martin and Jerry Lewis broke up the following year, and Jerry Lewis became the sole host of the second MDA telethon, held between November 30 and December 1, 1957. In an attempt to make the event even more accessible to viewers, Lewis moved it from a television studio stage to the Grand Ballroom at New York's Roosevelt Hotel. According to *New York Herald Tribune* writer Bob Salmaggi, the move gave the telethon "the air of a spontaneous party."

Q: Does the MDA Telethon still take place?

A: Yes. The Jerry Lewis MDA Telethon is a Labor Day tradition, televised worldwide and bringing in tens of millions of dollars for muscular dystrophy research. It has also proved beyond a doubt that telethons are a great way to make money quickly. Over the years, a wide variety of charities and organizations have jumped on the telethon bandwagon in some form or another, including St. Jude Children's Research Hospital, the Children's Miracle Network, and the Christian Broadcasting Network.

Q: Any other telethons I should know about?

A: National Public Radio and the Public Broadcasting Service use modified telethons (usually a few minutes of intense begging between features) as a way to help raise funds, and no less a body than the Democratic National Committee held three telethons between 1973 and 1975 to help pay off a $3.5-million debt.

Love 'em or hate 'em, telethons are probably here to stay. Critics often ridicule them (writer Cliff Jahr called them "institutionalized kitsch" in *New York* magazine), but the fact is, millions of people tune in to watch each year, many sticking around from beginning to end, and a good percentage of them are sufficiently moved to pledge a few bucks to a worthy cause.

Places & Landmarks
The Statue of Suez?

❖ ❖ ❖ ❖

Evidence suggests Lady Liberty has origins in a design originally intended for the Suez Canal.

In 1865, French sculptor Frédéric-Auguste Bartholdi (1834–1904) learned of his country's plan to create a gift for the United States. The present was intended to cement Franco-American friendship and commemorate the 100th anniversary of America's independence—still more than a decade away. The sculptor couldn't know it then, but he would go on to design this gift—now known as the Statue of Liberty. Surprisingly, evidence suggests Bartholdi's inspiration for the project came not from anything found in America, but rather from the Suez Canal, an engineering marvel that was in the works at the time.

A Grand Idea
Bartholdi's interest in the waterway came when he met fellow Frenchman Ferdinand-Marie, Vicomte de Lesseps, in Egypt. Bartholdi loved grand ideas, and de Lesseps's ambitious (or laughable, depending on your perspective) plan to channel through the desert from the Mediterranean Sea to the Red Sea was deliciously dramatic. With such shared passions fueling their friendship, the pair would become lifelong comrades.

By 1869, when the "laughable" Suez Canal was nearing completion, Bartholdi drew up plans for a commemorative statue. He envisioned a robed figure standing beside the canal's entrance, the lights within her headband and her torch guiding ships much like a lighthouse. Bartholdi deemed the figure "Progress," and presented his plans to Egyptian ruler Isma'il Pasha for funding. To his disappointment, the project was never commissioned.

Plan B
Soon thereafter, Bartholdi designed the Statue of Liberty, a great gift to America. It was erected on Bedloe's Island (later to become Liberty Island) just south of Manhattan and has since welcomed millions of immigrants to the New World.

Although Bartholdi denied any connection between Progress and Liberty, the uncanny similarities between the two are hard to ignore. Even so, the truth behind Liberty's lineage is mostly moot. This grande dame symbol of freedom and acceptance has been doing yeoman's duty in New York Harbor since 1886. The rest is just details.

Fun Facts About Lady Liberty

The statue's real name is "Liberty Enlightening the World."

Alexandre Gustave Eiffel was the structural engineer.

A quarter-scale bronze replica of Lady Liberty was erected in Paris in 1889 as a gift from Americans living in the city. The statue stands about 35 feet tall and is located on a small island in the River Seine, about a mile south of the Eiffel Tower.

There are 25 windows and 7 spikes in Lady Liberty's crown. The spikes are said to symbolize the seven seas.

Lady Liberty is 152 feet, 2 inches tall from base to torch and 305 feet, 1 inch tall from the ground to the tip of her torch.

There are 192 steps from the ground to the top of the pedestal and 354 steps from the pedestal to the crown.

The statue functioned as an actual lighthouse from 1886 to 1902. There was an electric plant on the island to generate power for the light, which could be seen 24 miles away.

The Statue of Liberty underwent a multimillion-dollar renovation in the mid-1980s before being rededicated on July 4, 1986. During the renovation, Lady Liberty received a new torch because the old one was corroded beyond repair.

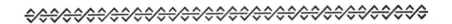

ACCIDENTAL INVENTIONS

We tend to hold inventors in high esteem, but many of their discoveries are the result of an accident or twist of fate. This is true for a surprising number of everyday items, including those that follow.

Play-Doh

One smell most people remember from childhood is the aroma of Play-Doh, the brightly colored, nontoxic modeling clay. Play-Doh was accidentally invented in 1955 by Joseph and Noah McVicker while trying to make a wallpaper cleaner. It was marketed a year later by toy manufacturer Rainbow Crafts. More than 900 million pounds of Play-Doh have been sold since then, but the recipe remains a secret.

Fireworks

Fireworks originated in China some 2,000 years ago, and legend has it that they were accidentally invented by a cook who mixed together charcoal, sulfur, and saltpeter—items commonly found in kitchens in those days. The mixture burned, and when compressed in a bamboo tube, it exploded. There's no record of whether it was the cook's last day on the job.

Potato Chips

If you can't eat just one potato chip (and who can?), blame it on chef George Crum. He reportedly created the salty snack in 1853 at Moon's Lake House near Saratoga Springs, New York. Fed up with a customer who continuously sent his fried potatoes back, complaining that they were soggy and not crunchy enough, Crum sliced the potatoes as thin as possible, fried them in hot grease, then doused them with salt. The customer loved them, and "Saratoga Chips" quickly became a popular item at the lodge and throughout New England. Eventually, the chips were mass-produced for home consumption, but since they were stored in barrels or tins, they quickly went stale. Then, in the 1920s, Laura Scudder invented the airtight bag by ironing together two pieces of

waxed paper, thus keeping the chips fresh longer. Today, chips are packaged in plastic or foil bags or cardboard containers and come in a variety of flavors, including sour cream and onion, barbecue, and salt and vinegar.

Saccharin

Saccharin, the oldest artificial sweetener, was accidentally discovered in 1879 by researcher Constantine Fahlberg, who was working at Johns Hopkins University in the laboratory of professor Ira Remsen. Fahlberg's discovery came after he forgot to wash his hands before lunch. He had spilled a chemical on his hands, and it caused the bread he ate to taste unusually sweet. In 1880, the two scientists jointly published the discovery, but in 1884, Fahlberg obtained a patent and began mass-producing saccharin without Remsen. The use of saccharin did not become widespread until sugar was rationed during World War I, and its popularity increased during the 1960s and 1970s with the manufacture of Sweet'N Low and diet soft drinks.

Post-it Notes

A Post-it Note is a small piece of paper with a strip of low-tack adhesive on the back that allows it to temporarily be attached to documents, walls, computer monitors, and just about anyplace else. The idea for the Post-it note was conceived in 1974 by Arthur Fry as a way of holding bookmarks in his hymnal while singing in the church choir. He was aware of an adhesive accidentally developed in 1968 by fellow 3M employee Spencer Silver. No application for the lightly sticky stuff was apparent until Fry's idea. The 3M company was initially skeptical about the product's profitability, but in 1980, Post-it Notes were introduced nationally. Today, the sticky notes are sold in more than 100 countries.

"To invent, you need a good imagination and a pile of junk."
—THOMAS EDISON

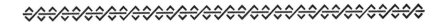

Law & Politics

Miranda Warning

❖ ❖ ❖ ❖

The violation of one man's rights becomes a warning to us all.

Most of us have never heard of Ernesto Miranda. Yet in 1963, this faceless man would prompt the passage of a law that has become an integral part of all arrests. Here's how it came to pass.

You Have the Right to Remain Silent

In 1963, following his arrest for the kidnapping and rape of an 18-year-old woman, Ernesto Miranda was arrested and placed in a Phoenix, Arizona, police lineup. When he stepped down from the gallery of suspects, Miranda asked the officers about the charges against him. His police captors implied that he had been positively identified as the kidnapper and rapist of a young woman. After two hours of interrogation, Miranda confessed.

Miranda signed a confession that included a typed paragraph indicating that his statement had been voluntary and that he had been fully aware of his legal rights.

But there was one problem: At no time during his interrogation had Miranda actually been advised of his rights. The wheels of justice had been set in motion on a highly unbalanced axle.

Anything You Say Can and Will Be Used Against You in a Court of Law

When appealing Miranda's conviction, his attorney attempted to have the confession thrown out on the grounds that his client hadn't been advised of his rights. The motion was overruled. Eventually, Miranda would be convicted on both rape and kidnapping charges and sentenced to 20 to 30 years in prison. It seemed like the end of the road for Miranda—but it was just the beginning.

You Have the Right to an Attorney

Miranda requested that his case be heard by the U.S. Supreme Court. His attorney, John J. Flynn, submitted a 2,000-word petition

for a writ of *certiorari* (judicial review), arguing that Miranda's Fifth Amendment rights had been violated. In November 1965, the Supreme Court agreed to hear Miranda's case. The tide was about to turn.

A Law Is Born

After much debate among Miranda's attorneys and the state, a decision in Miranda's favor was rendered. Chief Justice Earl Warren wrote in his *Miranda* v. *Arizona* opinion, "The person in custody must, prior to interrogation, be clearly informed that he has the right to remain silent, and that anything he says will be used against him in court; he must be clearly informed that he has the right to consult with a lawyer and to have the lawyer with him during interrogation, and that, if he is indigent, a lawyer will be appointed to represent him."

Aftermath

In the wake of the U.S. Supreme Court's ruling, police departments across the nation began to issue the "Miranda warning." As for Miranda himself, his freedom was short-lived. He would be sentenced to 11 years in prison at a second trial that did not include his prior confession as evidence. Miranda was released in 1972, and he bounced in and out of jail for various offenses over the next few years. On January 31, 1976, Miranda was stabbed to death during a Phoenix bar fight. The suspect received his Miranda warning from the arresting police officers and opted to remain silent. Due to insufficient evidence, he would not be prosecuted for Ernesto Miranda's murder.

"Good people do not need laws to tell them to act responsibly, while bad people will find a way around the laws."

—Plato

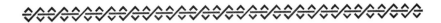

Fads & Fashion
When Fads Go Bad

♦ ♦ ♦ ♦

The leisure suit was created with the best of intentions.

The 1970s are often referred to as the "Me Decade"—and with good reason. Coming off the freewheeling, free-loving '60s, the people of this decade embraced social decadence with an enthusiasm not seen since the 1920s. Swinging, cocaine, pornography—whatever your vice, it was available for the taking.

There's no question that the decade produced more than its fair share of very bad things. But in the eyes of many, the true nadir of the Me Decade was the leisure suit, a ghastly fashion trend that tried to meld the respectability of the business suit with the comfort of "casual Friday," with predictably disastrous results.

As if the Polyester Weren't Bad Enough...

Almost always made of polyester, leisure suits had buttoned jackets with wide lapels and large pockets and pants that typically flared into bell-bottoms. Adding to their garish appearance was large, decorative stitching that sometimes contrasted with the suit's color.

And what colors! Unlike the muted tones of the traditional business suit, leisure suits were manufactured in a rainbow of hues, including burnt orange, cinnamon, crimson, pink, powder blue, saffron, tangerine, and umber.

Because leisure suits were designed for leisure, ties were a no-no. As a result, most men bold enough to wear a leisure suit complemented it with a silk or polyester shirt worn with the top buttons undone; the collars were worn outside the suit. This allowed for easy accessorizing with the '70s version of "bling."

Wardrobe for the Wealthy

Here's the really interesting thing about the leisure suit: While most closely associated with the '70s, it was actually introduced shortly after World War II as casual vacation wear for the rich. The first true

leisure suits were produced by Louis Roth Clothes and were made of wool gabardine. They had belted jackets with an inverted pleat in back; came in bright, nontraditional colors; and sold for a whopping $100, which was nearly four times what stores such as Sears charged for dress suits.

Leisure suits remained a fashion novelty until the 1970s, when they hit the scene like a brightly colored postmodern sledgehammer. Manufacturers produced them in innumerable styles, and leisure suits quickly became the polyester plumage of the hip and groovy. Leisure suits even appeared in television shows like *The Six Million Dollar Man* and futuristic movies like the 1975 James Caan hit *Rollerball*.

The timing was perfect because the leisure suit offered a nice compromise between the sloppy hedonism of '60s hippie wear and the stodgy formality of the traditional suit. At their height, they were sold in almost every department store and men's clothier and for a brief moment were ubiquitous on the business/social scene. Regardless of class or status, everyone was equal in a leisure suit.

Feeling Groovy?

Then came the inevitable backlash. First to rail against the leisure suit were respected fashion experts such as John Molloy, the author of *Dress for Success*, who declared leisure suits completely inappropriate for the office. (In a 1977 article, Molloy labeled such trends "fads for fools.")

But even more critical to the leisure suit's demise were dissatisfied wearers, who quickly realized the outfits weren't as groovy as they had been led to believe. Because they were made of polyester, leisure suits were uncomfortably hot, especially in the summer. They also had a tendency to stretch, bag, snag, and shrink. As a result, just a few short years after its second introduction, the leisure suit was consigned to the back of the closet, never to be worn again except as gag wear for '70s-themed costume parties.

Business
Banking's Crumple Zone: The Federal Reserve

The United States' first century was marked by periodic financial panics. The Federal Reserve System grew out of a need to weather them. Today, when the chairman of the Federal Reserve Board speaks, tremors ripple through the global economy.

Raison d'être

Anyone with a bank account can understand the problem that led to the Federal Reserve System (Fed). Say you have $1,000; you can keep it under a mattress or in a bank. The mattress method earns you no interest, but your access to the money is unquestioned. On the other hand, if you were sure you could withdraw your money on demand, you'd prefer to earn interest on it, so you'd deposit it.

However, the minute you suspect that your withdrawal privileges are endangered, you'll be at the teller's window to withdraw it all, right doggone now. Everyone tends to do that at once. When they do, it creates a run on banks—a panic. The antidote to panics is to assure the public that their deposits are safe and can be withdrawn at any time. Assured of that, the public doesn't withdraw cash en masse, and there's no crisis.

In the 1800s, the United States mostly lacked a central reserve bank and blundered along with a topsy-turvy monetary system; periodic panics demonstrated the need for reform. But it wasn't just about bank runs. If a central bank could easily contract or expand the money supply, government could moderate dizzy growth or meet liquidity needs. In the 1800s, many banks issued their own banknotes, which fell in value with distance from the bank's flagpole. Bank failures were unknown in Canada, eh, with its far more resilient monetary system. In fact, Canadian banknotes often circulated in parts of the United States.

Panic of 1907

The U.S. stock market went seriously south in 1906–07. This led to tighter credit and a run on trust companies—quasi-banks engaged

in riskier investments and market manipulations than conventional banks. When one bank stopped cashing checks drawn on the Knickerbocker Trust Company of New York, the dam burst. Soon everyone wanted their money out of the trusts. Only the intervention of J. P. Morgan, who formed a consortium to lend the trusts money—a move supported by Congress' Aldrich–Vreeland Act, which created emergency money, essentially doing what the Fed would later do—stemmed the tide of red ink.

Shhhh...It's at Jekyll Island

In 1910, the nation's banking kahunas met in secret at Jekyll Island, Georgia, to napkin-sketch what would become the Federal Reserve Act of 1913. This act created a Federal Reserve Board of Governors in Washington, D.C., supervising 12 regional Federal Reserve Banks (FRB). Banks would become shareholders of the Federal Reserve System, depositing cash in return for FRB stock. Fed branches would be able to lend banks money in a crisis.

World War I Crisis

The Fed began operations in November 1914, shortly after World War I began, but just a little too late to stem the financial crisis caused when the British began demanding loan payments in specie (gold). Although an extension of the Aldrich–Vreeland Act cushioned the blow, the lesson was clear: A central bank—the Federal Reserve System—was necessary for the financial stability of America.

Postwar

For the Fed, the postwar period was a time of learning by doing, as well as a time of shakeout: What could it legally do, and who would direct its actions? With banks failing all over, the Depression gave the Fed a full-immersion baptism in monetary policy. Also helping alleviate that situation was the Federal Deposit Insurance Corporation (FDIC), created to increase confidence in the banking system. The Fed and FDIC remain the primary bulwarks of public confidence in banking to this day.

Business
Amway's Humble Origins

❖ ❖ ❖ ❖

*When a couple of Michiganders started selling vitamins in the
1940s, they had no way of knowing they were onto something big.*

Take These ... They're Good for You! Seriously!

In the beginning, there was Carl Rehnborg, an American
businessman. Rehnborg went to China in the 1920s, where he saw
many undernourished persons. When he returned from China in
1927, he started mixing up vitamins. By 1934, Rehnborg was trying
to get his friends to take them. It was natural for people to be a little
skeptical about this new concept, and Rehnborg would return to find
the supplements untouched.

Rehnborg decided: no more freebies. He founded the California
Vitamin Corporation (CVC) to market his vitamins. When people
paid for them, they found they liked them—and bought more. The
multilevel marketing (MLM) business model began when Rehnborg's friends wanted him to sell to their friends. Instead, he invited
them to do the selling themselves, on commission.

In 1939, CVC became Nutrilite. Other than a rough patch,
where some of its salespeople went overboard with outlandish health
benefit claims, the company did well. In 1945, Nutrilite signed
Mytinger & Casselberry (M&C) to distribute its products. M&C
formalized and refined Nutrilite's MLM process.

Ja-Ri! Ja-Ri! Ja-Ri!

Jay Van Andel and Rich DeVos were friends and young
entrepreneurs from Michigan who came to maturity near the end
of World War II. Their best business was their Nutrilite vitamin
business, which they incorporated in 1949 as the Ja-Ri ("jah-ree")
Corporation. (Interestingly, numerous sources credit a Michael
Pacetti as a cofounder of Ja-Ri. Amway's own official history doesn't.
The (un?)reality of Pacetti's involvement remains one of Amway's
interesting mysteries.) DeVos and Van Andel worked hard and built
Ja-Ri into a thriving business, but change was on the horizon.

Business Divorce

By the 1950s, increasing government regulations on the industry began hurting sales. In 1958, Nutrilite fell out with M&C over business direction: Nutrilite wanted to branch into cosmetics, but M&C felt that such a move would hurt vitamin sales. When Nutrilite and M&C brought out competing cosmetics lines, Nutrilite saw the obvious: The marriage was over. Remembering Van Andel's skillful efforts at mediation, Nutrilite asked him to run its distribution network. Van Andel thought carefully. Why couldn't Ja-Ri run its own distribution network? In effect, it was already doing so.

Going Direct

In 1959, Van Andel and DeVos powwowed with several important Ja-Ri distributors. The group agreed to branch out into cleaning products. Why those? Because the government wasn't regulating soap success claims as stringently as it was monitoring health benefit claims for vitamins. Van Andel and DeVos believed, with reason, that enthusiasm sold products. If salespeople have to watch their claims, selling is tougher.

Van Andel, DeVos, and seven key distributors became Amway's first directors. Van Andel's original confidence proved well founded as the company grew. In 1972, Amway bought a controlling interest in Nutrilite, which it now owns outright. Today, Amway is a subsidiary of Alticor, a privately held corporation run by the Van Andel and DeVos families, with more than 10,000 employees and even more distributors.

Controversy

Amway's multilevel marketing method has been as widely attacked as it has been imitated. Those hostile to Amway accuse it of using rah-rah indoctrination seminars to hook people with the hope of a dream lifestyle few truly achieve. Its partisans deride the critics as negativist losers who didn't follow proven methods.

One fact is undebatable: Alticor is big. For fiscal year 2007, it reported global sales of $7.1 billion. That's a lot of vitamins and soap—plus hundreds of other products.

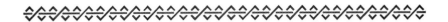

Sports
How the Marathon Didn't Get Started

❖ ❖ ❖ ❖

The primary connection between the modern race and the ancient messenger lies in a 19th-century poem that gets the details wrong.

The Basic Legend

Almost everyone has heard it: The Athenians paddled the Persians in the Battle of Marathon (490 B.C.), saving Greece from becoming a Persian province. Afterward, Pheidippides the messenger ran all the way to Athens to announce the elating news, then fell dead. Thereafter, a distance-racing sport called the Pheidippidaion became popular.

Okay, that wasn't its name. Can you imagine the "Boston Pheidippidaion"? It sounds like a tongue twister. And "Pheidippi-de-doo-dah" would never have caught on.

Did the run happen? We can't know for sure; it isn't impossible. Did the run inspire an ancient sport? No. Evidently, distance running was already an ancient sport if we believe Herodotus, since he clearly calls Pheidippides a professional distance runner. The longest race at the ancient Olympics was the well-documented *dolichos*, which literally means "long race" and was anywhere from 7 to 24 stades, or 1,400 to 4,800 meters. Pheidippides probably ran this race.

Ancient Sources

For those not steeped in the ancient world, Herodotus is revered as the "father of history"; antiquarians do not casually dismiss him. The story about Pheidippides usually gets pinned on Herodotus, but people garble what the great man actually wrote. Pheidippides (others name him "Philippides" or "Phidippides") was a professional distance runner sent to Sparta (which was also in for a stomping if Persia won) to ask for help.

Pheidippides returned, saying that the god Pan had waylaid him. "How come you ungrateful Athenians never worship Me? After all

I do for you, too. I hear you have a battle coming up; planned to pitch in there as well. The least you could do is throw Me a decent bash now and then," whined the deity. (Herodotus digresses that the Athenians responded to this come-to-Pan meeting by initiating annual ceremonies and a torch-race honoring him, mindful of his help in the battle.)

As for Spartan aid, Pheidippides relayed their lame excuse: Spartan law forbade them to march until the moon was full. That's a heck of a note for someone who purportedly just ran 135 miles in two days, then returned at the same pace. Gods only knew how quickly Pheidippides might have arrived had he not stopped to listen to Pan complain.

Herodotus says nothing of a messenger to Athens after the battle. (One wonders just how the Athenians had managed to reach 490 B.C. without acquiring a horse.) A few later Greek sources refer to the event, but none ever met living witnesses to this Marathon. Herodotus may well have met some elderly survivors, writing nearly half a century after the events.

More Recently...

As with numerous popular legends, this one owes its modern currency to a poet. In 1879, Robert Browning published "Pheidippides," in which the runner makes the run to Sparta and back *á la* Herodotus' histories, then the run to Athens where he announces Athens' salvation before keeling over.

People believed this, as they are apt to believe nearly any legend embellished by a poet. What's more, a philhellenic era was about to revive the ancient Olympics in modern form, minus the prostitutes and blood sports. In 1896, the modern Olympics restarted and included a marathon for men. It took 88 more years to include one for women. Marathon lengths have varied over the years but not by much: 40–43 kilometers (25–26.5 miles) was typical. The modern distance is 26.22 miles.

Today, of course, "marathon" has come to mean either an endurance footrace or any ultra-long event, such as an 18-inning baseball game or an office meeting that lasts until nearly every bladder present is about to rupture.

FOOD & DRINK

Weird Food Names

Most food names are pretty straightforward: No one has to ask what's in a ham and cheese sandwich, and there's no confusion when it comes to pasta marinara. But some names might cause the cautious to get some backstory before opening wide.

Deviled Eggs
Eggs may be smelly sometimes, but what is it that makes deviled eggs so evil? This dish—in which halved egg whites are filled with mashed-up egg yolk, sometimes topped with garnishes—was devilishly spicy in its original permutation. The mashed yolk is supposed to be blended and topped with an especially spicy ingredient, usually cayenne.

Shepherd's Pie
The story behind the name of this popular dish seems straightforward at first. Shepherd's pie is made of minced lamb, and shepherds herd lambs. The peculiar thing is it's not really a pie. The minced meat is covered with potatoes instead of crust, a practice that derives from the recipe's likely origin in peasant families of Northern England who made this "pie" out of cheap ingredients.

Baked Alaska
In 1804, physicist Benjamin Thompson Rumford discovered that stiffly beaten egg whites are resistant to heat. Thus began the creation of desserts in which ice cream was baked while covered in meringue, which is made from egg whites. The dessert would emerge from the oven, steaming hot but with rock-hard ice cream still frozen inside. Rumford deemed his invention "omelet surprise," but subsequent chefs of a more poetic inclination called it Baked Alaska.

Thousand Island Dressing
It turns out thousand island dressing owes its name to the "Thousand Islands" region in upstate New York, which actually boasts not 1,000 but 1,800 small islands that stretch up into Canada. Back in the early 1900s, then-famous actress May Irwin (born Ada May Campbell) was

served this scrumptious salad dressing while at a dinner party in the Thousand Islands area. She named the dressing and spread the word.

Sloppy Joes

This dish, which consists of ground meats mixed with sauce and spices and served up on a bun, is definitely sloppy, but no one's quite sure who Joe is. Sloppy Joes first became popular as a cheap sandwich in rural

areas, and from there became a staple at cheap diners. There was a popular restaurant called "Sloppy Joe's," which may be where the name came from, or it might just be an evocation of good old average Joe.

Grasshopper Pie

There are no insects in this pie filled with cream and créme de menthe, a mint-flavored alcohol. It was created in 1950s diners, at a time when mint milk shakes and liquors were also in vogue. A popular alcoholic beverage was also made with créme de menthe and also called a grasshopper. Some speculate that companies that wanted to promote their mint cream products invented the dessert.

What Do You Mean by That?

Cool as a Cucumber

Even on a warm day, a field cucumber stays about 20 degrees cooler than the outside air. Though scientists didn't prove this until 1970, the saying has been around since the early 18th century.

Egg on Your Face

During slapstick comedies in the Victorian theater, actors made the fall guy look foolish by breaking eggs on his forehead.

Spill the Beans

In ancient Greece, the system for voting new members into a private club involved secretly placing colored beans into opaque jars. Prospective members never knew who voted for or against them—unless the beans were spilled.

Science
Let's Talk About Sex, Baby

❖ ❖ ❖ ❖

Sex has always been a hot-button topic in America. But at the Kinsey Institute, located at Indiana University in Bloomington, Indiana, it's a subject of serious study and research.

The Kinsey Institute for Research in Sex, Gender, and Reproduction (its formal moniker) is named after Dr. Alfred C. Kinsey, a Harvard-trained professor of zoology who went on to become one of the world's most famous (and infamous) authorities on human sexuality.

How It All Began

In 1938, the Association of Women Students petitioned Indiana University for a course on sexuality for students who were married or considering marriage. Kinsey was tapped to coordinate the course, but he soon realized that there was little scientific data on human sexual behavior. The data that did exist was often value-laden or based on a small number of subjects.

Kinsey decided to gather his own data, and with the help of a small group of associates, he collected approximately 18,000 sexual histories based on in-depth, face-to-face interviews.

In 1947, the institute was established as a not-for-profit corporation affiliated with the university. Its primary purpose was to guarantee the confidentiality of Kinsey's interview subjects and to house the massive collection of interview data and other materials he had amassed on human sexuality.

Kinsey died in 1956 at age 62, but the institute continues his legacy of scholarly research. It is also a museum of sorts for Kinsey's amazing collection. His art and artifacts collection, for example, contains an estimated 7,000 items from the United States, Europe, South America, Africa, and Asia and spans more than 2,000 years of human history.

In addition, the institute's photography collection contains approximately 48,000 erotic images from the 1870s to the present, and includes works by such acclaimed artists as Pablo Picasso, Henri Matisse, Leonore Fini, and William Hogarth.

ACCIDENTAL INVENTIONS

Everyone Loves a Slinky

The story behind the toy that "walked" into our hearts.

In the post–World War II era, just about every kid owned one of these magical "walking" springs. It's no small wonder—folks of the day had every right to be mesmerized by a toy that actually performed feats of distraction. Hurray!

For those not familiar, a Slinky is an extraordinarily loose spring that will rest fully coiled in the palm of one's hand. If it stays in this dormant mode, people will wonder what all the fuss is about. Thankfully, it rarely does. Curiosity compels people to stretch it like an accordion and commit it to its greatest trick: walking down stairs.

It all started in 1943, with naval engineer Richard James. Laboring to develop a stabilization method for shipboard monitoring systems, James took notice when a spring accidentally fell from a shelf to a stack of books. As it uncoiled then recoiled, the spring "stepped" down to the next level. This was followed by another step to an even lower perch. James committed this life-changing moment to memory. In his spare time, he and wife Betty worked to devise the jumpy toy of the future. In 1945, the Slinky finally bounced onto the toy scene.

It would be wonderful to report that the husband-and-wife team used this invention as a springboard to advance their personal relationship, but such was not the case. In 1960, James recoiled from Betty and their six children, joined a missionary cult in Bolivia, and pumped a horde of Slinky profits into his new calling. Betty somehow managed to wrestle the suddenly floundering company back from her absentee husband, and the rest is history.

Slinky is now available in plastic and assorted colors, but the concept remains the same. According to the advertising jingle, "It's Slinky! It's Slinky! For fun it's a wonderful toy. It's Slinky! It's Slinky! It's fun for a girl and a boy." You betcha!

Science
Pangaea:
Putting the Pieces Together

❖ ❖ ❖ ❖

*Pangaea was a giant supercontinent that existed on Earth some
270 million years ago. Unlike the smaller, broken pieces of
contemporary continental plates, Pangaea had it all—literally.*

A History Lesson

The all-encompassing landmass known as *Pangaea* straddled the
equator in roughly the shape of a "C," grandly surrounded by one
of the largest (if not *the* largest) expanses of water ever to exist on
planet Earth: the Panthalassa Ocean. Only a few chunks of land lay
to the east, including bits of what we now call northern and eastern
China, Indochina, and part of central Asia. A smaller "sea," called
the Tethys Sea, was located within the "C" and is thought to have
been the precursor to today's Mediterranean Sea.

The climate was warm at this time, with no true polar ice caps.
Because of the high temperatures, life flourished during the Pangaea
years. Early amphibians and reptiles roamed the giant continent;
dinosaurs and archosaurs ran amok. When the supercontinent finally
broke apart, other plant and animal species arose, each developing
as a direct result of being cut off from their own species. In other
words, thanks to the breakup of Pangaea, our planet's organisms
became extremely diverse.

The Pangaea Puzzle

German meteorologist Alfred Wegener was the first to coin the
term *Pangaea* (which means "all earth" in Greek) in the early
20th century. He was also the first to publically propose and
publish—much to the dismay of the scientific community—the
idea that Earth's continents once lay together in the huge landmass
of Pangaea. Even more shocking was Wegener's theory that the
supercontinent broke apart over millions of years, with the pieces
ultimately reaching their current spots on Earth millions of years
later. His beliefs were based on many scientific discoveries of

his time, including identical fossils found on Africa and North America—and especially on the obvious giant jigsaw puzzle "fit" of the continents.

Now known as the "father of the continental drift theory," Wegener was a pariah in his own time. He was the victim of his own ideas, as he could not come up with a logical mechanism to explain the movement of the continents. Few of his contemporaries believed his idea, many of them citing the fact that Wegener was merely a meteorologist, not a geologist. But finally—almost three decades after his death in 1930—Wegener was vindicated, thanks to additional rock and fossil evidence and satellites that track the minute movements of the continents.

Getting the Drift of Continental Drift

Scientists now believe the shifting of the continental plates is caused by the moving mantle, the thick layer of viscous, liquid rock below Earth's crust. From the evidence provided by fossils, they believe two huge continents, Laurasia (to the north of the equator and made up of today's North America and Eurasia) and Gondwanaland (or Gondwana, to the south of the equator and made up of today's Africa, Antarctica, Australia, India, and South America) collided 270 million years ago during the Permian Period, forming Pangaea. Not long afterward—at least in terms of geologic time—around the Triassic Period 225 million years ago, the attraction waned.

This was the beginning of the end for the supercontinent, as a volcanic seam called a seafloor spreading rift (similar to today's Mid-Atlantic Ridge) ripped the continent apart. A second pair of continents formed, also called Laurasia and Gondwanaland; over the next tens of millions of years, they eventually plowed across the Earth, taking the positions we're so familiar with today. So far, there is no fossil or rock evidence that the supercontinent ever formed again. And although we will never know because our lifespans are so short, it's possible that as the continents move over the coming millions of years, another supercontinent may form.

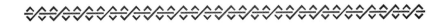

Toys & Games
From Pie Plate to Toy: The Frisbee

❖ ❖ ❖ ❖

For something that now seems so familiar, the
flying disc has an interesting story.

William Russell Frisbie

It all started with W. R. Frisbie, a bakery manager. In 1871, he
bought a Connecticut baking business, renamed the firm Frisbie
Pie Co., and got to work baking pies. When he passed away in 1903,
his son Joseph P. Frisbie donned the baker's hat. By the time of
Joe's death in 1940, the Frisbie Pie Co. had become a great regional
success. One example of Joe's savvy marketing: metal pie plates
stamped with "Frisbie's Pies," so that anyone keeping the plate
remembered the name.

Recreational Yalies

Yale University is a quick jog away from the Frisbie Pie Co.'s old
New Haven bakery. Like any self-respecting college students, Yalies
both loved a good feed and liked to find creative ways to amuse
themselves. After porking out on Frisbie's pies, they flung the empty
tins around for fun, quickly noting that they flew better if thrown
with a quick flick of the wrist to impart spin. If you threw them with
a spin, you could play catch with them. You could also accidentally
bonk Professor Stuffshirt upside the head, so they learned to yell
"Frisbie!"—as golfers holler "Fore!"—to warn of an incoming
hazard.

Morrison & Franscioni

Nope, that isn't a personal-injury law firm in Jersey. Walter "Fred"
Morrison was a World War II air combat veteran working for a
bottled gas company in California in the late 1940s. He brought
the idea for the frying plate to his employer, fellow vet Warren
Franscioni. They started experimenting on the side.

The partners soon learned that a streamlined plastic disk was
the ideal configuration. They began to make and market the Flyin'

Saucer—attempting to capitalize on budding American interest in UFOs—but the product didn't take off. In the meantime, the gas company tanked. Franscioni rejoined the Air Force and was relocated to South Dakota.

Wham-O

Morrison renamed the Flyin' Saucer the Pluto Platter. In 1957, he was demonstrating the projectile and caught the attention of a small slingshot company named Wham-O. Impressed, the Wham-O people offered to market the Pluto Platter, and they knew what they were doing. The toy sold well.

Not long thereafter, Wham-O cofounder Rich Knerr was giving out Pluto Platters at East Coast universities to build brand awareness and demand. At Yale, he saw students chucking metal pie tins around. When a tin was headed for a noggin, the Yalies yelled "Frisbie!," as tradition and safety demanded. (Irony: That same year, Frisbie's Pies shut down.)

Knerr soon renamed the Pluto Platter the Frisbee. Whether he changed the spelling for trademark reasons or thought that's how it was spelled, sales took off. Along with the Hula Hoop, the Frisbee became a Wham-O cash cow.

Morrison got royalties; Franscioni did not. He died in 1974 while still considering legal action. Wham-O's official histories of the Frisbee do not mention him.

❖❖❖❖❖❖❖

Wham-O was founded by Richard Knerr and Arthur "Spud" Melin in 1948. Their first product offering was a slingshot specifically designed to hurl bits of meat into the air to feed hawks and falcons.

Wham-O began marketing the Hula Hoop in 1957 and the Super Ball in 1964.

You can also thank Wham-O for the Slip-N-Slide, Silly String, and the Air Blaster—guaranteed to blow out a candle at 20 feet.

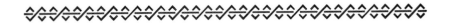

Sports
Whence Came the Knuckleball?

❖ ❖ ❖ ❖

*It's as hard to nail down the knuckler's origins as it is to
pitch, catch, or hit a good one. Legend hands the credit
to a guy named Toad, but does that hold up?*

The first knuckleball pitcher was probably some unknown, creative
sandlot kid in the 1800s who abandoned baseball in his teens. But
alas, today we can only search for someone who gained notoriety
from the pitch. Baseball lore indicates that Thomas H. "Toad"
Ramsey, a pitcher hopping around the old American Association in
the 1880s, threw the first knuckler.

The story goes that Toad was doing off-season masonry when he
severed a tendon in his pitching index finger. (Until the 1970s, most
ballplayers held off-season jobs.) Owing to this, Toad couldn't grip a
baseball in the normal fashion. The basic fastball grip, for instance,
requires two fingers to extend and grip the ball
on top, with two other fingers curled into the
palm. With a maimed index finger, Toad
couldn't grip the ball quite right, so he
curled the index finger down on the ball,
leaving three fingers curled behind the
ball and only one extended. Toad's pitch
acted like a natural sinker, which makes
sense if it was his index finger that was
injured—Hall of Famer Mordecai "Three-
Finger" Brown's missing index finger gave him a natural sinker.

In 1886, Toad struck out 499 men pitching 589 innings for Louis-
ville. That's impressive. Modern workhorses don't pitch half as many
innings. As for strikeouts, since 1887 no one has fanned 400, let
alone nearly 500.

Given that no two knuckleballers grip a baseball quite alike
anyway, Toad's reputed grip could possibly have produced a knuckler. But there's reason to doubt that. The knuckleball isn't a cheap
sinker; it's an anywhere pitch. The idea is to throw the ball slowly

with very little spin at all, so that air resistance on the seams makes the ball dance. Neither pitcher, catcher, nor hitter knows for sure where it's going, making the pitch tough to hit. If it starts spinning, of course, it becomes a high school batting practice pitch. Anyone could crush that.

Thrown naturally, a fastball's fierce backspin enables it to fly straight. To throw a knuckleball, one must defeat that backspin, so the pitcher curls the fingers behind a seam and flicks them forward when throwing. Having fewer functional fingers is no asset here—just ask Hall of Fame hurler Phil Niekro, a knuckleball specialist who had perfect use of all five digits.

If done perfectly, the forward flick cancels the backspin. Accounts of Toad's pitch do not describe a maddeningly slow floater that bobbed toward the plate. They describe a sinker, or perhaps a knuckle curve—a topspin pitch.

If Toad wasn't throwing a real knuck, who did it first? Some credit Lew Moren, who may have developed it as a comeback pitch in 1906–07 with the Philadelphia Phillies. Others credit Eddie Cicotte, who has quite a history. He was almost certainly the first pitcher to throw a true knuckler for sustained success. Given his 208 lifetime wins and his career 2.38 ERA, you'd expect to see him in the Hall of Fame. You never will. Cicotte was one of the infamous eight members of the 1919 Chicago White Sox who conspired to throw the World Series to the Cincinnati Reds at the instigation of mobster Arnold Rothstein. When the news broke, the "Black Sox" received lifetime bans from baseball.

Good knuckleball pitchers are rare. In any given year, there might be two or three active in the major leagues. Currently, Boston's Tim Wakefield is baseball's most recognizable knuckleballer; at age 42, you'd think he'd be looking to hang up his cleats. But that's one of the unique privileges of mastering the knuckler—the pitch is much easier on the arm and enables a longer career.

Language
The Ultimate Wordsmith

❖ ❖ ❖ ❖

*If there ever was any truth in the saying "The best
things happen when you least expect them," then the
story of Peter Mark Roget might just illustrate that point
perfectly. And if it doesn't illustrate it, then it may well*
demonstrate, exemplify, *or even* illuminate *that point.*

Monologophobians, Unite

Using the same word more than once can be an effective technique,
or it can plunge the thought into an unwanted abyss. The world may
never know if Dr. Peter Mark Roget suffered from *monologophobia,*
the obsessive fear of using the same word twice, but he did spend his
life compiling a classed catalog of words to facilitate the expression
of his ideas. His thesaurus, he claimed, would "help to supply [his]
own deficiencies." Roget's definition of deficiencies might conflict
with most, since he was an accomplished scientist, physician,
and inventor before he became one of the world's most famous
lexicographers.

Birth, Genesis, Nascency, Nativity, the Stork...

Roget was born in 1779 and became a physician at age 19. As a
young doctor, he influenced the discovery of laughing gas as an
anesthetic and published important papers on tuberculosis, epilepsy,
and the medical care of prisoners. As a scientist, he invented a log
slide rule to determine roots and powers of numbers (which was
used for more than 150 years—until the invention of the calculator)
and began a series of experiments concerning the human optic
system that would later aid the development of the modern camera.
While watching the wheels of a carriage through the blinds of a
window, he realized that the image of an object is retained on the
retina for about one-sixteenth of a second after the object has gone
out of view, a point he subsequently proved. This startling conclusion
helped lay the groundwork for a shutter-and-aperture device he
developed, an early prototype for the camera.

Amazingly, Roget also helped with the creation of the London sewage system and was an expert on bees, Dante, and the kaleidoscope. Achievements none too bad for a man who considered himself deficient!

The Logic and the Idea

It was only when Roget was 70 that he began putting together his first thesaurus (he borrowed the Greek word for "treasure house"), which would later bear his name. Roget's system, compiled from lists he had been saving most of his life, instituted a brand-new principle that arranged words and phrases according to their meanings rather than their spellings.

The thesaurus, now nearly 160 years in print, has sold more than 30 million copies worldwide and has become an institution of the English language. Despite critics' complaints that this reference book plunges people into "a state of linguistic and intellectual mediocrity" in which language is "decayed, disarranged, and unlovely," Roget set out to create a tool that would offer words that could express every aspect of a particular idea rather than merely list potential alternative choices. He also believed that people often just forgot the precise word they wanted and that his book would help them to remember.

"A Rose by Any Other Name"

- Roget's first thesaurus, released in 1852, contained 15,000 words; the sixth edition, published 149 years later in 2001, includes a whopping 325,000 words and phrases.
- Anyone can use the name *Roget* on their thesaurus, but only publisher HarperCollins has trademark-protected *Roget's International Thesaurus.*
- New editions of the thesaurus are greeted by the press and public as a mirror of the times in which we live. The 1980s brought into vogue such terms as *acid rain, creative accounting, insider trading, Cabbage Patch dolls,* and *bag lady.* The '90s ushered in new terms such as *eating disorder, Tamagotchi, double whammy, zero tolerance, air kissing, focus group, spin doctor, Prozac, road rage,* and *bad hair day.*

Television
The 30-Minute Scourge

❖ ❖ ❖ ❖

To quote a popular saying, you can run but you can't hide. This is especially true if you happen to be flipping through television channels. There, the dreaded infomercial will find you.

With a simple pen stroke and little fanfare, President Ronald Reagan signed off on the Cable Communications Policy Act of 1984. Among a host of other things, the act deregulated television and allowed cable stations to sell airtime to the highest bidders. Soon, the entire medium would be altered. The infomercial (information commercial) had been spawned.

Once upon a time, commercials were 15–60 seconds long. They could be an annoyance, sure, but viewers understood them to be a necessary evil. But then the infomercial, a "commercial on steroids," was born. The 30-minute marauder first invaded an overnight no-man's-land of postbroadcast test patterns and "snow." Today, the insidious beast can be found anytime and anywhere—often in disguise.

Current infomercials are often modeled after entertainment talk shows. It's part and parcel of the genre—infomercials strive to make us believe that we absolutely need the product being pushed, and they can get personal. (*Really* personal.)

But who's to say that we don't need the "breakthrough" items being hawked? Certainly a child with an unruly mane will benefit from a hair-cutting system that employs a filthy vacuum cleaner. What about a person suffering from "shameful" acne? Might they not benefit from an undisclosed "secret liquid formula" that purportedly flogs humongous craters into a smooth expanse? Of course, this doesn't even touch on "miracle" pills for men suffering from a humiliating "gravity" problem.

Hate them or hate them more, infomercials are here to stay. In 2003, the absurdly long advertisements raked in $91 billion in overall sales. That, as they say, ain't hay. The moral: Someone is buying those Ginsu knives and Ab Rollers . . . Take a wild guess as to who.

Clubs & Organizations
America at Its Best

✦ ✦ ✦ ✦

*"Chautauqua—a gathering that is typically American
in that it is typical of America at its best."*
—President Theodore Roosevelt

All but forgotten by a 21st-century public that depends on the information highway to stay informed, the Chautauqua of the 19th century was a traveling mode of education that circulated through the actual byways of America to edify, entertain, and enlighten.

The term *Chautauqua* actually refers to three types of educational organizations. The original Chautauqua Sunday School Assembly was founded in August 1874 by John H. Vincent, a Methodist clergyman, and Lewis Miller, a businessman, as a summer school for Sunday school teachers in Chautauqua Lake, New York. Over the next few years, the Chautauqua expanded into a lyceum and general amusement series, which included schools for languages and theology, as well as refresher courses for schoolteachers. Young students who wanted to broaden their cultural horizons joined clubs specializing in reading, music, the arts, physical education, and religion. The Chautauqua Institution still exists as a resort area with a summer program dedicated to the arts.

The Institution inspired the Chautauqua Literary and Scientific Circle, a correspondence school with courses in history, science, and the arts. Established in 1878, it still flourishes as a legitimate form of adult education.

Tent Chautauquas began around 1903, borrowing their name from the original institution though they had no official connection to the school. They traveled around America during the summers, setting up in tents on the outskirts of small towns for a few weeks, giving lectures, concerts, and recitals for adults. The tent Chautauquas survived until around 1930, when more pervasive forms of entertainment and popular culture, such as the cinema and radio, began to dominate the attention and leisure time of the public.

Law & Politics
License to Drive

❖ ❖ ❖ ❖

*No one needed a license to ride a horse or drive a
donkey cart. But then horses don't tend to slam into
one another at 30 miles per hour, nor has anyone ever
put his or her head through a horse's windshield.*

Early Chaos

Why did the government stick its nose into driving? To understand
this, it helps to consider the transition from animal to machine
transportation. In the 1800s, roads were designed for horse, wagon,
and foot traffic. While they were frequently dusty or muddy, they
served their intended purpose well enough. Buildings weren't far
from streets, so you couldn't make more room without knocking
something down.

Now add a daily-increasing flow of noisy early automobiles trying
to navigate the congestion without traffic control. The cars scared
the horses, and spooked horses scared the pedestrians. Things were
a mess.

Pressure for Change

By the late 1800s, any fool who could afford a motor vehicle was
entitled to operate one. Even then, vehicles routinely achieved
speeds that equaled that of a draft horse's gallop. But horseback
riders didn't typically gallop their mounts through busy city streets,
at least not any more than you would ride your mountain bike at full
speed through a crowded mall.

As 1900 loomed, traffic had gone from
being a mere annoyance to a growing public hazard. The new
motorcars could be lethal
(though on the positive
side, they didn't void
their bladders and bowels
in the streets). One

solution was to require drivers to obtain licenses, which could be revoked for bad driving.

Bringing Order

In the early 1900s, Germany and France became the first nations with mandatory licensing. The United States, which delegated the authority to individual states, proceeded slowly. In 1903, Massachusetts and Missouri became the first states to issue driver's licenses. By 1935, 39 states issued driver's licenses. Today all states do.

The driving test, which began in 1913 in New Jersey, gave the license meaning. Driver testing seeped into the system state by state, mainly between the 1930s and the 1950s. Of the first 48 states, South Dakota was the last to mandate licenses (1954) and driving tests (1959).

America's modern interstate highway system was designed in the 1950s during the Eisenhower administration. Its primary purpose was not to enhance casual driving over long distances but to provide for efficient movement of military vehicles if and when necessary.

Traffic lights were initially invented to control high horse-and-buggy traffic. The first, which only included red and green lights, was installed at a London intersection in 1868. Yellow was added in 1918.

The first Ford automobiles featured engines made by Dodge. John and Horace Dodge built engines for the Ford Motor Company at their shop in Detroit.

America's first federal gasoline tax, one cent per gallon, was created on June 6, 1932. By 2008, the rate was 18.4 cents per gallon.

Places & Landmarks
Reconstructing the Bermuda Triangle

❖ ❖ ❖ ❖

The mysterious origin of this famed locus of oceanic
tragedy suggests that the curse of the Bermuda Triangle
may be more maritime concoction than reality.

The Triangle's First Victims

It is 2:10 in the afternoon on December 5, 1945. Five Avenger
torpedo bombers take flight from the U.S. Naval Air Station in
Fort Lauderdale, Florida. The mission is a standard training flight:
13 students and their commander, Lieutenant Charles Taylor, are
scheduled to fly a short, triangular path over the sea and then return
to base.

But things did not go according to plan on that fateful afternoon.
About an hour and a half into the flight, a transmission was received
from Lieutenant Taylor. His compasses were not working properly,
and he was lost. In those days, pilots didn't have snazzy technology
like GPS to keep a constant update of their precise location, so in
the absence of a working compass, a pilot had to fly by the seat of
his pants. Taylor was an experienced pilot, but he was disoriented.
He was accustomed to flying westward from Florida instead of east
toward the Bahamas—the direction he was headed when he got lost.
From the snatches of radio transmission that were received, it seems
Taylor continued to lead his men farther out to sea, thinking that he
was headed for land.

Taylor and his men were never heard from again, and their aircraft were never recovered. The most likely scenario is that they
ran out of fuel and had to crash-land in the ocean. This tragedy
would likely have disappeared into the annals of naval disaster had
something very strange not happened next. A patrol plane, meant to
search for the missing Avengers, never returned from its search and
rescue mission. A merchant ship off of Fort Lauderdale reported

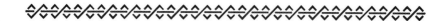

seeing a "burst of flames" in the sky soon after the rescue plane took off. The plane was a PBM Mariner; the aircraft were nicknamed "flying gas tanks" for their propensity to explode from a single spark.

Putting the Triangle Together

The tragedy of 1945 received a good deal of media coverage at the time, and some speculated that mysterious, possibly supernatural, forces were responsible for the disappearance of the planes. Rumors of strange magnetic fields, time warps, and even alien abduction began to circulate. It didn't help that Navy reports on the incident, which were requested by Taylor's mother, concluded the incident was due to "causes or reasons unknown."

Stories developed claiming that the Avengers disappeared over a particularly dangerous portion of the ocean. Not surprisingly, other accidents were found to have occurred in nearby stretches of sea. The exact dimensions of the Bermuda Triangle differ greatly depending on the source, but the three points are usually designated as Bermuda, Puerto Rico, and Miami, Florida. The Triangle's size is also in question; reports and studies list it as anywhere from 500,000 to 1.5 million square miles.

The area wasn't christened "the Bermuda Triangle" until the publication of a 1964 fiction story called "The Deadly Bermuda Triangle," written by Vincent Gaddis and published in *Argosy* magazine. A decade later, the Triangle leapt into popular culture with 1974's best-selling book *The Bermuda Triangle*, a sensationalized account of mysterious accidents that had occurred in the area.

More mundane explanations for the Triangle's deadly powers point to the statistical probability of more accidents occurring in an area that sees high traffic. The waters between Florida and the Bahamas are frequented by pleasure boats, which are often crewed by inexperienced tourists. In addition, aircraft and boats are also sometimes victim to short, unexpected storms that dissipate before reaching shore and thus seem mysterious or fantastic. Still, whether or not the Bermuda Triangle is really more dangerous than other patches of sea, the persistent legends of tragedy have certainly prevented many a weary traveler from entering its dreaded perimeter.

BIRTHDAYS OF THE RICH AND FAMOUS

Who can resist poking around to discover whether they share a birthday with a famous leader, legendary movie star, talented musician, or notorious celebrity?

The Force was with George Lucas when he was born on May 14, 1944.

The ageless Cher was born on May 20. Because she *is* ageless, we won't reveal her birth year!

Letterman or Leno? Which talk show host do you prefer? Both were born in April; Dave on April 12, 1947, and Jay on April 28, 1950.

The world became a bit brighter when iconic movie star Marilyn Monroe was born on June 1, 1926.

Johnny Depp, one of the best actors of his generation, was born on June 9, 1963.

Daniel Radcliffe, who became a star as the title character of the Harry Potter movies, was born on July 23, 1989. He owes his success to Harry Potter creator J. K. Rowling, who was born in the same month on July 31, 1965.

Mick Jagger, who was born on July 26, 1943, once said that he would rather be dead than sing "Satisfaction" when he was 45. Maybe we shouldn't tell him!

Which *Saturday Night Live* alum is funnier? Bill Murray, who was born on September 21, 1950, or Adam Sandler, who was born on September 9, 1966?

July 22, 1940. And the question is, "What is the birth date of *Jeopardy!* host Alex Trebek?"

How fitting that film director Alfred Hitchcock, who dealt in fear and murder as the master of suspense, was born in 1899 on unlucky August 13.

Famous and infamous, talented and troubled, King of Pop Michael Jackson moonwalked into this world on August 29, 1958.

We all love Lucy. Lucille Ball was born on August 6, 1911, the same date on which Hollywood man's man Robert Mitchum was born in 1917.

One giant leap for mankind! The first person to walk on the moon, Neil Armstrong, was born on August 5, 1930.

Famous Hollywood actor Robert De Niro was born on August 17, 1943. The man who helped make him a star, director Martin Scorsese, was born on November 17, 1942.

One of Latin music's most glamorous singers, Gloria Estefan, salsa-ed into this world on September 1, 1957.

Boo! Modern-day master of horror Stephen King was born on September 21, 1947.

Have a Big Mac on October 5 to celebrate Ray Kroc's birthday. The founder of McDonald's was born on that day in 1902.

In space, you can't hear her scream. Sigourney Weaver, resilient heroine of the *Aliens* series, touched down on Earth on October 8, 1949.

The Beatles changed the course of culture, not only influencing music but also clothing, movies, and sociopolitical attitudes. Celebrate the Beatles by commemorating their birthdays. Richard Starkey (a.k.a. Ringo Starr) was born on July 7, 1940; John Lennon on October 9, 1940; Paul McCartney on June 18, 1942; and George Harrison on February 24, 1943.

Roll over, Beethoven. Chuck Berry—the Prime Minister of rock 'n' roll—was born on October 18, 1926.

Happy trails to the King of the Cowboys and his queen. Roy Rogers was born on November 5, 1911, and Dale Evans was born on October 31, 1912.

Whoopi Goldberg, whose vocal stylings have benefitted her career as an actress, Broadway star, and talk show host, was born on November 13, 1955.

The counterculture of the 1960s produced two great comedians and social commentators: Richard Pryor, who was born on December 1, 1940; and George Carlin, whose birthday was May 12, 1937.

TomKat: Movie star Tom Cruise was born on July 3, 1962; wife Katie Holmes was born on December 18, 1978.

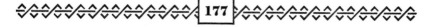

Miscellaneous
Origins: The History of Things

❖ ❖ ❖ ❖

*These intriguing stories offer insight into the
history of some everyday items, expressions, and
endeavors—stuff you never think to think about.*

The Latin Alphabet

People had been writing hieroglyphics (symbols that stood for objects
such as *dog, reed,* or *pyramid*) for at least a millennium before the first
glimmer of an actual alphabet appeared. Around 2000 B.C., a group of
Egyptian slaves (the Semitics) figured out how to communicate with
one another using symbols that represented sounds, not just things.
From this system, we eventually got the Phoenician and Aramaic
alphabets, as well as the Greek and Latin alphabets. Early Greek was
written right to left, before the "ox-turning" method (in which the
direction of writing changed with every line) was adopted. By the fifth
century B.C., the left-to-right method was in place.

The Evil Eye

The language of superstition is universal. From Europe to the
Middle East, from Mexico to Scandinavia, folktales have long
warned people against the power of the "evil eye." Essentially, the
evil eye is an unintentional look of envy from a person who covets
what the recipient possesses. At the very least, it's plain old bad
vibes; at its most potent, the evil eye is blamed for bad luck, disease,
and even death for the person who receives the look. Cultures that
fear the evil eye have developed various means of protection: A
common European custom is to wear a locket containing a prayer.
In India, small mirrors are sewn into clothing to deflect an evil
gaze and reflect it to the person who gave it; similarly, the Chinese
use a six-sided mirror called a *pa kua*. The Italians have developed
various hand gestures for protection. Sometimes the defense is
more elaborate: Folk healers in Mexico smear raw chicken eggs over
someone's body to keep him or her safe from the evil eye. In this
case, the person might just get a plain old dirty look.

The Jump Rope

Skipping and jumping are natural movements of the body (especially for kids), and the inclusion of a rope in these activities dates back to A.D. 1600, when Egyptian children jumped over vines as play. Early Dutch settlers brought the game to North America, where it flourished and evolved from a simple motion into the often elaborate form prevalent today: Double Dutch. With two people turning two ropes simultaneously, a third, and then fourth, participant jumps in, often reciting rhymes. Jumping techniques have become so complex that there are now worldwide organizations that sponsor Double Dutch competitions.

Quiche

Although similar concoctions date back to ancient Roman cheesecakes and medieval European tarts and pies, the modern quiche recipe comes from the Lorraine region of France. The original quiche Lorraine was an open-face pie filled with eggs, cream, and bacon. Cheese was later incorporated, along with any number of additions, from shallots to shellfish, depending on one's preference. In North America, quiche enjoyed its greatest popularity as a trendy 1970s food, joined by other notable offerings such as fondue and Caesar salad.

Taxicabs

Think of Cleopatra being carted around on a sedan chair, and you have the origins of the modern-day taxicab. Rickshaws replaced sedan chairs as a means of transporting people from one place to another, followed by horse-drawn carriages, which finally gave us poor humans a rest. At the end of the 19th century, automobiles started to fill the streets, and with the invention of the *taximeter* (an instrument that measures both the time and distance a vehicle has traveled), transport by cab became increasingly popular. Throughout the world, cab companies have painted their taxis particular colors, both for identification purposes and to cut down on the number of unofficial drivers. Today in New York City alone, taxis transport more than 200 million passengers almost 800 million miles every year.

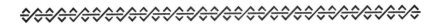

Language
The Beginnings of Braille

❖ ❖ ❖ ❖

*Once upon a time, a world without seeing meant a world
without reading. This changed forever when Louis Braille,
a precocious blind teenager, invented an ingenious system
that finally enabled the blind to read with ease.*

Blindness Before Braille

Throughout history, many different remedies, inventions, and
institutions have been developed to accommodate the blind. These
usually develop in cities where the blind population is large enough
to necessitate such programs. The first large-scale school for the
blind, called the Quinze-Vingts hospice, was endowed in 1260 by
Louis IX of France. The students there set off the extraordinary
chain of events that ultimately led to Braille.

In 1771, brilliant French linguist Valentin Haüy watched men
from the Quinze-Vingts hospice perform in front of a mocking crowd.
Haüy was enraged that instead of receiving a good education, blind
students were reduced to performing in the street. As the story goes,
a few years later, Haüy gave a coin to a blind beggar, who determined the denomination of the money by feeling the bumps on its
face. Haüy was inspired, and in 1784, he opened his own school for
the blind, The Royal Institute for Blind Youth, in Paris. He made
embossed, oversize books with raised letters, usually round and
cursive, that the blind could feel, one by one, as they read. Embossed
books made reading slow and difficult, but Haüy's students were
grateful to be able to read at all.

Braille Enters the Scene

Around the same time Haüy was teaching his pupils in Paris, Louis
Braille was born in Coupvray, a village located east of France's
capital. Louis injured his eye at the age of three while playing with
his father's tools. The injury became infected, and the infection
quickly spread to the other eye. Eventually, young Louis went blind.
It was clear to everybody in Coupvray that Louis was a special

child—he showed a genius for music and craftsmanship, and in 1819, at the age of ten, he was awarded a scholarship to the school Haüy had founded.

Louis was amazed by the embossed books he found at his new school. Haüy's books were cumbersome and expensive, so there were only 14 in the entire library. Louis read them all, but the process was laborious: Each letter had to be felt individually, so by the time Louis reached the end of a sentence, he could barely remember how the sentence had begun. He began experimenting with ways to improve on Haüy's method.

Braille Meets Barbier

Louis's moment of insight came from an unexpected source. Charles Barbier de la Serre, an entrepreneur and soldier in the French army, visited Haüy's school in the 1820s. Barbier had devised a system of touch-based communication while serving as a captain under Napoleon. During battle, it was necessary for officers to communicate quickly at night amid loud artillery fire. Barbier devised a technique called "night writing," in which pages were embossed with a system of dots rather than raised letters.

Louis was amazed. Raised dots would be easier to feel than raised letters, and if the dots were small, several of them could be felt at once against a fingertip. Louis set to work on his own dot-based alphabet. In 1824, at the age of 15, Louis perfected the system that is now known as Braille. Each Braille character is called a *cell*, and there are one to six dots in a six-position cell. The given letter or punctuation mark depends on which dot is raised, in which position, within the cell.

Louis taught his invention to his fellow students, who learned it quickly. The superiority of Louis's method was immediately obvious to anyone who used it. Louis also developed a Braille code for music. Today, standardized Braille codes have been developed for languages the world over, and it is the best and most popular form of reading for the blind.

Fads & Fashion
What's that in Your Hair?

✦ ✦ ✦ ✦

*A Midwestern hairdresser enters a magazine
contest and creates an iconic look.*

When Margaret Vinci-Heldt set out to win a contest run by a beauty
magazine in 1960, the 42-year-old hairdresser from Elmhurst,
Illinois, had no idea she was about to create a look that would be
adopted by women all over the world. With just a few hours of teas-
ing and *lots* of hairspray and bobby pins, she unleashed one of the
biggest fashion trends of the decade—the beehive hairdo. Also
known as the B-52 for its resemblance to the bulbous nose of the
famous World War II aircraft, her distinctive design piles the hair
into a high dome resting on the crown of the head. Famous fash-
ionistas of the era, including Brigitte Bardot and Jacqueline Kennedy Onassis, began sporting the elaborate 'do for the cameras, and
women throughout the Unites States and Europe began rushing to
the beauty salon on a weekly basis to get theirs.

Why All the Buzz?

It's difficult to pin down why the style became so popular. Some
say it's the classic look; others point to the fact that the piled-
high coif makes the wearer look taller; and still others note that it
requires relatively little maintenance (though sleeping in one does
involve some elaborate preparation). Whatever the reason, the
beehive quickly became the iconic look of the pre-counterculture
1960s. Audrey Hepburn famously sported a beehive in what was
unquestionably her most famous role—Holly Golightly in *Breakfast
at Tiffany's*. The look was also seen regularly on *Star Trek*, worn by
the secondary character Yeoman Janice Rand, and it even became
the centerpiece of an episode of *The Flintstones*.

Though the style's popularity waned toward the late '60s, it
remained a familiar part of pop culture for decades. The sassy
Southern waitress Flo on the sitcom *Alice* was never seen without
her trademark beehive, and virtually all of the matronly women who

populated Gary Larson's world-famous *The Far Side* cartoons wore one. The style was the trademark look for arguably the worst TV mom in history, Peg Bundy of *Married...with Children*, as well as for everyone's favorite cartoon mom, Marge Simpson. The B-52's, a popular 1970s New Wave band, took their name from the slang term for the hairstyle—two of the band's female singers were known to sport the 'do. And John Waters lovingly put the beehive at the center of his 1988 cult movie *Hairspray.* More recently, British singer Amy Winehouse created her distinctive look in part by wearing elaborate variations of the beehive, which has actually led to a resurgence of the style in Britain and Australia.

Hairy Moments

While some have touted the beehive as "the last great hairdo" to be invented, the style has also had its share of low moments. In a survey sponsored by a British hair products company in 2005, the beehive was voted the third-worst hairstyle of all time, behind only the Mohawk and the mullet. A year later, an American woman traveling from Amsterdam to Cork was arrested by Irish customs officials for smuggling cocaine, which she had secreted in her beehive. Even at the height of the craze in the 1960s, there was a degree of backlash against the style. Persistent urban legends told of spiders or ants nesting in women's highly piled hair. Hatmakers of the era were also not fans of the beehive—many of them blamed the popularity of the new hairstyle for driving women's hats out of vogue.

Although the beehive may have had its detractors, it remains a thoroughly distinctive and original look that will forever be recognized as a symbol of its era.

"If I want to knock a story off the front page, I just change my hairstyle."

—Hillary Clinton

Language
Forged Jury

✦ ✦ ✦ ✦

The skills of the blacksmith are not usually equated with speed, so it may seem ironic that the term "strike while the iron is hot" was forged to describe swift and timely action.

The phrase "strike while the iron is hot" is a reference to acting quickly, moving swiftly, and forging ahead with an idea, plan, or opportunity while conditions are favorable for success. In other words, snooze and you lose, go in and you win. It's similar to the old adage "make hay while the sun shines." The proverb's roots are decidedly European, with its first recorded use occurring in the 14th century. The saying itself refers to the act of forging and shaping iron in a blacksmith's shop. The blacksmith would heat a piece of iron in the fire until the tip of the rod became red-hot. After removing the tongs from the flames, the smith had to hammer or strike the iron into the desired shape and mold it while it was still hot. Once the metal cooled, it became brittle and was impossible to manipulate. So, speed, precision, a steady hand, and a keen eye are key ingredients for success, whether one is forging iron or pursuing a potentially prosperous path in life or business.

The phrase is used to describe any number of situations—be it politics, real estate, or the stock market. Bands and artists such as Kenny Neal, the Vigilantes of Love, and Orange and Lemons have written songs using the phrase, and the group Born Hammers borrowed the maxim as the title of their 2003 album. The jury is still out on the quality of these recordings.

Personal Hygiene
Soap Floats

❖ ❖ ❖ ❖

Ivory Soap's buoyancy doesn't have anything to do with purity.
Here's the lowdown on one of America's favorite bars of soap.

Perhaps one of the most memorable lines in commercial advertising is the following: "It's 99 and $^{44}/_{100}$ percent pure!" Whenever viewers heard this line uttered on television, they knew a pure-white bar of Ivory Soap would soon make an appearance, its distinctive etched lettering positioned for maximum impact. Print ads also capitalized on the soap's purity with the tagline "Ivory Soap. It floats."

Of course, a more discriminating viewer—let's call him "I. M. Sinical"—might sometimes watch TV with his wife Jane, with a decidedly different reaction. "What is this soap trying to hide?" the curmudgeon would demand. "I want to know what's in the $^{56}/_{100}$ percent! And what's with this 'so pure it floats' malarkey? Dog droppings sometimes float, and I'm not about to bathe in them!"

The Pure Truth?

As the story goes, in 1879, a "White Soap" producer at Procter & Gamble neglected to turn off his mixing machine at lunchtime. Fearing punishment, he allowed the air-enriched batch of soap to be shipped. Soon, customers were asking for more "soap that floats," a fun by-product of the error. The worker came clean, company officials complied, and Ivory Soap was born.

It's a great story. But it isn't true. In 2004, Procter & Gamble discovered records dating back to 1863, which indicated that the floating soap was indeed intentional. Anyone who has ever lost a bar of soap while taking a bath can see why the company thought floating soap might be a good idea.

To conclude, we'll answer Mr. Sinical's probing questions with established facts: It is air that makes Ivory Soap float, *not* purity. And the composition of the suspect $^{56}/_{100}$ths? Uncombined alkali, carbonates, and mineral matter—each an *impurity*. How's that for truth in advertising?

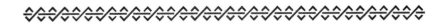

Toys & Games
The Real Origin of the Barbie Doll

◆ ◆ ◆ ◆

*It didn't take long for the Barbie doll to become not only
an iconic toy, but a symbol of adult style and ambition
as well. Where exactly did Barbie come from?*

When Barbie appeared in 1959, she was the first adult-styled toy for
young girls. Previously, girls were offered stuffed animals and vinyl
baby dolls, presumably meant to evoke their maternal instinct. But
Barbie was a creature to which a young girl could *aspire*—albeit one
that was, er, rather statuesque.

German Influences

Before Barbie, there was a doll called Bild Lilli, a provocative copy
of a cartoon character in the German newspaper *Bild.* Clad only
in a short skirt and tight sweater, Bild Lilli was sold to grown men
through tobacco shops and bars.

Ruth Handler, the genius behind Barbie, instinctively understood
that young girls wanted to enter the adult world years before their
time. Handler had noticed her own daughter, Barbara, assigning her
paper dolls grown-up roles while playing with them. When Handler
spotted Bild Lilli in Europe during a family vacation, she recognized
the doll's possible commercial potential and purchased several examples, each in a different outfit.

Barbie's earliest appearance, although toned down from Bild
Lilli, still owed much to her forerunner: She was pale, with pouty
red lips and heavily made-up eyes that cast a knowing sidelong
glance, not to mention her absurd measurements (which, on a
human counterpart, would equal 38″-18″-32″). Barbie was also a
protofeminist icon, holding at least 95 different careers. Her original
job description as "a teenage model dressed in the latest style" (even
though she looked at least a decade older) later evolved into non-
specific "career girl," with astronaut, ballerina, doctor, pilot, attorney,
paleontologist, and presidential candidate versions, to name a few.

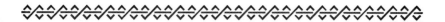

The Barbie Empire Grows

Millions of baby-boom children grew up imagining themselves as Barbie, who went on to acquire boyfriend Ken, close friend Midge, little sister Skipper, and a wardrobe that any Hollywood star would envy. Actually, "acquire" could have been Barbie's middle name (although it was really Millicent). She needed everything. At first, it was just a trunk to hold her irresistibly detailed clothes and teeny accessories. Then came furniture and a beach house, accessed via luxury cars (pink Cadillac, red Porsche). Her features and hair softened; her other friends (Stacey, a British pal, and Christie, her African American girlfriend) came and went; and, after the longest engagement in history, she finally dumped Ken (named after Handler's son). Just like real life, only writ small.

During the past half-century, Barbie has reflected both fashion and social history. Charlotte Johnson, who originally dressed the doll, took her job seriously, interpreting the most important clothing trends of each successive era. Barbie also inspired top designers, including Armani, Christian Dior, Dolce & Gabbana, John Galliano, Gucci, Alexander McQueen, and Vivienne Westwood, to create exclusive originals for her; Philip Treacy designed her hats, and Manolo Blahnik her shoes.

The Decline of the Barbie Era

But what was once cutting-edge has now become rather staid. What excites little girls nowadays is the hypersexualized, even more cartoony-looking Bratz dolls, who come off as even poorer role models. In comparison, Barbie looks square and has accordingly lost market share. Her future seems to be more as a nostalgic collectible for adults. Indeed, a complete collection of early Barbies, plus friends and outfits, was auctioned for record prices at the venerable Christies in late 2006; a single doll, Barbie in Midnight Red, sold for $17,000. In order to retain value, collectors keep limited editions in their original boxes.

In an odd way, Barbie has come full circle: From her sordid, bar-hopping start as Bild Lilli, Barbie has once again become a toy for grown-ups only.

BAND NAMES

As the saying goes, you can't judge a book by its cover. But what about judging a band by its name? Although a band's chosen name might not clue you in to whether or not you'll like their music, it sometimes offers an indication of a group's roots.

ABBA
There is no cryptic significance behind the name of this smash Swedish group that topped the worldwide music charts from the mid-1970s to the early 1980s. ABBA is merely an acronym formed from the first letters of each group member's first name: Agnetha Fältskog, Björn Ulvaeus, Benny Andersson, and Anni-Frid Lyngstad.

Bee Gees
Already performing as the Rattlesnakes, the brothers Gibb met radio DJ Bill Gates (not *that* Bill Gates!) and racetrack promoter Bill Goode. The trio of young singers was rebranded the "B.G.'s" after the initials of the two promoters—but the group's mother was also named Barbara Gibb, and the fact that they were often called the Brothers Gibb just reinforced the name, which evolved to become the Bee Gees.

Joy Division
There is little happiness in the name, sound, or even legacy of Manchester, England's Joy Division. The group originally took the name Stiff Kittens but eventually settled on the name Warsaw—a reference to the song "Warszawa" by David Bowie. This led to confusion with a London punk band named Warsaw Pakt, so the group instead took the name of the prostitution wing of a Nazi concentration camp mentioned in the 1955 novel *The House of Dolls.*

New Order
Following the suicide of Joy Division's lead singer, Ian Curtis, the group decided not to continue under its original name. While there had already been a punk band called The New Order, the group's manager found a reference to "The People's New Order of Kampuchea" in *The Guardian* newspaper. Despite the undertones given the origin of the name Joy Division, the group has disavowed any fascistic connotations.

Blue Öyster Cult

With songs of mythology and the occult, It is no surprise that the group that first billed themselves as Soft White Underbelly would look for a more cryptic name. They ultimately settled on Blue Öyster Cult, a name taken from a poem—written by their manager, Sandy Pearlman—that told of how aliens secretly controlled Earth and guided humans through history.

Chicago

One of the leading U.S. singles-charting groups in the 1970s and beyond, Chicago originally formed as a cover band called The Big Thing. Made up of DePaul University students, the group ended up working on original songs and changed their name to Chicago Transit Authority. The actual Chicago Transit Authority threatened legal action, so the boys from Chicago simply took the name of their hometown.

Led Zeppelin

The group that was once jokingly predicted to crash and burn instead became one of the most popular and influential rock bands of all time. Bass player Jimmy Page joined The Yardbirds in 1966, replacing original bassist Paul Samwell-Smith. By 1968 most of the other members had left the group, but the band was contractually obligated to complete its Scandinavian tour, which it did as The New Yardbirds. The popular story is that Page tried to recruit former Yardbird Jeff Beck along with The Who's Keith Moon and John Entwistle to form a supergroup that would go down like a "lead zeppelin."

Soundgarden

Seattle grunge pioneers Soundgarden took their name from a public work of art located at the National Oceanic and Atmospheric Administration adjacent to Magnuson Park in their Washington hometown. Created in 1982 by Doug Hollis, the sculpture catches the wind to create a unique sound.

UB40

The British reggae band UB40 began as a group of friends in the English city of Birmingham, where unemployment was rampant in the 1970s. In 1978, the group took the name off a form from the UK government's Department of Health and Social Security, the Unemployment Benefit, Form 40. The hard-working group has released more than 50 singles in the past 30 years.

Signs & Symbols
The Swastika: Sacred Good, Nazi Evil

❖ ❖ ❖ ❖

For thousands of years, the swastika stood as a sacred symbol of fortune and vitality—until Adolf Hitler adopted its eye-catching geometry to lead his rise to power, turning the swastika into the 20th century's ultimate emblem of evil.

Originating in India and Central Asia, the swastika takes its name from the Sanskrit *svastika,* which means well-being and good fortune. The earliest known examples of the swastika date to the Neolithic period of 3000 B.C. A sacred symbol in Hinduism, Buddhism, and Jainism, the swastika was most widely used in India, China, Japan, and elsewhere in Asia, though archaeological examples have also been found in Greco-Roman art and architecture, in Anglo-Saxon graves of the pagan period, in Hopi and Navajo art from the American Southwest, and in Gothic architecture in Europe. Synagogues in North Africa and Palestine feature swastika mosaics, as does the medieval cathedral of Amiens, France.

For thousands of years, the swastika was a symbol of life, the sun, power, and good luck, though in some cultures a counter-clockwise mirror image of the swastika, called a *sauvastika,* meant bad luck or misfortune. Pointing to evidence in an ancient Chinese manuscript, astronomer Carl Sagan theorized that a celestial phenomenon may have given rise to the swastika's use around the world. The phenomenon he was referring to took place thousands of years before; gas jets shooting from the body of a passing comet were bent into hooked forms by the comet's rotational forces—a shape similar to that of the swastika. Other scholars believe that the symbol was so widely known because its geometry was inherent in the art of basket weaving.

The modern revival of the swastika in the Western world began with the excavation of Homer's Troy on the shores of the Dardanelles in the 1870s. German archaeologist Heinrich Schliemann

discovered pottery and other artifacts at the site decorated with swastikas. Schliemann and other scholars associated the finds with examples of the symbol uncovered on ancient artifacts in Germany. They theorized that the swastika was a religious emblem linking their German-Aryan ancestors to the ancient Teutons, Homeric Greeks, and the Vedic civilization. German nationalists, including anti-Semitic and militarist groups, began using the symbol at the end of the 19th century. But with its connotations of good fortune, the swastika also caught on in Western popular culture. Swastikas were used to decorate cigarette cases, postcards, coins, and buildings throughout Europe. In the United States, they were used by Coca-Cola, the Boy Scouts, and a railroad company. The U.S. Army's 45th Division used the symbol during WWI, and Charles Lindbergh painted one inside the nose cone of the *Spirit of St. Louis* for good luck.

In 1920, Adolf Hitler adopted the symbol for the Nazi Party's insignia and flag—a black swastika inside a white circle on a field of red—claiming he saw in it "the struggle for the victory of the Aryan man." With Hitler's appointment as chancellor, the Nazi flag was raised alongside Germany's national flag on March 14, 1933, and it became the nation's sole flag a year later. The symbol was used ubiquitously in Nazi Germany—on badges and armbands, on propaganda material, and on military hardware. By the end of the war, much of the world identified the symbol only with Hitler and the Nazis. Its public use was constitutionally banned in postwar Germany. Though attempts have been made to rehabilitate its use elsewhere, the swastika is still taboo throughout the Western world.

In Asia, however, the swastika remains a part of several religious cultures and is considered extremely holy and auspicious. In India, it is a symbol of wealth and good fortune, appearing not only in temples and at weddings but on buses, on rickshaws, even on a brand of soap. Hindus in Malaysia, Indonesia, and elsewhere in Southeast Asia also continue its use. In China, the left-facing Buddhist swastika is the emblem of Falun Gong. In 2005, the government of Tajikistan called for adoption of the swastika as a national symbol.

Toys & Games
Raising the Stakes

❖ ❖ ❖ ❖

*We're willing to bet you're interested in learning how a
lowly token came to supplant both money and sanity.*

You have to hand it to the inventor of the poker chip. Here's an
item that spends like money, bets like money, even has people lust-
ing after it like money, yet it doesn't quite *feel* like money. Ask any
gambler—they'll tell you that poker chips, or gaming chips as they're
now called, seem like Monopoly money when compared to the real
thing. This is especially true when you're down on your luck because
the mystical quality of the chip makes the reality of losing hard-
earned dollars a little fuzzy. What evil genius devised such a thing?

The fact is, nobody seems to know for sure. History records
evidence of substitute money being used as betting chips as far back
as the 18th century, but the modern chip that we've come to love or
loathe (depending upon individual luck) didn't make an appearance
until the early 20th century.

Although such crude chips (generally made from ivory, bones, or
clay) represented a breakthrough in gaming convenience, they also
invited attempts at forgery. Industrious types would simply manufacture similar-looking bits at home and smuggle them into gaming
parlors. But necessity fosters invention, and soon, the modern poker
chip was born.

Today, gaming chips are constructed of composite materials and
feature such high-tech extras as microchips within the chip to foil
would-be forgers. Thanks to mass production, casino-
quality chips are now available to home
gamblers as well, which should
be just the thing for those who
wish to lose their shirts without
the associated guilt, shame, and
anguish of blowing real money.
Ladies and gentlemen, lay
down your bets.

Language
Cutting the Red Tape

❖ ❖ ❖ ❖

Everyone hates it; Dr. Seuss helped the government reduce it.

Q: Where did the term "red tape" originate?
A: Actual red tape originated as an antifraud measure, similar to wax seals in ancient times. The goal was to ensure that a document received by its intended recipient was the exact same one sent by its author or authors. So it had to be secured in such a way that any tampering would be revealed. Anyone seeking to alter an official document would have to break the wax seal and untie the red tape.

The Vatican archives preserve about 85 copies of Henry VIII's petition to Pope Clement VII for a divorce from his first wife, Catherine of Aragon, wrapped with official red tape. But red tape was probably in use for many, many years before that. The Vatican itself used red tape, as did the British Parliament and other European chanceries and courts.

Q: So what happened next in this "tacky" story? Why did the term stick?
A: Around 1736, "red tape" became synonymous with pointless bureaucratic procedure and obstruction. Some scholars suggest that frustratingly hard-to-access American Civil War veterans' records were bound in red tape. Today, red tape is alleged to frustrate scientists, keep economies from achieving their potential, prevent start-up companies from succeeding, and block the efforts of charities. All politicians campaign against it. All officials promise to cut it—at least until some of them are accused of fostering it. Red tape, it seems, is an evil growth, entwining and frustrating everyone's best efforts.

Q: What does Dr. Seuss have to do with any of this?
A: During World War II, newspapers published a series of articles dubbed the "Society of Red Tape Cutters." The intention was to commend those individuals who kept bureaucracy (red tape) from deterring the war effort. Theodor Geisel (a.k.a. Dr. Seuss) illustrated the certificate for the award, which went to such notables as Franklin D. Roosevelt, Harry S. Truman, and Admiral Chester W. Nimitz. Since then, other groups have taken the same name, including a Society of Red Tape Cutters in Northfield, Illinois, that consists of volunteers who help senior citizens get government services.

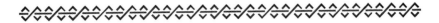

Personal Hygiene
One Sharp Guy

❖ ❖ ❖ ❖

*King Gillette never ruled a country—he did better
than that. He oversaw a disposable kingdom.*

There's a quirky billboard currently plastered along America's
byways. It reads "Failed, failed, failed. And then..." Alongside the
cryptic message is a photograph of Abraham Lincoln. It may take
a few seconds, but the message ultimately becomes clear. The billboard is a variation of a popular maxim that we learned as children:
"If at first you don't succeed, try, try again." Sounds like a page lifted
from the life of King Camp Gillette (1855–1932).

As a boy, Gillette amused himself by watching his parents tinker.
His dad, a patent agent, was forever inventing ways to do things
better, and his mom, a homemaker, concocted wonderful recipes
through experimentation. Their efforts planted a seed in the mind of
young Gillette. He fantasized about inventing something that would
make him rich and famous.

A Close Shave
By his mid-30s, Gillette had little to show for his efforts and was
becoming increasingly bitter. Despite having poured his heart
and soul into countless projects throughout the years—even
earning several patents along the way—Gillette still hadn't found
his breakthrough invention. Then, at age 40, while working as a
salesman, he was given the advice to invent something disposable.
Gillette was intrigued.

A Cutting-edge Idea
It hit him while shaving one
morning: Why bother to
sharpen a razor if you could
replace it with a disposable
blade? *Voilà!* Gillette put
his nose to the grindstone

and began his quest. In 1903, at age 48, Gillette started selling his perfected disposable razor blades, and Gillette Safety Razor Company was born.

The King's Noble Vision

Over the years, King Gillette's disposable safety blade would become wildly successful. Always the innovator, Gillette started giving his razors away free of charge. This "get them hooked" strategy was ahead of its time and only added to the company's success. By 1999, the renamed "Global Gillette" had mushroomed into a $9.9 billion company. King Camp Gillette's magnum opus had finally been realized.

The safety razor is at least partly responsible for a personal hygiene trend among women. Underarm hair used to be no big deal. But the invention of the safety razor, combined with the acceptance of scantier clothing styles, changed all that. In fact, Gillette produced a razor designed especially for women, called the Milady Décolletée, in 1916.

Let's be grateful King Camp Gillette wasn't around to witness this cutting mistake: The brass at Gillette thought they'd come up with a great idea. For the cost of only one million dollars, they were able to supply Mach3 razors for all welcome bags given out to delegates at the 2004 Democratic National Convention. Unfortunately, security officers worried that the razors presented a threat to attendees and promptly confiscated any that were carried into the convention hall.

Food & Drink
America's Favorite Dessert Comes from Humble Beginnings

❖ ❖ ❖ ❖

*Whether you love it or hate it, there's no denying that
JELL-O is one of the world's best-known product names—
not to mention America's best-selling dessert.*

JELL-O dates back to 1845 when an inventor and philanthropist named Peter Cooper obtained a patent for a flavorless gelatin dessert. Cooper packaged the product in convenient boxes—complete with instructions—but did little to promote it. As a result, most people continued to make gelatin the old-fashioned way, which was very labor-intensive.

In the 1890s, Pearl B. Wait, a carpenter and cough medicine manufacturer from Le Roy, New York, perfected a fruit-flavored version of Cooper's gelatin dessert. Wait's wife, May, called the product JELL-O and offered it in lemon, orange, raspberry, and strawberry flavors. But Wait had little luck selling the stuff. In 1899, Wait sold the business to his neighbor and owner of the Genesee Pure Food Company, Orator Frank Woodward, for $450. At the time, Woodward's company was best known as the manufacturer of a popular coffee substitute called Grain-O.

A savvy promoter, Woodward advertised JELL-O in such magazines as *Ladies' Home Journal,* calling it "America's Most Famous Dessert." Sales soared. In 1904, Woodward introduced the iconic JELL-O Girl, the brand's first trademark. Usually depicted playing with boxes of JELL-O, the character was based on Elizabeth King (the daughter of Franklin King, an artist for Genesee's advertising agency) and was drawn by Rose O'Neill. JELL-O ads featuring Kewpie dolls, another O'Neill creation, debuted in 1908.

Competitors tried valiantly to stop JELL-O's skyrocketing popularity but to no avail. One competing gelatin manufacturer even ridiculed the "sissy-sweet salads" made with JELL-O, apparently unaware that it was JELL-O's reputation as an easy-to-make,

nonthreatening, tasty dessert that made it so popular across ethnic and social lines.

In fact, JELL-O quickly became a must-have on American dinner tables. And since it cost only ten cents a box, it was within everyone's budget. In 1912, a booklet was published featuring JELL-O recipes from six of America's most famous cooks. Later booklets, which numbered in the hundreds, included *Thrifty JELL-O Recipes to Brighten Your Menus; JELL-O, Quick Easy Wonder Dishes;* and the perplexingly titled *What Mrs. Dewey Did with the New Jell-O!* One booklet even included recipes from celebrities such as Ethel Barrymore and opera singer Madame Ernestine Schumann-Heink. JELL-O had become so popular that during the first quarter of the 20th century, samples of the undulating dessert were given to immigrants arriving at Ellis Island as a special "welcome to America."

JELL-O slowly expanded from its original four flavors and is available today in a taste-tempting array that includes apricot, cherry, cranberry, lemon, lime, watermelon, and even margarita, piña colada, and strawberry daiquiri.

Indeed, new and daring flavors have done much to maintain JELL-O's reputation as America's favorite dessert. And its amazing versatility hasn't hurt either. In addition to enjoying JELL-O as a dessert unto itself, fans often jazz it up with mixed fruit, whipped cream, crushed cookies, and other goodies. Some home cooks even make it a dinner side dish by adding a medley of mixed vegetables. (Spring this on your family at your own risk.)

Today, JELL-O is owned by Kraft Foods, which has expanded the JELL-O brand with a huge array of JELL-O pudding products (famously advertised by comedian Bill Cosby) and other items. But it is JELL-O gelatin that remains the company's biggest seller, moving about 300 million boxes a year—a true testament to the world's fascination with desserts that shimmy and shake.

Religion
Christian Science

❖ ❖ ❖ ❖

Mary Baker Eddy believed that she was learning to evoke Christlike healing powers in the modern day, regaining humanity's gift from the divine. Agree or disagree with her, that's original.

Something About Mary

Mary Baker was born into a Congregational (Calvinist) New Hampshire family in 1821. Growing up, she was often ill, which was particularly unfortunate in an era when doctors did as much harm as good. They found little in the way of modern medicine to heal her.

Young Mary had an independent religious streak. She was devoted to Christianity, but she questioned core Calvinist tenets such as original sin and predestination. Even as a little girl she seemed to have a healing gift, though evidently not one that could cure her own chronic illnesses.

Mary's young adulthood brought such pain and calamity we might well be amazed she maintained any enthusiasm for life. Her first husband died in 1844 when she was pregnant with their son. She moved back home to live with her parents, but her mother died five years later. Mary was never in robust health, and at times her chronic illness required her to foster her son with family acquaintances. Her second husband abandoned her in 1866.

Just when it seemed Mary couldn't catch a break, she did.

Healing Powers?

Since doctors had never provided Mary much medical relief, she experimented at developing her own therapies. She tried diets, homeopathy, mentalism, placebo, therapeutic touch, and other nontraditional healing methods. While most of these techniques draw harrumphs from some of today's medical professionals, in Mary's day they had one great advantage over doctors: They rarely did harm.

In 1866, Mary slipped on a patch of ice and injured her back. Bedridden, she asked to be brought her Bible. As she studied pas-

sages about Jesus' healing episodes, she noticed her back pain fading. She considered it a manifest miracle of divine healing—like those the New Testament attributed to Jesus of Nazareth.

Mary was convinced that humanity could rediscover this art. For the next nine years, she researched the art and science of spiritual healing. In 1875, she published her findings in a guide, *Science and Health with Key to the Scriptures.*

Church of Christ, Scientist
She hoped, perhaps a bit naively, that Christian churches would welcome her healing methods. It wasn't happening, so in 1879 she started the Church of Christ, Scientist (CS). Its mission: "reinstate primitive Christianity and its lost element of healing." (The Church still bases its procedures upon Mary's manual.)

Like most new Christian sects, CS sought to rediscover the Christian knowledge from which modern churches had wandered. While tens of thousands of people were drawn to her message, many others opposed it—some quite vociferously—on moral, ethical, or spiritual grounds.

Nonetheless, the message spread, and more and more Christians were attracted to it. Church of Christ, Scientist, got its first actual church building in Boston in 1894. Today, about 2,000 churches exist worldwide.

Spreading the Word
Since Mary was doing a lot of writing, it made sense for CS to start a publishing house. The Christian Science Publishing Society is still around. You're probably familiar with one of its publications: *The Christian Science Monitor,* an internationally respected (and mostly secular) newspaper founded in 1908. This too was Mary's idea. The 20th century opened in an atmosphere of "yellow journalism." Sensationalized stories were used by newspaper bigwigs to manipulate the opinions of their readers. Yellow journalism disgusted Mary, especially when it took swipes at CS. The *Monitor's* goal was, and is, "to injure no man, but to bless all mankind" (in short, to present news as news, free of bias and sensationalism).

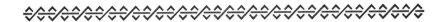

Household Items

The Fountain Pen: Mightier than, at Least, the Quill

❖ ❖ ❖ ❖

*The story of how an inconvenient mess ended
up making a mark on history.*

Rumors of a writing instrument that had a reservoir for ink go all the way back to the tenth century, but we'll stick to the more recent past. The first truly operable fountain pen, which had a leak-proof reservoir, a steady writing nib, and a reliable ink flow, didn't come about until 1884, well after the invention of two critical components: hard rubber and iridium.

From Ink Stain to Invention

As the story goes, New Yorker Lewis Waterman, an insurance broker, had been using pens of a lesser quality for years when he lost an enormous contract to a competing broker, all because of a massive blot from his writing instrument. In a gesture that might have been accompanied by outraged screaming, he vowed to create his own pen—one that wouldn't leak. In 1884, after years of experimentation, he patented a pen that held ink in a reservoir, allowing it to flow at a conservative rate through a gold-and-iridium nib. Waterman's pen was far less complicated than earlier pens had been, consisting of only four parts made entirely of hard rubber.

The "Write" Stuff

Four short years later, another American, George Parker, a professor of telegraphy in Janesville, Wisconsin, encouraged all of his students to buy fountain pens, but he found himself consistently having to improve or repair these writing implements. Parker decided to invent and sell his own line of pens, which rapidly began to outsell those offered by Waterman's New York company.

By the early 1900s, many improvements were on the horizon: W. A. Scheaffer, a jeweler, created a pen that could be filled by raising and lowering a lever on the shaft of the pen, eliminating any need to dirty one's fingers. Meanwhile, the German ink company Pelikan introduced the piston feed, which allowed users to rotate a cap at the end of the shaft and fill the pen that way.

Waterman did not keep up with the times and fell rapidly behind in sales, but in a twist of history, Sanford, a Midwestern company that started out in the ink and glue business, now distributes both Parker and Waterman writing instruments.

Ink has been around almost 6,000 years. Ballpoint pens were invented less than 150 years ago.

John J. Loud patented the ballpoint pen in 1888, but since he used it only to mark leather, he neglected to consider its wider commercial possibilities. In later legal skirmishes over the right to claim the invention, his limited patent was ignored. And you think you have tough luck.

"The very ink with which history is written is merely fluid prejudice."

—MARK TWAIN

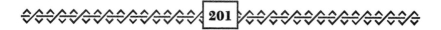

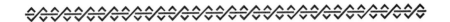

Places & Landmarks
The Long, Slow Struggle to Borrow a Book

❖ ❖ ❖ ❖

While libraries have been around almost as long as civilization,
they've only recently become a public enterprise.

Most of us take the library for granted. We rely on the fact that we can stroll into a building conveniently located in our neighborhood; browse thousands of books, movies, or audio recordings; and borrow the selection of our choice for a few weeks. But this wasn't always the case. Although libraries in one form or another have existed for thousands of years, public lending libraries are a relatively recent invention.

The Early Days
The earliest known library was actually more of an archive for government and public records. Housed in a temple in the Babylonian city of Nippur some 5,000 years ago, the collection included thousands of clay tablets stored in several rooms. The ancient Greeks took a long stride toward our modern notion of a library by creating collections of writings on literature, philosophy, history, and mathematics that were kept in the famous schools established by great thinkers such as Plato and Aristotle. Libraries also flourished during this same period in China, particularly around 206 B.C. under the Han Dynasty, which charged its extensive civil service system with collecting, storing, and categorizing their collections.

Of course, these early libraries were not open to just anyone, and the notion of lending out scrolls and tablets would have been preposterous. With everything written meticulously by hand, items were simply too precious to ever consider letting them leave the building.

The ancient world's crowning achievement in book collecting was undoubtedly the great library at Alexandria in Egypt. Established by the Ptolemy Dynasty, the collection included several hundred thousand scrolls. This library was known to lend out part of its collection

to other respectable institutions—but only if substantial security deposits were given to offset the possible loss of the works.

The Roman Empire also had its share of libraries—though many of their works were actually pilfered from Alexandria when Julius Caesar conquered Egypt—that served scholars and scientists. Roman baths also often contained library rooms with small collections that were available for patron use on-site.

During the Middle Ages in Europe, various monastic orders, particularly the Benedictines, kept extensive libraries that focused on spiritual works. They commonly lent works to one another, initiating what was probably the first formal interlibrary loan system. The Middle East saw significant growth in libraries between 700–1000 B.C., and many classical works of Greece and Rome survived only in these Islamic collections. With the coming of the Renaissance and its emphasis on learning and literacy, public and private libraries flourished beginning in the 1600s, particularly in the many new universities established in Europe.

The Newest Thing

The 1700s saw the rise of two new trends—circulating libraries, which were profit-seeking ventures run by printers and book merchants who essentially rented books to customers, and social libraries, which were private clubs whose paid members shared books among themselves. The first social library in America was said to have been founded by Benjamin Franklin in 1731.

It wasn't until 1833, when the New Hampshire legislature agreed to support a library in the town of Peterborough, that the first publicly funded, open-access library appeared in the United States. Boston opened the first of the massive city libraries in 1854, and other local governments followed suit over the next several decades, though they often faced opposition. Many felt it was a waste of taxpayer dollars to make books available to the uneducated masses. Thankfully, industrialist Andrew Carnegie had a different view. The father of the American public library system, Carnegie was a self-made millionaire who believed that education and hard work gave anyone a shot at the American Dream. He began bankrolling public libraries in 1886 and eventually donated more than $40 million to build libraries around the country.

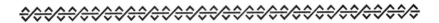

Fads & Fashion
Hot Pants

❖ ❖ ❖ ❖

*The 1970s saw more than its share of bad fashion
trends, but few did more to set back the burgeoning
women's liberation movement than hot pants.*

Basically just really short shorts, hot pants were typically made of
satin or some other clingy fabric. It took a certain physical build
to look good in hot pants, but they were amazingly popular nonetheless.

Hot pants were introduced in Paris and London in the late 1960s
and early 1970s in response to the midi skirt, a calf-length dress
that fashion designers were promoting as a more mature answer to
the miniskirt. But young women didn't want to show less leg—they
wanted to show more. Hot pants allowed them to do just that.

It took a while for hot pants to go mainstream. Fashion magazines were reluctant to promote them, so at first hot pants were
worn primarily by women who felt empowered by the clothing's out-
rageous sensibility. Only later did European magazines finally admit
to their popularity.

The story was completely different in the United States, where
the skimpy shorts were an immediate hit. In fact, Bloomingdale's
was literally mobbed when the store first started selling them in
January 1971.

It was *Women's Wear Daily* that first coined the term "hot pants,"
and it didn't take long for the short shorts to become high fashion.
Celebrities such as Marlo Thomas and former First Lady Jackie
Onassis were photographed wearing the daring duds, and designers
were soon producing them in every style, from mink to sequins.

But like most fashion fads, hot pants quickly lost their appeal
and—as with the leisure suit—were banished to the back of the
closet. Today, the only place you're likely to see hot pants is on NFL
cheerleaders.

Inventions
All That and a Corkscrew, Too?

❖ ❖ ❖ ❖

A nation known for its neutrality comes up with the most versatile piece of military technology ever known.

Switzerland is certainly no military powerhouse. In fact, when it comes to international disputes, this European country is best known for not getting involved. It's hard to imagine how its army would become associated with what may be the best known, most beloved, and most commonly used piece of military hardware in the world—the Swiss Army Knife.

The distinctive multitool pocketknife was the brainchild of Swiss cutlery manufacturer Karl Elsener. A true patriot, Elsener bristled at the fact that Swiss soldiers got their standard-issue knives from a German manufacturer, and he set out to win the contract from his government. In the 1890s, he designed a unique spring mechanism for pocketknives that allowed the handle to hold several blades. That was clever enough in and of itself, but Elsener's true moment of genius came when he decided that rather than adding extra blades, he would include several basic tools in his knife—a can opener, a hole punch, and a screwdriver. According to some sources, it was the screwdriver that won over the Swiss military brass; the nation's infantry had just begun using a new type of rifle, and soldiers needed screwdrivers to perform basic maintenance on the weapon.

Elsener dubbed his creation the "Soldier's Knife" and followed it up with a lightweight version with a few more tools called the "Officer's and Sports Knife." Before long, handymen around the world were carrying them in their pockets, but it wasn't until World War II—when American GIs dubbed it the Swiss Army Knife—that the tool got the name we use today.

Elsener's company, Victorinox, is still in business, producing 34,000 knives a day in some 300 configurations. Almost any tool you can imagine can be found on one model or another: corkscrew, wire strippers, toothpick, fish scaler, ruler, nail file, saw, chisel, magnifying glass, flashlight—even a ballpoint pen or a tracheotomy knife!

SPORTS

Defining Moments in Sports Terminology, Part Two

Fore: This term is likely borrowed from the military. When artillery shells were fired from cannons situated behind friendly troops, a warning cry of "beware before" was often used to warn the soldiers. The term was shortened to *fore* and used to warn link-side duffers that wayward golf balls were headed their way.

Slam Dunk, Air Ball, Charity Stripe, Finger Roll: Although the term *dunk* was commonly used to describe the action of propelling a basketball through the hoop from above the rim, the phrase *slam dunk* was coined by the late Los Angeles Lakers announcer Francis "Chick" Hearn. The colorful commentator also originated the terms *air ball* (ball that misses the entire backboard), *charity stripe* (foul line), and *finger roll* (rolling the ball off the fingertips).

Gridiron: The playing field for football is marked with a series of parallel lines that form a grid. In the early years of the game, an astute—and presumably sober—football fan noticed that the pattern of lines resembled a gridiron, a grate used to grill or broil foods. The name stuck.

Baltimore Chop: When he was playing for the Baltimore Orioles in the 1890s, baseball pioneer John McGraw would often slap or chop down on the ball, causing the stitched orb to bounce high in the air off the hardened area of dirt around home plate. The technique often allowed the speedy tactician to reach first base safely and became a useful offensive strategy.

Can of Corn: The phrase, which describes a pop fly that is easy to catch, comes from the era of the old-time grocery store. To reach an

object on a high shelf, the grocer would use a pole or a stick to knock the item—such as a can of corn—off its perch and catch it in the fold of his apron, which he fanned out like a net firefighters might use.

Birdie, Eagle, Albatross: The terms *birdie* and *eagle* originated in the United States in 1899. When a duffer struck the dimpled orb particularly well or knocked the pill close to the pin, he was said to have hit "a bird of a shot." Soon, making a score under par on a hole was dubbed a *birdie*. In keeping with the feathery phonetics, a score two shots better than par was called an *eagle*. A double eagle, a hole played three strokes under par, is also known as an *albatross*, the rarest of birds.

Sudden Death: The origin of the term in sports comes from the wild, wild West but not from the gunslingers of the era. Gamblers used the phrase *sudden death* to describe any outcome that was decided by a single or final toss of the dice or flip of a coin. Mark Twain is often credited with originating the expression when he used it in an article he wrote describing "rot gut whiskey."

Underdog: The origin of the term is debatable but its meaning is clear. The favorite to win—be it best in show or first in the race—is the top dog. All others are bottom—or under—dogs. The first known use of the phrase comes from a poem printed in various American newspapers in 1859 called "The Under Dog of the Fight." The key passage reads: "I shall always go for the weaker dog,/For the under dog in the fight."

Red Sox Nation: The blame for the name "Red Sox Nation" can be laid on the desk of *Boston Globe* feature writer Nathan Cobb. The fanatical fraternity was first mentioned on October 20, 1986, in an article Cobb wrote about how baseball fans in Connecticut were divided in their devotion to the Boston Red Sox and New York Mets during the 1986 World Series.

Places & Landmarks
The Old-school JELL-O Belt: The State of Deseret

❖ ❖ ❖ ❖

The "JELL-O Belt" (yes, so-called due to the abundance of JELL-O found at today's Latter-day Saints church functions) runs through the U.S. Mountain West. But founder Brigham Young's ideas ran a bit bigger than JELL-O salad.

Pioneers

In 1846, Brigham Young led a large group of Mormons (almost all of them, in fact) west across America to what is now Utah, with the hope of being left alone to build their own society. (You may recall another American group that description once fit: the Pilgrims.) The Latter-day Saints (LDS), as they called themselves, had grown sick of persecution. They also expected a cataclysmic wipeout of the wicked, sinful world, and they didn't care to be in the path of the spiritual cyclone.

Modern Utahans call these early settlers the Pioneers, and they're a key part of LDS cultural lore. But, cataclysm or no, in 1848, the treaty that ended the Mexican War ceded the Pioneers' turf (along with most of the modern Southwest) to the United States. Young's Pioneers had gotten busy setting up a functional government, but now they would have to come to terms with Washington.

Politics

In 1849, Young proposed that the U.S. Congress admit to the Union the State of Deseret. The name came from a term in the Book of Mormon meaning *honeybee,* which symbolized hard work. The name fit well because the Pioneers had been working very hard to gain ground against unfamiliar and frustrating conditions: icy winters, frosty springs, foreign soil, hungry crickets, and other headaches.

Young's suggested state would have included nearly all of modern Nevada and Utah; small parts of southern Oregon and southern Idaho; big pieces of western Wyoming, Colorado, and New Mexico;

most of Arizona; and much of southern California—a total area significantly larger than modern France.

But the Mormons had underestimated national anti-LDS prejudice, especially against the practice of polygamy. In hindsight, it's rather astonishing that they thought they'd get their way, especially after being persecuted and even assaulted all across the Ohio Valley until a lynch mob murdered their founder, Joseph Smith, in 1844. By 1849, American opinion firmly opposed the notion of a state run by the LDS Church. In 1850, California gained statehood, and a far smaller portion of proposed Deseret became the Utah Territory. The name was something of an in-your-face by the U.S. government, given the conflicts the Pioneers had experienced with Ute Indians.

This Isn't Over

Young's Pioneers weren't going to give up on Deseret so easily. They maintained an active Deseret Legislature and a sort of shadow government, mainly run by the same people governing the Territory. Mormon leaders bucked U.S. sovereignty. An armed Mormon militia wasn't always kind to non-LDS people passing through, as evidenced by some violent incidents and the very ugly 1857 Mountain Meadows massacre.

In 1857, President Buchanan sent the U.S. Army to apply some pressure to the Mormons of Deseret. The Pioneers' militia readied for action, and Young swore to burn the Temple in Salt Lake City rather than see it occupied by the heathens. But in the end, the "Utah War" saw very little armed conflict. It also put the kibosh on the State of Deseret idea, though the shadow government remained until well after the Civil War.

Legacy

It took 46 years for Utah to go from territory to state (1896). Neighboring Nevada had been admitted in 1864, Colorado in 1876. If you suspect that this long delay had much to do with the LDS practice of plural marriage, you paid attention. The practice was discontinued in 1890, and the modern LDS Church utterly disavows it.

Even today, however, Utah is known as the Beehive State, and its state highway signs and highway patrol cars depict a beehive. Its second-largest daily newspaper goes by the name of *Deseret News*.

ADVERTISING

A True Ad Pitch(er)

❖ ❖ ❖ ❖

Could a pitcher with a face on it become an
advertising icon for the ages? Oh yeah.

Big corporations will use anything to sell product: Recall Mrs.
Butterworth, the grandma of pancake syrup. Or Snap, Crackle, and
Pop, the elves that live in your breakfast cereal.

Every once in a while, though, they get it right. In 1953, food
giant General Foods bought Kool-Aid from inventor Edwin Perkins. Perkins's creation started out as a bottled liquid named Fruit-
Smack, but the cost of bottle breakage and shipping forced Perkins
to come up with a way to remove the liquid from his formula,
resulting in a powdered concentrate that Perkins called "Kool-Ade"
and later renamed Kool-Aid.

Legend has it that Marvin Potts, art director for General Food's
advertising agency, was charged with coming up with a smart way
to sell the powder. He had his best idea while watching his son
draw smiley faces on a frosty window. It occurred to him that a
friendly, frosty pitcher might be the perfect emblem for the drink.
The smiley face is perhaps indicative of Perkins's good nature;
during the Great Depression, he cut the cost of Kool-Aid in half
so that everyone would be able to afford a tall glass of refreshment
despite the dire economic circumstances.

The higher-ups at General Foods loved Potts's idea, and ads with
a smiling pitcher started to hit the general public. It wasn't until 1975,
though, when Kraft acquired General Foods, that the pitcher spouted
arms and legs and donned some youthful blue jeans and sneakers.

The Kool-Aid Man has inspired so much loyalty that the town of
Hastings, Nebraska, where Perkins launched his invention, hosts an
annual Kool-Aid Days celebration. It is, after all, the official drink
of Nebraska.

Fads & Fashion
The "Fasten"-ating History of Suspenders

❖ ❖ ❖ ❖

As the saying goes, "You don't want to be caught with your pants down!" It's a sentiment with which Albert Thurston clearly agreed.

Belts are fine and dandy, and they were all a man needed until the early to mid-19th century. Around that time, men's pants started to feature high waistlines. In one of the few historical instances where men bent to style conventions, British designer Albert Thurston, who was also a purveyor of luxury, custom-made items for men, stepped in.

His invention, unveiled in 1822, involved two straps that buttoned onto trousers to keep them from falling down. The rest of the world quickly caught on, and suspenders made of everything from velvet to rubber became de rigueur, even as fashion moved on and men's waistlines lowered again.

Nearly half a century later, one of America's most celebrated authors got into the game by creating a new way to adjust and fasten the suspenders using buttons and buckles and straps made of elastic. Yes, yes, Mark Twain could write. But did you know that he was also an inventor?

Still later, American firefighter George C. Hale created a set of suspenders that had a fire-retardant cord sewn loosely into the straps. When pulled, the cord would come loose, thereby allowing the wearer to lower his suspenders down from the flaming building in which he was trapped. The firefighters below could then attach a rescue rope to the suspenders. The lucky owner of the suspenders would retrieve the rescue rope, tie it to some nonflaming part of the building, and climb down to safety. Incidentally, Hale is the inventor of several other very successful fire-escaping and firefighting devices, including the water tower.

Toys & Games
Days Gone By: Pinball

❖ ❖ ❖ ❖

*Once considered an untoward distraction, pinball survived
early disapproval and even banishment to become the
popular predecessor to today's video games.*

Prohibition

Pinball was invented in the 1930s, inspired by the 19th-century
game *bagatelle,* which involved a billiards cue and a playing field
full of holes. Some early pinball arcades "rewarded" players for
high scores, and in the mid-1930s, machines were introduced
that provided direct monetary payouts. These games quickly
earned pinball a reputation as a fun diversion—and as a gambling
device. Thus, starting in the 1940s, New York City Mayor Fiorello
LaGuardia declared pinball parlors akin to casinos ("magnets for
the wrong element"), ushering in an era of pinball prohibition.
Chicago, Los Angeles, and other major American cities followed
suit with their own pinball bans. New York's pinball embargo lasted
until 1976, and city officials destroyed 11,000 machines before the
prohibition was lifted. The turning point: Writer and pinball wizard
Roger Sharpe called his shots during a demonstration in front of the
New York City Council, proving that pinball was indeed a game of
skill. The council members voted 6–0 to legalize pinball in the Big
Apple.

Rise and Fall

Despite the fact that pinball was banned in the United States'
three largest cities, it became a favorite pastime among adolescents
and teens in the 1950s. This changed in 1973 with the advent of
the video game, but pinball enjoyed the first of several revivals
later in the 1970s, thanks to its association with such rock-and-
roll luminaries as The Who, Elton John, and KISS. The last
pinball renaissance peaked with Bally's *The Addams Family* game,
introduced in 1991 to tie in with the release of the movie. *The
Addams Family* became the best-selling pinball game of all time,

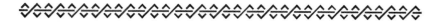

with 22,000 machines sold. In the 1990s, the bottom dropped out of the pinball market, and as of 2007, Stern Pinball was the only American manufacturer.

Origin of the Flippers

Gottlieb's *Humpty Dumpty,* designed by Harry Mabs in 1947, was the first pinball game to feature flippers (three on each side) that allowed the player to use hand-eye coordination to influence gravity and chance. Many pre-flipper games were essentially dressed-up gambling contraptions, and players could just tilt the machines to rack up points. *Humpty Dumpty* and the thousands of flipper games that followed were true contests of skill. In 1948, pinball designer Steven Kordek repositioned the flippers (just two) at the bottom of the playfield, and the adjustment became the industry standard.

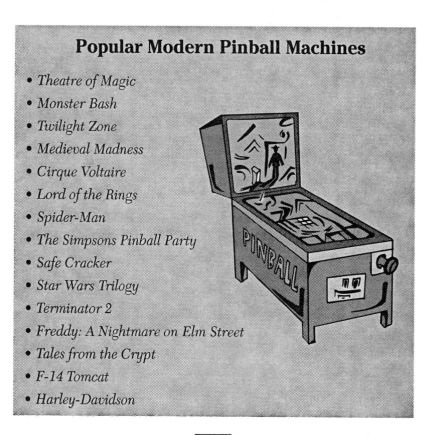

Popular Modern Pinball Machines

- *Theatre of Magic*
- *Monster Bash*
- *Twilight Zone*
- *Medieval Madness*
- *Cirque Voltaire*
- *Lord of the Rings*
- *Spider-Man*
- *The Simpsons Pinball Party*
- *Safe Cracker*
- *Star Wars Trilogy*
- *Terminator 2*
- *Freddy: A Nightmare on Elm Street*
- *Tales from the Crypt*
- *F-14 Tomcat*
- *Harley-Davidson*

REAL NAMES OF THE RICH AND FAMOUS

Entertainers, actors, musicians, and other celebrities change their names for many reasons. Some prefer to use nicknames; some have unusual names that are not glamorous or sophisticated; others allowed managers, studio executives, or agents to change their names. Entertainers from previous generations "Americanized" ethnic-sounding names to appeal to a wide audience. Uncovering a celebrity's real name often provides insight into his or her career and background.

Basketball legend Kareem Abdul-Jabbar was born Ferdinand Lewis Alcindor Jr.

Actor Alan Alda's real name is Alphonso Joseph D'Abruzzo.

Woody Allen began life as Allen Stewart Konigsberg.

Beautiful Ann-Margret was born Ann-Margret Olsson.

Lighter-than-air dancer Fred Astaire's real name was Frederic Austerlitz Jr.—nothing light about that last name!

Velvet-throated Tony Bennett is really Anthony Dominick Benedetto.

Rocker David Bowie was christened David Robert Jones.

Funnyman Mel Brooks was originally Melvin Kaminsky.

Nicolas Cage changed his name from Nicholas Coppola so that he could get acting jobs without taking advantage of the family name.

Kate Capshaw, actress and real-life wife to Steven Spielberg, was born Kathleen Sue Nail.

Writer Truman Capote, subject of two Hollywood films, began life as Truman Streckfus Persons.

Glamorous dancer Cyd Charisse of the Golden Age of Hollywood was born Tula Ellice Finklea.

Comic actor Chevy Chase is really Cornelius Crane Chase.

Computers & Cyberspace
Making Book on the Internet

❖ ❖ ❖ ❖

*A good idea and a better name resulted in one
of the Web's biggest success stories.*

Jeff Bezos was never a slouch. Class president and valedictorian of
his high school, he graduated from Princeton University summa
cum laude in 1986. After graduation, Bezos distinguished himself,
first at a high-tech firm, then with financial services companies.
But it wasn't until Bezos applied his unique combination of skills—
computer nerd and financial whiz—that he really found his niche.
He decided that e-commerce would be the next big thing.

But what to sell? Starting with a list of 20 possible products,
Bezos eventually settled on books, a market that no single company
dominated and one that comprised more than one million products.

In 1994, Bezos launched what would eventually become the
world's largest online store, Cadabra.com, which was supposed
to sound like "abracadabra." Unfortunately, it also sounded like
"cadaver"—not a great association for a new startup.

Bezos decided he needed a new name, and he wanted one that
would come up first in an alphabetical search. In 1995, he changed
his site to Amazon.com, naming it after the largest river in the
world—a more fitting namesake for what he hoped would become
the largest channel of books on the Internet.

The very first book sold by Amazon.com was *Fluid Concepts
and Creative Analogies: Computer Models of the Fundamental
Mechanisms of Thought,* which probably isn't going to be made into
a movie any time soon. Nevertheless, during its first month of business, Amazon.com filled orders in all 50 states and 45 countries from
the garage of Bezos's Seattle home.

Amazon.com soon became one of the most-visited sites on the
Web, though the company didn't actually make a profit until the end
of 2003—Bezos was too busy plowing money back into the company
and buying new businesses. Today, the site sells everything from
lawn mowers to watches.

Health & Medicine
The Evolution of the Cesarean Section

❖ ❖ ❖ ❖

Today the cesarean section is considered a fairly routine surgery.
But there was a time when it was a tragic procedure of last resort.

What's in a Name?

The history of the cesarean section is shrouded in mystery. Legend has it that Julius Caesar was born by cesarean section in an era when the procedure was only done as a last-ditch effort to save the infant if its mother was dead or dying. However, historians debate whether Caesar was born via cesarean. There are references to his mother, Aurelia, being alive during his life, which would probably have been impossible had she undergone a cesarean. The procedure's name might alternatively derive from a Roman law called "Lex Caesarea," which dictated that if a woman in labor was dead or dying, the baby must be saved so the population of the state would grow as much as possible.

A Look Back

The cesarean's history is difficult to trace because two lives are at stake during the procedure, so the exact circumstances were either intentionally kept hush-hush or were mixed up with religious birthing and funereal ceremonies. In ancient times, cesareans were usually postmortem procedures: Deceased babies were removed from deceased mothers so that both could have a proper funeral. It was probably pretty rare for an emergency cesarean operation to be done on a dying woman during labor, since few would want to be responsible for determining when and if the mother's chance of survival was hopeless.

References to cesarean sections can be found in ancient pictures and texts the world over. There is some evidence that the surgery was performed on living women; scattered accounts indicate that some women may even have survived the procedure. Cesareans have also been reported in hunter-gatherer and tribal cultures. In fact,

one Western report dated to 1879 describes a Ugandan tribal healer who used banana wine to sanitize his hands and the woman's abdomen as well as to intoxicate the woman before practicing a strategy to massage the uterus and make it contract. The woman survived, and the Western observer concluded the procedure was old and well established.

The cesarean's Western rise to popularity began with the Renaissance, when precise anatomical studies improved all surgeries. It was the development of anesthesia in the 19th century that made the cesarean possible as a procedure intended to preserve the mother's life during a difficult labor: If the mother was not conscious during the procedure, the risk of her dying of shock was removed. Additionally, the development of antiseptics lowered the risk of infection. The cesarean slowly began to replace a tragic procedure called a *craniotomy*. During long and painful childbirths—or in cases when it was clear that the infant had died in the womb—the baby had to be removed without killing the mother. A blunt object would be inserted through the woman's vagina in an effort to crush the baby's skull. The infant was then removed, piecemeal. This was a dangerous procedure that the woman often did not survive.

At Last, Success

Although the cesarean ultimately replaced the craniotomy, maternal mortality remained high. A groundbreaking change came with the realization that the uterine suture—stitching up the uterus—which had once been considered dangerous, was actually the key to a successful cesarean. This, combined with other advances, made the cesarean a feasible option during problematic labor. In fact, the cesarean has become so common that women sometimes elect a cesarean over a vaginal birth, even if there is no difficulty with their labor. This modern practice has led to a peculiar problem: Assuming there is no medical reason for the cesarean, it is safer for a woman to stick with a vaginal birth. The cesarean has thus completed its amazing transformation from an almost impossible option to one that, if anything, is used too frequently.

Food & Drink
SPAM: Revolution in a Can

❖ ❖ ❖ ❖

The story of how a "miracle meat" swept the nation—and the world.

It has been an American dinnertime staple, a wartime savior, and the subject of a catchy *Monty Python* ditty. Since its introduction in 1937, SPAM has revolutionized global gastronomy and become a cultural icon both praised and derided. But how did this unlikely combination of ground pork shoulder, ground ham, and various spices come to be?

The story of SPAM dates to 1926, when the Geo. A. Hormel & Co. came out with the nation's first canned ham. Eleven years later, the company unveiled something even more revolutionary: a canned meat product that didn't require refrigeration. Developed by Jay C. Hormel, the son of the company's founder, it was marketed under the name "Hormel Spiced Ham" to overwhelming public apathy.

Indeed, to say that Hormel Spiced Ham didn't exactly set the canned meat market on fire would be an understatement. Adding to the problem was the fact that many other canned meat lunch products were being produced by competitors, which cut sharply into Hormel's market share. In an effort to generate greater public interest in its product, Hormel offered a $100 prize for a catchier name. The contest winner suggested SPAM, which may have been a shortened form of "shoulder of pork and ham." Of course, over the years, people have had fun with the name, suggesting it stands for "Something Posing as Meat" or "Spare Parts Animal Meat."

Hormel reintroduced its canned luncheon meat and its new name in mid-1937 with a national advertising blitz that touted SPAM as appropriate for any meal, including breakfast. In 1940, Hormel started advertising SPAM with what some experts consider the first singing commercial. The lyrics were simplicity itself: "SPAM, SPAM, SPAM, SPAM/Hormel's new miracle meat in a can!/Tastes fine, saves time/If you want something grand/Ask for SPAM!"

In a brilliant move, Hormel also became a major sponsor of an extraordinarily popular radio show starring George Burns and Gracie

Allen. Ad spots during the radio program introduced the public to "SPAMMY the Pig" in 1940. Almost immediately, Americans took to SPAM as if it were manna from heaven, and sales skyrocketed.

SPAM Goes to War

SPAM was especially popular during World War II, both at home and on the front lines. It wasn't subject to wartime rationing like beef, so it became a dinner staple in many American households. The military liked SPAM because it required no refrigeration. SPAM fed many an Allied soldier throughout the war and was even credited by Soviet Premier Nikita Khrushchev with helping save the starving Soviet army.

Here to Stay?

Decades later, SPAM still sells well and has achieved a certain cultural panache. And while Americans consume their share of the spiced canned meat, SPAM has developed an even more passionate following in South Korea, where it is sold in gift packs and used as an ingredient in a variety of traditional Korean dishes.

In recent years, of course, *spam* has also become a universal word for unsolicited e-mail. Understandably, this negative connotation does not sit well with Hormel Foods, which has gone to court to keep companies that deal in the prevention of unwanted e-mail from using its trademark. "It's really important that SPAM doesn't get confused with anything else," Vice President Julie Craven told ABC News. "I think any time [the name is] used inappropriately, it is under assault."

But that's not to suggest that Hormel Foods doesn't have a sense of humor when it comes to SPAM. The company has expressed appreciation for a popular Monty Python sketch that extols the product at length and is even a sponsor of the musical *Monty Python's SPAMALOT,* a stage play based on the movie *Monty Python and the Holy Grail,* which itself includes a SPAM reference.

Such allusions only go to prove SPAM's long and far-reaching cultural influence—a heady accomplishment for a product originally developed as a quick and easy meal for harried housewives.

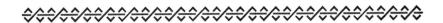

Music
The Little Disc that Could

❖ ❖ ❖ ❖

Digital downloads may have hurt the traditional record store, but the CD remains the world's most popular medium for audio recordings. Not only that, but the technology also changed the way digital data is stored.

Compact discs first hit the market in 1982. After little more than a decade, the format dominated the market, quickly replacing the vinyl records that had been the mainstay for decades. Although music purists and audiophiles maintain that vinyl has a richer or "warmer" sound, the compact disc has superior advantages—notably that repeated playback causes virtually no wear to the surface of the disc; the recordings sound the same after 10 plays or 10,000 plays.

The compact disc was invented by James T. Russell in the late 1960s. Russell patented the technology in 1970.

The first player, Sony's CDP-101, was released in Japan in October 1982 and arrived in the United States the following spring. The compact disc quickly became a breakthrough format for popular music. The 1985 album *Brothers in Arms* by Dire Straits was the first compact disc to sell one million copies.

The CD ultimately lent itself to more than just music. The same digitally encoded data that made music storage possible also worked as a storage device for computers. In 1990, the CD-ROM (read-only memory) and recordable CDs (for music and data) were introduced. And while the MP3 may slowly be stealing the spotlight from the music CD, the discs will live on through volume, if nothing else; to date, more than 200 billion discs have been sold worldwide.

❖❖❖❖❖❖

"I've got hundreds of ideas stacked up—many of them worth more than the compact disc. But I haven't been able to work on them."
—JAMES T. RUSSELL

War & Military
The U.S. Attack on Pearl Harbor

❖ ❖ ❖ ❖

In an improbable twist of fate, a U.S. rear admiral's
attack plan is used against America.

On December 7, 1941, the Japanese bombed Pearl Harbor. This
tragedy prompted President Franklin Delano Roosevelt's "infamy"
speech, which credited "naval and air forces of the Empire of
Japan" with the surprise attack that ultimately launched the United
States into World War II. However, as is often the case with pivotal
moments in history, there's more to the story.

On February 7, 1932—nearly a full decade before the attack—
U.S. Navy Rear Admiral Harry Yarnell sought to prove his theory
that aircraft carriers, not battleships, should operate as the principal
arm of a well-prepared navy. With a fleet comprised of two carriers
and more than 150 warplanes, Yarnell positioned an armada 60 miles
northeast of Oahu and commenced war game exercises. The end
result would prove eye-opening, to say the least.

"Attacking" Pearl Harbor before dawn on a Sunday morning,
Yarnell's surprise assault hypothetically knocked stationary U.S.
aircraft completely out of commission and sunk or damaged a multi-
tude of warships. The exercise was so effective that a reporter from
The New York Times observed that Yarnell's planes "made the attack
unopposed by the defense, which was caught virtually napping."
After the exercise, pro-carrier admirals argued that Yarnell's victory
prompted a reassessment of naval tactics, but a majority of battleship
admirals voted the notion down. And with that, the stage was set for
future tragedy.

Japanese observers who had witnessed the American exercise
forwarded a comprehensive report to Tokyo. By 1936, the revealing
data found its way into a report entitled "Study of Strategy and Tactics in Operations Against the United States." It concluded: "In case
the enemy's main fleet is berthed at Pearl Harbor, the idea should be
to open hostilities by surprise attack from the air." Five years later—
on a date that will live in infamy—the Japanese did just that.

Media & Communication
Frequency Modulation (FM Radio)

❖ ❖ ❖ ❖

A fearless innovator's marvelous invention is tarnished by betrayal.

Fame and riches are supposed to go to those visionaries that build the better mousetraps. But with the invention of frequency modulation (FM radio), things didn't quite work out that way. Edwin H. Armstrong (1890–1954) invented a new transmission medium that left the former giant, amplitude modulation (AM radio), quivering in its wake. For most people, such a lofty achievement would bring a degree of satisfaction—not to mention a stack of cash. For Armstrong, it would bring mostly heartache.

Before this underappreciated genius found his way to FM, he made other worthy contributions. Two of Armstrong's inventions, the regenerative circuit of 1912 and the superheterodyne circuit of 1917, would set the broadcasting world on its ear. When combined, they would produce an affordable tube radio that would become an American staple. Armstrong was on his way.

Soon afterward, the inventor turned his attentions to the removal of radio static, an inherent problem in the AM circuit. After witnessing a demonstration of Armstrong's superheterodyne receiver, David Sarnoff, the head of the Radio Corporation of America (RCA) and founder of the National Broadcasting Company (NBC), challenged the inventor to develop "a little black box" that would remove the static. Armstrong spent the late 1920s through the early 1930s tackling the problem. Sarnoff backed the genius by allowing him use of a laboratory at the top of the Empire State Building. This was no small offering—in the broadcasting game, height equals might, and none came taller than this 1,250-foot giant, which has since been named one of the seven wonders of the modern world.

In 1933, Armstrong made a bold announcement. He had cracked the noise problem using frequency modulation. With a wider frequency response than AM and an absence of background noise, the new technology represented a revolutionary step in broadcasting.

Armstrong's upgraded system had the ability to relay programming from city to city by direct off-air pickup by 1936. Without knowing it, the inventor had effectively boxed himself in. NBC, and by extension Sarnoff, was the dominant force in conventional radio during this time. With America mired in an economic depression, NBC wasn't interested in tooling up for a new system. Even worse for Armstrong, television loomed on the horizon, and NBC was pouring most of its resources into the new technology. Instead of receiving the recognition and financial rewards that he so rightly deserved, Armstrong was fired unceremoniously by his "friend" Sarnoff. It seemed like the end of the line—but Armstrong's battle was only just beginning.

In 1937, a determined Armstrong erected a 400-foot tower and transmitter in Alpine, New Jersey. Here, he would go about the business of perfecting his inventions. Unfortunately, without Sarnoff's backing, his operation found itself severely underfunded. To make matters infinitely worse, Armstrong became embroiled in a patent battle with RCA, which was claiming the invention of FM radio. The broadcasting giant would ultimately win the patent fight and shut Armstrong down. The ruling was so lopsided that it robbed Armstrong of his ability to claim royalties on FM radios sold in the United States. It would be hard to find a deal rawer than this.

To fully appreciate Armstrong's contribution, compare AM and FM radio stations: The difference in transmitted sound will be pronounced, with FM sounding wonderfully alive and AM noticeably flat in comparison. Even "dead air" sounds better on FM because the band lacks the dreaded static that plagues the AM medium. Without a doubt, FM technology is a tremendous breakthrough. But it came at a terrible cost. On January 31, 1954, Armstrong— distraught over his lack of recognition and dwindling finances—flung himself from the 13th-floor window of his New York City apartment.

"The world, I think, will wait a long time for Nikola Tesla's equal in achievement and imagination."

— EDWIN H. ARMSTRONG

Language
Misfire Caught Fire—as a Metaphor

❖ ❖ ❖ ❖

*The expression "flash in the pan" ignited from a
weapon known for its frequent malfunction.*

The origin of the expression "flash in the pan" is most frequently
traced to the flintlock musket. This firearm was introduced around
1610 and was last used by U.S. soldiers in the early days of the Civil
War. Pulling the trigger on a flintlock sparked a small charge of
gunpowder, which ignited a flame. The flame would then shoot up
a touchhole and ignite a more significant charge of gunpowder. It
was this charge that fired the lead ball ammunition. But if the flame
failed to create enough of a spark to fire the ball—because of wet
gunpowder, too little gunpowder, or for some other reason—the
result would be nothing more than a flash in the pan. Literally.

As an expression, "flash in the pan" suggests the disappointment
of expecting a result that does not materialize. It is often used to
describe a promising career that goes nowhere or a hopeful start to
a project that doesn't deliver. (After all, if you're in a situation where
you need to fire a flintlock, don't you fervently hope that you'll see
more than a flash in the pan?)

You'll sometimes see the phrase traced to other origins, such as the
California gold rush, where it is said to refer to a flash of gold in a pan.
But the flintlock origin is the most plausible and is well documented.

⟨⟩⟨⟩⟨⟩⟨⟩

*"I thought it was all a flash in the pan. It wasn't until Broadway
came along that I felt I had really made it."*
—JULIE ANDREWS

"Television won't last. It's a flash in the pan."
—MARY SOMERVILLE, RADIO PRESENTER, IN 1948

Inventions
People Mover

◆ ◆ ◆ ◆

The Segway was born to revolutionize urban transportation.

Inventor Dean Kamen lives to solve problems. His fertile mind has produced a pocket-size infusion pump to deliver insulin and other medications, a wheelchair that can climb stairs, and the Segway Human Transporter, a two-wheel standing scooter that promises to change the way people get around in the big city.

The key to the Segway's function is balancing technology, which is comprised of microprocessors and gyroscopes that prevent the user from falling over. To go forward, the user leans slightly forward; to go backward, he or she leans slightly back. A "LeanSteer" handlebar is used to turn left or right. The vehicle has a maximum set speed of 12.5 miles per hour—though police vehicles can go twice as fast—and can travel about 24 miles on a single battery charge.

Kamen and his team began developing the Segway in the mid-1990s at a cost of $100 million. The device was finally unveiled, to tremendous publicity, in December 2001.

Kamen conceived the Segway as an innovative way to relieve city traffic congestion and began lobbying governments in the United States and abroad to allow the unique motorized vehicle to be driven on city sidewalks. Many municipalities have given their approval, though others have expressed concern that the vehicles could potentially be dangerous on crowded sidewalks.

The Segway is especially popular among people who like both its futuristic design and its environmental friendliness. It has also gained favor among some police departments, which use it to patrol city streets and common areas. It has even been evaluated by the United States Postal Service as an assistive device for delivering the mail.

In the end, it seems Kamen's invention offers a unique solution to a common problem associated with urban life. What more could an inventor hope for?

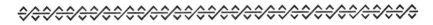

Food & Drink
The McDonald's Kingdom

✦ ✦ ✦ ✦

*In the restaurant industry, there is probably no greater success
story than that of McDonald's. But while the franchise of
golden arches fame has certainly had its share of supporters,
there are plenty of people who believe the introduction of
the "take-away meal" has ruined Americans' health. Still,
regardless of which side of the bun you're on, there's no
denying that McDonald's origins make for a great story.*

Setting the Record Straight

If you thought Ray Kroc opened the first McDonald's, you'd be
wrong. In 1940, two brothers, Dick and Maurice (Mac) McDonald,
opened the first McDonald's on Route 66 in San Bernardino,
California. As was common at the time, carhops served hungry teens
with made-to-order food. But that all changed in 1948, when the
McDonalds fired the carhops and implemented their innovative
"Speedee Service System," a technique that streamlined the assembly
process and became the benchmark for premade hamburgers.
Additionally, this process allowed profits to soar. . . the brothers could
now sell hamburgers for 15 cents, or half what a dinner would cost.

In 1953, Dick and Mac decided to franchise their restaurant, and
the second McDonald's opened in Phoenix, Arizona. It was the first
Mickey D's to sport the famous golden arches. A year later, an entrepreneur and milkshake-mixer salesman named Ray Kroc visited. He
was impressed with the McDonalds' enterprise, and he immediately
joined their team. In 1955, he founded the current McDonald's
Systems, Inc., and opened the ninth McDonald's restaurant in Des
Plaines, Illinois. Six years later, Kroc bought the business from the
McDonald brothers for $2.7 million. The poorly constructed deal
stipulated that Dick and Mac could keep the original restaurant but
somehow overlooked their right to remain a McDonald's franchise.
Because of this error, Kroc opened a restaurant down the block from
the original store, and within a short time he drove the brothers out
of the hamburger business.

Two All-beef Patties

Kroc's many marketing insights included the introduction of Hamburger University—where the graduates are presented with bachelor's degrees in Hamburgerology—ads targeting families, and the creation of Ronald McDonald and "McDonaldland." Feeling the need to adapt, the company altered the menu for the first time in 1963, adding the Filet-O-Fish, followed by such famous additions as the Big Mac and apple pie.

McDonald's spread like wildfire and, in 1967, the first McDonald's restaurant outside the United States opened in Richmond, British Columbia. Ten years later, McDonald's was operating on four continents. It completed its world domination in 1992 by opening an African restaurant in Casablanca, Morocco.

In 1974, along with Fred Hill of the Philadelphia Eagles, McDonald's founded the Ronald McDonald House, an organization that caters to families of critically ill children seeking medical treatment. As of 2008, there were 259 outlets.

Hold the Mayo

All has not gone smoothly for the Mc-empire over the past several years, however. In 2000, Eric Schlosser published *Fast Food Nation,* a critical commentary on fast food in general and McDonald's in particular. This was followed by several lawsuits: one on obesity (claiming McDonald's "lured" young children into their restaurant with their playgrounds) and others asserting various claims of damaged health due to saturated fats.

A huge sensation followed the 2004 release of the film *Supersize Me.* This documentary accused fast-food restaurants of ignoring America's escalating obesity crisis. Later that year, in response to the public's desire for healthier food, McDonald's did away with its super-size meals and implemented more chicken and fish options. In 2005, they added a range of salads and low-sugar drinks and agreed to put nutritional information on all their packaging.

In addition to its new health-conscious menu, McDonald's has also tightened its belt by closing restaurants to compensate for occasionally sagging financial reports. But not much deters McDonald's, which, for the foreseeable future, remains the king of the world's fast-food empire.

The City That Rose from the Sand

❖ ❖ ❖ ❖

Over the past 50 years, Dubai has transformed from a small trading outpost to one of the most powerful cities in the world. The area's exponential growth can be traced to the investment sense and tenacious imagination of the city's ruling royal family.

The stunning cityscape of Dubai, a Middle Eastern city perched on the Persian Gulf, seems almost surreal in its splendor. Dubai is home to the world's largest indoor ski resort, only seven-star hotel, and a set of humanmade islands shaped like a palm tree that can be seen from space. In the making are the world's largest mall, largest theme park, and a cluster of islands shaped like a map of the world. And let's not forget Burj Dubai, a building set to become the tallest in the world—beating the current record holder by 1,000 feet. Investment bankers and real estate moguls from both the West and the Middle East are drawn to this bastion of tourism and wealth.

Descended from the Desert

But things didn't always look this way. The area around Dubai is a sparse desert landscape. Over the millennia, the various nomadic tribes that inhabited the area were involved in trade, especially with nearby India. The modern historical trajectory of Dubai didn't begin until 1833, when 800 members of the Bani Yas tribe made the city an outpost for pearl trading and sea trade. Descendants of this same tribe still rule the city today, but now the family is established as a constitutional monarchy.

Dubai is one emirate in a nation called the United Arab Emirates (UAE). The city itself is technically called Dubai City and lies within the Dubai emirate. The UAE was formed in 1971, when the British officially abandoned their colonial influence over the region. The wealth of Dubai is inextricably linked with the oil wealth of Abu Dhabi, another of the UAE's emirates. Dubai traded in oil extracted from Abu Dhabi, and then in 1966, oil was discovered in Dubai itself. In the following years, the population of Dubai continued to grow.

Transformation Takes Flight

But Dubai's more recent exponential growth comes from investment income, not oil wealth. Back in 1985, Dubai became a pet project of the UAE's then-prince, now Prime Minister Sheik Mohammed bin Rashid Al Maktoum. It

all started with the well-known plight of travel inconvenience: One day, Maktoum's flight out of Dubai was cancelled. Because of this, Maktoum decided to invest his money in a new international airline. Today, this airline is known simply as Emirates, and it is the world's second most profitable airline.

The royal family realized the potential of investing their own money to make Dubai a center of finance and tourism. They hosted international sporting events, established zones that have special tax-free trading and finance laws, and sought foreign capital in real estate and other ventures. In order to make this all happen, an influx of immigrant construction and service workers, especially from southern Asia, inundated the city. Liberal laws were established so that foreign citizens of Dubai would not be subject to the region's religious traditionalism. Islam is the official religion of the UAE, but immigrant workers are allowed religious freedom.

The royal family's plans were immediately successful. In 1985, the population of Dubai was 370,800; today it is 1.4 million. As with other cities that were created out of nothingness through sudden wealth investment, the population of Dubai is oddly lopsided. Almost 90 percent of Dubai's population comes from outside the UAE. Still, UAE nationals are granted special rights and privileges, especially when it comes to land ownership. Living side by side with the affluent nationals and foreign investors that came to Dubai for its promise of wealth is a much larger population of poor migrant families, who built the city from the desert up in a blink of the metaphorical eye.

Media & Communication
Don't Touch That Dial

✦ ✦ ✦

*The history of American broadcasting is associated with so
many call letters, it might as well be alphabet soup. Here's
a brief look at the early days of radio and television.*

Blue Radio
The major TV networks, CBS and NBC, both began as radio
networks. NBC actually had two networks, which it called the Red
and Blue Networks (despite the fact that radio can't broadcast color).
Due to antitrust litigation, NBC was forced to sell off the Blue
Network, which became the American Broadcasting Company, or
ABC.

The Fourth TV Network
When Fox launched in October 1986, it was dubbed "the fourth
network." But it was not the original fourth network. This honor
goes to the DuMont Television Network—the first commercial TV
network. It began operation in 1946 and lasted until 1956, when it
ceased broadcasting. Interestingly enough, two of the TV stations
that had been owned and operated by DuMont are now part of Fox.

Low-definition TV
Today's high-definition television (HDTV) features up to 1,080 lines
of resolution. In contrast, the first live television broadcasts in
1928 featured 48-line images. This first live and scheduled TV was
produced from Hugo Gernsback's New York City radio station.
To make sure that people would tune in, Gernsback published a
magazine with TV schedules called *Television*.

Not-so-famous First
While it is no surprise that the first video on MTV was "Video Killed
the Radio Star" by The Buggles, the first live event on cable sports
channel ESPN was a double header of two slow pitch softball World
Series games.

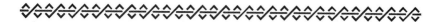

Inventions
Neon Signs: Bright 'n' Gassy

❖ ❖ ❖ ❖

The neon sign serves both art and function.

The neon sign is one of advertising's most effective tools. Its colorful, often soothing light is pleasing to the eye and effortlessly draws our attention to products ranging from automobiles to beer.

The neon sign has been an American advertising icon for decades, but the science behind it dates back to the turn of the century. Neon, derived from the Greek word *neos* (meaning "new") is a relatively rare gaseous element first identified in 1898 by British researchers William Ramsay and M. W. Travers. However, it was French engineer Georges Claude who, around 1902, discovered that a glass tube filled with neon gas glowed brightly when electrically charged. Claude realized the glow would make an effective light source, and he debuted the first neon lamp in Paris in December 1910.

Neon glows fire-red when hit with electricity, but Claude learned that different colors could be produced by mixing neon with other gases such as argon and mercury. He also found that the glass tubes could easily be shaped into letters and designs. This discovery led to the development of the neon sign.

In 1923, Claude introduced his innovative invention to the United States. The first two neon signs, reading "Packard," were sold to Earle C. Anthony, who owned a Packard dealership in Los Angeles.

Neon signs took America by storm and quickly became an integral part of indoor and outdoor advertising. The signs were such a novelty at first that people would literally stop and stare at them.

Like all great inventions, there have been some amazing spin-offs from the neon sign. In the 1930s, for example, the concept led to the development of the fluorescent lightbulb. And the very first experimental color television receivers used neon to produce the color red, complemented by mercury-vapor and helium tubes for green and blue.

Written Word
Oxford English Dictionary

✦ ✦ ✦ ✦

*One of the English language's most esteemed
reference books has links to madness.*

There's no disputing that dictionaries are valuable tools. But did
you ever stop to wonder who originally compiled the words in these
syllabic storehouses? Certainly, anyone vying to be the authoritative
word on, well, words, would need credentials above reproach. Right?

Wrong. The decidedly highbrow *Oxford English Dictionary
(OED)*—the reference book of note that many turn to when they
wish to mimic the King's English—was created in part by a mur-
derer. In fact, this madman was one of the book's most prolific contributors. Who knew?

Inititally called the *New English Dictionary (NED)*, the compen-
dium was a project initiated by the Philological Society of London
in 1857. It was a daunting task by any yardstick. From 1879 (the
year real work on the *NED* began) until its 1928 completion, tens
of thousands of definitions would be culled from a small army of
donors. One of these contributors was Dr. William Chester Minor,
a retired American surgeon who had served the Union Army during
the Civil War. During his military stint, the surgeon would witness
horrible atrocities at the famed Battle of the Wilderness. This experience, along with other horrifying wartime encounters, would inflict
emotional scars that would eventually drive the good doctor completely over the brink.

Answering an ad seeking literary contributions, Minor first came
to the attention of Professor James Murray, the *NED*'s chief editor
from 1879 until his death in 1915. Impressed by the neat, well-
researched quotes that Minor had mailed to him, Murray accepted
the material for inclusion in the dictionary. As a sensationalized
account of the story goes, after a few such go-rounds, Professor
Murray asked the man to meet him in Oxford so they could discuss
future work. Each time the editor made the gesture, he was politely
rebuffed. This baffled Murray. He knew that Minor was located just

50 miles away at the Broadmoor Criminal Lunatic Asylum and had assumed that he was one of their doctors. Surely the physician could take a brief leave from his duties to discuss the Dictionary in person?

But Minor wasn't part of Broadmoor's staff. He was a patient whose grip on reality was tenuous at best. Minor killed a laborer whom he thought meant him harm and was consequently judged insane and permanently confined to the asylum.

Eventually, Minor relented and allowed Murray to meet him at the facility. One can only imagine the editor's shock when he arrived to discover that his prized contributor was a homicidal madman. After allowing the truth to gel, Murray was undeterred. It was obvious that Minor, despite his demons, was meticulous in his research and gifted in his application. It was also obvious that he could use a friend.

Murray would continue to accept Minor's dictionary contributions and visit him regularly until 1910, the year the troubled man was relocated to the United States. In the end, Minor was one of the most prolific contributors to the *NED*. Why had Murray been so keen to accept contributions from a stark, raving madman? As any seasoned editor will tell you, ability is where you find it—and when you find it, you hang on tight. Minor had the stuff, and Murray knew it. And, as it now happens, so do you.

The 1928 version of the NED, *published under the title* A New English Dictionary on Historical Principles, *contained more than 400,000 words and was divided into ten volumes.*

The New English Dictionary *became the* Oxford English Dictionary *in 1933.*

William Chester Minor was ultimately diagnosed with schizophrenia.

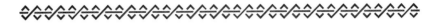

Music

Punk Rock: A British Phenomenon Born in the U.S.A.

❖ ❖ ❖ ❖

*Punk rock exploded onto the music scene in
1977 with a distinctively British bent that overshadowed
the music's fundamental American origins.*

They were a British rock 'n' roll band that crashed their way into the United States, playing a brash, stripped down, and rough-edged style of music. Their lyrics angrily denounced the Queen and British society and nihilistically declared that their generation had no future. Menacing, vulgar, and confrontational, they were the complete antithesis of The Beatles and they made The Rolling Stones look like choir boys.

They were the Sex Pistols—and with their seminal 1977 recording *Never Mind the Bollocks, Here's the Sex Pistols* and a short, chaotic, and highly publicized U.S. tour in January 1978, they introduced mainstream America to the furious, frenzied sound of punk rock.

"(I'm Not Your) Stepping Stone"

But the music the Sex Pistols were importing wasn't all that new, nor did it originate in Britain. Known for its bare-bones, primal musical form and antiestablishment lyrics, punk rock actually germinated in the United States.

Punk rock emerged in the early 1970s at a time when rock 'n' roll seemed to be veering a million miles from its simple original form and rebellious spirit. Progressive rock—popularized by groups such as Pink Floyd, Yes, and Genesis—featured long, opuslike compositions that were artistically complex and heavily layered. The mainstream rock churned out by performers ranging from the Eagles, Doobie Brothers, and James Taylor was safe and tame. These two genres dominated the American rock music scene.

"Today Your Love, Tomorrow the World"

On the fringes, however, was a different sound created by a new generation of American bands who scolded contemporary rock as

pompous, excessive, and lame. They were heavily influenced by garage rock—a raw and unpretentious musical style rooted in rock's original form. Garage rock had been around since the early 1960s, and although it gained some prominence through bands such as The Kinks and The Who, it generally remained underground. Now, groups such as The Velvet Underground, MC5, the New York Dolls, and the Stooges (fronted by Iggy Pop) were stripping the music back to basics—and influencing others to do the same.

Among those feeding off the gritty new sound were two New York City musicians named Tom Verlaine and Richard Hell, who in 1973 formed the band Television. In March 1974, Television began playing a regular Sunday night gig at a seedy, hole-in-the-wall club on the edge of New York's East Village called CBGB.

Television quickly gained a loyal local following that gravitated to the band's thoroughly antiestablishment style and demeanor as much as to their music. Band members sported short cropped hair, T-shirts, tight jeans, leather jackets, and bondage gear—completely rejecting the hippie-influenced look of their rock contemporaries (Richard Hell later added a unique accessory to the look: the safety pin). They brandished an edgy, screw-the-world attitude that resonated with their audiences.

Throughout 1974, numerous bands followed in Television's footsteps at CBGB, including the Patti Smith Group, Blondie, and the Talking Heads. The Ramones also played at CBGB, and their short, three-chord, ultrafast songs would come to characterize the provocative new sound people were labeling "punk rock." CBGB became Ground Zero for the burgeoning—albeit still mostly underground—punk movement.

One man attuned to the vibrant punk scene and subculture was a London entrepreneur named Malcolm McClaren. Hanging around New York in 1974, McClaren met several artists spearheading the new movement. Inspired, he returned to London in May 1975 and began managing a little-known local band, which he reinvented in the punk style and renamed the Sex Pistols.

A year later, The Ramones played in London—an event that galvanized the nascent U.K. punk scene led by the Pistols and such future punk icons as The Clash, The Stranglers, and the Buzzcocks.

Punk was about to turn the rock establishment on its ear.

Religion
The Intergalactic Journey of Scientology

❖ ❖ ❖ ❖

*There are few who don't know about the aura of mystery
and scandal that surrounds the Church of Scientology,
which boasts a small membership and a seismic pocketbook.
Scientology frequently graces the headlines, with stories
ranging from accounts of Tom Cruise tomfoolery to an endless
stream of lawsuits and accusations of bribery and abuse.*

The fantastical elements to the saga of Scientology were perhaps
written into the religion from its beginning, given that Scientology
sprang from the fertile mind of its late creator, pulp fiction writer
turned religious messiah, L. Ron Hubbard. Hubbard, born in 1911,
began his writing career in the 1930s after flunking out of college.
Hubbard had always preferred imagination to reality: Accounts of
his past reveal hallucinogenic drug abuse and an obsession with
black magic and Satanism. In between prolific bouts of writing,
Hubbard served in the Navy during World War II, became involved
in various start-up ventures, and, of course, dabbled in black magic
ceremonies. Allegation has it that Hubbard and wealthy scientist
friend John Parsons performed a ritual in which they attempted to
impregnate a woman with the antichrist. The woman was Parsons's
girlfriend, but she soon became Hubbard's second wife—though he
was still married to his first wife.

Down to a Science
In 1949, Hubbard developed a self-help process that he called
Dianetics. All of humanity's problems, according to Dianetics,
stem from the traumas of past lives. These traumas are called
engrams, and Hubbard's own e-meter (a machine using simple lie
detector technology) can identify and help eliminate these engrams.
Getting rid of engrams can have amazing results—from increasing
intelligence to curing blindness. The first Dianetics article appeared
in a sci-fi publication called *Astounding Science Fiction.* In 1950,

Hubbard opened the Hubbard Dianetic Research Foundation in New Jersey, and in that same year *Dianetics: The Modern Science of Mental Health* was published and sold well.

Hubbard and his followers attempted to establish Dianetics as an official science. But the medical profession didn't appreciate Dianetics masquerading as science. The Dianetic Research Foundation came under investigation by the IRS and the American Medical Association. Hubbard closed his clinics and fled New Jersey.

Actually, It's a Religion...

Dianetics wasn't making the cut as a scientific theory, so Hubbard played another card. Years before, Hubbard is reputed to have told a friend "writing for a penny a word is ridiculous. If a man really wants to make a million dollars, the best way would be to start his own religion." After fleeing Jersey, Hubbard moved to Phoenix, Arizona, declared Dianetics an "applied religious philosophy," and, in 1954, Hubbard's organization was recognized as a religion by the IRS and granted tax-exempt status.

Thus the Church of Scientology was born. Hubbard added new stories to the original Dianetics creation, and by the 1960s, humans were spiritual descendants of the alien Thetans, who were banished to live on Earth by the intergalactic terrorist dictator Xenu 75 million years ago. Scientologist disciples must not only expel the traumas of past lives but of past lives on different planets. Discovering these traumas is an expensive process, so the Church actively recruits wealthy devotees. As for Hubbard, he died in 1986, soon after the IRS accused him of stealing $200 million from the Church. Today, Scientology and its various offshoot nonprofit groups and private business ventures continue to hold a vast fortune, and Scientology's ongoing litigation with the IRS, the press, and ex-devotees (hundreds of lawsuits are pending) are so bizarre, they seem almost out of this world.

Toys & Games
The Early Days of Video Games

❖ ❖ ❖ ❖

*Today's die-hard video gamers might chuckle at the
thought of playing a simple game of table tennis on a
TV screen. But without* Pong, *there might not be* Grand
Theft Auto. *Read about the early history of the video
game and marvel at how far the industry has come.*

Spacewar
At MIT in 1962, Steve Russell programmed the world's first video
game on a bulky computer known as the DEC PDP-1. *Spacewar*
featured spaceships fighting amid an astronomically correct screen
full of stars. The technological fever spread quickly, and by the end
of the decade, nearly every research computer in the United States
had a copy of *Spacewar* on it.

Pong
Nolan Bushnell founded Atari in 1972, taking the company's name
from the Japanese word for the chess term "check." Atari released
the coin-operated *Pong* later that year, and its simple, addictive
action of bouncing a pixel ball between two paddles became an
instant arcade hit. In 1975, the TV-console version of *Pong* was
released. It was received with great enthusiasm by people who could
play hours of the tennislike game in the comfort of their homes.

Tetris
After runaway success in the Soviet Union in 1985 (and in spite of
the Cold War), *Tetris* jumped the Bering Strait and took over the
U.S. market the next year. Invented by Soviet mathematician Alexi
Pajitnov, the game features simple play—turning and dropping
geometric shapes into tightly packed rows—that drew avid fans in
both countries. Many gamers call *Tetris* the most addictive game of
all time.

Space Invaders
Released in 1978, Midway's *Space Invaders* was the arcade
equivalent of *Star Wars*: a ubiquitous hit that generated a lot of

money. It also presented the "high score" concept. A year later, Atari released *Asteroids* and outdid *Space Invaders* by enabling the high scorer to enter his or her initials for posterity.

Pac-Man
This 1980 Midway classic is the world's most successful arcade game, selling some 99,000 units. Featuring the yellow maw of the title character, a maze of dots, and four colorful ghosts, the game inspired rap songs, Saturday morning cartoons, and a slew of sequels.

Donkey Kong
In 1980, Nintendo's first game marked the debut of Mario, soon to become one of the most recognizable fictional characters in the world. Originally dubbed Jumpman, Mario was named for Mario Segali, the onetime owner of Nintendo's warehouse in Seattle.

Q*bert
Released by Gottlieb in 1982, this game featured the title character jumping around on a pyramid of cubes, squashing and dodging enemies. Designers originally wanted Q*bert to shoot slime from his nose, but it was deemed too gross.

From 1988 to 1990, Nintendo sold roughly 50 million home-entertainment systems. In 1996, the company sold its billionth video game cartridge for home systems.

In 1981, 15-year-old Steve Juraszek set a world record on Williams Electronics' Defender. *His score of 15,963,100 got his picture in* Time *magazine—and it also got him suspended from school. He played part of his 16-hour game when he should have been attending class.*

Atari opened the first pizzeria/arcade establishment known as Chuck E. Cheese in San Jose in 1977. Atari's Nolan Bushnell bought the rights to the pizza business when he parted ways with his company in 1978, then he turned it into a nationwide phenomenon. It was later acquired by its primary competitor, ShowBiz Pizza.

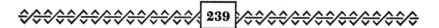

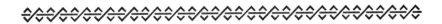

Language
Commendable Condiment

❖ ❖ ❖ ❖

While an apple a day may keep the doctor away, taking something
with a grain of salt will make that flavorful fruit—and any other
advice that lurches on the ledge of logic—easier to swallow.

Unlike many of the phrases that originated in the era when recording history was lightly regarded and often ignored, the exact genesis
of "take it with a grain of salt" has not been lost in the murky sands
of time. Its meaning refers to administrating caution before accept-
ing the validity of a claim, and its roots can be traced to first-century
Rome, thanks to the well-documented works of scholar and natural-
ist Gaius Plinius Secundus, who is better known as Pliny the Elder.

His most famous offering was a comprehensive compilation
entitled *Historia Naturalis,* an exhaustive encyclopedia completed in
A.D. 77 and the largest tome of its type from the time of the Roman
Empire to survive through the centuries.

Pliny's production consists of 37 books and includes virtually everything that the Romans knew about the natural world in the fields of
mathematics, geography, anthropology, zoology, botany, pharmacology,
mining, mineralogy, cosmology, astronomy, metallurgy, and agriculture.
It also includes an ancient antidote for poison that states a person can
survive poisoning if they combine the ingredients (walnuts, figs, and 20
leaves of rue) with a pinch of salt. Over the centuries, that advice was
moderated to mean that a grain of salt can act as a measure of prevention against any injurious substance, be it poison or bad advice.

The Oxford English Dictionary dates the usage of the expression
"with a grain of salt" to 1647.

❖❖❖❖❖

"A wise woman puts a grain of sugar into everything she says to a
man, and takes a grain of salt with everything he says to her."
—HELEN ROWLAND, WRITER

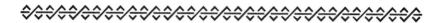

Household Items
When Broken Dishes Mean Business

❖ ❖ ❖ ❖

Not every tale of invention is a rags-to-riches story.
This one is more of a "dishes-to-riches" story.

Josephine Cochran came from a line of inventors—her great-grandfather was John Fitch, inventor of the steamboat. She also came from money. Like many society women of her time, Mrs. Cochran liked to entertain. What she didn't like was the way her servants handled her good china while washing it after parties, often chipping or breaking it.

Mrs. Cochran decided that the world needed a mechanical dishwasher. Patents had already been issued for such devices, first to Joel Houghton in 1850 for a hand-cranked model and then to L. A. Alexander in 1865, but these were clumsy affairs that didn't do a very good job of washing dishes. "If nobody else is going to invent a dishwashing machine," Mrs. Cochran is reported to have said, "I'll do it myself."

And so she did. In a shed behind her home, she measured her plates, cups, and saucers, then fashioned wire baskets to fit them. The baskets were loaded into a wheel inside a copper boiler, where hot water rained down upon them as the wheel turned.

Mrs. Cochran's friends were so impressed with her invention, they encouraged her to market it. She founded her own company— Cochran's Crescent Washing Machine Company—and received a patent for her "dish-washing machine" in 1886.

The first customer for her dishwasher was the historic Palmer House in Chicago, the city where her invention also took a first prize at the legendary World's Columbian Exposition of 1893.

Mrs. Cochran's dishwashers quickly became popular with restaurants and hotels—which went through a lot of dishes—but they were too expensive for most homeowners. It wasn't until much later—in the middle of the 20th century—that electric dishwashers caught on. Mrs. Cochran's company changed names over the years, but it lives on as KitchenAid.

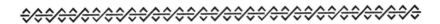

Holidays & Traditions
Happy Birthday, Dear Valentine?

❖ ❖ ❖ ❖

*Why do we celebrate St. Valentine's birthday? We
don't. Instead, we commemorate his martyrdom.*

Who was St. Valentine? The Catholic Church says there were
actually three St. Valentines, and all were martyrs. So which one
does Valentine's Day honor? The most likely candidate was a Roman
priest during the reign of Claudius II, emperor of Rome from A.D.
268 to 270. Desperate for men to fight his wars, Claudius forbade
soldiers to marry. According to the legend, young lovers came to
Valentine to be married, and these unauthorized marriages led to his
imprisonment. While awaiting his execution, he fell in love with his
jailer's daughter. Shortly before his death on February 14, he wrote
her a letter and signed it "From Your Valentine."

The problem is that there's no proof that any of this actually
happened. Valentine's name is not on the earliest list of Roman
martyrs, and there's no evidence that he was put to death on
February 14. In fact, in 1969, the Catholic Church removed
Valentine's Day from the list of official holy days.

**How did Valentine become associated with a celebration
of love?** It may be that February 14 was chosen by the early
Church to replace a Roman fertility festival called Lupercalia, which
fell on the same date. Another explanation is that the sentimentality
of Valentine's Day can be traced to the Middle Ages, an era fixated
on romantic love. It was popularly believed that birds chose their
mates on February 14, a legend Geoffrey Chaucer referenced in his
poem "Parliament of Foules": "For this was on St. Valentine's Day,
when every fowl cometh there to chooses his mate."

What about all the flowers and chocolates? These fairly
recent additions to the Valentine story have more to do with the
power of retailers than the passion of romance.

What Do You Mean by That?
The Animal Edition

Blind as a Bat
Actually, bats' vision isn't all that bad. They are color-blind (as are many humans), but they also have supersharp night vision and can find their way around very well by using echolocation, a form of natural sonar. While in flight, bats emit sounds that bounce off nearby surfaces, and they use those echoes to judge distances.

Sweaty as a Pig
When humans get too hot, we sweat. We release perspiration through approximately 2.6 million (give or take a few) sweat glands in our skin, and that perspiration evaporates and cools us down. Pigs, however, have no sweat glands and can't sweat at all, which is why they attempt to lower their body temperature by wallowing in mud.

Slimy as a Snake
Although a snake's scales are shiny and often appear slimy, the reptile's body is dry to the touch. People may confuse snakes with amphibians such as frogs and salamanders, which have thin skins that are moist to the touch. And worms are definitely slimy.

Dirty as a Rat
Even before the Black Death in the 14th century, rats had a reputation for being filthy. Due to their lack of an assertive PR department, they haven't been able to point out that fleas were actually the responsible party. Rats, in fact, are quite clean and tidy. They spend 40 percent of their time washing themselves (more than the average house cat), searching out water for grooming, and compulsively cleaning their habitats.

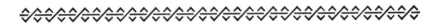

Film
Lights, Camera, Technicolor

❖ ❖ ❖ ❖

Moving pictures were astonishing to the audiences
who first saw them. It wasn't too hard to get used to
seeing them in black and white. But when movies went
to color, all of a sudden, that was like real life.

Tripping the Shutter

The marvel of moving pictures was first demonstrated by Californian
Eadweard Muybridge, who set up a series of 24 still cameras
at a racetrack in Palo Alto, California, in 1878. The shutter of
each camera was connected to a string; as the horse galloped by,
the strings were tripped, and each camera captured an image.
Muybridge fashioned a crude process to project the images in
sequence, demonstrating his method to an art society in San
Francisco in 1880.

In 1891, inventor Thomas Edison set up a lab in West Orange,
New Jersey, and patented a 35mm motion-picture camera called the
Kinetograph. The novelty of moving pictures quickly became big
business in the entertainment world at the turn of the 20th century.
Edison hired Edwin S. Porter, a camera technician, in 1900. Porter
realized that entire stories could be told with film, and he proceeded
to do just that. Other major film studios opened in Chicago, but by
the mid-teens, inclement weather and labor issues there drove filmmakers to sunny Southern California.

Problems Persist

As the film industry continued to grow, several issues remained. The
cinema was silent and images were black and white—hardly realistic.
During the 1920s, films were usually accompanied by live piano or
organ music, improvised by the theater musician as action unfolded
on the screen. Some studios tried to increase the visual experience
by hand-tinting certain scenes in various washes of color.

Color movies had been tried with limited success in England.
Known as *Kinemacolor,* the process involved special cameras and

projectors that used black-and-white film with two colored filters. But the result was questionable, producing fringed and haloed effects that distracted from the projected image. Even so, more than 50 American films were produced with the Kinemacolor process by the late teens.

The Color of Money

Technicolor picked up where Kinemacolor left off. Three chemical and mechanical experts named Kalmus, Comstock, and Wescott recognized the need for a realistic color film stock and created the Technicolor Company in 1915 (taking "Tech" from their alma mater, Massachusetts Institute of Technology). Their two-color dye process gained limited use for some sequences in epics from the 1920s, including *The Phantom of the Opera, The Ten Commandments, King of Kings,* and *Ben-Hur.* By 1933, the two-color process had reached talking pictures with *The Mystery of the Wax Museum.*

Still, Technicolor was garish and didn't look real. Kalmus convinced Walt Disney to try a new, refined three-color Technicolor process on his animated short *Flowers and Trees.* The result was a breathtaking success: an Academy Award for Disney and a contract to produce all future Disney films in Technicolor (which remained in force until the Hollywood Technicolor plant closed in 1975).

The new Technicolor process used a series of filters, prisms, and lenses to create three films: a red, blue, and green record. The three were then combined, and the result was a three-strip print. The success of this film stock was not lost on Hollywood, as budgets were increased to allow for color productions. While black-and-white features such as *Citizen Kane, Casablanca,* and *The Treasure of the Sierra Madre* became classics from the 1930s and '40s, Technicolor became part of the visual story for such '30s blockbuster films as *Robin Hood, The Wizard of Oz,* and *Gone with the Wind.*

Aging Somewhat Gracefully

By the 1950s, television had taken a large bite out of moviegoing America. By the 1970s, the cost for Technicolor prints had become very high, and the dye process was too slow to serve the country's theaters with enough prints. *The Godfather* and *The Godfather: Part II* were among the last films to use the Technicolor process.

Language
Oll Korrect!

❖ ❖ ❖ ❖

"OK" may be America's most successful export—it has the
distinction of being the most understood word on Earth.

There seems to be no limit of probable explanations for OK's origins. The Finnish word for *correct* is *oikea*. School papers used to be
marked with the Latin *Omnis Korrecta* (OK). A telegraph symbol
that meant "open key" was often abbreviated to "OK." Alas, none of
these theories are accepted as OK. When etymologists study word
meanings, they follow strict guidelines to authenticate a word's
source. It isn't enough to say a word was once used in a certain way.
It must be found in writing and in the correct context.

An 1830s craze for wordplay in New York and Boston ultimately
provided the written proof needed to establish OK's origin. Long
before the age of text messaging, this fad had people intentionally
misspelling words and stringing initials together to form comical
acronyms. (Examples include "N.C." for *nuff ced* and "K.Y." for
know yuse.) OK was first found in print in 1839. A Boston newspaper story about the anti-bell ringing society (A.B.R.S.) used O.K.
as an acronym for the intentionally misspelled "oll korrect." Its use
spread a year later in the 1840 presidential campaign. The incumbent Martin Van Buren's nickname was "Old Kinderhook" (based
on the name of his birthplace: Kinderhook, New York). Van Buren's
supporters began forming "Democratic O.K." clubs and used "OK"
as an insider's campaign slogan.

Today, this tiny pronouncement is one of the most useful words
in the English language. It can be a noun, a verb, or an adjective and
is understood everywhere from the Amazonian jungles to the deserts
of Mongolia. Few expressions will get you further than "OK."

❖❖❖❖❖❖❖

"One out of four people in this country is mentally unbalanced. Think
of your three closest friends. If they seem OK, then you're the one."
—ANN LANDERS

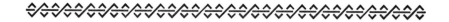

Presidential Nicknames

Old Kinderhook isn't the only presidential nickname to become popular over the decades. Here are the origins of a few more.

Sam: President Hiram Ulysses Grant earned this nickname at West Point. He enrolled as Ulysses Hiram Grant (a move some say was an attempt to avoid having the initials HUG embroidered on his clothing). Somehow, the name was entered as Ulysses S. Grant instead. Grant's classmates were the first to call him "Sam" based on his newly acquired middle initial.

The Phrasemaker: President Woodrow Wilson was known as an acclaimed historian who seldom used speechwriters.

Washington of the West: President William Henry Harrison was a general, like George Washington, and was remembered for his victories at the Battle of Tippecanoe and the Battle of the Thames.

Young Hickory: President Andrew Jackson was "Old Hickory," so his protégé President James Knox Polk became Young Hickory.

The Abolitionist: President John Quincy Adams routinely brought up the issue of slavery and earned the nickname after returning to Congress following his presidency.

The Negro President: President Thomas Jefferson earned this nickname following his victory in the 1800 election, which he won because of the Three-Fifths Compromise.

The American Cincinnatus: Known as the Father of His Country, George Washington was often compared to that famous Roman, who also became a private citizen instead of a king.

Ten-cent Jimmy: President James Buchanan earned this nickname because of a campaign claim that 10 cents was enough for a man to live on.

Food & Drink
Who Put the PB in PB&J?

❖ ❖ ❖ ❖

What goes equally well with jelly, bacon, marshmallow fluff,
chocolate, and banana? Peanut butter, of course. And most schoolkids
think that George Washington Carver is the man behind that magic.

The Well-traveled Peanut

The myth that George Washington Carver invented peanut butter
has spread as easily as this spreadable favorite. But by the time
Carver was born in 1864, peanuts were being crushed into a paste on
five continents. Peanuts have been grown for consumption in South
America since 950 B.C., and the Incas used peanut paste in much of
their cooking. Fifteenth-century trade ships took peanuts to Africa
and Asia, where they were assimilated into local cuisines, often
as a paste used for thickening stews. In the 18th century, peanuts
traveled back across the Atlantic Ocean to be traded to North
American colonists. In 1818, the first commercial peanut crop was
produced in North Carolina. Today, there are approximately 50,000
peanut farms in the United States, and 50 percent of the peanuts
produced on these farms are turned into peanut butter.

A Popular Nut Paste

So the Incas, not Carver, must be credited with first grinding of
peanuts into a paste. But the forefather of modern-day peanut butter
was an anonymous doctor who, in 1890, put peanuts through a meat
grinder to provide a protein source for people with teeth so bad they
couldn't chew meat. A food-processing company saw the potential in
the doctor's product and started selling the nut paste for $0.06 per
pound. Dr. John Harvey Kellogg (the inventor of corn flakes) had
been feeding a similar paste made from steamed, ground peanuts to
the patients at his sanatorium in Battle Creek, Michigan. In 1895, he
patented his "process of preparing nut meal" and began selling it to
the general public.

The nut paste caught on, and peanut-grinding gadgets became
readily available, along with cookbooks full of recipes for nut meals,

pastes, and spreads. In 1904, visitors at the St. Louis World's Fair bought more than $700 worth of peanut butter. In 1908, the Krema Nut Company in Columbus, Ohio, began selling peanut butter—but only within the state because of problems with spoilage.

Carver's Contributions

So how did George Washington Carver get in the middle of this peanutty story? Carver was an agricultural chemist, inventor, and innovator who had a strong interest in peanut production and a firm belief that it could benefit American agriculture. Although born to slaves, Carver worked and studied hard. He earned master's degrees in botany and agriculture from Iowa Agricultural College (now Iowa State University), and he became the director of agriculture at the Tuskegee Normal and Industrial Institute for Negroes in 1897.

At the Tuskegee Institute, Carver researched and developed approximately 290 practical and esoteric uses for peanuts, incorporating them into foods, cosmetics, ink, paper, and lubricants. He didn't patent any of these products, believing that the earth's crops and their by-products were gifts from God. Although he published several works about the benefits of peanuts in agriculture, industry, and cuisine, he became nationally associated with the crop only late in his career.

Influential Nonetheless

The story of Carver's humble beginnings, talents, and professional success took on mythic proportions. A number of articles and biographies generously (and erroneously) credit him with everything from inventing dehydrated foods to rescuing the South from crushing poverty by promoting peanut products. At some point, the invention of peanut butter was attributed to him.

Schoolchildren everywhere are entranced by Carver's personal success story and his contributions to American agriculture. He is a role model despite the fact that he didn't invent peanut butter. Giving credit where it's due—to the Incas—does not diminish the value of Carver's accomplishments.

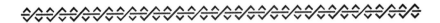

Television
Reality TV: Watching Others Look Foolish Since 1950

❖ ❖ ❖ ❖

It became the TV craze of the early 21st century, but reality TV dates back to television's infancy. Of course, in those days, networks didn't have to blur/bleep out as many body parts and profanities.

Early Days

In 1950, NBC in New York first aired *Truth or Consequences,* a television program that challenged ordinary people to answer trivia questions; participants were required to perform screwball stunts when they blew the answers. Little did the producers realize the size of the boulder they had set rolling.

American Idol isn't a new concept. *Arthur Godfrey's Talent Scouts* did a similar thing beginning in 1948: People would perform (some notable participants include Patsy Cline, Pat Boone, and Lenny Bruce), and audience applause would determine the victor. A similar show, *Ted Mack & the Original Amateur Hour,* came to TV in 1948. Several reality TV shows evolved from reality radio shows; for example, *Candid Camera* was originally *Candid Microphone.*

"Smile! You're Pranked on National TV!"

That was the theme of Allen Funt's groundbreaking *Candid Camera,* which debuted in 1948. Sometimes the victim was an average Joe or Jane; sometimes it was a celebrity such as Buster Keaton or Ann Jillian. The show would contrive zany situations, and a hidden camera would film people's reactions. Sample stunts included:

- Collecting tolls on hiking trails

- Offering to vaccinate workers against a computer bug

- Watching people's interactions with an attendant in a restroom without plumbing

- Chaining restaurant silverware to the table

For the most part, people took it in good fun—and still do. *Candid Camera* has run intermittently since its debut.

The First Golden Age

In the post–WWII era, reality TV looked like the wave of the future. Game shows mingled the reality concept with prize competitions: *This is Your Life, You Asked For It, Beat the Clock, Truth or Consequences,* and *What's My Line?* all contained reality elements, albeit with some contrivance behind the scenes. Which leads us to reality TV's eternal, dirty secret: There is always some level of stage-managing—often far more than producers want us to realize.

While game shows thrived throughout the 1960s and were technically a form of reality TV, they ultimately formed their own entertainment genre. Reality TV faded into a niche for many years.

1988 and Beyond

Professionals are expensive and may "withhold their professional services" (strike). Amateurs are cheap and will line up for the opportunity to be on television. So went the networks' thinking during the 1988 Writer's Guild of America strike, which messed up the whole fall schedule. Fox debuted a modern TV version of a 1950s reality radio show called *Night Watch: Cops* in which ride-along cameras filmed real police work. In 1992, MTV launched *The Real World,* cramming seven strangers into a house for months at a time. It was an early example of modern mainstream reality TV in the United States.

Many modern reality show concepts, most notably *Big Brother* and *Trading Spaces,* started in Europe in the 1990s before U.S. networks mimicked them.

Outwit! Outplay! Outlast!

Survivor, The Amazing Race, Fear Factor, Big Brother USA, and *American Idol: The Search for a Superstar* all debuted in the early years of the new millennium. With these shows and dozens of imitators/variants, reality TV became as great a sensation as it ever was in its 1950s infancy.

Evidently, we love to watch ordinary people's suffering and triumph. And networks like reality because it's cheaper to produce than scripted TV. Talk about a win-win situation!

Language
Penny-saving Piggies

✦ ✦ ✦ ✦

The piggy bank sprang from a play on words.

The piggy bank is one of America's favorite ways to save. Kids love to hoard their pennies in them, and adults often use them to hold spare change. But the origin of the venerable piggy bank has nothing to do with pigs. It can actually be traced to an English play on words that dates back hundreds of years.

According to historians, the concept of the piggy bank most likely started in England around the mid-1500s. Back then, metal was precious and quite expensive, so the average family used dishes, jars, and cookware made from an inexpensive orange clay called *pygg*, which was probably initially pronounced "pug."

It was common for families to keep extra coins in a pygg jar, which eventually came to be known as the "pygg bank." Centuries later, in the 1700s, the name evolved to "piggy bank." Amused British potters started making clay banks in the shape of pigs, and that's how the piggy bank as we now know it was born.

People quickly became enamored with piggy banks, and their popularity soared throughout England. The earliest piggy banks were ceramic and had to be broken to retrieve the money inside. Later versions came with a hole or other retrieval method so that the banks could be used over and over.

Piggy banks eventually spread outside of England to equal popularity. Adults found them a good way to instill a sense of financial responsibility among children, and versions of the piggy bank can now be found throughout the world.

Fads & Fashion
Nylon Evolution

❖ ❖ ❖ ❖

Back in the day, it took a lot of effort for women to look sexy and stylish. They had to put on their underwear, then hosiery, then a garter belt or other support device to hold up the hosiery. Sometimes the garter belt would snap or the hosiery would bag, resulting in unattractive "elephant knees." What was a woman to do?

The solution came with the development of pantyhose, a convenient one-piece garment that combined panties and stockings. Actress-dancer Ann Miller, who starred in such films as *Easter Parade* (1948) and *Kiss Me Kate* (1953), claims to have worn the first pantyhose in the early 1940s as a time-saver when filming dance numbers. At that time, stockings were commonly sewn directly to costumes because garter belts were impractical for dancers. But when the stockings tore, a new pair had to be resewn. So Miller asked a hosiery manufacturer to sew the stockings to a pair of briefs. The first attempt was too short for Miller's long gams, but the second pair fit just right.

In 1959, Allen Gant Sr. of North Carolina–based Glen Raven Mills introduced pantyhose to the American public, revolutionizing the foundation garment industry. In 1965, Glen Raven Mills introduced the first seam-free pantyhose, which conveniently coincided with the advent of the mini-skirt. Over the years, numerous other styles have been produced, most notably "Control Top" pantyhose, which contain a reinforced panty to make the wearer appear more slender.

Pantyhose were a huge success from the moment they were introduced because women found them convenient and comfortable. Today, the hosiery industry produces an estimated two billion pair of pantyhose each year. And while the majority of wearers are women, men have also been known to slip into a pair. Football players and other athletes occasionally wear pantyhose to help them stay warm, to reduce chafing, and to improve circulation.

Places & Landmarks
At the Center of It All

❖ ❖ ❖ ❖

A stroll through New York City's Central Park might lead you to believe that it is the one remaining slice of nature amid the towering skyscrapers of steel and glass that flank it. But, in fact, this urban park was almost entirely humanmade. And even though Manhattan's northern half was laid out in the early 19th century, the park was not part of the Commissioners' Plan of 1811.

Between 1821 and 1855, the population of New York nearly quadrupled. This growth convinced city planners that a large, open-air space was required. Initial plans mimicked the large public grounds of London and Paris, but it was eventually decided that the space should evoke feelings of nature—complete with running water, dense wooded areas, and even rolling hills.

The original park layout included the area stretching from 59th to 106th streets and also included land between 5th and 8th avenues. The land itself cost about $5 million. This part of Manhattan featured an irregular terrain of swamps and bluffs and included rocky outcrops left from the last Ice Age 10,000 years earlier; it was deemed unsuitable for private development but was ideal for creating the park that leaders envisioned. However, the area was not uninhabited. It was home to about 1,600 poor residents, most of them Irish and German immigrants—though there was a thriving African American community there as well. Ultimately, these groups were resettled, and the park's boundaries were extended to 110th street.

In the 1850s, the state of New York appointed a Central Park Commission to oversee the development of the park. A landscape design contest was held in 1857, and writer and landscape architect Frederick Law Olmsted and architect Calvert Vaux won with their "Greensward Plan."

Olmsted and Vaux envisioned a park that would include "separate circulation systems" for its assorted users, including pedestrians and horseback riders. To accommodate crosstown traffic while still

maintaining the sense of a continuous single park, the roads that traversed Central Park from East to West were sunken and screened with planted shrub belts. Likewise, the Greensward Plan called for three dozen bridges, all designed by Vaux, with no two alike. These included simple granite bridges as well as ornate neogothic conceptions made of cast iron. The southern portion of the park was designed to include the mall walk to Bethesda Terrace and Bethesda Fountain, which provided a view of the lake and woodland to the north.

Central Park was one of the largest public works projects in New York during the 19th century, with some 20,000 workers on hand to reshape the topography of nearly 850 acres. Massive amounts of gunpowder (more, in fact, than was used in the Battle of Gettysburg) were used to blast the rocky ridges, and nearly three million cubic yards of soil were moved. At the same time, some 270,000 trees and shrubs were planted to replicate the feeling of nature.

Despite the massive scale of work involved, the park first opened for public use in 1858; by 1865, it was receiving more than seven million visitors a year. Strict rules on group picnics and certain activities kept some New York residents away, but by the 1880s, the park was as welcoming to the working class as it was to the wealthy.

Over time, the park welcomed a number of additions, including the famous Carousel and Zoo, and activities such as tennis and bike riding became part of the landscape. Today, Central Park plays host to concerts, Shakespeare plays, swimming, and ice-skating. It also features a welcoming bird sanctuary for watchers and their feathered friends alike and is a pleasant urban retreat for millions of New Yorkers.

"One belongs to New York instantly, one belongs to it as much in five minutes as in five years."

—Thomas Wolfe

Inventions
The Origin of Water Pipes

◆ ◆ ◆ ◆

The luxury of a "civilized" life would not
be possible without water pipes.

Humble hollow tubes have been improving our quality of life for thousands of years. As it turns out, the piping of water in and out of living spaces originated in many different ancient civilizations. Plumbing technology was often developed only to be lost until it was reinvented from scratch. Lead pipes have been found in Mesopotamian ruins, and clay knee joint piping has been traced to Babylonia. The Egyptians used copper piping. But the most sophisticated ancient waterworks flourished at the hands of the Harappan Civilization (circa 3300–1600 B.C.) in the areas of present-day India and Pakistan.

The Harappans boasted of a network of earthenware pipes that would carry water from people's homes into municipal drains and cesspools. Archeological excavation in the 1920s uncovered highly planned cities with living quarters featuring individual indoor baths and even toilets. Thanks to the Harappans' advanced ceramic techniques, they were able to build ritual baths up to 29 feet long and 10 feet deep—as big as modern-day swimming pools.

While the Romans can't be credited with the invention of water pipes, their mastery of pipe-making influenced plumbing up to the 20th century. (The word *plumbing* comes from the Latin word for lead, *plumbum*.) Pipes were made by shaping sheets of the easily malleable (and highly toxic) molten lead around a wooden core. Plumbers then soldered the joints together with hot lead. It could be said that they were largely responsible for "civilizing" Rome, making it a place where homes had bathtubs as well as indoor toilets that flushed into underground sewage systems. Fresh water was piped directly into kitchens, and there were even ways of "metering" how much water was being used by the width of the pipe installed. (Even then, convenience had its price!)

BAND NAMES

Deep Purple

Heavy metal pioneers Deep Purple went through nearly as many name changes in their early days as lineup changes in the years to follow. After taking such names as The Flower Pot Men and Their Garden, The Ivy League, and Roundabout, guitarist Ritchie Blackmore suggested the name Deep Purple, which had been his grandmother's favorite song—a 1933 tune that began as a piano composition before being scored for a big band orchestra.

Lynyrd Skynyrd

This Southern rock band has had its share of triumph and tragedy—including a plane crash that took the life of founding member Johnny VanZant. It was VanZant who had suggested a new name for the group, which had originally been known as The Noble Five and later My Backyard. The group finally settled on a mocking play on the name Leonard Skinner, a gym teacher at Robert E. Lee High School in Jacksonville, Florida, who was known for a strict policy against boys having long hair.

U2

While it is sometimes rumored that the Irish quartet was named after the American U-2 spy plane, the fact is that the members—who had been playing under the name The Hype—chose their moniker because it was ambiguous and somewhat open-ended. When Dik Evans, brother of guitarist The Edge, a.k.a. Dave Evans, left the group, the remaining members actually just picked a name they disliked the least.

AC/DC

The group has a rather simple explanation for the origin of their name—that of the electrical "alternating current/direct current." Members say they saw the abbreviation on the back of a sewing machine and felt it described their then-aspiring group's raw energy.

Computers & Cyberspace
IBM Before It Was IBM

◆ ◆ ◆ ◆

*IBM has cast a long shadow on American life and industry
since the 1920s, but its ancestor companies were bound up
with workplace automation from the concept's earliest days.*

Roots

In 1896, Herman Hollerith formed the unimaginatively named
Tabulating Machine Company (TMC) to market a punch-card
tabulating device that had already revolutionized the U.S. Census.
Held once per decade, the Census was taking about eight years to
tabulate. Hollerith's system trimmed that time to less than two years.
Unfortunately, the brilliant inventor proved a lousy businessman. By
1911, TMC needed a bailout.

Meanwhile, in 1891, the also creatively named Computing Scale
Company (CSC) began making sophisticated computing scales—
essential to all businesses that measured product by weight. CSC
acquired several competitors in the early 1900s and was successful
but not dominant in its niche.

Late 1800s labor law was minimal, and companies went to great
lengths to wring maximum work from their wage dimes. In 1889,
the Bundy Manufacturing Company (BMC) cashed in with the first
industrial time clock. For slackers who showed up late and/or left
early, the party was over. By 1911, BMC had bought several competitors and had grown into International Time Recording Company
(ITRC), a leader in the field.

Consolidation

In 1911, financier Charles Flint arranged to merge ITRC, CSC, and
TMC as the Computing-Tabulating-Recording Company (C-T-R).
C-T-R's time clock and data tabulation businesses thrived. In 1914,
Flint hired Thomas J. Watson Sr. to manage C-T-R. Watson was a
veteran of National Cash Register (NCR) and had actually done a
year in jail for NCR's antitrust violations before his conviction was
overturned on a technicality.

Whatever his past, Watson established key elements of IBM's future corporate culture. Everyone (even Watson) would punch in and out on a time clock. The marketing uniform was a dark suit and white shirt: no exceptions. C-T-R prized company loyalty and customer service above all else. Within a year of his hire, Watson was named president; within four years, C-T-R's revenues had doubled. The company was going places.

Expansion

In 1917, C-T-R set up shop in Canada as International Business Machines Company, Ltd., though the U.S.-based parent didn't change its name. Watson emphasized leasing rather than sales, which conferred several advantages. It meant steady, predictable cash flow for C-T-R. It tied up less of customers' capital. And when C-T-R developed new products, clients weren't stuck with the old ones; they could lease C-T-R's new gear.

By 1924, C-T-R produced an ever-widening array of equipment. Some, like electric keypunch adding machines, survive today in advanced form. With European and Canadian offices, C-T-R had truly gone international, so Watson renamed the company International Business Machines Corporation (IBM). Under his savvy leadership, IBM actually grew through the Depression—though it also became somewhat cultlike, even introducing its own hymnal for employees with songs rhapsodizing over Watson's leadership.

Explosion

World War II enhanced IBM's prestige tremendously, even though two-thirds of its facilities shifted production to military weapons. Watson continued the salaries of employees called to war, a generous and patriotic step. And IBM's equipment was essential enough to the navy that its enlisted crewmen had their own rating, "IBM Operator," like "Machinist's Mate" or "Chief Yeoman."

Most important for IBM, WWII drove demand for its information processing technology. Thomas Watson Jr. took over IBM in 1952 and steered the company into computing, a field it owned for 30 years. He retired in 1971. In 1981, IBM introduced the IBM Personal Computer.

Sports
Bragging Rights

❖ ❖ ❖ ❖

*"Faster, higher, stronger" may be the motto for the
modern Olympic Games, but it's also an apt description
for the athletes who stretched the boundaries of human
endurance and initiated the Ironman competition.*

The old cliché "anything you can do, I can do better," along with a
spirited discussion over the true meaning of "better," ultimately led
to the creation of the Ironman Triathlon. During the awards ceremony for the 1977 Oahu Perimeter Relay, a running race for five-person teams held in Hawaii, the winning participants, among them
both runners and swimmers, became engrossed in a debate over
which athletes were more fit.

As both sides tossed biting barbs, rousing rhetoric, and snide
snippets back and forth, a third party entered the fray. Navy Commander John Collins, who was listening to the spirited spat, mentioned that a recent article in *Sports Illustrated* magazine claimed
that bike racers, especially Tour de France winner Eddy Merckx,
had the highest recorded "oxygen uptake" of any athlete ever measured, insinuating that cyclists were more fit than anyone. Collins
and his wife, Judy, suggested the only way to truly bring the argument to a rightful conclusion was to arrange an extreme endurance
competition, combining a swim of considerable length, a bike race
of taxing duration, and a marathon foot race. The first Ironman
Triathlon was held on February 18, 1978, in Honolulu, Hawaii.
Participants were invited to "Swim 2.4 miles! Bike 112 miles! Run
26.2 miles! Brag for the rest of your life." This rousing slogan has
since become the registered trademark of the event.

But the Ironman competition was not the first triathlon event.
The first competition to combine swimming (500-yard race), bike
racing (5-mile course), and running (2.8 miles) was held on September 25, 1974, in San Diego, California.

Toys & Games
The Truth About Monopoly

♦ ♦ ♦ ♦

When the nation was in the depths of the Great Depression, people needed a distraction. If they couldn't corner the stock market in the real world, why not become property moguls on the game board?

Monopoly is as American as apple pie or Norman Rockwell. Yet the story of how the most commercially successful board game came to be is a rather sordid tale. Apparently, the game's manufacturer, "creator" Charles Darrow, was not its true inventor at all. Darrow actually passed off Elizabeth Magie Phillips's concept as his own.

On January 5, 1904, Phillips, a.k.a. Lizzie J. Magie, received a patent for The Landlord's Game. It was based on economist Henry George's belief that landowners should be charged a single federal tax to extend equality to renters, from whom landlords were, in George's opinion, disproportionately profiting. Magie created an educational game, demonstrating how a single tax would control land speculation.

Except for the fact that properties were rented rather than purchased, The Landlord's Game was suspiciously identical to Parker Brothers' Monopoly, which premiered almost 30 years later. Through the years, The Landlord's Game was passed through communities, evolving along the way. It eventually picked up the name Monopoly, despite Magie's intention that the game be a teaching tool against the very idea of monopolies. The Atlantic City–inspired properties were also incorporated. This chain of events led to Charles Darrow, who learned the game at a hotel in Pennsylvania.

Enthralled, Darrow produced his own copies of the game and subsequently patented and sold "his" idea to Parker Brothers. The company conveniently forgot its refusal to buy the same game (under its old name) from Magie years earlier and promptly covered those tracks. It slyly bought out Magie's patent for a paltry $500, paid off at least three other "inventors" who had versions circulating, and cranked up its propaganda machine. Monopoly has since sold in excess of 250 million copies.

Inventions
Smile: You're on Camera Obscura
❖ ❖ ❖ ❖

Photography didn't begin with the daguerreotype (1839),
but Louis Daguerre's gadget was the breakthrough step.

Pinhole Cameras

Ironically, no photos exist of the earliest known camera pioneer, a
Chinese man named Mo Ti. It would be nice if his likeness had been
captured on film for the world to remember, but alas, technology in
China circa 400 B.C. was not quite there yet. Ancient history credits
Mo with uncovering a simple key principle: Light traveling through
a small hole will cast an image onto a surface. Unfortunately, there
was no efficient way to capture the image—which explains the lack
of paparazzi photographs of Mo.

Camera Obscuras

In about A.D. 1015, it came to light (so to speak) that a closed box
placed behind a pinhole camera makes a *camera obscura* (Latin:
"dark chamber"). At that time, Arab scholar Abu Ali al-Hasan ibn
Al-Haytham published a landmark optics text describing how the
device could project an image onto paper, enabling one to sit and
trace/draw the image. Limited, but useful.

The situation improved in the 1500s, when clever pioneers added
a magnifying lens to the pinhole. It inverted the image, but one
could later flip the sketch upright and paint in the colors. This was
impossible to do while tracing the image because the room's dark-
ness made it difficult for the artist to tell the paint colors apart.

Fixing the Image

During the 1700s, researchers discovered that light could change
certain substances, particularly silver compounds. In 1826, a
Frenchman named Joseph Niépce used a camera obscura and
about eight hours of exposure to fix an image onto bitumen (natural
asphalt). Where the light hit the bitumen, it hardened, and Niépce
dissolved away the unfixed remainder.

The image wasn't very clear, but it was a beginning. The oldest surviving example of what's called a *heliograph* evidently dates to about 1826, when the image was much improved. But a clever chap named Louis Daguerre grabbed onto Niépce's coattails a few years before Niépce's death in 1833. Since Daguerre also grabbed the credit, few people outside of France have ever heard of Niépce.

Daguerreotyping

Daguerre kept experimenting with chemicals until 1837 when he found a suitable light-sensitive combination involving iodine and mercury vapor. The subjects now had to stand still for "only" half an hour, which seems like forever—until you consider that the alternative was a much longer portrait sitting. Nearly all the earliest surviving photos of American icons such as Dolley Madison, young Horatio Alger at Harvard—even early pornography—are daguerreotypes.

Daguerre's camera was to photography what the first self-assembled mail-order Altair 8800 PC would become to young computer nerds in the late 1970s (including twenty-something Bill Gates). It set numerous clever souls to fiddling with camera technology. With the invention of negatives in 1835, multiple copies of photos became feasible. By 1871, image plates no longer required immediate development.

From Mainstream to Mass Market

George Eastman, whom you may accurately connect with Eastman Kodak, patented photo emulsion–coated paper and rollers in 1880. Farewell to cumbersome plates! Photography was about to go mainstream.

Kodak's Brownie, a $1 mass-market camera, hit the shelves in 1900. The 1900s would become photography's democratic age, where any fool could preserve whatever he or she wished on film. Before long, camera nuts would keep whole families waiting in the Model T so this or that fascinating item could be recorded for all posterity in the family album.

For whatever reason, the paparazzi wouldn't get saddled up until the 1930s. Sure took them long enough.

Television
Tutoring TV

❖ ❖ ❖ ❖

By combining daring documentaries and captivating commentary with educational programming and inventive entertainment, PBS helped transform television from boob tube to brain train.

The origin of the Public Broadcasting Service (PBS) can be traced to the very beginning of television. The network was originally founded as the Educational Television and Radio Center (ETRC) in November 1952, with funds provided by the Ford Foundation's Fund for Adult Education. The ETRC was originally intended to be a visual library of sorts, where educational programs produced by local television stations were exchanged and distributed to other stations. The network did not produce any material by itself.

In 1958, the network was renamed the National Educational Television and Radio Center (NETRC) and eventually increased its daily on-air broadcasting coverage from five to ten hours by adding programming that was originally produced by the BBC in England. In 1963, the network renamed itself National Educational Television (NET) and began airing controversial and biting documentaries and news programs, including its centerpiece show, the *NET Journal*. The network also provided a nationwide forum for innovative children's programming including *Mister Rogers' Neighborhood* (produced by WQED in Pittsburgh) and *Sesame Workshop* (produced by the Children's Television Network). However, the content of NET's more controversial programming and the expense of keeping the network operating caused the Ford Foundation to cut its funding, putting the future of the broadcaster in peril. In 1967, the U.S. government created the Corporation for Public Broadcasting, which eventually led to the creation of the PBS network on November 3, 1969. PBS began broadcasting on October 5, 1970, with NET staples such as *Sesame Street* and *Mister Rogers* in their lineup.

Unlike America's other networks, PBS does not air commercials to help pay the bills. They rely on government funding, corporate sponsorship, and public donations to keep the cameras rolling and the viewers satisfied.

Fads & Fashion
Birkenstocks

❖ ❖ ❖ ❖

Birkenstock sandals may be icons of the 1960s granola-munching crowd, but the company that makes them is more than 200 years old.

The Birkenstock company traces its roots to the German village of Langen-Bergheim, where in 1774 Johann Birkenstock was registered as a "Shoemaker." In 1897, his grandson, Konrad Birkenstock, introduced a major advance—the first contoured shoe lasts, which enabled cobblers to customize footwear.

At the time, there was a debate regarding whether it was healthier to train your feet to fit your shoes or to wear shoes that were made to support the foot's natural shape. The Birkenstock company worked to promote the second idea. By 1902, Birkenstock's flexible arch supports were being sold throughout Europe. During World War I, Birkenstock employees worked in clinics to design shoes especially for injured veterans.

It took the aching feet of a tourist to bring the Birkenstock sandal to America. In 1966, Margot Fraser came across Birkenstocks during a visit to a German spa. The shoes soothed her foot ailments, and she was hooked. Fraser secured the distribution rights and set out to sell these strange-looking German sandals back at her California home.

At first, the only places that would carry her Birkenstocks were health food stores. In the 1970s, as health food became more popular, people discovered Birkenstocks at the same time that they discovered tofu and alfalfa sprouts. Birkenstocks' association with "granola" and "hippies" came directly out of this.

Although the company has attempted to bring its sandals into the realm of high-end fashion (model Heidi Klum has designed her own line of Birkenstocks), this is one brand of footwear that keeps its "crunchy" connotations. Interestingly, researchers have discovered shoes more than 8,000 years old in a cave in Missouri, and the modern shoe that these most resembled was the Birkenstock! Crunchy or not, comfort never goes out of style.

REAL NAMES OF THE RICH AND FAMOUS

Entertainers, actors, musicians, and other celebrities change their names for many reasons. Some prefer to use nicknames; some have unusual names that are not glamorous or sophisticated; others allowed managers, studio executives, or agents to change their names. Entertainers from previous generations "Americanized" ethnic-sounding names to appeal to a wide audience. Uncovering a celebrity's real name often provides insight into his or her career and background.

Elvis Costello must have taken the first name of the world's most famous rock 'n' roller for a reason, but he doesn't like to talk about it. His real name is Declan Patrick MacManus.

Tom Cruise shortened his name from Thomas Cruise Mapother IV.

Doris Mary Ann Von Kappelhoff came to Hollywood and became sunny Doris Day.

Johnny Depp was born John Christopher Depp II.

Movie star Kirk Douglas was christened Issur Danielovitch.

Folk-rock legend Bob Dylan was Robert Zimmerman back in Minnesota.

Sean O'Fearna traveled to Hollywood and became one of America's greatest film directors, John Ford.

Spunky Judy Garland, who played Dorothy Gale in *The Wizard of Oz* (1939), was born with an unlikely name—Frances Ethel Gumm. It just doesn't have the same ring, does it?

It should be no surprise that Whoopi Goldberg is not the entertainer's real name. She was born Caryn Elaine Johnson.

When Archibald Alexander Leach hit the shores of America, he quickly evolved into Cary Grant.

Clothing designer Roy Halston Frowick thought one name, Halston, would be enough.

Paul Rubenfeld became Paul Reubens before settling on Pee-Wee Herman. We're not sure that change was for the better!

Food & Drink
The Birth of Good Humor

✦ ✦ ✦ ✦

*There is surprising controversy behind
this beloved slice of Americana.*

American suburbia: laughing children, lemonade stands, sprinklers, and, of course, that ice-cream truck emitting its soothing jingle.

In 1920, Harry Burt, an ice-cream shop owner in small-town Ohio, invented the first ice-cream confection on a stick. His store was selling a lollipop called the Jolly Boy Sucker as well as an ice-cream bar covered in chocolate. Inserting a wooden stick into the ice-cream bar made it "the new, clean, convenient way to eat ice cream."

Burt quickly patented his manufacturing process and started promoting the "Good Humor" bar in accordance with the popular belief that one's palate affects one's mood. He then sent out a fleet of shiny white trucks, each stocked with a friendly Good Humor Man and all the ice-cream bars kids could eat. By 1961, 200 Good Humor ice-cream trucks wound their way through suburbia.

Not Without a Little Bad Humor

The ice cream on a stick suddenly found itself facing solid competition from other be-sticked frozen treats. First there was Citrus Products Company, champion of the frozen sucker. Then came Popsicle Corporation, home to the Popsicle. Good Humor took these companies to court, alleging that Good Humor's patent gave them exclusive rights to frozen snacks on a stick. Popsicle countered that Good Humor only owned the rights to ice cream on a stick, whereas Popsicles were flavored water. When Popsicle attempted to add milk to its recipe, a decade-long court battle ensued, centering on what precise percentages of milk constitute ice cream, sherbet, and flavored water.

Popsicle and Good Humor have settled their differences and are now owned by the same corporation. As for the Good Humor Man, he's endangered but not extinct. Good Humor stopped making its ice-cream trucks in 1976, but they are still owned by smaller distributors.

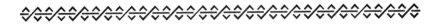

Language
X Marks the Spot

◆ ◆ ◆ ◆

Born in an era of peaceful paranoia, the offspring of the Cold War period of prosperity have been described as "underemployed, overeducated, intensely private, and unpredictable." However, the generation is best known by a single letter: X.

In mathematics, the letter *X* is used to represent a value that is unknown and unpredictable. The variable was easily transposed to indicate the uncertain characteristics of the generation of post–Baby Boomers brought into this world between 1965 and 1982.

The term "Generation X" actually dates to the December 1952 edition of a now-defunct travelogue magazine called *Holiday*. But it wasn't until 1964 that the phrase first started gaining steam. British author Jane Deverson was commissioned by *Woman's Own* magazine to conduct a series of interviews with teenagers of the time. Her study ascertained that the current generation of teenagers, dubbed "Generation X," slept together before they were married, didn't believe in God, disliked the Queen, and didn't respect their parents—conclusions the publishers deemed too controversial for use in their magazine. Deverson, with the cooperation and support of Hollywood correspondent Charles Hamblett, decided to publish her findings in book form. Their novel, titled *Generation X*, was a lively description of the trials and tribulations of a select group of children who would come of age in the 1960s and 1970s. Of course, today we know this generation as the Baby Boomers.

Although Deverson and Hamblett's book was published in 1964, the term Generation X didn't achieve worldwide acclaim until 1991 when author Douglas Coupland wrote his own novel entitled *Generation X: Tales for an Accelerated Culture.* Coupland's version is a fictional account of three strangers who distance themselves from society to get a better sense of who and what they are. Coupland describes the characters as "underemployed, overeducated, intensely private, and unpredictable." It was at this point that Generation X came to describe the generation born between 1965 and 1982.

Education
America Goes to Kindergarten

❖ ❖ ❖ ❖

*Kindergarten—which literally means "children's garden"
in German—is now considered a normal transition
between home and full-time schooling for young children.
But initially, America was slow to warm to the idea.*

Friedrich Froebel first conceived of kindergarten in 1840 as an introduction to art, mathematics, and natural history—a preeducation for
children of all classes, as opposed to the custodial religious services
that had been created for the offspring of the very poor. But after
kindergarten became associated with radical feminist ideals in its
German homeland and in Prussia, authorities became upset that
women's nurturing skills might be translated into a wider commercial sphere, and kindergarten was soon banned.

You Can't Keep a Good Idea Down

German liberals in exile, however, exported the idea to other
countries: Bertha Ronge took it to England, and her sister
Margarethe Meyer Schurz opened the first American (even if it was
German-speaking) kindergarten in Wisconsin in 1856. Elizabeth
Palmer Peabody created the first English-speaking kindergarten
three years later in Boston. But it was Susan Elizabeth Blow who
established the first public kindergarten, Des Peres School in St.
Louis, Missouri, in 1873. She taught children in the morning and
gave seminars to teachers in the afternoon. By 1883, a mere ten
years later, every St. Louis public school had a kindergarten, making
the city a model for the nation.

The movement really garnered momentum after Commissioner
of Education William Harris spoke to Congress on February 12,
1897, in support of public kindergartens: "The advantage to the
community in utilizing the age from four to six in training the hand
and eye...in training the mind...will, I think, ultimately prevail
in...the establishment of this beneficent institution in all the city
school systems of our country."

ACCIDENTAL INVENTIONS

A Magnetic Curiosity

It might surprise you to learn that a melted candy bar led to the invention of the microwave.

Percy Spencer didn't set out to find a faster way to make popcorn. A self-educated engineer, Spencer had contributed greatly to the Allied efforts in World War II by developing a speedier way of manufacturing *magnetrons,* the crucial element in radar systems used by Allied bombers.

One day in 1945, Spencer was standing near a magnetron at the Raytheon Company in Waltham, Massachusetts, when he noticed that the candy bar in his pocket was melting. Spencer wasn't the first person to notice the phenomenon, but he was the first to wonder what caused it. This was typical of Spencer's insatiable curiosity, which had led him from the Maine farm where he grew up to a career as the world's foremost authority on microwave radiation.

Spencer suspected that the melting was caused by microwaves emitted by the magnetron. To test his theory, he fetched a package of uncooked popcorn and held it near the magnetron. Sure enough, the popcorn heated and popped. Next, he tried cooking an egg—which exploded in the face of a curious coworker who got too close.

Soon after discovering this effect, Spencer patented and built the first microwave oven, the Radarange, a monster of an appliance that stood more than five feet tall, weighed 750 pounds, and cost $5,000—more than $40,000 by today's standards.

How does a microwave oven work? Simply put, microwave radiation causes the molecules in food to move, bumping into each other and causing heat. Objects whose molecules are too far apart (like air) or locked together (like a teacup) do not heat up.

The U.S. Navy gave Spencer the Distinguished Public Service Award for his work on military uses of the magnetron. But Spencer's greatest public service—as far as the rest of us are concerned—was developing the technology that enables us to cook popcorn, or nearly anything else, in a couple of minutes.

Holidays & Traditions
What About the Football Game?

❖ ❖ ❖ ❖

Most people were taught that Thanksgiving originated with the Pilgrims when they invited local Native Americans to celebrate the first successful harvest. Here's what really happened.

There are only two original accounts of the event we think of as the first Thanksgiving, both very brief. In the fall of 1621, the Pilgrims, having barely survived their first arduous year, managed to bring in a modest harvest. They celebrated with a traditional English harvest feast that included food, dancing, and games. The local Wampanoag Indians were there, and both groups demonstrated their skill at musketry and archery.

So that was the first Thanksgiving, right? Not exactly. To the Pilgrims, a thanksgiving day was a special religious holiday that consisted of prayer, fasting, and praise—not at all like the party atmosphere that accompanied a harvest feast.

Our modern Thanksgiving, which combines the concepts of harvest feast and a day of thanksgiving, is actually a 19th-century development. In the decades after the Pilgrims, national days of thanksgiving were decreed on various occasions, and some states celebrated a Thanksgiving holiday annually. But there was no recurring national holiday until 1863, when a woman named Sarah Josepha Hale launched a campaign for an annual celebration that would "greatly aid and strengthen public harmony of feeling."

Such sentiments were sorely needed in a nation torn apart by the Civil War. So, in the aftermath of the bloody Battle of Gettysburg, President Lincoln decreed a national day of thanksgiving that would fall on the last Thursday in November, probably to coincide with the anniversary of the Pilgrims' landing at Plymouth. The date was later shifted to the third Thursday in November, simply to give retailers a longer Christmas shopping season.

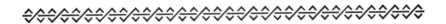

Written Word
A Dark and Stormy Night

❖ ❖ ❖ ❖

On a searingly bright, sunny, and radiant day that could only hold gently forth the promise of good things to come, an incredibly overdressed, overthinking Victorian baron named Edward George Bulwer-Lytton started his novel Paul Clifford *with these words: "It was a dark and stormy night." The rest, as they say, is history.*

A more discriminating modern editor might have argued that stormy nights are usually dark and, therefore, summarily thrown Bulwer-Lytton's book into the reject—or, at least, rewrite—pile. Bulwer-Lytton apparently didn't have that kind of working partner: His novels and plays were published intact—florid prose, overwrought descriptors, and all.

Nevertheless, "It was a dark and stormy night" is likely the most famous opening line in the world, perhaps on par with Herman Melville's "Call me Ishmael." It's also the key to Bulwer-Lytton's lasting but questionable reputation: His name is now synonymous with bad writing, as is evidenced by a California university's annual Bulwer-Lytton Fiction contest in which "wretched writers are welcome," and a judging panel collects and scrutinzes tremendously bad writing. Winners and especially noteworthy contestants are immortalized in a widely available book.

Perhaps a better illustration of Bulwer-Lytton's legacy is the fact that his line has been appropriated by two world-famous authors. Children's novelist Madeleine L'Engle started her book *A Wrinkle in Time* with "It was a dark and stormy night," and comic fans may remember that Snoopy's novel, which he was forever writing from his workstation on his doghouse roof, began the exact same way. L'Engle's book went on to win the Newbery Medal and had sold more than six million copies at the time of her death in 2007.

Given Bulwer-Lytton's influence on the literary world, perhaps it's better that he be remembered by another of his lines, taken from his play *Richelieu:* "The pen is mightier than the sword." Indeed!

REAL NAMES OF THE RICH AND FAMOUS

Entertainers, actors, musicians, and other celebrities change their names for many reasons. Some prefer to use nicknames; some have unusual names that are not glamorous or sophisticated; others allowed managers, studio executives, or agents to change their names. Entertainers from previous generations "Americanized" ethnic-sounding names to appeal to a wide audience. Uncovering a celebrity's real name often provides insight into his or her career and background.

He-man wrestler Hulk Hogan was christened with the feminine-sounding Terry Gene Bollea.

Actress Diane Keaton was born Diane Hall, which is alluded to in the title of her most famous film, *Annie Hall*, directed by former romantic partner Woody Allen.

Original movie Batman Michael Keaton was born Michael Douglas, but since there was already an actor named Michael Douglas, he changed his name.

CNN talk-show favorite Larry King changed his name from Larry Zeiger.

Even animal celebrities change their name once they arrive in Hollywood. The original Lassie was named Pal.

Director Spike Lee has a memorable name, shortened from Shelton Lee.

Superstar Madonna needs only one name, but she was christened Madonna Louise Veronica Ciccone.

Chico, Groucho, Harpo, and Zeppo Marx were born Leonard, Julius, Adolph, and Herbert.

Marilyn Monroe's name was fabricated by her studio; she was born Norma Jean Mortensen.

Demi Moore is actually Demetria Guynes. Her young husband was born Christopher Ashton Kutcher but shortened his name to star in *That '70s Show*. Her former husband and action superstar Bruce Willis likewise shortened his name from Walter Bruce Willis.

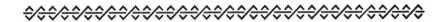

Business
The Power of the Wish Book

❖ ❖ ❖ ❖

*Every day, hundreds of thousands of people shop at Sears, but
few customers realize that this retail institution ushered in the
era of mass consumption that marked the 20th century.*

Sears, Roebuck and Co. began in 1886 when railroad station
agent Richard Sears founded the R. W. Sears Watch Company in
Minneapolis, Minnesota, to sell watches through the mail.

In 1887, Sears moved his watch business to Chicago, where
he hired young Alvah Roebuck to be the company's official watch
repairman. The following year, Sears wrote the company's first
catalog, the R. W. Sears Watch Co. catalog, which was sent to rural
communities around the country. The catalog offered potential
customers watches, diamonds, and jewelry, all with a money-back
guarantee. The latter was important to Sears's sales tactics because it
gained the trust of farmers and rural residents who had been swin-
dled by unscrupulous traveling salesmen.

In 1889, Sears sold his successful business to become a banker in
Iowa. But he ultimately became restless and missed the mail-order
business that he helped to pioneer. He returned to Minnesota and
repartnered with Roebuck. By 1893, the pair had moved to Chicago
as Sears, Roebuck and Co., and the Sears Catalog had grown to
196 pages. It expanded to 507 pages in 1895. In addition to jewelry
and watches, the catalog now offered sewing machines, furniture,
clothing, tools, saddles, shoes, musical instruments, and much more.

The Wish Book
Having worked on the railroad, Richard Sears knew what rural
communities were like, and during this era, roughly 65 percent
of Americans lived in rural areas. He knew that they had only the
local general store or the occasional traveling salesman to fill their
needs. The Sears Catalog, which customers began calling the "Wish
Book," allowed country folk a taste of the urban life. It transformed
the look, tastes, and attitudes of rural residents faster than anything

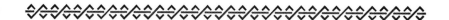

prior to the automobile. Sears wrote the descriptions for the catalog items in a folksy style, addressing each of his customers as "Kind Friend." The initiation of rural free mail delivery in 1896 and parcel post in 1913 enabled the company to send merchandise to the most isolated customers. By the turn of the century, Americans rated the Sears Catalog as their favorite book after the Bible. Most important, it allowed the rural population to take part in the mass consumption that defined the 20th century.

In 1895, Roebuck sold his interest in the company to Julius Rosenwald, who made the company stronger with his administrative skills. The company constructed a new $5 million mail-order plant on Chicago's West Side in 1906, with more than three million square feet of floor space, making it the largest business building in the world.

Sears retired from active participation in the company around 1908–1909, due to either poor health or a falling out with Rosenwald over the advertising budget. By the time he died in 1914, the catalog had evolved into a slick-looking publication with factual descriptions instead of the folksy-sounding tone preferred by Sears.

Sears Stores

Initially, Sears, Roebuck and Co. was solely a catalog business, and its success was dependent on rural America. However, by the early 1920s, the urban population outnumbered rural residents for the first time. Sears's new vice president, Robert E. Wood, lobbied for retail expansion, and in 1925, the first Sears store opened in Chicago. By 1933, the retail operation had grown to 400 stores, and store sales had topped mail-order revenue for more than two years. By that time, some of the mail-order merchandise was sold under the Sears brand name. This was the beginning of the Sears-associated lines known as Craftsman, Kenmore, and Die Hard.

The Sears "Big Book" catalog was discontinued in 1993.

Clubs & Organizations
Now They Have to Kill Us: The Bavarian Illuminati

❖ ❖ ❖ ❖

Before delving into the intracacies of the Illuminati's
origin, we'd recommend donning a tinfoil hat. It will
protect you against the New World Order conspiracy.

Q: What does *Illuminati* actually mean?
A: "The Enlightened." Like many religious faiths and secret societies, the original Bavarian Illuminati were founded in search of enlightenment. Prior groups with similar ideas used similar names.

Q: Did earlier Illuminati groups evolve into the Bavarian Illuminati?
A: Well, let's examine some earlier groups. Spain's *Alumbrados* ("enlightened") dated to the time of Columbus (1490s), suffered from the Inquisition, and developed a following in France (as the *Illuminés*) that endured until the late 1700s, when the French Revolution sat on them. The Rosicrucians started in Germany in the early 1600s, claiming lineage from the Knights Templar; by the late 1770s, their theme was becoming increasingly Egyptian. Many Rosicrucians were also Freemasons, a group with unbroken lineage to the present day.

They all had ideas in common with the Bavarian Illuminati; however, the Bavarian Illuminati sprang from the fertile mind of an iconoclastic law professor, not from a previous group. At most, the Bavarian group experienced some cross-pollination with other similar groups (notably Freemasonry), but that doesn't equal ancestral continuity.

Q: How'd the Bavarian group get going?
A: It began in Ingolstadt, Bavaria, with a German 20-something named Adam Weishaupt. In 1775, Weishaupt accepted a natural and canon law professorship at the University of Ingolstadt that had recently been vacated by an ejected Jesuit. Weishaupt was a maverick prone to anticlerical utterances: the anti-Jesuit, if you will. He soon managed to convince himself, without irony, that he was destined to lead humanity out of superstition toward enlightenment. Unsurprisingly, the Jesuits hated his guts.

Evidently, Weishaupt couldn't afford the Masons' fees, so he launched the Perfectibilists (later the Bavarian Illuminati) on May 1, 1776 (this would

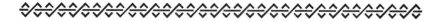

later fuel plentiful conspiracy theories about May Day celebrations). Fascinated with Egyptian stuff, he assigned his society a pyramid as its symbol.

Q: Did this group extend tentacles into business, government, and church?
A: To extend tentacles, one must first possess some. The Illuminati concerned themselves mostly with secret degrees and titles, plus absolute obedience to the chain of command with Weishaupt at the top. There is no evidence the group ever controlled anything. Illuminati were supposed to spurn superstition and strive toward rationalism to help perfect each other's mentalities. The meta-goal was clearing the earth of inhumanity and stupidity. It actually sounds more than a little like modern Scientology, at least in terms of stated goals (as opposed to reality).

Q: That sounds like the vision of a new world order.
A: It is. The modern conspiracy question rests not in the nature of the original Bavarian Illuminati, which is well documented, but rather to what degree it has survived to exert control over modern affairs. As any nightly news broadcast will show, their work didn't make a lasting dent in either inhumanity or stupidity.

Q: Why not?
A: Because inhumanity and stupidity are so very human, perhaps? Think of the Illuminati as a die intended to mint enlightened persons. This die possessed one fundamental crack: Its concept of enlightenment categorically discouraged questioning the autocratic leader. That's no way to run a freethinkers' group. In such groups, true freethinkers drift away, leaving only quasi-freethinkers who don't argue with the Maximum Leader.

Q: But the organization still grew. Why?
A: It only grew for a brief time, and that had much to do with the work of Baron Adolph Knigge, who joined in the 1780s. Knigge was both well-known and a capable administrator who gave the Illuminati a great deal of practical Masonic wisdom, helping sort out Weishaupt's rather rinky-dink organization. By its peak in 1784, it had several thousand members.

Q: What sent it downhill?
A: First there was the inevitable squabble between Weishaupt and Knigge, which ended with Knigge telling Weishaupt where to shove his little fiefdom. It's tempting to blame the whole thing on Weishaupt, but the evidence indicates that Knigge had an ego to match Weishaupt's and could be just as great a horse's posterior. The deathblow came when Duke Karl Theodor of Bavaria banned all unauthorized secret societies.

Q: Did that simply shatter the organism into many pieces that grew independently?
A: Evidence suggests that the ban, plus police raids, shattered the Illuminati into dying pieces rather than living ones. Sacked from teaching, Weishaupt fled to a neighboring state and died in obscurity. Others tried to keep Illuminati islets alive, without evident success. Like witchcraft of an earlier age, the actual practice became far rarer than the accusation—and official paranoia over secret societies and sedition kept the term *Illuminati* cropping up.

Q: So, why does the intrigue linger?
A: Perhaps for the same reason the Freemasons, Knights Templar, and so forth keep showing up in conspiracy theories: When someone wants to point to a potential conspiracy, he or she can usually find some bit of circumstantial evidence hinting a connection to one of the above. Those who disagree, of course, must be toadies of the conspiracy! It's an argument that can't end.

But insofar as we are guided by actual evidence, the Bavarian Illuminati did end. Whatever world conspiracies there might be today, it's doubtful any descend directly from Weishaupt's ideological treehouse club.

"But I would have executed much greater things, had not government always opposed my exertions, and placed others in situations which would have suited my talents."
—ADAM WEISHAUPT

"This is the great object held out by this association; and the means of attaining it is illumination, enlightening the understanding by the sun of reason which will dispel the clouds of superstition and of prejudice."
—ADAM WEISHAUPT

Household Items
Clothes Encounters

❖ ❖ ❖ ❖

This was the way we washed our clothes…

Once upon a time, people washed clothes by hand, pounding them against stones or using such high-tech gadgets as washboards. It was an arduous process that involved hauling or pumping water, heating it in large kettles, and scrubbing with caustic substances such as lye soap. No wonder the *Lady's Book* of 1854 said, "Our spirits fall with the first rising of steam from the kitchen, and only reach a natural temperature when the clothes are neatly folded in the ironing basket." It's also no wonder that lots of folks tried to come up with gadgets that would make washing clothes easier.

In 1797, a man named Nathaniel Briggs was granted the first U.S. patent for "an improvement in washing clothes." Unfortunately, the records of the patent were destroyed when a fire broke out at the patent office in 1836, so we have no idea what that device looked like.

The early washing machines that we do know about were rotating drums with an attached crank—you put in the soap, water, and clothes, closed the door, and started cranking. C. H. Farnham received a U.S. patent for a hand-cranked washing machine in 1835. From there, it was an obvious leap to attach a motor to the crank and power it with steam, electricity, or gasoline.

Who gets credit for first attaching an electric motor to a washing machine and thereby "inventing" the electric washer? Hard to tell. Many sources credit Alva J. Fisher, who received a patent for such a washer in 1910. But other people had received patents for motor-driven washers before Fisher, and Fisher did not claim to have invented the electric washer in his patent. Oddly, the Hurley Machine Company had been selling the electric Thor washer, designed by Fisher, since 1907. While Hurley is no longer in business, two companies that began selling electric washers about the same time are Maytag and Whirlpool.

Television
Tune In Next Week...

❖ ❖ ❖ ❖

What's on television tonight? Nowadays, this question
might send you to the Internet or to your cable network's
on-screen guide. But once upon a time, viewers relied
on the TV Guide *to answer this age-old question.*

TV Guide is the iconic American weekly magazine that lists television programming for the upcoming week. In addition to series
listings, *TV Guide* includes feature articles, industry gossip, and
interviews with television stars and behind-the-scenes personnel.

Launched in 1953, the magazine was the brainchild of Walter
Annenberg, the owner and publisher of Triangle Publications. His
goal was to provide a service for viewers, increase their enjoyment
of the medium, and serve the television industry. Annenberg got
the idea when he noticed *TV Digest*, which had been listing Philly's

TV programming since 1948, as well
as Chicago's *TV Forecast* and New
York's *TV Guide.* He envisioned a
larger-scale magazine that would
provide the same information on a
national level.

Annenberg purchased the *TV
Digest, TV Forecast,* and *TV Guide,*
and he contracted with TV magazine
publishers in other cities to buy his
nationally based guide. Annenberg
quickly gained control of television-guide publishing, gathered staffs
in each major city, and established his associate Merrill Panitt as the
editorial director. What might have been a logistical nightmare for
other publishers—gathering and organizing data in different time
zones for different markets—was right up Triangle Publications'
alley; it already published such data-driven guides as *The Daily Racing Form,* which listed every horse in every race at various tracks in
different regions across the country.

The first issue of *TV Guide* featured Lucille Ball's new baby on the cover, commemorating one of the most popular events in television history. The handy 5-by-7½-inch guide sold one and a half million of the debut issue at fifteen cents per copy. By the 1960s, *TV Guide* was the most read and circulated magazine in the United States. With its familiar red-and-white logo immediately recognizable, the guide was sold at the counters of grocery stores, making it as accessible and indispensable as milk. The company was sold in 2008 for a single dollar—an amount less than the cost of a single issue.

10 Countries with the Most Televisions

Country	Number of Televisions per 1,000 People
1. Bermuda	1,010
2. Monaco	771
3. United States	741
4. Malta	703
5. Japan	679
6. Canada	655
7. Guam	629
8. Virgin Islands	626
9. Germany	624
10. Finland	613

SOURCE: CIA WORLD FACTBOOK

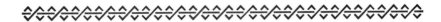

Food & Drink
Sushi: The Hallmark of Japan's Fast-food Nation

*While the combination of fish and rice has been a
mainstay in Asian cuisine for millennia, sushi as we
know it today began with an entrepreneurial mind, lots
of street carts, and a little bit of sumo wrestling.*

Complexities in Fish Fermentation

Modern sushi consumers are accustomed to sushi of the fast-food
variety—throw rice on seaweed, add a strip of fish, and presto, you
have a snack that is both nutritious and delicious. Yet the earliest
type of sushi, known as *Narezushi,* took more than six months to
prepare and was so smelly that it was eventually replaced by the
stink-free sushi that we know today.

The sushi prototype actually originated in China and was then
perfected in Japan. Before the days of refrigeration, innovations in
fish preservation abounded. One popular method was to press fish
between layers of salt for months at a time. At some point, it was
discovered that fish would ferment faster if it was rolled in rice *and*
pickled with salt. After the fermentation was complete, the rice was
discarded, and the fish was eaten alone.

This method of fish preservation was popular in China and
Southeast Asia, but it was only in Japan that the process eventually
evolved into the snack-size morsels of sushi. The original Narezushi
was created by a complex process that involved salting and pickling
fish for more than a month, piling the pickled fish in between layers of cool rice, sealing everything into a barrel, then pickling some
more. This drawn-out exercise created a sourness that was awful to
smell but delectable to the taste buds.

It's difficult to popularize a food that's six months in the making, but this all changed with the invention of rice vinegar, which
decreased fermentation time. Sushilike dishes were popular during Japan's Muromachi Period (1338–1573) and again during the
Azuchi-Momoyama period (1574–1600). The first type of sushi to

gain widespread popularity was the Oshizushi of Osaka, which was rectangular in shape and consisted of alternating layers of rice, fish, and sometimes pickled vegetables. Yet even this popular sushi, quite literally, stank.

Sushi Served Up Fast

The process of fermentation had to be abandoned completely before sushi could come out smelling like roses—or at least not like old fish. It wasn't until the rise of a large urban city, where fish could be caught and consumed in plenty within a 24-hour time frame, that modern sushi became possible. In late 18th-century Edo (Tokyo), it became common to place a strip of raw fish on a mound of rice. This is called *nigiri-zushi,* or handmade, sushi.

The popularization of nigiri is usually attributed to early 19th-century entrepreneur and chef Yohei Hanaya. Legend has it that he was throwing a dinner party in 1824 when he realized he didn't have enough fish to go around. As a solution, he placed small slabs of fish on large mounds of rice. The entrepreneur in Hanaya realized he'd just discovered a gold mine.

Hanaya transformed his off-the-cuff innovation into a fast-food phenomenon. He sold his nigiri sushi in carts throughout the streets of Edo, and soon others opened sushi carts of their own. Hanaya opened his first cart in front of Ryukoku Temple, where frequent sumo wrestling tournaments created an ongoing glut of pedestrians. The idea was that sushi is a finger food that can quickly be prepared and eaten, right on the street. The fish in these early sushi were often cooked, marinated, or heavily salted, so dipping in soy sauce was not necessary. Sushi went from food carts to restaurants throughout Edo to restaurants throughout Japan and eventually gained its current status as a worldwide food favorite.

The word sushi *actually refers to the pickled or vinegared rice, not the fish itself.* Sashimi *refers to the raw fish.*

Mythology & Folklore
Reward: One Lost Island

❖ ❖ ❖ ❖

*Did the legendary island of Atlantis ever really
exist? Or did Plato make the whole thing up?*

It's hard to believe that Plato, an early Greek philosopher, was the
type to start rumors. But in two of his dialogues, *Timaeus* and *Critias,* he refers to what has become one of the most famous legends of
all time: the doomed island of Atlantis.

In *Timaeus,* Plato uses a story told by Critias to describe where
Atlantis existed, explaining that it "came forth out of the Atlantic
Ocean, for in those days the Atlantic was navigable; and there was
an island situated in front of the straits which are by you called the
Pillars of Heracles; the island was larger than Libya and Asia put
together, and was the way to other islands . . . ." Not only that, but
Plato also divulges the details of its fate: "afterwards there occurred
violent earthquakes and floods; and in a single day and night of
misfortune all your warlike men in a body sank into the earth, and
the island of Atlantis in like manner disappeared in the depths of
the sea. For which reason the sea in those parts is impassable and
impenetrable, because there is a shoal of mud in the way; and this
was caused by the subsidence of the island." In *Critias,* the story
revolves around Poseidon, the mythical god of the sea, and how the
kingdom of Atlantis attempted to conquer Athens.

Although many ascribe Plato's myth to his desire for a way to
emphasize his own political theories, historians and writers perpetuated the idea of the mythical island for centuries, both in fiction and
nonfiction. After the Middle Ages, the story of the doomed civilization was revisited by such writers as Francis Bacon, who published
The New Atlantis in 1627. In 1870, Jules Verne published his classic
Twenty Thousand Leagues Under the Sea, which includes a visit to
sunken Atlantis aboard Captain Nemo's submarine *Nautilus.* And
in 1882, *Atlantis: The Antediluvian World* by Ignatius Donnelly was
written to prove that Atlantis did exist—initiating much of the Atlantis mania that has occurred since that time. The legendary Atlantis

continues to surface in today's science fiction, romantic fantasy, and even mystery stories.

More recently, historians and geologists have attempted to link Atlantis to the island of Santorini (also called Thera) in the Aegean Sea. About 3,600 years ago, one of the largest eruptions in the history of planet Earth occurred at the site of Santorini: the Minoa, or Thera, eruption. This caused the volcano to collapse, creating a huge caldera or "hole" at the top of the volcanic mountain. Historians believe the eruption caused the end of the Minoan civilization on Thera and the nearby island of Crete, most likely because a tsunami resulted from the massive explosion. Since that time, most of the islands, which are actually a complex of overlapping shield volcanoes, grew from subsequent volcanic eruptions around the caldera, creating what is now the volcanic archipelago of islands called the Cycladic group.

Could this tourist hot spot truly be the site of the mythological island Atlantis? Some say that Plato's description of the palace and surroundings at Atlantis were similar to those at Knossos, the central ceremonial and cultural center of the Minoan civilization. On the scientific end, geologists know that eruptions such as the one at Santorini can pump huge volumes of material into the air and slump other parts of a volcanic island into the oceans. To the ancient peoples, such an event could literally be translated as an island quickly sinking into the ocean. But even after centuries of study, excavation, and speculation, the mystery of Atlantis remains unsolved.

Dan Brown's blockbuster novel The Da Vinci Code *reignited public interest in Atlantis in a roundabout way. Brown's story referenced the Knights Templar, an early Christian military order with a dramatic history that involved bloodshed, exile, and secrets—one of which was that they were carriers of ancient wisdom from the lost city of Atlantis.*

What Do You Mean by That?

Bringing Home the Bacon

This expression is used to denote the person in a marriage who earns the larger monetary share of household income, but it once meant exactly what it says. In the 12th century, at the church of Dunmow in Essex County, England, a certain amount of cured and salted bacon was awarded to the couple that could prove (we're not quite sure how) that they had lived in greater bliss than any of their competitors. The earliest record of this contest was 1445, but evidence exists that the custom had already been in effect for at least two centuries. In the 16th century, proof of devotion was determined through questions asked by a jury of unmarried men and women. The curious pork prize continued, albeit in irregular intervals, until the late 19th century.

Gone to Pot

This phrase, meaning not much good for anything, originated in the Elizabethan era with the forerunner of beef stew, when any tidbit of meat too small for a regular portion was thrown into a big pot always boiling over the fire.

Clean as a Whistle

Since when has the whistle been synonymous with cleanliness? Back in the prehistoric day when reeds were used to make whistling sounds, they had to be free of all debris to attain the desired tone.

In Cahoots

When two or more people are up to no good, they're said to be "in cahoots." The phrase may well come from France, where a small cabin was called a *cahute*. If these cabins were occupied by bandits and robbers planning a heist, the name of the cottages may have become a sort of shorthand to signify what went on inside them.

Running Amok

When a crowd of people begins to panic, it's said to "run amok." The phrase comes from the Malay word *amok*, which means "violent and out of control." It is said that this is what the excited Malaysians yelled when they first encountered Europeans.

Computers & Cyberspace
The Floppy Disk Story

❖ ❖ ❖ ❖

Two engineers walk into a bar…

The personal computer was made possible by two crucial developments: the microprocessor and the floppy disk. The first provided the PC with its brains. The second gave it a long-term memory—one that would last after the computer was turned off.

But who invented the floppy disk? Dr. Yoshiro Nakamatsu claims he developed the basic technology—a piece of plastic coated with magnetic iron oxide—back in 1950 and later licensed the technology to IBM. IBM has never acknowledged these claims, but it does own up to an "ongoing relationship" with Dr. Nakamatsu, who holds more than 3,000 patents and also claims to have invented the CD, DVD, and digital watch.

At any rate, IBM made the first floppy disks, which were eight inches in diameter, encased in a paper jacket, and held a whopping 80 kilobytes of memory. But these disks were too big for personal computers, so in 1976 two engineers sat down in a Boston bar with An Wang of Wang Labs to discuss a new format. When they asked Dr. Wang how big the new floppies should be, he pointed to a cocktail napkin and said, "About that size." The engineers took the napkin back to California and made the floppies exactly the same size as the napkin: 5¼ inches.

The 5¼-inch floppy became standard in early personal computers, but they were easy to damage or get dirty, and as PCs got smaller and smaller, the disks were still too large. Various companies released smaller formats, but it wasn't until Apple Computer incorporated a 3½-inch floppy drive in its Macintosh computer that things began to change. The new disks had a stiff plastic case and a sliding metal cover to protect the data surface, and they stored 360K, 720K, and later 1.44 megabytes. The writing was on the disk, and these days, the original floppies have gone the way of carbon paper and mimeograph machines.

Personal Hygiene
Paleolithic Children Did Not Have to Brush Their Teeth Before Bed

If modern dentistry's mandate to brush three times a day seems excessive, it becomes even more so compared to zero times a day. The origins of toothbrushing lie with the Neolithic Revolution, when humans switched from hunting and gathering to agriculture.

A world without toothpaste, toothbrushes, and biannual visits to the dentist may be difficult for the contemporary mind to grasp, but there was a time when modern exercises in dental hygiene were simply not necessary. The primary purpose of toothbrushing is to rub abrasive substances against the teeth so as to dislodge food and scratch away plaque. Before agriculture, the hunter-gatherer diet included harder, uncooked foods that worked as natural abrasives. This diet was also low in the types of carbohydrates and sugars that lead to cavities. Hunter-gatherer groups dislodged food from their mouths with sharpened sticks, and they chewed on substances with antiseptic properties to reduce oral infection, but toothbrushing as we know it wasn't done.

Junk Food Gets the Brush-off
And then came the Neolithic Revolution, with its carbohydrate-rich staple crops and an abundance of soft, cooked foods. As dental cavities became a widespread problem, innovations in toothbrush and toothpaste developed. Since the very beginnings of the written word, references to dental cavities and the multifarious ways to get rid of them can be found. The ancient Egyptians probably used their fingers in lieu of a toothbrush and made abrasive tooth powders from the ashes of ox hooves, myrrh, burnt and powdered eggshells, and pumice. The ancient Greeks and Romans were fond of toothpaste that included crushed bones and oyster shells. Ancient Persian records indicate the use of, among other things, the burnt shells of snails. Meanwhile, in China, the ingenious use of the chew stick became popular around 1600 B.C. One end of a

stick was chewed down into a frayed brush, while the other end was sharpened into a toothpick: brushing and flossing in one easy-to-use tool.

China also appears to be one early source of the bristled tooth-brush. The bristles were made of the hairs of wild boar, which were placed into a carved bone or bamboo handle. Early toothbrushes—no matter where in the world they popped up—were usually made from bone and animal hair. By the early 1800s, bristled toothbrushes were widespread in Europe and Japan. Yet even at this time, it was still popular to simply use a toothpick and homemade toothpaste. Toothbrushing as it is known today began with the mass manufacture and commercialization of toothbrushes and toothpaste.

Uncle Sam Wants YOU to Brush Your Teeth!

It was William Addis of late 18th-century England who first developed a toothbrush that was meant for mass manufacture. The toothbrush was patented in the United States in 1857, and in 1939, the first electric toothbrush was developed in Switzerland. Synthetic materials, particularly nylon, came to replace animal hair as bristles, and bone handles were replaced with plastic handles. Yet even with all these innovations, toothbrushing was not pervasive in the United States until after World War II, when GIs were mandated to brush their teeth daily. Since then, advances in toothbrush and especially toothpaste technology have powered ahead at incredible speed, as companies compete to create the perfect product of oral hygiene—fresh mint, whitening, plaque control, you name it. Meanwhile, organizations such as the American Dental Association and the National Institute of Dental and Craniofacial Research keep busy to ensure best practices in oral hygiene are followed nationwide. Thus, children in the United States don't garner much sympathy when they refuse to brush their teeth before going to bed, even if their Paleolithic peers got away with it.

Places & Landmarks
The Not-so-windy City

❖ ❖ ❖ ❖

Called the "Windy City" for well over a century, Chicago is famed for its swirling wind currents. But all may not be as it seems. Both the city's nickname and the assumptions behind it are "airy" affairs.

Perhaps the most interesting aspect of Chicago's "Windy City" nickname is the fact that there's no certainty about its origin. But there are theories. One possible explanation appeared in an article in the September 11, 1886, edition of the *Chicago Tribune*. It claimed that the nickname referred to the "refreshing lake breezes" blowing off Lake Michigan. Another explanation completely ignores climate and credits 19th-century Chicago promoters William Bross and John Stephen Wright with inspiring the phrase. In this colorful version of the story, witnesses to the duo's loud boasts eventually branded them "windbags." The backhanded term "Windy City" grew from this, and the rest is history.

A Lot of Hot Air

The origin of Chicago's nickname may be up for debate, but the veracity of its claim is not. One need only consult weather records that display average annual wind speeds for U.S. cities. Certainly, if Chicago's "Windy City" tag derives from its much-celebrated wind currents, this would be the place to confirm it.

According to National Climatic Data Center findings from 2003, Blue Hill, Massachusetts, blows harder than all other U.S. cities, with a 15.4-mile-per-hour average annual wind speed. Dodge City, Kansas, and Amarillo, Texas, nab second- and third-place honors, with wind speeds of 14.0 mph and 13.5 mph, respectively. Lubbock, Texas, comes in tenth on the center's top-ten list with a 12.4-mph clocking. How fast do air currents move in the notorious Windy City? With average annual winds pushing the needle to just 10.3 mph, it appears Chicago's blustery status is full of hot air.

Food & Drink
The Toll House Mystery

❖ ❖ ❖ ❖

*We know who invented the chocolate chip cookie, and
we know when. But we're not exactly sure how.*

In the 1930s, Ruth Wakefield and her husband operated the Toll
House Inn near Whitman, Massachusetts. Wakefield was a dietitian,
cookbook author, popular food lecturer, and an excellent cook.

One day, she was mixing up a batch of Butter Drop cookies, a
popular sugar cookie found in recipe books dating back to the colonial days.

According to oft-repeated legend, the recipe called for baker's
chocolate, but Ruth didn't have any, so she used a bar of Nestlé
semisweet chocolate instead. But why would a sugar cookie recipe
include baker's chocolate? Who knows? In any event, Wakefield
broke up the bar and added it to the dough.

Or did she? George Boucher, who was head chef at the Toll
House Inn, told a different story. According to Boucher, the chocolate accidentally fell into the mixing bowl from a shelf just above it,
knocked off by the vibrations of the electric mixer. Mrs. Wakefield
was going to throw the batter out, but Boucher convinced her to try
baking it, and the rest is cookie history. (Doubters might wonder
why the chocolate would be sitting on a shelf unwrapped, just waiting to fall into the mix, but never mind them.)

The official Nestlé version of the story states that Wakefield
expected the chocolate to melt and was surprised when it didn't. But
as she was an experienced cook and knew her way around a kitchen,
it seems more likely that she was intentionally trying to create a new
recipe and added the semisweet chocolate on purpose.

Of this there is no doubt: In 1939, Nestlé invented chocolate
chips specifically for the cookies and printed the recipe on the bag.
Today, Toll House Cookies are perhaps the most popular cookie in
history.

Clubs & Organizations
Girl Scout Beginnings: Southern Dames and Warfare Games

❖ ❖ ❖ ❖

Youth movements and bloody wars generally don't go hand in hand, but the origin of the scouting movement for both girls and boys is inextricably linked with patriotism and war.

The founder of Scouting, Robert Stephenson Smyth Baden-Powell, doesn't have much in common with the founder of the Girl Scouts in the United States, Juliette Gordon Low—at least not on paper. For one, Baden-Powell, an Englishman, started his career as a military officer. He fought in many wars in the late 1800s, and as a military leader, he often incorporated wilderness survival skills to help his men survive. When his troops were besieged in the Second Boer War, a group of local youths helped out by carrying messages and supplies. This got Baden-Powell to thinking about hands-on youth education. If youth were taught survival and leadership skills, basic military maneuvers, and community service, then not only would the community as a whole benefit, but youth would learn about team-work and civic responsibility.

And thus the Boy Scouts were born. In 1908, Baden-Powell published *Scouting for Boys,* which is considered the first edition of the *Boy Scout Handbook.* From there, the Boy Scouts took off, and troops formed throughout the United Kingdom and around the world. The Scouting movement was international in focus from the beginning, since Baden-Powell's philosophy included multicultural acceptance and the benefits of physical and mental growth for all children, everywhere. So it's not surprising that soon after the formation of the Boy Scouts, girls were enthusiastically welcomed into the movement as well.

The first Girl Scouts came in the form of Girl Guides, a group that was formed in 1910 by Agnes Baden-Powell, Robert's sister. And then, in 1912, Juliette Gordon Low founded the Girl Scouts in the United States. By the time Low learned about the Scouting move-

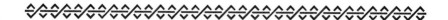

ment, she had spent a lifetime in community service. She was born in Savannah, Georgia, and had spent most of her young years traveling, learning, and serving her community. When she met Agnes Baden-Powell in 1911, her plan had been to emigrate to France. But after learning about the new youth movement, she moved to Scotland to lead a Girl Scout troop. She soon realized, however, that she wanted to bring what she had learned back to the United States.

Low wasted no time. Once back in Savannah, Georgia, she called a friend and is reported to have exclaimed "I've got something for the girls of Savannah, and all of America, and all the world, and we're going to start it tonight!" On March 12, 1912, Low convened the first meeting of the American Girl Guides. The name was changed to Girl Scouts the following year.

The movement spread with dizzying speed. There was an excitement in encouraging girls to take part in activities that were so different from the mechanic drudgery of school lessons. From outdoor adventure activities to bake sales to volunteer work at hospitals, girls were expected to do it all. Education was transformed from writing and copying to doing. The philosophy was learning through experience and making the community a better place in the process. Not only that, the Girl and Boy Scout movements actively recruited minority members as well as those with physical and mental disabilities. An effort was made to create groups in poorer areas.

World War I broke out soon after the creation of the Girl Scouts, and the movement's root in helping one's country during war was immediately put to practical use. Girl Scout troops volunteered in hospitals, sold war bonds, and learned how to conserve resources. Since that time, the Girl Scouts have become the largest worldwide educational organization for girls—and it all began with one spirited troop in Savannah.

"Ours is a circle of friendships united by ideals."
—Juliette Gordon Low

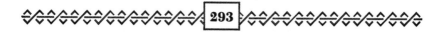

Toys & Games
The Game of Kings

❖ ❖ ❖ ❖

Chess is a game where protecting the king is key. So it should come
as little surprise that it may once have been a favorite of royalty.

Often called the "royal game," chess is one of the world's most popular games and is enjoyed by millions of people. It is played informally by friends, in clubs, in tournaments, and even in international championships. In its design and strategy, chess delightfully meshes simplicity with complexity and has attracted competitors the world over; by phone, by mail, and now by Internet, players carry on long, thoughtful games that can last years.

Chess has its roots in India and dates to the sixth century A.D. It arrived in Europe in the tenth century, where it soon became a court favorite of the nobility. Europe is the likely origin of the modern pieces, which include a king and queen and other notable ranks of the Middle Ages—eight pawns, a pair of knights, a pair of bishops, and a pair of rooks. The latter pieces were called *chariots* in the Persian game before transforming to the castle pieces in the Westernized version.

The game is played on an eight-by-eight board of 64 squares. Players take alternating turns, and the game continues until one player is able to "checkmate" the opponent's king, a strategic move that prevents the king from escaping an attack on the next turn. The game can also end in a draw in certain scenarios. Each piece moves according to specific rules that dictate how many squares it can traverse and in what direction. The queen is generally considered the most powerful piece on the board—perhaps a nod to the power the queen wielded when the game arrived in Europe.

The first modern chess tournament was held in London in 1851 and was won by Adolf Anderssen, who would become a leading chess master. Since then, computer programmers have developed game strategy using artificial intelligence, and for years there were attempts to create a computer that could defeat the best human players. This finally happened in 1997 when a computer defeated world champion Garry Kasparov.

PATENT WARS

So you think the origins of some things—the sewing machine, the modern airplane, the cotton gin, office chairs—ought to be pretty clear-cut? Think again: Patent wars have been around almost as long as the patents system itself.

The Wright Brothers vs. Glenn Curtiss: Even Alexander Graham Bell got involved in this battle over the invention of a critical piece of airplane machinery. Graham Bell's company, the Aerial Experiment Association, hired aeronaut Glenn H. Curtiss to create an airplane. Despite being warned off by Wilbur and Orville Wright, Curtiss went ahead with his design, which led the Wrights to file several lawsuits against him and his company. Curtiss eventually lost the case; his company, the Curtiss Aeroplane & Motor Company, Ltd., merged with the Wright Aeronautical Corporation just before Curtiss's death in 1930.

Elias Howe vs. Isaac Singer: Something as small as a needle's eye was the lynchpin to this case. Isaac Singer's sewing machine was the first commercially successful sewing machine. However, his machine used the same stitch as Elias Howe's sewing machine, and Howe sued Singer for use of the stitch. Howe won the case, and Singer was forced to pay him a per-use royalty fee.

Netflix vs. Blockbuster: While customers of Netflix and Blockbuster were busy enjoying the fact that both companies offered home delivery of movies, the two were duking it out in court. Netflix challenged Blockbuster for patent infringement of its system; Blockbuster claimed that the former had never patented the method by which it would lease out its movies. The argument eventually fizzled out less than a year later: Both companies agreed to settle out of court.

Herman Miller vs. Teknion: Herman Miller's Aeron chair, which was designed in the mid-1990s, has made a lot of office workers very comfortable, and it has made Herman Miller a lot of money. Ergonomic chairs became practically de rigueur in the workplace, and other companies were quick to jump on the bandwagon. But Herman Miller didn't become an industry leader for nothing: When Teknion, a Japanese company that also makes office furniture, introduced their own version of the Aeron, Herman Miller was quick to sue over a long list of design-oriented patents. The suit was settled in 2007.

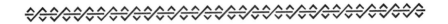

Fads & Fashion
Popular Hairstyles Through the Ages

❖ ❖ ❖ ❖

Humans are the only animals to willingly and consciously cut their hair, and although this ability definitely has its perks, it has also been the source of many woes and bad decisions. Here are some of the more extreme, time-consuming, gravity-defying looks that have graced our crowns through the ages.

Powdered Wigs

In the 18th century, hygiene was hardly what it is today, and head lice were a rampant problem, so wigs were worn to cover shaved heads. But powdered wigs themselves were hotbeds for lice, roaches, and other critters. Still, wigs were worn until the end of the 18th century, when an expensive tax on white powder made the trend die down.

Pompadour

In a pompadour, the hair is gelled back, giving it a sleek, wet look, and the front is pushed forward. The look is often associated with the 1950s, when it was worn by the likes of Elvis Presley and Johnny Cash. But Madame de Pompadour, a mistress to King Louis XV and a fashionista in her time, originally donned the look in the 1700s. The style is still worn by retro rockabilly types, including Brian Setzer.

The Flip

This spunky, youthful style was mega-popular among hordes of modern women throughout the 1960s. Shoulder-length hair was back-combed or teased slightly at the top, then the ends were curled up in a "flip" with rollers or a curling iron. Depending on the age of the woman and her willingness to push the envelope, the flip was combined with the bouffant, which meant that it got bigger and puffier. Mary Tyler Moore sported the classic flip on *The Dick Van Dyke Show,* and Jackie Kennedy had her own more conservative version, too. Later, the style became so ubiquitous it was nicknamed "beauty pageant hair" or "Miss America hair," because for years nearly every contestant sported flip after perfect flip.

The Mop Top

The influence of The Beatles on popular culture was unlike anything the world had ever seen. Girls and boys alike mimicked the boyish charm of these Liverpool lads, especially when it came to hairstyles. Longer, over the ears, shaggy, and generally floppy on all sides, the mop top was also sported by another mega-band of the time, The Rolling Stones.

Afro

Birthed by the black pride movement, the afro represents a time when African Americans stopped applying harsh chemicals to achieve something close to Caucasian texture and style to their hair. In the 1960s, the afro was a political statement, but today it is worn as fashion. Anyone with extremely curly hair can adopt the style.

Mohawk

Originally worn in Native American cultures, the mohawk reappeared sometime in the 1970s, along with the punk rock movement. At its most extreme, the mohawk, called the *mohican* in the United Kingdom, featured a stripe of hair sticking straight up and running down the middle of the head, with the sides shaved. It made a statement about not giving in to social standards. However, with the advent of the metrosexual "fauxhawk" (small spike, not shaved on sides), the mohawk of today is much more watered-down.

Mullet

Also appearing sometime in the 1970s, the mullet soared to popularity in the '80s among rockers and rednecks. But the origins of the short-on-the-top-and-sides, long-and-free-in-the-back look are a bit mysterious. Some say that hockey players originated the 'do, and others think it's an offspring of rock 'n' roll (David Bowie was an early adopter)—but most agree that the style should be retired.

BIRTHPLACES OF THE RICH AND FAMOUS

Was someone famous born in your hometown?

Brooklyn, the most fabled of New York City's five boroughs, is the birthplace for hundreds of the rich and famous, especially those in show business. Perhaps the reason is that Brooklyn natives are street-smart and savvy. Comedians Eddie Murphy, Zero Mostel, Curly and Moe Howard of the *Three Stooges*, Charlie Callas, Jackie Gleason, Buddy Hackett, Joan Rivers, and Jerry Seinfeld all hail from Brooklyn.

On the other end of the artistic spectrum, composers Aaron Copland and George Gershwin were born in Brooklyn.

Brooklyn was also home to actors Tony Danza, Martin Landau, Veronica Lake, Susan Hayward, Mary Tyler Moore, Mickey Rooney, Barbara Stanwyck, Eli Wallach, Mae West, and Barbra Streisand.

Many entertainers who have become household names in the United States were born in Canada, including Michael J. Fox of Edmonton, Dan Aykroyd of Ottawa, William Shatner of Montreal, Martin Short of Hamilton, Fay Wray of Alberta, Peter Jennings of Toronto, Lorne Michaels of Toronto, Mack Sennett of Quebec, Donald Sutherland of Saint John, Art Linkletter of Saskatchewan, Guy Lombardo of London (Ontario), Mary Pickford of Toronto, and Neil Young, also of Toronto.

Alabama contributed several civil rights leaders to history, including Ralph Abernathy from Linden, Coretta Scott King from Marion, and Rosa Parks from Tuskegee.

One of the most influential performers in the history of country music, singer-songwriter Hank Williams was born in tiny Mount Olive West, Alabama.

Sally K. Ride of Encino, California, has the perfect name for an astronaut.

Born in Hollywood, California, Leonardo DiCaprio may have been destined to become a movie star.

Actor and director Clint Eastwood was once mayor of Carmel, California, but he was actually born in San Francisco.

Language
Ju Idealisma Origino da Esperanto

❖ ❖ ❖ ❖

"What we've got here is failure to communicate."
—Cool Hand Luke, *1967*

*It's been the world's lament, but one man
was certain he had a solution.*

What Do Words Say?

As a boy living in Bialystok in Russian-controlled Poland in the 1860s
and '70s, Ludwik L. Zamenhof was keenly aware of the endless
bickering that preoccupied neighborhood kids and grown-ups.
Everybody talked, and if they listened at all, they only grew angrier
because nobody could understand what the others were saying. That
was because Bialystok was dominated by three groups: Jews, who
spoke mainly Yiddish; White Russians, who spoke Belarusian; and
Germans, who spoke, well, German. This central inefficiency of local
communication was aggravated because the language of government
administration was Russian. Young Ludwik may have appreciated
the small mercy that Person A likely never realized that Person B
had just let loose with a withering insult, but he had no doubt that
sometimes language isn't an advantage, but an awful impediment.

As Zamenhof grew into young adulthood, he became an oph-
thalmologist and perfected his understanding of Russian, Yiddish,
and German. He also immersed himself in Latin, English, French,
Hebrew, and Greek. His thoughts soon turned to the creation of a
universal language that could easily be learned, spoken, and written,
eliminating the enormous linguistic barriers that impaired relation-
ships not just in Poland, but across the globe. Zamenhof reasoned
that without such a language, civilization would forever be defined
by endless ethnic strife and war.

In 1887, when Zamenhof was just 28, he published *Lingvo
Internacia,* the first textbook of his new language, which he called
Esperanto ("hopeful one"). The book's primary text was written in
Russian, and authorship was attributed to "Dr. Esperanto."

How It Works

Although Esperanto was designed to be culturally neutral, it shares qualities with European languages—no surprise, given Zamenhof's background. What sets Esperanto apart is its internal consistency. The alphabet has 28 letters. There are no silent letters and no variations in pronunciation. All words put stress on the next-to-last syllable: "ess-per-AHN-toe." The language functions with only 16 rules—no exceptions. Suffixes identify parts of speech: All nouns end in *O*, all adjectives in *A*, adverbs in *E*. The letter *J* forms the plural and *N* indicates a direct object.

Zamenhof gave up all claims to ownership of Esperanto, making it his gift to humanity. This is unvarnished idealism, so Zamenhof was greatly disappointed when the Russian tsar banned Esperanto as a tool of sedition. Even so, freethinkers and linguists across Europe, particularly in France and Germany, became excited about Esperanto. Many famous works were translated into the new language, and 1889 brought the first magazine written entirely in Esperanto, *La Esperantistto*. Zamenhof himself published the first Esperanto dictionary in 1894.

The first World Esperanto Congress attracted 688 linguists and other enthusiasts to Boulogne, France, in 1905. Three years later, the Universal Esperanto Association was established.

Tragedy and Triumph

Ludwik Zamenhof died in 1917; his wife, Klara, passed away in 1924. A decade later, Hitler outlawed Esperanto across the Third Reich, claiming it was part of the imaginary world Jewish conspiracy. In a particularly ugly irony, all three Zamenhof children were ensnared in the web of Hitler's Holocaust and killed.

Esperanto has outlived its detractors. Across Europe and the Middle East, plaques, busts, and street names honor Zamenhof. A minor planet discovered in 1938 is called Zamenhof.

Since it was first embraced by enthusiasts, Esperanto has been regularly spoken by anywhere from 100,000 to 2 million persons. All dialogue in *Incubus,* a 1965 movie starring William Shatner, is in Esperanto. British comic Spike Milligan famously remarked, "I can speak Esperanto like a native." Conventions and publications are common, and the language's proponents now lobby for its adoption as the official language of the European Union.

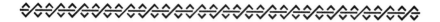

Sports
Hockey's Other Hat Trick

✦ ✦ ✦ ✦

*One might logically assume that NHL great Gordie Howe invented
the "Gordie Howe Hat Trick." Then again, when you assume…*

Mr. Hockey did not invent the three-pronged feat that bears his
name. In fact, the term used to describe the art of recording a goal,
an assist, and a fight in a single hockey match didn't enter the sport's
lexicon until 1991. That's a full ten years after the game's longest-
serving veteran hung up his blades.

Honoring a Hockey Great

Make no mistake: Gordie Howe was more than capable of achieving
all three elements necessary to complete the celebrated triple play.
He was a wizard at putting the biscuit in the basket, a magician at
deftly slipping a pass through myriad sticks and skates and putting
the disc on the tape of a teammate's stick, and he wasn't opposed to
delivering a knuckle sandwich to a deserving adversary. However,
the tattered pages of the NHL record books show that he recorded
only one Howe Hat Trick in his 32-year career in the NHL and
the World Hockey Association. On December 22, 1955, in a game
against the Boston Bruins, Howe (playing for the Detroit Red
Wings) scored the tying goal, set up the winning 3–2 tally, and
bested Beantown left winger Lionel Heinrich in a spirited tussle.

The Record Holder

The Gordie Howe Hat Trick isn't an official statistic—in fact, the
San Jose Sharks are the only franchise that lists the achievement in
its media guide—but it is a widely acknowledged measurement of a
skater's ability to play the game with both physical skill and artistic
grace. The New York Rangers' Brendan Shanahan is the NHL's all-
time leader in "Howe Hats." According to *The Hockey News*, Shanny
scored a goal, recorded an assist, and had a fight nine times in the
same game.

BAND NAMES

Kiss and Makeup

Why were protective parents around the globe convinced that the name of the rock band KISS was really an acronym for Knights in Service of Satan?

Branding a Band

Onstage, they looked like they'd come straight from the gates of hell, dressed head-to-toe in black, their faces adorned with macabre makeup. When KISS hit the concert circuit in 1973—the group drew a sitting-room-only crowd of three people to their first gig—rock 'n' roll was undergoing an image transformation. The emergence of androgynous rockers such as David Bowie and Marc Bolan, along with the popularity of glam groups such as Mott the Hoople and the New York Dolls, forced bands to find new, exciting, and controversial methods to market their product. When four young rockers from New York City decided to combine comic book characters and colorful costumes with a morbid mentality, they needed an appropriate handle to describe themselves, one that was easy to spell and mysterious enough to keep their fans confused. Drummer Peter Criss had been in a group called Lips, which prompted the crew to dub themselves KISS.

What's in a Name?

According to the boys in the band, the name was spelled in capital letters to make it stand out and was never meant to be an acronym for anything. But that revelation didn't stop members of religious flocks—who considered rock 'n' roll to be synonymous with the sounds of Satan—from claiming that the group's moniker was a devilish derivation. In fact, the KISS name has spawned several acronymic identities, including Keep it Simple, Stupid; Kids in Satan's Service; and Korean Intelligence Support System. Judging from the millions of records they've sold in their 35 years in the business, as well as their relentless licensing of KISS-related merchandise, the band might find a more appropriate name in CASH.

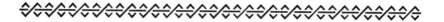

Toys & Games
Fad Inventions
❖ ❖ ❖ ❖

*If we could figure out the next hottest trend, we'd all be
millionaires, right? Here are some seemingly crazy ideas
that turned out to be both lasting and lucrative.*

Hacky Sack
Mike Marshall created this version of the footbag in 1972 to help
his friend John Stalberger rehabilitate an injured leg. After they
marketed it, the Hacky Sack rehabilitated their bank accounts
as well. In Oregon in 2006, Tricia George and Paul Vorvick set a
doubles record of 1,415 footbag kicks in ten minutes.

Pet Rock
Its genesis makes sense when you consider the occupation of its
inventor. In the mid-1970s, advertising executive Gary Dahl packaged ordinary beach stones in an attractive box and sold them with
instructions for their care and training. They cost a penny to manufacture and sold for $3.95, and though the fad lasted less than a year,
it made Dahl millions.

Super Soaker
The giant water gun was invented in 1988 by aerospace engineer
Lonnie Johnson. An intriguing feature was the incorporation of
air pressure, which enabled more water to be sprayed at greater
distances. Some of today's pump-action models can "shoot" water
accurately as far as 50 feet.

Yo-Yo
The first historical mention of the yo-yo dates to Greece in 500 B.C.,
but it was a man named Pedro Flores who brought the yo-yo to the
United States from the Philippines in 1928. American entrepreneur
Donald Duncan soon bought the rights from Flores. Sales of the toy
peaked in 1962, when more than 45 million units were sold.

Science
History of Taxidermy

◆ ◆ ◆ ◆

Want a rat torso, an evil eye, or a dried turkey head? How about an end table with the base made from an elephant's foot or a thermometer (it really works!) made from a freeze-dried deer foot? Before you decide to buy a mounted, two-headed calf at an auction, take a look at the process that got it there.

I'm Stuffed, Thank You

Taxidermy, Greek for "the arrangement or movement of the skin," is a general term that describes various procedures for creating lifelike models of animals that will last a long, long time—possibly even forever. The models, or representations of the animals, could include the actual skin, fur, feathers, or scales of the specimen, which is preserved and then mounted.

A quick search on the Internet will certainly reveal the odd, the bizarre, and many sideshow items, some of which are even for sale. The main focus of taxidermy, however, is the integrity of the final product, and getting the best results might require a far greater range of skills and crafts than simply stuffing and mounting. Those in the know consider it a precise art.

Take This Job and Stuff It

By the early 1800s, hunters began bringing in their trophies for preservation. The process usually began with an upholsterer skinning the creature. Then, the hide was removed and left outside to rot and self-bleach. Once this stage was complete, the tanner stuffed the hide with rags and cotton and then sewed the skin closed to replicate the live animal.

These rough methods of taxidermy are a far cry from modern-day processes. Today, professional taxidermists abundantly prefer the term *mounting* over *stuffing,* and rags and cotton have been replaced by synthetic materials.

They Don't Have to Sing for Their Supper

Dermestid beetles can be used to clean skulls and bones before mounting. As one might guess, these beetles clean by eating anything organic left on the bones, but at least they eliminate the need to use large cooking pots to boil the skulls clean. But wait, before you judge too harshly, it should be pointed out that this same method of turning the beetles loose is used by museums on delicate skulls and bones.

Cryptic as It May Sound

Freeze-drying is the preferred method for preserving pets. It can be done with reptiles, birds, and small mammals, such as cats, large mice, and some dog breeds. However, freeze-drying is expensive and time-consuming—larger specimens require up to six months in the freeze dryer.

But taxidermy can be even more creative than preserving animals. In crypto-taxidermy brand-new animals—dragons, jackalopes, unicorns—can be made. The subjects can also be extinct species, such as dinosaurs, dodo birds, or quaggas.

Some taxidermists have an impish side, as well. One popular practice places animals in human situations, building entire tableaux around them. This is called *anthropomorphic taxidermy.* Walter Potter has created a number of such works. *The Upper Ten,* or *Squirrels Club,* for example, features a group of squirrels relaxing at an upper-crust men's club. Another well-known work, *Bidibidobidiboo* by M. Cattelan, shows a suicidal squirrel dead at its kitchen table—definitely a conversation-starter in any home or business.

A new trend is the creation of entirely artificial mounts that do not contain any parts of the animal at all: for instance, re-creations of fish taken from pictures by catch-and-release anglers. This technique is called *reproduction taxidermy,* and although it is not traditional, it is definitely a more environmentally savvy method of preservation.

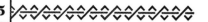

Film

The Real-life Explorers Who Made *King Kong*

❖ ❖ ❖ ❖

Long before Jurassic Park, The Blob, *or even* Godzilla *terrorized big-screen audiences, a prehistoric gorilla by the name of Kong served up its own enormous case of king-size quivers to the moviegoing masses.*

Monkeys are a mainstay of zoos today, but in the early 20th century, when Merian C. Cooper's original *King Kong* came out, few zoos held displays of the entertaining and excitable creatures. Capitalizing on that void and incorporating his own anthropological background, Cooper coupled with fellow filmmaker and friend Ernest B. Schoedsack to parlay their nature documentary into a feature film. Little did they know at the time how their "creature feature epic," the first of its kind, would change the landscape of cinematic and pop culture.

Thrilling Adventure

Cooper lived an exciting life before creating one of the most adventurous epics of all time. As a U.S. Army officer and bomber pilot in World War I, he traveled the globe and was a prisoner of war. His initial filmmaking career was devoted to creating nature documentaries for Paramount Pictures. As such, much of his time was spent exploring exotic locales. Always the innovator, even with these documentaries, he incorporated technological techniques to ensure that action-packed sequences were the main features of his works. Unlike the typical nature documentary, Cooper always insisted that stage-set action sequences accompany the nature footage to ensure just the right feel of excitement.

Schoedsack, too, was an ardent fan of technological advancements in filmmaking. Schoedsack and Cooper met while both were providing military service in Ukraine. Upon their return to the United States, they forged a working relationship that combined their mutual interests in nature, adventure, and filmmaking innovations. Their initial collaborations continued their previously estab-

lished work in the documentary genre, but their united efforts on *King Kong* put Cooper and Schoedsack on the cinematic map.

It's All in the Script

From the start, the filming of *King Kong* was riddled with odd and unexpected roadblocks. The original scriptwriter commissioned by Cooper fell ill and died before producing a workable text. Even though scriptwriter Edgar Wallace is credited as a writer on the film, Cooper, Schoedsack's wife, Ruth Rose, and James Ashmore Creelman were forced to quickly rework the entire script to get it done in time for production. Creelman was hired to reconstruct Wallace's unedited draft to Cooper's liking. Although Creelman's changes were pleasing to the perfectionist Cooper, he still thought that the script lacked snap. Thus, Rose was asked to jump into the screenwriting process. Cooper was pleased with her adjustments but, of course, felt compelled to imprint his own voice, as well.

Another marked change in the film's production revolved around its name. *King Kong* went through several name changes before its release. The movie went by *Kong, King Ape, The Beast, The Ape,* and *The Eighth Wonder* before finally being released as *King Kong*. In fact, even as press release packets were being sent out in anticipation of the release, the film was referred to as *The Eighth Wonder.* Only one known pamphlet—which brought $11,000 at auction in 2005—exists with this designation.

Pushing Film Technique Forward

Several technologically innovative methods were employed in *King Kong*'s production. One technique, stop-motion, was a new trick in which objects were filmed at different locations and positions in many frames to mimic movement. This animation method was utilized to create special effects involving the film's prehistoric creatures—dinosaurs and the ape himself. By today's standards, the choppiness of the technique might appear hokey, but at the time, stop-motion was a cutting-edge means to meet the movie's needs.

Another method employed, rear-projection, was combined with the magic of stop-motion to create the illusion that Kong was tromping through scenes alongside the live actors. To achieve this technique, a camera projects a previously recorded background onto

the scene's backdrop while live action takes place in front of it. This technique was not a first choice—in fact, multiple alternate routes were explored fully. However, just as filming was scheduled to start, an advanced version of rear-projection was discovered, and Cooper jumped on the innovation.

Although some have suggested that Kong was, at times, portrayed by a man in an ape suit, all scenes with the prehistoric beast were made utilizing stop-motion, rear-projection, and other special effects with one of the four Kong models crafted in various sizes. Although the differing dimensions could not produce a consistently accurate Kong, whether the gigantic ape terrorized at 18 feet or the 24 feet he appeared to be while menacing Manhattan, each rendition was produced by a miniature model made from crude materials including aluminum, rubber, and wire.

Boffo Box Office

King Kong, released in 1933, had the biggest opening weekend of its time. It became the highest-grossing film of the year and the fifth of the entire decade. Not bad considering that 1933 was, by many accounts, the lowest point of the Great Depression. The film's great success brought the production company that carried it, RKO (Radio-Keith-Orpheum), back from the brink of bankruptcy.

Critics and the public were in love with the mammoth gorilla. In fact, the film was so popular that it was rereleased three more times in the next 20 years. But with each new showing, the strong arm of censorship took its toll. Through the years, various images deemed too horrifying were cut out, piece by piece. For instance, scenes featuring the giant gorilla taking a few nibbles of a New Yorker and causing a person to plummet to his death were removed. By modern standards, these scenes might seem fairly tame, but such gruesomeness was uncommon then. In 1971, however, the original film was pieced back together and rereleased, yet again, in its entire form.

Since *King Kong* popped into pop culture, countless monster movies have been created, including those manufactured during the great giant monster genre surge in the 1950s. But it was the great Kong and the technological ambitiousness of its creators, Cooper and Schoedsack, that set the stage for the special effects and terrifying monsters that scare audiences right out of their seats today.

Sports
Baseball—They Used to Be The...

❖ ❖ ❖ ❖

*What and where were some of today's major league baseball
teams? Some borrowed the names of defunct teams but
have no other continuity with the ghosts of old.*

Atlanta Braves (National Association/National League): formerly
the Boston Red Caps and Red Stockings (1876–1882), then the
Bean-eaters (until 1906), then Doves (to 1910), then Rustlers (for
1911). In 1912, they stopped the insanity, becoming the Boston
Braves. After a 38–115 season in 1935, they played as the Boston
Bees from 1936 to 1940. Just before the 1953 season, they lit out for
Milwaukee and stayed 12 years, moving to Atlanta in 1966. In 1977,
they began playing for owner Ted Turner.

Boston Red Sox (American League): founded as the Boston
Americans in 1901, unconnected with the Boston Red Stockings,
who became the modern Atlanta Braves. They've been playing as
the Boston Red Sox since 1908. Other early names, such as Pilgrims,
were in fact rarely used and not official.

Baltimore Orioles (AL): started play as the Milwaukee Brewers
in 1901 (finishing last), then became the St. Louis Browns. Deciding
that 52 years of bad baseball in one place would suffice, the team
became the Baltimore Orioles in 1954—honoring a rough-and-
tumble 1890s team by that name, though without direct succession.

Chicago Cubs (NA/NL): once the Chicago White Stockings
(1876–1889), then Colts (1890–1897), then Orphans (1898–1901). In
1902, they finally settled on the name they still carry today.

Chicago White Sox (AL): grabbed the Cubs' old nickname
(White Stockings) in 1901 on their founding, then took the official
abbreviation of White Sox in 1904. If you want to have fun with Sox
fans, just point out that their name is actually an old Cubs nickname.

Cincinnati Reds (American Association/NL): formerly the Red Stockings (1882–1889), then the Reds. During the McCarthy years (1954–1958), they quietly became the Cincinnati Redlegs, lest a team playing the American national pastime hint at a Bolshevik takeover. They soon resumed the nickname "Reds."

Cleveland Indians (AL): born the Cleveland Blues in 1901, called Broncos in 1902, then became the Naps in 1903 to honor star Nap Lajoie. After trading Lajoie in 1914, the team took its current name.

Los Angeles Angels (AL): began play in 1961, but in 1965 they became the California Angels, now playing in Anaheim. Thirty years later it was time for a change, so they became the Anaheim Angels. Since 2005, the team has officially been the Los Angeles Angels of Anaheim.

Los Angeles Dodgers (AA/NL): began as the Brooklyn Atlantics in 1884 and were often called the Trolley Dodgers. They would play as the Grays, Bridegrooms, Grooms, Superbas, Infants, and Dodgers—all before World War I! In 1914, they became the Robins (after manager Wilbert Robinson), then went back to Dodgers in 1932. After the 1957 season, their owner moved them to Los Angeles.

Milwaukee Brewers (AL/NL): started as the Seattle Pilots in 1969. After giving Emerald City ball fans a season of futile baseball in Sicks Stadium (today the spot is a hardware store), they fled to Milwaukee in haste for the 1970 season. When major league baseball expanded in 1998, a team had to switch leagues, and the Brew Crew moved to the National League.

Minnesota Twins (AL): began in the District of Columbia as the Washington Senators but were also periodically called the Nationals—from 1905 to 1906 the name even appeared on their jerseys. How could this nebulous situation be? Especially before 1920, nicknames were more fluid, and teams were often called by their city names: "The Bostons defeated the Detroits." In 1961, the Senators/sometime Nationals moved to their current Minneapolis home.

New York Yankees (AL): began (in 1901) as one of several Baltimore Orioles franchises in Major League Baseball. Moving to the Bronx in 1903, they became the New York Highlanders. The name Yankees gradually supplanted Highlanders, becoming official in 1913.

Oakland Athletics (AL): started play as the Philadelphia Athletics in 1901. In 1955 they became the Kansas City Athletics, a big-league team that seemd to act like an informal Yankee farm team by sending promising players to the Bronx in exchange for declining veterans. They moved to Oakland in 1968, then became a dynasty. They've also been called A's since they began.

Philadelphia Phillies (NL): started as the Philadelphia Quakers in 1883, but by 1890 the popular Phillies nickname was official. It has stayed that way except for 1943–1944, when they were called the Blue Jays.

Pittsburgh Pirates (AA/NL): Go Alleghenys! In 1882, that's how they were born—just Alleghenys, spelled thus, not Pittsburgh anything. Soon the Pittsburgh designation took over. Briefly called Innocents in 1890, they were then called Pirates for supposedly stealing a player from another team. That name sticks to this day.

St. Louis Cardinals (AA/NL): used to be the Brown Stockings (1882)—those were the days of flamboyant, creative, egomaniacal owner Chris von der Ahe. The team quickly became the Browns. In 1899, someone decided to rename them the Perfectos, but that was too dumb to stick. The next year they became Cardinals.

Washington Nationals (NL): started in 1969 as les Expos de Montréal but never quite seemed to fit there. In 1977, they took bad baseball locations to the next level by moving to Stade Olympique, with its dysfunctional retractable roof. Local interest got so bad that from 2003 to 2004, they played some home games in Puerto Rico. The ownership disconnected the Expos from the Montreal respirator for the 2005 season, moving to D.C. and reviving the old Nationals name.

REAL NAMES OF THE RICH AND FAMOUS

"A rose by any other name" is supposed to smell as sweet, but while that may be true in love, it isn't always so in show business. Below are the real names of some famous faces—see if you can match the real name to the alias.

1. Reginald Kenneth Dwight	a. John Wayne
2. Paul Hewson	b. Cary Grant
3. Mark Vincent	c. Woody Allen
4. David Robert Jones	d. Elton John
5. Caryn Elaine Johnson	e. Mark Twain
6. Nathan Birnbaum	f. Freddie Mercury
7. Archibald Leach	g. Bob Dylan
8. Eleanor Gow	h. George Michael
9. Samuel Langhorne Clemens	i. Whoopi Goldberg
10. Tara Patrick	j. Bono
11. McKinley Morganfield	k. Jason Alexander
12. Farrokh Bulsara	l. Demi Moore
13. Frances Gumm	m. Vin Diesel
14. Robert Allen Zimmerman	n. George Burns
15. Demetria Gene Guynes	o. David Bowie
16. Marion Morrison	p. Muddy Waters
17. Allen Konigsberg	q. Judy Garland
18. Georgios Panayiotou	r. Elle MacPherson
19. Jay Scott Greenspan	s. Carmen Electra

1. d; 2. j; 3. m; 4. o; 5. i; 6. n; 7. b; 8. r; 9. e; 10. s; 11. p; 12. f; 13. q; 14. g; 15. l; 16. a; 17. c; 18. h; 19. k

Language
Pet Precipitation

❖ ❖ ❖ ❖

While the idiom "raining cats and dogs" might conjure images of domestic denizens being heaved from the heavens, the conception of the cliché is more down-to-earth.

While there is considerable speculation as to the exact genesis of the idiom "raining cats and dogs," there is no doubt about one thing: It describes a vicious storm where all kinds of solid materials are spewed and strewn about by the sheer velocity of the downpour. But things get murky from there. Some theorists claim the phrase originated in the Middle Ages. Back then, tenuous, almost transparent thatched roofs covered many domestic dwellings. These anemic canopies consisted of intertwined batches of vented vegetation such as straw, heather, and other porous particles. It was common for dogs and their feline brethren to climb into the comblike confines of these roofs in an effort to keep warm and dry. However, in a downpour, these rickety roofs would often give way, causing pets to plunge down from their lofty lairs, creating the illusion that they were raining from the sky.

Another theory offers a more gruesome justification for the origin of this phrase. In the Middle Ages, it wasn't uncommon to dispose of perished pets by simply dumping them in a street-side gutter or a garbage-strewn alley. Since sewer systems at the time were inadequate at best, a thundering rainstorm would deluge the drains and swamp the alleys, causing the deceased pets to drift down the streets and give the impression that their untimely demise was associated with and caused by the harsh rain.

Jonathan Swift, the Anglo-Irish author best known for his tall tale *Gulliver's Travels,* may also be responsible for introducing the lifeless litter to literature. In his satirical poem "A Description of a City Shower," first published in the October 17, 1710, edition of *Tatler Magazine,* Swift writes of "Drown'd Puppies, stinking Sprats, all drench'd in Mud, Dead Cats and Turnip-Tops come tumbling down the Flood." And it's on that cheerful note, that we take leave of this discussion. Keep those umbrellas handy!

Holidays & Traditions
The Creation of Kwanzaa

❖ ❖ ❖ ❖

When the holiday season arrives in the United States, offices and shopping malls are decked with posters that celebrate Christmas, Hanukkah, and Kwanzaa. Yet many don't realize how recently the secular holiday of Kwanzaa originated.

It doesn't take long to trace the birth of Kwanzaa—one need only go as far back as Los Angeles in 1966, when Ron Karenga, a young political activist and scholar, invented the holiday. Karenga was a leader of the wide-ranging Black Nationalist movement. He intended Kwanzaa to be a replacement for Christmas, which he and his followers perceived as a vehicle of white power and commercialism.

Kwanzaa was officially inaugurated on December 26, 1966, when Karenga and his family and friends gathered together to light a candle that represented unity. According to Karenga, Kwanzaa "was chosen to give a Black alternative to the existing holiday and give Blacks an opportunity to celebrate themselves and history, rather than simply imitate the practice of the dominant society." Over time, Karenga reinvented Kwanzaa as a holiday meant to supplement, rather than replace, other holidays. The official Kwanzaa Web site states that Kwanzaa "is not an alternative to people's religion or faith but a common ground of African culture."

Kwanzaa is observed each year from December 26 through January 1. The symbols and practices of the holiday derive from a conglomeration of various African religions. Each day of

celebration is devoted to one of the seven principles, or *Nguzo Saba*, which are unity, self-determination, collective work and responsibility, cooperative economics, purpose, creativity, and faith. The seven candles of the candleholder, or the *Kinara*, represent these seven principles. Throughout Kwanzaa, African heritage and identity is discussed and celebrated through artwork.

The word *Kwanzaa* means "first fruits" in Swahili, an East-African language. The colors of Kwanzaa are black, red, and green: black for the people, red for the struggle, and green for the future and for the hope that comes from struggle. Many Kwanzaa traditions are inspired by the first harvest celebrations of Africa. Kwanzaa is a time for family and friends to gather in celebration, thus strengthening community and cultural bonds. Celebrants typically have one large feast, and the final day of Kwanzaa is reserved for reflection and self-evaluation.

Some controversy surrounds Kwanzaa, as it is tied up with the actions and political views of Karenga. He spent four years in prison for the 1971 assault and torture of two women who were involved with The Organization Us, a Black Nationalist group that Karenga founded in 1965. It was after Karenga was released from prison in 1975 that he repudiated some of his more extreme views. Today, Karenga remains the leader of The Organization Us. According to this organization's Web site, the heart of their project is "the continuing quest to define and become the best of what it means to be both African and human in the fullest sense."

It is difficult to gauge the popularity of Kwanzaa among African Americans and other groups worldwide. The majority of African Americans do not celebrate the holiday at all; some celebrate it as a replacement for other religious holidays, whereas others incorporate it to varying degrees into Christmas celebrations. A 2004 study by the National Retail Foundation found that 13 percent of African Americans celebrate Kwanzaa. Most celebrants value Kwanzaa as a vehicle for uniting disparate African American identities and as a way to reaffirm, revive, and study African, African Diaspora, and African American cultural traditions.

Personal Hygiene
Listerine: Inventing the Need

❖ ❖ ❖ ❖

Some 40 years after Listerine's invention, marketing gurus finally figured out how to sell it to Jane and Joe Average: Tell Jane that if she didn't cure her toxic breath, Joe wouldn't kiss her.

Not by Lister?

Surgery was a filthy business in the 19th century. U.S. President James Garfield died from the crude probings of his doctors' bare, germy fingers as they scrounged around his abdomen trying to fish out an assassin's bullet—and Garfield had the finest medical care of the day. The worst was a Dante's *Inferno* of squalor, amputation, infection, and gangrene. In wartime, a bullet to the gut generally meant an agonizing death that surgery would merely hasten.

Into that breach stepped Dr. Joseph Lister, an English doctor who advised doctors to wear gloves, wash their hands, and sanitize their instruments. It was that simple. The mortality rate dropped so far that a grateful Queen Victoria made Lister a baron. But later generations would most frequently associate him with a mouthwash he didn't invent and probably never used.

Then Who Did?

Dr. Joseph Lawrence and Jordan Lambert first whipped up a batch of surgical disinfectant in 1879—a blend of thymol, menthol, eucalyptol, and methyl salicylate in grain alcohol. It needed a name. Did the inventors name it after Lister to honor him or to ride on his famous coattails? That depends on your opinion of the inventors' motives, but the profit motive surely drove Listerine's invention and marketing. There's no evidence that Dr. Lister ever received a penny for the appropriation of his name, nor that he complained or cared. A devout man of science and medicine, Lister didn't seek riches.

Here Comes the Marketing

In 1884, Lambert formed the Lambert Company to sell Listerine. By 1895, it was clear that Listerine did a quick, safe job of wiping out

oral bacteria, so Lambert started hawking it to dentists as well. One might say that Western medicine washed away centuries of sin with a baptism in Listerine.

If Duels Were Still Legal, Your Breath Could Win

By 1914, Lambert's son Gerard was calling the shots for Listerine. In an era of snake-oil concoctions with names like Spurrier's Powders, Kvak's Pills, and Boga's Tonic, which promised to cure anything from baldness and "female complaints" to rheumatism and colds yet conferred no actual health benefit, Listerine was the exception—*it actually did something useful.*

Gerard started selling Listerine over the counter as a mouthwash, thus inventing the category... and soon realized he had to invent the problem. His new advertising focused on halitosis, or bad breath, and played on the idea (often well-founded, granted) that oblivious persons with poor dental habits might be offending everyone with their dragon breath.

The cure? You know what it was. Americans started rinsing their mouths with medical disinfectant. The Lambert Company's annual revenues went from $115,000 to $8 million in seven years. Wish we could bust a marketing move like Gerard Lambert.

Today, Listerine comes in a variety of flavors, but you can still buy the old-school version. It hasn't changed much, if at all, since Jordan Lambert started selling it as a surgical sanitizer.

Listerine tasted nasty, so even during Prohibition (1920–1933) you had to be a pretty desperate alcoholic to swallow the stuff.

One claim Listerine eventually had to back off of was that it helped fight colds. The makers got away with that one for 50 years before the FTC made them quit.

Science
Benjamin Franklin
Flies a Kite

❖ ❖ ❖ ❖

As it turns out, Benjamin Franklin did not discover electricity.
What's more, the kite he famously flew in 1752 while
conducting an experiment was not struck by lightning. If
it had been, Franklin would be remembered as a colonial
publisher and assemblyman killed by his own curiosity.

Before Ben

Blessed with one of the keenest minds in history, Benjamin Franklin
was a scientific genius who made groundbreaking discoveries in the
basic nature and properties of electricity. Electrical science, however, dates to 1600, when Dr. William Gilbert, physician to Queen
Elizabeth, published a treatise about his research on electricity and
magnetism. European inventors who later expanded on Gilbert's
knowledge included Otto von Guericke of Germany, Charles Francois Du Fay of France, and Stephen Gray of England.

The Science of Electricity

Franklin became fascinated with electricity after seeing a demonstration by an itinerant showman (and doctor) named Archibald
Spencer in Boston in 1743. Two years later, he bought a Leyden
jar—a contraption invented by a Dutch scientist that used a glass
container wrapped in foil to create a crude battery. Other researchers had demonstrated the properties of the device, and Franklin set
about to increase its capacity to generate electricity while testing his
own scientific hypotheses. Among the principles he established was
the conservation of charge, one of the most important laws of phys-
ics. In a paper published in 1750, he announced the discovery of the
induced charge and broadly outlined the existence of the electron.
His experiments led him to coin many of the terms currently used
in the science of electricity, including *battery, conductor, condenser,*
charge, discharge, uncharged, negative, minus, plus, electric shock,
and *electrician.*

As Franklin came to understand the nature of electricity, he began to theorize about the electrical nature of lightning. In 1751, he outlined in a British scientific journal his idea for an experiment that involved placing a long metal rod on a high tower or steeple to draw an electric charge from passing thunder clouds, which would throw off visible electric sparks. A year later, French scientist Georges-Louis Leclerc successfully conducted such an experiment.

The Kite Runner

Franklin had not heard of Leclerc's success when he undertook his own experiment in June 1752. Instead of a church spire, he affixed his kite to a sharp, pointed wire. To the end of his kite string he tied a key, and to the key a ribbon made of silk (for insulation). While flying his kite on a cloudy day as a thunderstorm approached, Franklin noticed that loose threads on the kite string stood erect, as if they had been suspended from a common conductor. The key sparked when he touched it, showing it was charged with electricity. But had the kite actually been struck by lightning, Franklin would likely have been killed, as was Professor Georg Wilhelm Richmann of St. Petersburg, Russia, when he attempted the same experiment a few months later.

The Lightning Rod

Although Franklin did not discover electricity, he did uncover many of its fundamental principles and proved that lightning is, in fact, electricity. He used his knowledge to create the lightning rod, an invention that today protects land structures and ships at sea. He never patented the lightning rod but instead generously promoted it as a boon to humankind. In 21st-century classrooms, the lightning rod is still cited as a classic example of the way fundamental science can produce practical inventions.

"An investment in knowledge always pays the best interest."
—BENJAMIN FRANKLIN

Clubs & Organizations
The First United Nations

❖ ❖ ❖ ❖

When a group of nations band together for collective security,
it's an alliance or coalition. When a great many nations band
together for global security, it's the United Nations (UN). But
there was a UN before the UN: the League of Nations.

Genesis

Founded in 1919 and now almost forgotten, the League of Nations
was the UN's forerunner. World War I's devastation suggested that the
next war would be even bloodier; might it obliterate all civilization?
Forty-four nations banded together to form the League, which
was headquartered in Geneva, Switzerland. The League sought to
influence nations to take the following actions (and failed because):

- Stop arming themselves to the teeth. (If someone wouldn't disarm,
  and the League couldn't or wouldn't arm to disarm them, so much
  for disarmament.)

- Let peoples govern themselves as they chose. (Unless they chose
  Communism, which left out the Soviet Union—a rather big puzzle
  piece.)

- Abandon sleazy secret maneuvers in favor of open international
  dialogue. (Fine, provided nations stopped doing sneaky things.
  They didn't.)

- Trust the League for security rather than military power blocs. (A
  military is needed for authentic security, and the League had none.)

When it came to keeping the peace, humanity talked a better
game than it played. The League faltered when authoritarian nations
rearmed, suppressed national self-determination, began secret
political maneuvering, and forged military power blocs.

Exodus

The United States never joined the League. Domestic "it's not
our problem" sentiment disappointed President Woodrow Wilson,

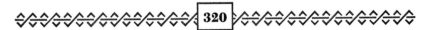

who pinned all his personal prestige on the League's promise. The League ebbed into a genteel, useless debate club as other powers withdrew:

- Japan invaded Manchuria in 1931. Fed up with lectures, resurgent Japan left the League in 1933 and invaded China proper in 1937. Little was done.

- The League fidgeted but did little as Hitler remilitarized the Rhineland, slurped up Austria, browbeat Czechoslovakia out of existence, and started the Holocaust.

- Mussolini's Italy used chemical weapons against Abyssinia (Ethiopia). Lectured but not thwarted, Italy quit the League in 1937.

- In 1939, the League expelled the Soviet Union (which had finally been admitted in 1934) for invading Finland. Stalin didn't care. He'd only joined to annoy Hitler anyway.

World War II came, and its death toll of 72 million confirmed the League's founding fears while standing as a tombstone for its failures. The League's rump membership took the organization behind an Alp and euthanized it in 1946. The Palace of Nations, its Geneva HQ, later became a UN office.

Legacy
The League wasn't all failure. It reduced slavery, aided POW repatriation, developed passports for stateless persons, and ran other errands of mercy. It resolved some dangerous regional conflicts. It established that larger and wealthier nations should help improve the world, while giving smaller and poorer nations a voice. Despite the League's glaring failures, humanity needed an international peace and humanitarian organization. Another would come.

Successor
At the height of World War II, Franklin D. Roosevelt and Winston Churchill first used "United Nations" as a synonym for "The Allies." The United Nations agreed not to seek or accept separate peaces with the Axis (Germany, Italy, Japan, and minor allies) and kept that commitment. After the war (1945), the United Nations became a formal, funded organization.

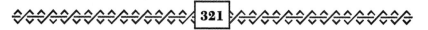

After the lessons from the League experience, the UN has compiled a better track record. While it obviously didn't eliminate regional power blocs, there hasn't been a WWIII, and most people think that's good. The UN's six official languages (Arabic, Chinese, English, French, Russian, and Spanish) better reflect the world than did the League's French, English, and Spanish. Major powers understand that if they quit the UN in a huff, the remaining membership will simply decide without them. It's imperfect, but it has seen its 60th anniversary. Its ancestor, the League of Nations, never celebrated a 30th.

Continuing to Work Together

As of this writing, 192 member states represent virtually all recognized independent nations. The first session of the general assembly convened January 10, 1946, in the Westminster Central Hall in London under the auspices of acting Secretary-General Gladwyn Jebb, a prominent British diplomat. On February 1, Norway's Trygve Lie was chosen to be the United Nations' first secretary-general. The secretary general is appointed for a renewable five-year term; to date no secretary general has served more than two terms.

Today the United Nations is headquartered at an 18-acre site on New York's Manhattan Island. The land was purchased in 1946 through a donation from John D. Rockefeller Jr.; even though it's physically located in New York City, it is considered international territory. The United Nations is comprised of six principal operating organs: the General Assembly, the Security Council, the Economic and Social Council, the Secretariat, the International Court of Justice, and the Trusteeship Council. The General Assembly operates on a one-state-one-vote system, and a two-thirds majority is required to pass many resolutions. The organization has twice been honored with the Nobel Peace Prize.

Food & Drink
Ugly but Delicious:
The Chocolate Truffle

❖ ❖ ❖ ❖

*Chocolate truffles may look like grubby little mushrooms,
but that's where the resemblance ends.*

Named for their physical resemblance to the fungus so treasured
by chefs around the world, chocolate truffles have their origin in
France, where chocolatiers originally set them out as Christmastime
goodies. Because of the high cream and butter content of the treats,
and because refrigeration wasn't always de rigueur, truffles were only
offered for a short time—typically during the winter months, when
it'd be easier to keep them from spoiling.

Traditional truffles are made of chocolate paste (chocolate,
cream, eggs, and butter) and then rolled in cocoa powder. They may
be flavored with brandy, rum, vanilla, cinnamon, or coffee. Americans do it a little differently: We like ours in a hard chocolate shell
and flavored with everything from ginger to jalapeño.

No one really knows where or how the truffle came into being,
but we do know that pastry chef Alice Medrich, who first sampled
a chocolate truffle when she was living in Paris in the '60s, is largely
credited with bringing this little treasure to the United States via her
San Francisco store Cocolat. Now, *haut-chocolat* houses from coast to
coast offer them: Vosges Haut-Chocolat, which offers retail locations
in Chicago, New York, and Las Vegas, showcases savory flavors, while
you can still find traditionally flavored truffles at Jacques Torres's
Brooklyn, New York–based chocolate factory. Even
middle-of-the-road chocolate com-
panies offer their version of the
truffle, although you won't
find flavors such as "gold leaf"
among their offerings.

Fads & Fashion
A Chronicle of Kissing

✦ ✦ ✦ ✦

Smooching, necking, spit-swapping, lip-locking—whatever you call it, kissing can be one of life's more pleasurable experiences. We've uncovered the history and naughty little secrets of the kiss.

The First Kiss
Although human nature suggests that the first kiss would have been shared much earlier, anthropologists have traced the first recorded kiss to India in approximately 1500 B.C. Early Vedic documents report people "sniffing" with their mouths and describe how lovers join "mouth to mouth."

"With This Kiss, I Thee Wed"
The tradition that inspired the phrase "You may kiss the bride" probably originated in ancient Rome. To seal their marriage contract, couples kissed in front of a large group of people. The Romans had three different categories of kisses: *osculum,* a kiss on the cheek; *basium,* a kiss on the lips; and *savolium,* a deep kiss.

The Holy Kiss
In the early Christian church, congregants would greet one another with an *osculum pacis,* or holy kiss. This greeting was said to transfer spirits between the kissers. In the 13th century, the Catholic Church provided something called a "pax board," which the congregation could kiss instead of kissing each other. Until the 16th century, the holy kiss was part of the Catholic mass, though kissing the Pope's ring is something that's still practiced.

Butterfly Kiss
The strange but sweet butterfly kiss is named for its similarity to a butterfly's fluttering wings. Simply put your eye a whisper away from your partner's eye or cheek, and bat your lashes repeatedly.

Performance High
The adrenaline rush you get when you jump out of a plane or run a marathon is essentially the same rush you get from kissing. The neurotransmitters that fire when you're kissing cause the heart to beat faster and the breath to become deeper.

Kissing Competitions
Sideshows at the Olympic games of ancient Greece included kissing competitions. How one would have judged such a thing is hard to know, but similar competitions still crop up from time to time, usually for fund-raising purposes or simply for spectacle's sake.

Germ Theory
The human mouth is coated with mucus that is chock-full of microscopic bacteria. When you lock lips with someone, between 10 million and 1 billion bacterial colonies are exchanged. The good news: Saliva also contains antibacterial chemicals that neutralize the spit, preventing the transfer of germs.

The scientific name for kissing is philematology.

More than 5,300 couples kissed for at least ten seconds in the Phillipines on Valentine's Day in 2005.

The first on-film kiss occurred between John C. Rice and May Irwin in the movie The Kiss *(1896).*

In the 1927 movie Don Juan, *Estelle Taylor and Mary Astor received a total of 127 kisses from John Barrymore.*

People spend an average of two weeks of their lives kissing.

Media & Communication
The Only Semi-Bookish Beginnings of National Geographic

❖ ❖ ❖ ❖

Little has changed at National Geographic since its inception, when a bunch of trailblazing academics, adventurers, and entrepreneurs united in the simple desire to spread their love of knowledge and discovery.

National Geographic is a challenge to classify: It walks like a duck, but it doesn't really quack like one. Most know National Geographic only through its monthly publication, *National Geographic* magazine. Yet the magazine is only the tip of a very large iceberg. National Geographic is actually a blanket term for the National Geographic Society, a nonprofit organization that funds scientific research and educational programs and is involved with projects that range from educating the public about global poverty to funding scientific research that seeks to end poverty.

National Geographic is scientific, yet its magazine targets everyday readers. The magazine's articles are based on scholarship, yet they read like creative journalism. National Geographic funds research, yet it is not an academic institution. National Geographic's hodgepodge of media subdivisions, from television channels to documentaries to radio shows, has the flavor of a pop culture empire—but with philanthropic goals. In short, National Geographic is one of those rare organizations that, through its ability to resist society's typically rigid divisions, is also able to transcend them.

This combination of lowbrow and highbrow was built into National Geographic from the beginning. The Society was founded mostly by academics, yet their goal was to include everybody, no matter their education level, in the pursuit of knowledge. In 1888, scientists and adventurers from all over the United States met at the Cosmos Club in Washington, D.C., right across from the White House. Included in this group were teachers, lawyers, geographers, explorers of various stripes, and even military officers. All of these

individuals were united by their passion to discover truths about the world, whether they be the location of the world's highest mountain peak or the customs of a different culture.

In those days, much of the earth was uncharted territory. Colonialism had only recently introduced the world to the vast multiplicity of human culture. The founders of the National Geographic Society wanted people to be informed of the exciting new discoveries that were taking place. The founders resolved that inclusion in the society should be "on as broad and liberal a basis in regard to qualifications for membership as is consistent with its own well-being and the dignity of the science it represents." The National Geographic Society was officially incorporated on January 27, 1888.

The first issue of *National Geographic Magazine* (later shortened to just *National Geographic*) was published nine months after the Society was founded. The founders decided that a magazine would be the best way to educate the public about scientific findings. Unlike academic journals with their obscure language and esoteric references, *National Geographic Magazine* was intended to unite people in a curiosity for the world. Gilbert Hovey Grosvenor, Alexander Graham Bell's son-in-law, was the magazine's first editor, and from the outset he established an all-encompassing criteria for geographic knowledge as "embracing nations, people, plants, animals, birds, fish. It enters into history, science, literature, and even the languages."

National Geographic's renown for publishing startlingly beautiful photographs commenced in 1905, when Grosvenor had a deadline and 11 blank pages to fill. On a whim, he published 11 pages' worth of photographs of Tibet, and from there on out made photographic journalism a focus of the publication. The first issue of *National Geographic* was sent to 165 people; today, *National Geographic* is published in more than 30 languages, with a circulation of more than 8 million. The National Geographic Channel has more than 65 million viewers, and the National Geographic Society is one of the world's largest and most influential nonprofit organizations.

Signs & Symbols
Zero: To Be or Not to Be

❖ ❖ ❖ ❖

*You might think that zero is an insignificant little
number worth nothing. But you'd be wrong.*

The origin of the number "zero" was not as neat as the subtraction of
one minus one. In fact, there was no symbol for zero for centuries.
Before a symbol was used for zero, most archeologists believe various cultures used an empty space to stand in zero's stead.

It is thought that the Babylonians were the first to use a placeholder for zero in their numbering system in 350 B.C. But it was not
a zero; instead, they used other symbols, such as a double hash-
mark (also called a *wedge*), as a placeholder. Why the need for a
placeholder—or a number that holds a place? Merchants and tax
collectors in particular needed such a tool. After all, their numbers
became larger as trade developed and more taxes were levied. The
placeholder became extremely necessary; for example, the number
5,000 implies that the three places to the right of the 5 are "empty"
and only the thousands column contains any value.

The first crude symbol for zero as a placeholder may have been
invented around 32 B.C. by Mesoamericans in Central America—
most notably in a calendar called the Long Count Calendar. No one
really agrees if it was the Olmecs or the Mayans who first used a
shell-like symbol for zero. Either way, the idea of using a symbol for
zero remained a secret for centuries, as isolation hindered the Mesoamericans, never allowing their concept of zero to be spread around
the world.

More than 100 years later, another symbol for zero was invented
either in Indochina or India. In this case, the culture was not averse
to spreading their number system—including the concept of zero—
around the world in trade and commerce. And by around A.D. 130,
Greek mathematician and astronomer Ptolemy, influenced mainly
by the Babylonians, used a symbol representing zero along with the
alphabetic Greek numerals—not just to hold a place, but as a
number.

But because zero technically means nothing, few people accepted the concept of "nothing" between numbers. Not every culture ignored the idea, though; Hindu mathematicians often wrote their math in verse, using words similar to "nothing," such as *sunya* ("void") and *akasa* ("space"). Finally, around A.D. 650, zero became an important number in Indian mathematics, though the symbol varied greatly from what we think of as our modern zero. The familiar Hindu-Arabic symbol for zero—essentially an open oval standing on one end—would take several more centuries to become accepted.

Why all the excitement after zero was "invented"? It turns out that all the wonderful, exotic properties of zero made it a necessity to the development of science and technology over time—in everything from architecture and engineering to our checkbooks. The properties are many: You cannot divide by zero (or in other words, divide something by nothing); zero only in the numerator (top number) of a fraction will always be equal to zero; it's considered an even number. Probably its most endearing quality is that when zero is added or subtracted from any number, the result is that number. Add nothing, subtract nothing, and you get the original number—a handy device to have when it comes to counting on anything.

"The importance of the creation of the zero mark can never be exaggerated. This giving to airy nothing, not merely a local habitation and a name, a picture, a symbol, but helpful power, is the characteristic of the Hindu race from whence it sprang. It is like coining the Nirvana into dynamos. No single mathematical creation has been more potent for the general on-go of intelligence and power."

— G. B. HALSTED

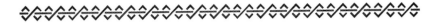

Inventions
Worth the Paper It's Printed On: The Origins of Paper

◆ ◆ ◆ ◆

Three cheers for Ts'ai Lun! Without him, there would be no daily gazette. Without him, there would be no dollar bills. Without him, nobody could let their fingers walk through the local phone directory. Without him, no one could read this very book. Thanks to this gentleman from Lei-Yang, China, the world enjoys the gift of paper.

Where's the Paper, Boy?

Ts'ai Lun's invention of paper dates to A.D. 105. However, paperlike papyrus had been produced in Egypt for more than 3,000 years prior. The word *paper* is even derived from *papyrus*. Ancient Egyptians developed it by hammering strips of the papyrus plant into a unified sheet for writing. They even sold it to the Greeks and Romans until around 300 B.C. With their papyrus supply cut off, Greeks and Romans turned to parchment, made from the skins of a variety of animals.

Paper on a Roll

Ts'ai Lun was a member of the imperial court who became fascinated with the way wasps made their nests. Using that knowledge as a starting point, he took a mash of wood pulp and spread it across a coarse cloth screen. The dried fibers formed a sheet of pliable paper that could be peeled off and written on.

The new material quickly became a staple for official government business, for wrapping, and for envelopes. By the seventh century A.D., the Chinese had even invented toilet paper. A Chinese scholar at the time showed good judgment, observing, "Paper on which there are quotations or...the names of sages, I dare not use for toilet purposes."

Paper Goes International

The art of papermaking remained in Asia for several centuries, spreading to Korea and Japan. Around A.D. 1000, papermaking

reached the Middle East. Arabians used linen fibers in place of wood pulp, creating a higher-quality paper. These superior products were in high demand, and exports increased. In this way, the art of papermaking reached Europe and flourished—particularly in Italy—by the 13th century.

The Italians took their papermaking very seriously, using machinery and standardized processes to turn out large amounts of top-notch paper. They used water power to run paper mills, created higher-quality drying screens, and improved the sizing process. A new coating was also developed to improve paper strength and reduce water absorbency.

(Don't) Stop the Presses!

When a German named Johannes Gutenberg developed the movable type printing press in the mid-1400s, the world of papermaking was changed forever. Books that were once hand-copied were now available in a mass-produced format. As the appetite for new books grew, so did the need for paper.

The New World was introduced to papermaking in the late 1600s, when the first paper mill was built in Mexico. A German immigrant named William Rittenhouse started the first paper plant in the British colonies in Philadelphia in 1690. In less than a century, 20 mills were producing paper in the colonies.

All the News(paper) That's Fit to Print

Much of the paper being produced in the mills was made from old rags, clothing, and other textiles, making a thick paper. Around 1840, a Canadian named Charles Fenerty used a fine wood pulp to create a thin, inexpensive paper known as "newsprint." However, he didn't pursue a patent for his work and his claim of invention was lost to others. Still, Fenerty's invention enabled newspapers to be printed more frequently.

It's In the Bag

Paper has proved to be a versatile material in uses that go far beyond writing and printing. Following the Civil War, veteran Charles Stilwell returned to his home in Ohio and became a mechanical engineer. He noticed that paper bags used to carry groceries were not well made and wouldn't stand up on their own. He solved the problem, patenting a machine in 1883 that made paper grocery bags with a flat bottom and pleated sides. The style remains largely unchanged in the paper bags used today.

If Ts'ai Lun were still alive, he would most likely be amazed by how widespread his humble invention has become. In the modern world, it is virtually impossible to pass a day without picking up a book, a newspaper, an envelope, or a paper bag. Readers, writers, and even shoppers owe him a debt of gratitude for making their world an easier place in which to live.

By 1995, worldwide sales of toilet paper had reached $3.5 billion.

In 1999, the United States used approximately 800 pounds of paper per person.

The world's largest producers of paper and paper products are Canada and the United States.

Recycling just one ton of paper saves 17 trees.

Computers & Cyberspace
The Invention That Clicked

❖ ❖ ❖ ❖

*It's the input device we really couldn't live without. While you may
be able to control some of your computer via keyboard "hot keys,"
the point-and-click mouse is still an essential component. In fact, it
would be all but impossible to use most computers without one.*

Q: How does a mouse work?
A: A computer mouse functions by detecting two-dimensional motion. This
allows you to move the pointer around the screen to open documents,
launch applications, and click on Web sites. It is even the primary means
of control for many computer games.

Q: Why is it called a *mouse*?
A: Care to take a guess? It's called a mouse
because it resembles one. When the
device was developed at the Stanford
Research Institute (SRI), it had a cord
attached to its rear—much like the
tail on a mouse.

Q: Who invented the mouse?
A: SRI inventor and engineer Douglas
Engelbart is generally considered the father of the first PC mouse. But it
was Bill English, an engineer who assisted with the construction of Engelbart's original designs, who first created the now-familiar inverted track-
ball system, which replaced the multiwheels used in Engelbart's device.
English's innovation became the predominant model for more than three
decades. It was also the basis of the first marketed integrated mouse,
which was intended for personal computer navigation and was first sold in
1981 with the Xerox 8010 Star Information System. English can also be
credited with adding the word *mouse,* as a computer term, to the English
lexicon. He included it in his 1965 publication *Computer-Aided Display
Control.*

While Engelbart's motion controls soon improved, his other contributions
have remained a core part of the mouse. Most notable is his single-button
design, a feature that remained part of Apple systems until 2005 (PC mice
commonly have three or more buttons).

Film
A Star Is Born

❖ ❖ ❖ ❖

A publicity stunt catapulted actress Florence Lawrence to fame as the first movie star. But her story doesn't have a happy ending.

Long before the age of cinema, featured performers in theater, vaudeville, and even sports were recognized and admired as stars in the public eye. But it was the movie industry that would glamorize and exploit the concept of stardom to such a degree that film actors and actresses were ultimately turned into fantasy figures idolized by an adoring public. Ironically, the American film industry did not immediately employ a star system and was actually even slow to credit the actors who appeared in its movies.

In the early days, performing in front of the camera was not considered a special talent by many production companies, which often required their casts to also serve as crew members by building sets, making costumes, or helping with other chores. Despite the relative anonymity of movie actors, audiences wrote to production companies to express interest in certain performers whether they knew their names or not.

Around 1908–1909, production companies began to hold their performers in higher regard and consider them on par with theater actors. As a result, small-scale efforts to tout actors or at least identify them emerged. In January 1909, Kalem released a photo of their cast roster to the *New York Dramatic Mirror*, listing the actors' names beneath the photos; in the fall, the Edison Company became the first to announce the cast of their films onscreen. Both efforts were in response to the public's interest in their performers and were a bid to generate more attention.

The First Star and the First Major Publicity Stunt

Against this backdrop, an incident occurred that immediately boosted the popularity of one actress, propelling her into full-fledged stardom. Florence Lawrence had been a popular actress for American Biograph and was recognized by the public as the

Biograph Girl, though her real name was unknown. In late 1909, she left Biograph and signed with a rival upstart, IMP Moving Picture Co., owned by Carl Laemmle.

Laemmle wanted audiences to know that the Biograph Girl now worked for IMP. In the December 1909 issue of *Moving Picture World,* a photo of Lawrence appeared in an ad for her film *Lest We Forget.* Written across her photo in bold was "She's an IMP!" Though the ad did not mention Lawrence by name, it traded on the public's recognition of her as the Biograph Girl and then mischievously let them know that IMP had snapped her up.

In March 1910, Laemmle escalated his publicity efforts. On March 12, he placed an ad in *Moving Picture World,* claiming that rival production companies had spread rumors in St. Louis, Missouri, newspapers that Florence Lawrence (the IMP Girl, formerly the Biograph Girl) had been killed in a streetcar accident. He lambasted his enemies for spreading lies and reassured the public that she was doing the best work of her career for IMP. Laemmle's claims regarding the newspaper article were probably false; no such article has ever been discovered. His goal was to direct attention to Lawrence in a large-scale way, reveal her real name to the public, and tout her films for IMP so that audiences would flock to see them.

This publicity stunt worked and became the archetype for promotion tactics of the future. It generated articles about Lawrence in major newspapers, and when the IMP Girl came to St. Louis the following month to appear at the premiere of her latest film, she was mobbed.

Lawrence did become the first movie star as a result of Laemmle's publicity stunt, though her fame was short-lived. After she was badly burned in a 1915 fire, her popularity was eclipsed by Mary Pickford, among others. Lawrence was relegated to bit parts and was soon forgotten. In 1938, she committed suicide—a victim of the star system she helped create.

Visual Art
The American Quilt

❖ ❖ ❖ ❖

*Whether you curl up for a nap under your grandmother's
quilt or do a little quilting yourself, rest assured, your
interest in this beloved bedding is steeped in tradition.*

The First Few Stitches

Quilting is the process of sewing together layers of fabric and filler.
The bottom layer is called the *backing,* the middle layer is the filling
or *batting,* and the top layer is called, well, the *top.* The layers are
sewn together to create cozy bedding or clothing.

People have been quilting—but not necessarily making quilted
blankets—for a long time. An ivory carving from around 3600 B.C.
depicts a king in a quilted cloak. Excavation of a Mongolian cave
revealed a quilted linen carpet, and a pair of quilted slippers found
near the Russia/China border was probably from the eighth or ninth
century.

Patchwork, the process of piecing together scraps of fabric to
make a larger whole, was widely practiced in Europe through the
1600s because it was economical. Old clothes and blankets were
often recycled into something entirely new.

Early Amish Influence

The roots of the traditional quilt began to take hold in Europe and
the United States in the 18th century. The oldest existing piece is the
Saltonstall quilt. It was made in Massachusetts in 1704 and, though
tattered, provides a window into the quilt-making styles of the era.
Amish settlers arrived in Pennsylvania in the early 1700s, and their
quilts, known for jewel-toned fabrics and striking geometric patterns, surfaced in the 1800s. Our concept of patchwork quilts, patterns, and blocks has been greatly influenced by Amish quilters.

An Industrial Revolution

By the end of the 18th century, the textile industry in England had
been fully mechanized, and the French were coming up with better,

faster, and cleaner ways to dye fabric. Large quantities of colorfast, printed cottons became readily available, much to the delight of people everywhere.

By the time the War of Independence rolled around, the vast English textile industry was exporting thousands of tons of cotton to America. These fabrics made up the majority of the clothes and quilts of the era.

Social Hour

It's a misconception that people made quilts just for practical purposes. In fact, most quilters engaged in the hobby because they loved the craft—not because they needed a blanket. By 1820, sewing groups were widespread, allowing people to work together to sew quilts that were pulled across large frames. Many of the close-knit community sewing bees (or "sewing circles") of yesterday still function as quilting guilds and clubs today.

Patterns and Designs

Though some quilters specialize in whole-cloth quilts, most of the quilts made today are of the patchwork variety. Pieces of fabric are sewn together to make a single block; multiple blocks are then stitched to each other, creating the quilt top.

One of the most admired quilt styles comes from Hawaii. These quilts incorporate just two colors—usually red and white—and one large cutout design sewn directly onto the quilt top. The striking geometric shapes and intricate stitching have made Hawaiian quilts popular among quilters and quilt admirers for two centuries.

Modern-day Quilts

Quilting in the United States experienced a revival in the 1970s, largely due to the country's 200th birthday. As part of the celebration, women and men alike took a renewed interest in quilting and in folk art and crafts in general.

The surge in the popularity of quilting turned this humble pastime into the $3.3-billion-a-year industry it is today. The current movement toward more simple, eco-friendly lifestyles will likely keep quilting alive for years to come.

Religion
Grandpa, Stick Around a While: The Origins of Mummification

❖ ❖ ❖ ❖

*Turns out that the Egyptians—history's most famous embalmers—
weren't the first. By the time Egyptians were fumbling with the
art, Saharans and Andeans were veterans at mortuary science.*

Andes

In northern Chile and southern Peru, modern researchers have
found hundreds of pre-Inca mummies (roughly 5000–2000 B.C.) from
the Chinchorro culture. Evidently, the Chinchorros mummified all
walks of life: rich, poor, elderly, didn't matter. We still don't know
exactly why, but a simple, plausible explanation is that they wanted
to honor and respect their dead.

The work shows the evolution of increasingly sophisticated, artistic techniques that weren't very different from later African methods: Take out the wet stuff before it gets too gross, pack the body
carefully, dry it out. The process occurred near the open-air baking
oven we call the Atacama Desert, which may hold a clue in itself.

Uan Muhuggiag

The oldest known instance of deliberate mummification in Africa
comes from ancient Saharan cattle ranchers. In southern Libya,
at a rock shelter now called Uan Muhuggiag, archaeologists found
evidence of basic seminomadic civilization, including animal
domestication, pottery, and ceremonial burial.

We don't know why the people of Uan Muhuggiag mummified
a young boy, but they did a good job. Dispute exists about dating
here: Some date the remains back to the 7400s B.C., others to only
3400s B.C. Even at the latest reasonable dating, this predates large-
scale Egyptian practices. The remains demonstrate refinement and
specialized knowledge that likely took centuries to develop. Quite
possibly some of this knowledge filtered into Egyptian understanding given that some of the other cultural finds at Uan Muhuggiag
look pre-Egyptian as well.

Egypt

Some 7,000 to 12,000 years ago, Egyptians buried their dead in hot
sand without wrapping. Given Egypt's naturally arid climate, the
corpse sometimes dehydrated so quickly that decay was minimal.
Sands shift, of course, which would sometimes lead to passersby
finding an exposed body in surprisingly good shape. Perhaps this
inspired early Egyptian mummification efforts.

As Egyptian civilization advanced, mummification interwove
with their view of the afterlife. Professionals formalized and refined
the process. A whole industry arose, offering funerary options from
deluxe (special spices, carved wood case) to budget (dry 'em out and
hand 'em back). *Natron*, a mixture of sodium salts abundant along
the Nile, made a big difference. If you extracted the guts and brains
from a corpse, then dried it out it in natron for a couple of months,
the remains would keep for a long time. The earliest known Egyptian mummy dates to around 3300 B.C.

Desert Origins

It's hard to ignore a common factor among these cultures: proximity
to deserts. It seems likely that ancient civilizations got the idea from
seeing natural mummies.

Ice and bogs can also preserve a body by accident, of course, but
they don't necessarily mummify it. Once exposed, the preservation
of the remains depends on swift discovery and professional handling.
If ancient Africans and South Americans developed mummification
based on desert-dried bodies, it would explain why bogs and glaciers
didn't lead to similar mortuary science. The ancients had no convenient way to deliberately keep a body frozen year-round without
losing track of it, nor could they create a controlled mini-bog environment. But people could and did replicate the desert's action on
human remains.

Today

We make mummies today, believe it or not. An embalmed corpse
is a mummy—it's just a question of how far the embalmers went in
their preservation efforts. To put it indelicately: If you've attended
an open-casket funeral, you've seen a mummy.

Inventions
Barbed-wire Revolution

❖ ❖ ❖ ❖

In 1915, Robert Frost gave the world the line "Good fences
make good neighbors." But fences have often meant much
more than that; to the brave men and women defending their
property against the wilderness, they meant nothing less than
safety and survival. But what makes a "good" fence?

In the American West, the answer was barbed wire—an invention
that left its mark on an entire continent. As America's settlers spread
out into its vast heartland, they tried to take their fences with them.
However, in comparison with the rock-strewn fields of New England
or the lush pine forests of the South from whence they came, the
pioneers found their new environs to be lacking in suitable material
with which to build the barriers that would protect their land. At the
time, it was the responsibility of landowners to keep roving animals
out of their fields (rather than it being incumbent upon the owner of
the animals to keep them controlled). As a result, farmers were left
to deal with the problem of how to protect their crops in conjunc-
tion with the impossibility of building their traditional fences. A new
solution simply had to be found. The answer came from the state of
Illinois, which was on the border between the civilized East and the
wild West.

An Idea Whose Time Had Come
In 1873, a farmer named Henry Rose was desperate to control a
"breachy" cow. His original idea was to attach a board covered with
metallic points directly to the head of his cow; when the cow ran into
a fence, the points would prick the cow and cause it to retreat. It
came as a surprise to Rose (though probably not to anyone else) that
requiring his cow to wear a plank all the time proved impractical; he
then decided to attach the boards to his fence rather than to the cow.
The solution seemed promising, and Rose proudly showed off his
invention at a county fair where it caught the attention of a number
of other inventors, including Joseph Glidden.

Glidden, working with a hand-cranked coffee mill in his kitchen, soon found that by twisting two lengths of wire together with a shorter piece in between to form a prickly barb, he could make a fence as effective as Rose's. He put up a test fence demonstrating his new invention, and word quickly spread. Isaac Ellwood, who had also seen Rose's display at the county fair and had been working on his own version, drove out to see Glidden's fence only to ride off in a rage when his wife commented that Glidden's barrier was superior to his. Ellwood was a shrewd businessman, however, and after he cooled down, he purchased an interest in Glidden's invention, and the two went into business together making barbed-wire fencing. Joseph Haish, also inspired by the Rose invention, introduced a rival barbed-wire fence around the same time.

All that was left was to convince a doubtful public that a few strands of thin wire could hold back determined cattle. The innumerable herds of Texas would be the proving ground, as barbed-wire salesmen threw up enclosures and invited ranchers to bring their most ornery cattle. To the amazement of the onlookers, barbed wire proved equal to the task again and again, and sales skyrocketed.

Don't Fence Me In

Ironically, even though barbed wire's most obvious use was to protect farmers' fields, it wasn't until the cattle ranchers seized on barbed wire that it began to transform the West. Large ranches quickly realized that by fencing off grazing land they could effectively control the cattle industry, and miles of fencing sprang up across Texas and other territories. The fences weren't always well received; they injured cows and were sometimes put up without regard to traditional pasture or water rights. The winters of 1885 to 1887 were particularly brutal; free-range cattle in northern ranges, accustomed to moving south in the face of impending blizzards, found their way blocked by the strange new fences. The cows froze to death by the thousands—carcasses stacked 400 yards deep against

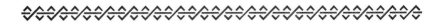

the fences in some places—in an event forever remembered as the Big Die-Up. Tempers naturally ran high, and there were open hostilities across the West as armed factions cut down rival fences and put up new ones.

Despite the controversy, however, it proved impossible to reverse the trend to fence in land. Within about 25 years of the introduction of barbed wire, nearly all of what had previously been free-range land was fenced and under private ownership. The open land of the West, at one time considered an inexhaustible resource for all to use, was divided up and made off-limits to the general public. The new invention channeled people into fixed paths of transit centered on railroads and towns. These patterns evolved into the interstate highways and cities we know today. It's no exaggeration to say that barbed wire is responsible for the shape of the modern West as we see it today—and it can all be traced back to farmer Henry Rose's breachy cow.

❖❖❖❖❖❖❖

"Where a new invention promises to be useful, it ought to be tried."
—THOMAS JEFFERSON

"An amazing invention—but who would ever want to use one?"
—RUTHERFORD B. HAYES UPON MAKING A CALL FROM WASHINGTON TO PENNSYLVANIA
WITH ALEXANDER GRAHAM BELL'S TELEPHONE, PATENTED ON MARCH 7, 1876

"Our inventions are wont to be pretty toys, which distract our attention from serious things. They are but improved means to an unimproved end."
—HENRY DAVID THOREAU

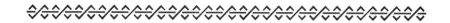

REAL NAMES OF THE RICH AND FAMOUS

Entertainers, actors, musicians, and other celebrities change their names for many reasons. Some prefer to use nicknames; some have unusual names that are not glamorous or sophisticated; others allowed managers, studio executives, or agents to change their names. Entertainers from previous generations "Americanized" ethnic-sounding names to appeal to a wide audience. Uncovering a celebrity's real name often provides insight into his or her career and background.

Ringo Starr was the only Beatle to change his name. He was born Richard Starkey.

Rock singer Sting of The Police was known as Gordon Matthew Sumner back when he was a young soccer fan in England.

Before Tina Turner stormed the stage in her micro-minis and stiletto heels, she was Anna Mae Bullock.

Everyone's favorite lunatic character actor, Christopher Walken, was originally Ronald Walken.

Tough cowboy star John Wayne could not have captured as many bad guys with his original name, Marion Michael Morrison.

Anna Mae Wong, Hollywood's first Asian star, was born Wong Liu Tsong.

Tony Orlando has inspired thousands of Americans to tie yellow ribbons around oak trees. Would he have had as much success with the name Michael Anthony Orlando Cassavitis?

The given name of talented young actress Natalie Portman is Natalie Hershlag.

Actor Martin Sheen was born Ramon Estevez, creating identity crises for his actor sons. Like his father, Charlie Sheen changed his name—from Carlos Irwin Estevez—while another son stuck with his birth name: Emilio Estevez.

Food & Drink
Fun with Food

❖ ❖ ❖

Hungry to know where your favorite foods originated?
Take a bite out of this tasty treatise!

Pizza

It might be considered American fast food today, but pizza originated in the South Italian region around Naples, where flat yeast-based bread topped with tomatoes was a local specialty. In 1889, baker Raffaele Esposito made pizzas for the visiting Italian King Umberto I and Queen Margherita. The queen's favorite was a pizza that featured the colors of the Italian flag—green basil leaves over white mozzarella cheese and red tomatoes. This dish soon became known as margherita pizza and was the taste of Italy around the world.

Sandwich

This lunchtime favorite likely dates back to the ancient Hebrews, who may have put meat and herbs between unleavened bread during Passover. But it was an 18th-century British noble that gave it its name. John Montagu, 4th Earl of Sandwich, was a keen card player and commonly ate meat between pieces of bread to keep from getting the cards greasy.

Pretzel

Monks in southern France or northern Italy, possibly dating back to the seventh century, can be credited with giving baked dough as a reward to children who learned their prayers, hence the shape, which is meant to resemble a person in prayer. The salty snacks gained popularity in southern Germany in the 12th century, where folded, baked bread was called *Brezl*.

Caesar Salad

It is a salad fit for a Roman emperor, but it isn't named after Julius or even Augustus. It is the creation of Italian-born Mexican chef Caesar Cardini, who according to one story, whipped up the salad when faced with a shortage of ingredients for a Fourth of July celebration in 1924. Another tale attests that Cardini made it for a gourmet contest in Tijuana. Either way, the salad is worthy of his name!

Steak Tartare

The nomadic Tartar warrior tribe was known for eating raw meat, which was usually pressed underneath the saddle of a horse, but the raw meat dish today, which is usually chopped beef or horsemeat with a liberal amount of seasoning and spices, may take its name from the Italian word *tartari,* which means raw steak.

Ranch Dressing

One of the most popular salad dressings in the United States actually did start out on a ranch—a dude ranch in Santa Barbara, California. Opened in 1954 by Steve and Gayle Henson, the "Hidden Valley Ranch" served a special house dressing that was so popular visitors came just to buy it.

Pasty

The forerunner of the potpie was originally cooked up as a lunch meal by Cornish miners, who were unable to return to the surface to eat or even clean up. The pastry crust allowed the miners—as well as other laborers—the ability to eat the contents, which typically included meat, vegetables, and gravy, and then discard the shell.

TV Dinner

The advent of the microwave has changed the frozen food market, but in 1953, Swanson's TV Brand Frozen Dinner was a popular prime-time meal. However, it may come as a surprise that frozen dinners predated Swanson's by nearly a decade, when William L. Maxson devised a prepackaged frozen meal for airplanes in 1944. Still, clever marketing and better distribution ensured that the TV Dinner from Swanson became the nationally recognized leader in frozen food.

Taco

The handheld Mexican favorite can be considered one of the first "fusion" foods—and it is as much a mix of cultures as the Mexican people today. The native Nahuatl people ate fish served in the flat corn bread, but it was 16th-century Spanish explorers who gave the bread the name *tortilla* and began to fill it with beef and chicken as well.

Nachos

One of today's cheesiest snacks made its debut during World War II. When several U.S. soldiers stopped in at the Victory Club, just south of the Texas-Mexico border, chef Ignacio "Nacho" Anaya found he had little food to serve beyond tortillas and cheese. Cut into triangles and fried, the tortilla chips were served with the cheese. Over the next three decades, the dish spread throughout Texas until sportscaster Howard Cosell gave kudos to the dish during a taping of *Monday Night Football* in 1977.

Waffles

During the Middle Ages, a thin crisp cake was baked between wafer irons. Oftentimes, the irons included designs that helped advertise the kitchen that produced the waffle. Early waffles were made of barley and oats, but by the 18th century, the ingredients changed to the modern version of leaven flour.

Pop Tarts

Kellogg's brand name for toaster pastries was actually developed in response to a product from Post Cereals that used a process initially used for dog food. Post had created a food-in-foil process for canine chow and then adapted it for a breakfast food the company introduced as "Country Squares." But Kellogg jumped on the bandwagon with its own sugary filling in a pastry crust, and thus Pop Tarts won the battle of the toasters.

What Do You Mean by That?

Up for Grabs

This phrase, which means that something is available to anyone who wants it, is a fairly recent expression, dating back to the Great Depression, when restaurants saved every scrap of excess food. The leftovers were put into bags and set at the end of the counter, where any person in need could take one without suffering the indignity of having to beg.

Mad as a Hatter

The Mad Hatter was popularized in Lewis Carroll's *Alice's Adventures in Wonderland,* but Carroll did not coin the phrase. Making hats had already been linked with madness. During the early days of processing felt to use in hatmaking, the toxic substance mercury was used, which resulted in many industry workers developing mental or neurological disturbances. From this unfortunate situation, the phrase "mad as a hatter" came to indicate anyone who had gone insane.

Crocodile Tears

When someone is said to be crying "crocodile tears," they are feigning sorrow. This phrase actually does come from crocodiles and specifically refers to a peculiarity in which crocodiles shed tears while eating. This is caused by food pressing against the roof of the animal's mouth, which activates the lachrymal glands that secrete tears, making crocodiles appear to be crying without really being sad at all.

It's Greek to Me

This phrase, used by someone to indicate that he or she doesn't understand a word of what's being said, is really a quotation from the first act of William Shakespeare's *Julius Caesar.* The character Casca, one of the plotters who participates in Caesar's assassination, describes overhearing Cicero, who was speaking in Greek to deter eavesdroppers. The ploy obviously worked.

Sports
Lacrosse—As American as Apple Pie

❖ ❖ ❖ ❖

*Lacrosse is Canada's national summer sport and is the fastest
growing high school and college sport in the United States.
Along with basketball, it is arguably the most North American
game there is—First Nations (Native Americans) invented it.*

First Nations Origins

Algonquins called lacrosse *baggataway,* and the Iroquois called it
teewaarathon. Natives played the game to honor the Great Spirit
of revered elders or to celebrate. Lacrosse also served a diplomatic
role. Suppose you were a Mohawk elder, and you learned that the
Oneidas were fishing on your side of the lake (violating your long-
standing agreement). Rather than sending your warriors to fight
the Oneida, you'd send an emissary to challenge them to settle the
dispute with a teewaarathon match. These early games, which were
quite violent, took place on fields that were miles long and involved
as many as 1,000 participants. We can thank French Canadians for
the game's name: *La crosse* means "the bishop's staff," because that's
what the stick looked like.

Settlers' Adoption

Europeans' first record of a lacrosse match dates to the 1630s in
southern Ontario, when missionary Jean de Brébeuf watched the
Hurons play. By the 1800s, the game was popular with French-
Canadian settlers. In 1867, the same year Canada became a dominion,
Canadian dentist W. George Beers standardized the rules of lacrosse.
By 1900, the Canadian game had spread well across its native land and
into the United States, with both men's and women's versions.

The Game Today

There are two primary forms of lacrosse today: box (indoor) and field
(outdoor). Box lacrosse is largely a Canadian sport, but Canadians
also compete well in men's and women's field lacrosse. The game
values speed and agility above brawn. The crosse (stick) takes skill

to manipulate as players move the ball around. Play flow is similar to hockey or soccer; a team tries to control the ball and send it past a goaltender into the net. Fouls are similar to those in hockey, as is the penalty box. Lacrosse is a physical, speedy, demanding game that requires the toughness of rugby and the stamina of soccer.

First Nations in the Game

Only one First Nations team is sanctioned for international sport competition: the Iroquois Nationals, in field lacrosse. They're even sponsored by Nike!

Positions in Men's Lacrosse

Attack: *There are three attackers on the field at one time. The attackers use "short-sticks" and must demonstrate good stick-handling with both hands; they must know where their teammates are at all times and be able to handle the pressure of opposing defense. Attackers score most of the goals.*

Defense: *Three defensive players with "long-poles" and one long-stick midfielder are allowed on the field at a time, using their sticks to throw checks and trying to dislodge the ball. One of the "long-poles" may also play midfield as a strategic defender, a.k.a. a long-stick middie. Teams usually use this to anticipate losing the face-off and to be stronger on defense.*

Midfield: *Three "middies" are allowed on the field at once. There are two types of midfielders, defensive and offensive. The two can rotate by running off the sidelines. Midfielders are allowed to use short-sticks and up to one long-pole. While on offense, three short-sticks are generally used for their superior stick-handling. While on defense, two short-sticks are used with one long-pole. Some teams have a designated face-off middie who takes the majority of face-offs and is usually quickly substituted after the face-off is complete.*

Goalkeeper: *Goalies try to prevent the ball from getting into the goal, and they also direct the team defense.*

Television

Where No Show Had Gone Before: The Origin of *Star Trek*

❖ ❖ ❖ ❖

Star Trek is so integrated into modern American geek culture that it's hard to believe the original series more or less flopped. But flop it did, lasting only three seasons before deteriorating into sharp cheddar. In fact, the series almost wasn't made at all.

Concept

Science fiction wasn't new in 1960, as any Edgar Rice Burroughs devotee will tell you, but it was on the brink of going mainstream. A creative producer named Gene Roddenberry wanted to produce a science fiction TV series about space exploration, loosely based on C. S. Forester's classic *Hornblower* seafaring novels. Roddenberry didn't have much luck selling the concept until 1964, when he pitched it to Herb Solow, a senior production executive at Desilu Studios.

> *Early fact: Comedienne Lucille Ball was a key part of* Trek, *though she never appeared in an episode. She owned Desilu.*

A Tough Sell

Solow and Roddenberry tried to sell the networks a pilot (in TV-speak, a sample episode). Only NBC bought. The episode, "The Cage," bore modest resemblance to the later series and was in fact later melded into another episode as a backstory. NBC didn't buy *Star Trek* based on "The Cage," but some aspects of it impressed them. Other details, such as the "guy with the pointed ears" (Leonard Nimoy's Mr. Spock), didn't go over quite as well. The network ordered a second pilot.

> *Early fact: For a brief time, the series concept was called* Gulliver's Travels, *and the captain was Gulliver. Then everyone sobered up.*

In 1965, Desilu produced the second pilot, "Where No Man Has Gone Before." Most of the cast was new. NBC still had misgivings

about the Spock character: They felt he looked diabolical enough to alienate devout Christians. Nonetheless, the network ordered a season of *Trek* for 1966–67. The U.S.S. *Enterprise* was finally spaceworthy.

Early fact: Trek *actresses' scanty costuming was inspired partly by pulp magazines and partly by Roddenberry's vast libido.*

"These Are the Voyages..."
Trek presented immense challenges to prop, costume, and set designers. As a result, it was chronically overbudget. The show depended on heroic improvisations by the crew, turning salt shakers into surgical implements and scrap Styrofoam into futuristic fixtures.

Early fact: Due to the high cost of union labor, the crew maintained a nonunion costume sweatshop nearby.

Trek also showed up at precisely the right time to find a following. In those days of civil rights strife, antiwar protests, the space race, and Cold War fear, Star Trek portrayed future humanity unified behind high ideals. Their United Federation of Planets refused to interfere with other planets' cultures. The crew's ethnic and gender mix supported the impression, for in addition to a nonhuman, Enterprise officers included an African woman, a Japanese man, and by the second season, a Russian man. While the Enterprise ran on naval lines, it acted more like an exploration ship than a heavy cruiser. Star Trek was what the late 1960s counterculture wanted to see.

Early fact: Trek's *third and final season depicted the first interracial (white/black) kiss on American TV.*

Downfall
Unfortunately, *Trek* never earned stellar ratings. The third season aired in the "banana peel" slot: 10 P.M. Fridays. Not even a(nother) massive letter-writing campaign could save the show.

But its fans wouldn't let go, and in 1979 came *Star Trek: The Motion Picture.* Then came scores of novels, more movies, and even several new *Trek* TV series. In 2009, yet another new *Star Trek* movie was released to the delight of fans everywhere.

Clubs & Organizations
Utopian Societies

❖ ❖ ❖ ❖

In 1516, Sir Thomas More coined the term utopia *in a book of the same name. In it he refers to an ideal, imaginary island where everything is lovely all the time. For centuries since then, groups of people (often led by fanatical figures) have broken off from society to develop their own communities intended to bring peace, harmony, and spiritual enlightenment to all their citizens—and ultimately the whole world. Unfortunately, utopian societies seldom work out as planned.*

Founder: Charles Fourier

Plan: In the mid-19th century, Fourier contacted out-of-work New Englanders with the proposition of joining communal-living groups he called *phalanxes.* These groups would be arranged hierarchically according to members' trades or skills. Children are good at digging in the dirt, for example, so they would be in charge of maintaining the garbage dumps. Group members would be compensated for their contributions to the community.

Outcome: Fourier died in Paris before he saw the development of any phalanxes. In the early 1840s, a group of devotees, or Fourierists, founded the North American Phalanx on farmland in New Jersey and kept it going until disputes over women's rights and abolition drove many away. A fire destroyed buildings on the site in 1854, and operations ceased completely in 1856.

Founder: Robert Owen

Plan: Owen called his version of utopia New Harmony and hoped his "empire of goodwill" would eventually take over the planet. His attempt at communal bliss started in Indiana in 1825.

Outcome: Hundreds of devoted followers lived according to Owen's ideals, with individual members plying their crafts and contributing to the community (even if that meant there was no one with the ability to spin the wool shorn by an abundance of sheepshearers).

With no sound economic plan, New Harmony was in chaos from the start. There were five constitutions drafted in the first year alone. Not surprisingly, New Harmony failed within two years.

Founder: The Spiritualists

Plan: The Mountain Cove Community was the Spiritualists' attempt to create their own idea of harmony. They founded their group in Virginia in 1851 on a spot once considered to be the Garden of Eden. The group insisted that no one individual would be allowed to dictate to others; all the direction anyone needed would come from "the spirits."

Outcome: As part of their introduction into the community, members were required to give up all their possessions, again leaving issues such as finances to the spirit world. Not surprisingly, the experiment lasted less than two years.

Founder: Etienne Cabet

Plan: Cabet's *Voyage en Icarie,* written in 1840, depicted an ideal society, the Icarians, in which an elected government controlled all economic activity as well as social affairs. Cabet decided to make his dream a reality and set sail for America.

Outcome: In 1848, the group landed outside New Orleans on swampland not fit for settlement. Malaria and starvation took many of this group of Icarians, and the rest deserted around 1856.

Founder: The Shakers

Plan: The Shakers were an 18th-century religious denomination of Protestants who decided to leave the immoral world behind and create a pious place in which to live and serve God.

Outcome: By the mid-1800s, the Shakers had built 19 communal settlements in New England, Kentucky, and Ohio that attracted some 200,000 followers. Their numbers gradually dwindled, but their simple way of life continues to attract widespread interest. The Shakers are generally considered to be one of the few successful utopian societies.

Inventions
An Uplifting Tale: The Origin of the Elevator

❖ ❖ ❖ ❖

When Elisha Graves Otis and his sons began their elevator business in the 1850s, the solid brick buildings of America's cities had four-story height limits. By the 1920s, with the widespread adoption of safe, power-driven lifts, skyscrapers had replaced church steeples as the hallmark of urban design.

Elevators to lift cargo have been around since the pyramidal ziggurats of ancient Iraq. In 236 B.C., the Greek scientist Archimedes used his knowledge of levers to deploy beast- and slave-drawn hoists. In 1743, technicians of French King Louis XV devised a "flying chair," with pulleys and weights running down the royal chimney, to carry his mistress, Madame de Pompadour, in and out of the palace's upper floor.

An Uplifting Background

A descendant of American Revolutionary James Otis, Elisha Otis won a hard-earned path to success. Born in Vermont in 1811, Otis was a stereotype of Yankee ingenuity. In the 1840s, as a senior mechanic in a bedstead factory in Albany, New York, he patented a railroad safety brake, critical to quickly and safely hauling freight in and out of the factories of the Industrial Revolution. By 1852, Otis was a master mechanic at another bedstead firm in Yonkers, New York. He began tinkering with a safety lift for its warehouse, but the company went belly-up. Otis was mulling a move to California's Gold Rush country when a furniture maker asked him to build two safety elevators. A pair of workers at the manufacturing plant had died when a cable to their lift broke. Fighting off chronically poor health, Otis established his own company and set to work.

All Safe

In 1854, Otis—looking quite distinguished in a full beard and top hat—took to a platform at the Crystal Palace exposition in New York. A rope had pulled his newfangled "hoisting apparatus" high up a

354

shaft, its side open to public view. With a flourish, he waved an ax toward the nervous onlookers crowding the hall. Then, with a quick motion, Otis cleaved the rope with the ax. The onlookers gasped as the elevator began its downward plunge—only to suddenly stop after a three-inch fall.

Elisha Otis tipped his hat and proclaimed: "All safe, gentlemen, all safe."

Otis's means of making his freight elevators safe was straightforward. He attached a wagon wheel's taut springs to the elevator ropes. "If the rope snapped," explained *Smithsonian* magazine, "the ends of the steel spring would flare out, forcing two large latches to lock into ratchets on either side of the platform."

Otis soon patented an elevator driven by a tiny steam engine, permitting small enterprises like retail stores to purchase their own lifts. Modern department stores with multiple floors, such as Macy's, began to appear.

Despite his technical wizardry, Elisha Otis's commercial success and business sense were limited. Two years after his successful demonstration—despite a follow-up exhibit at P. T. Barnum's Traveling World's Fair—sales of Otis elevators totaled less than $14,000 a year. Even if proceeds picked up, wrote Otis's son Charles, "Father will manage in such a way [as] to lose it all," going "crazy over some wild fancy for the future." Five years later, in 1861, Otis died at age 49 of "nervous depression and diphtheria." He left his two sons a business that was $3,200 in the red.

Success

Charles and Norton Otis proved better businessmen and rivaled their father as technicians, making important improvements to their useful device. By 1873, Otis Brothers & Company, revenues soaring, had installed 2,000 elevators into buildings. Replacing steam-powered lifts, their hydraulic elevators sat on steel tubes sunk into shafts deep below the buildings. An influx of water pushed the platforms up. Reducing the water pressure lowered the elevators.

Where hotel guests previously had preferred the accessible first floor, they now opted to "make the transit with ease"—as an Otis catalog boasted—to the top floors, which offered "an exemption from noise, dust and exhalations of every kind."

Though taken for granted today, elevators were the height of opulence then. The Otis elevator in Gramercy Park, New York, which dates from 1883 and is still running, was decorated with upholstered seating and walnut paneling. Another elevator from that era in Saratoga Springs, New York, was outfitted with chandeliers and paneled in ebony and tulipwood.

Riding the skyscraper boom, the Otis firm went from one noted project to another. In 1889, the firm completed lifts for the bottom section of the Eiffel Tower. Around 1900, it bought the patents to a related invention, the escalator. In 1913, the Otis firm installed 26 electric elevators for the world's then-tallest structure, New York's 60-story Woolworth Building. In 1931, Otis installed 73 elevators and more than 120 miles of cables in another record-breaker, the 1,250-foot Empire State Building.

Setting the Ceiling

All the while, along with enhancements such as push-button controls, came improvements in speed. Cities constantly changed their elevator "speed limits"—from a leisurely 40 feet a minute for Elisha Otis's original safety lifts, to a speedy 1,200 feet a minute in the 1930s, to today's contraptions, which at 2,000 feet per minute can put a churning knot of G-force in the stomachs of passengers hurtling to their destination.

"That's probably as much vertical speed as most people can tolerate," says an Otis engineer.

Along the way, the elevator industry quashed early fears that speedy lifts were bad for people. In the 1890s, *Scientific American* wrote that the body parts of elevator passengers came to a halt at different rates, triggering mysterious ailments. Like the earlier notion that fast trains would choke passengers by pushing oxygen away from their mouths, that theory has since been debunked.

Prolific Producers

These "movers and shakers" are responsible for more than their fair share of the world's greatest accomplishments.

For those who believe that **Hollywood** produces the greatest number of films worldwide, hold onto your cellulose. **Bollywood,** the informal name bestowed upon India's movie industry, reels out roughly 1,000 films per year—*twice* as many as the much-celebrated Tinseltown. More formulaic than American movies, Indian films generally feature romantic musicals, love triangles, and a good-trumps-evil angle. Actress Aishwarya Rai and actor Amitabh Bachchan represent Bollywood royalty.

Speaking of Bollywood, **Daggubati Ramanaidu** is the producer to end all movie producers. Between 1963 and 2008, Ramanaidu generated some 110 films. This works out to an astounding 2.5 films per year for 45 years and ranks Ramanaidu as the most prolific movie producer in the world.

When it comes to NFL football, no one has scored more points than place kicker **Morten Andersen.** The 6' 2", 225-pound dynamo had amassed 2,544 career points by the end of the 2007 season. He officially retired in December 2008.

The "Wizard of Menlo Park," **Thomas Alva Edison** was so fruitful in dreaming up new devices, he referred to his West Orange, New Jersey, workplace as an "invention factory." Items such as the phonograph, alkaline storage battery, and moving pictures sprang from Edison's unique assemblage of talent and tenacity. "Genius is one percent inspiration and ninety-nine percent perspiration," the practical inventor would often say. Edison's U.S. patents, all 1,093 of them, attest to his foresight and fortitude.

Eyeing Edison's model and upping the ante in volume, Japanese inventor **Shunpei Yamazaki** has secured more U.S. patents than anyone. As of January 2008, Yamazaki held in excess of 1,700 patents (mostly in the field of computer science) with hundreds still pending. At a comparatively young 65 years of age, the potential to raise that number seems quite likely.

Places & Landmarks
Get Your Kicks

◆ ◆ ◆ ◆

Route 66 calls forth that part of the American spirit that is restless, adventurous, and longs to hear the song of the open road.

Route 66 is arguably the most famous highway in the United States, celebrated in history, novels, and songs. As such, it carries a mystique that no modern interstate can surpass.

During the 1920s, the American Association of State Highway officials recognized that the country's road system was not advancing at the same rate as automobile ownership. Cyrus Avery, a member of the Association, thought the existing system of named roads (such as the Lincoln Highway and the National Road) was antiquated and should be replaced by an integrated network of numbered interstate routes. He also pushed for an east-to-west route that would stretch more than 2,000 miles from Chicago to California, passing through his home state of Oklahoma. This roadway was formally proposed in 1925. By the following year, it had been approved, allocated the number "66," and opened.

In 1926, much of the highway was still unpaved, but it connected small towns to larger cities, making it easier for rural residents to escape failed farms for better luck in urban centers. As dirt roads gave way to new pavement, a network of motels, diners, gas stations, and oddball attractions sprang up to make long-distance travel along Route 66 not only possible but also comfortable and entertaining.

The Mother Road in American Pop Culture
Writer John Steinbeck was the first to immortalize Route 66 in American culture when he nicknamed it the "Mother Road" in his 1939 novel *The Grapes of Wrath*. Thousands of farmers had left the southern Great Plains region because of the natural devastation caused by dust storms and the financial ruin caused by the Depression. Steinbeck chronicled their situation through the fictional Joad family, who, like their real-life counterparts, packed up everything they owned and hit Route 66 seeking better opportunities

in California. After World War II, Route 66 continued its identity as the road to golden opportunities when returning soldiers and their families traveled West to make new lives for themselves.

In 1946, band leader Bobby Troupe celebrated the Mother Road in his song "Route 66," which invited the listener to get their "kicks" by taking to the highway and heading for California. A quarter-century later, the rock band the Eagles paid tribute to Winslow, Arizona—a major stop on Route 66—while extolling the virtues of the open road in their song "Take It Easy."

The roadway's mythic status reached a zenith in 1960 when the television drama *Route 66* debuted. The premise of the series captured the footloose spirit of American youth, following two friends who leave behind the drudgery of the nine-to-five world to tool around the country in a 1960 Corvette, reveling in their freedom while finding adventure and romance on the road.

Pull Up and Have a Rest at Wigwam Village

Another reason for the legendary status of Route 66 was the number of unique, privately owned restaurants, motor camps (motels), and attractions along the way. Unlike the chain restaurants and motels of today, these establishments were all one-of-a-kind and afforded travelers of the postwar era memories that have steeped Route 66 in nostalgia. From the Launching Pad Drive-In restaurant in Wilmington, Illinois, with its giant fiberglass spaceman in the parking lot, to the Wigwam Village motor court in Holbrook, Arizona, where guests stay in concrete teepees, Route 66 is lined with colorful and charming examples of Americana.

Beginning in the 1950s, interstates began to replace Route 66, and by 1984, the last part of the original highway was finally bypassed. Sections of the old highway are still maintained as "Historic Route 66," and the spirit of the fabled roadway is embedded in every American who revels in the freedom of the open road.

Science
Phrenology: Bumps in the Night

❖ ❖ ❖ ❖

*What if we told you that the bumps on your noggin could
be mapped to reveal insight into your true character?*

Phrenology got its start in 1796 when Austrian physician Franz
Joseph Gall proposed the shocking notion that the brain controlled
mental function, a science he initially called *cranioscopy*. Although
this idea was groundbreaking, it was not universally well-received,
especially by the religious community. Suggesting that it was the
brain—and not the soul—that controlled reason was the height of
hypocrisy. Consequently, Austrian Emperor Francis I asked Gall to
stop lecturing about his brain research in 1802.

   This bump in the road didn't stop Gall. In 1805, he published *On
the Activities of the Brain,* correctly stating that various points within
the brain are responsible for different functions. But he incorrectly
asserted that the shape of a person's skull allows a physician to study
the internal workings of the brain. Gall believed that there were
some 26 "organs" on the surface of the brain that affected the con-
tour of the skull—and even pointed out a "murder organ."

   By 1808, Gall had presented his most famous theory, that the
bumps on one's skull reveal the true character of its owner, a theory
that gave birth to modern phrenology. Others followed Gall's lead,
but phrenology truly grew to new heights during the Victorian era,
as snake-oil charmers and con men used the idea to profit from an
unsuspecting public by opening phrenology parlors and using the
practice to do all manner of things, from diagnosing illness to determining suitable marriage partners or appropriate careers. In 1931,
Henry C. Lavery cut out the middleman by inventing an automated
phrenology machine that he called the *psychograph.* The device was
showcased at the 1933–34 Chicago World's Fair.

   Of course, phrenology was ultimately rejected and relegated to
the role of "pseudoscience." With today's technology, scientists can
now chemically detail the brain—without the use of bumps.

Food & Drink
The Good Old Days of Soda Fountains

❖ ❖ ❖ ❖

In an age when drive-through coffee shops are serving up iced mochachinos, it's easy to forget that chrome-topped soda fountains once held a place of distinction in American culture.

The Golden Age

In 1819, the first soda fountain patent was granted to Samuel Fahnestock. This nifty invention combined syrup and water with carbon dioxide to make fizzy drinks—and they caught on instantly.

The first soda fountains were installed in drugstores, which were sterile storefronts originally intended only to dispense medicines. To attract more business, pharmacists started to sell a variety of goods, including soda drinks and light lunch fare. That way, customers could come in to shop, take time out for some refreshment, and possibly do extra shopping before they left.

Typical soda fountains (the name for both the invention and the shops where the fountains could be found) featured long countertops, swivel stools, goose-neck spigots, and a mirrored back bar, all of which helped attract the attention of young and old alike. Soda fountains were also installed in candy shops and ice-cream parlors. Before long, freestanding soda fountains were being built across the country.

Two of the world's most popular beverages got their start at soda fountains. In 1886, Coca-Cola was first sold to the public at the soda fountain in a pharmacy in Georgia. Pepsi's creator, Caleb Bradham, was a pharmacist who started to sell his beverage in his own drugstore in 1898.

Soda fountain drinks had to be made to order, and this was typically done by male clerks in crisp white coats. Affectionately referred to as "soda jerks" (for the jerking motion required to draw soda from the spigots), these popular, entertaining mixologists were the rock stars of the early 1900s. Think of a modern-day bartender juggling bottles of liquor to make a drink: Soda jerks performed roughly the same feats, except that they used ice cream and soda.

Birth of the Brooklyn Egg Cream

In Brooklyn, New York, candy shop owner Louis Auster created the egg cream, a fountain drink concoction that actually contained neither eggs nor cream.

You make an egg cream any way you like it, but a basic recipe combines a good pour of chocolate syrup with twice as much whole milk, along with seltzer water to fill the glass. (In New York, an egg cream isn't considered authentic unless it's made with Fox's "U-Bet" chocolate syrup.)

The foam that rises to the top of the glass resembles egg whites, which may be how the drink got its name. Some claim that the original chocolate syrup contained eggs and cream; others say "egg cream" comes from the Yiddish phrase *ekt keem,* meaning "pure sweetness"; still others believe that when kids ordered "a cream" at the counter, it sounded like "egg cream." Whatever the etymology, the drink is legendary among soda fountain aficionados. Auster claimed that he often sold more than 3,000 egg creams a day. With limited seating, this meant that most customers had to stand to drink them, prompting the traditional belief that if you really want to enjoy an egg cream, you have to do so standing up.

Several beverage companies approached Auster to purchase the rights to the drink and bottle it for mass distribution, but trying to bottle an egg cream was harder than they thought: The milk spoiled quickly, and preservatives ruined the taste. Thus, the egg cream remained a soda fountain exclusive.

Sip and Socialize

Prohibition and the temperance movement gave soda fountains a boost of popularity during the 1920s, serving as a stand-in for pubs. Booze became legal again in 1933, but by that time, fountains had become such a part of Americana that few closed shop. During the 1950s, soda fountains became the hangout of choice for teenagers everywhere.

It wasn't until the 1960s that the soda fountain's popularity began to wane. People were more interested in war protests and puka beads than Brown Cows and lemon-lime-flavored Green Rivers. As more beverages were available in cans and bottles and life became increasingly fast-paced, people no longer had time for the leisurely pace of the soda shop.

Some fountains survived and still serve frothy egg creams to customers on swivel stools, and many of these establishments attempt to appeal to a wide audience by re-creating that old-fashioned atmosphere.

Recipes

Brown Cow

4 scoops ice cream (chocolate for a Brown Cow, vanilla for a White Cow)
4 tablespoons flavored syrup (usually chocolate)
1½ cups milk

Whirl in a blender until smooth. Share, or not.

Green River

3 ounces lemon-lime syrup
10 ounces seltzer water

Stir. Add ice, if desired.

Hoboken

½ cup pineapple syrup
A splash of milk
Seltzer water
Chocolate ice cream

Blend and enjoy!

Catawba Flip

1 scoop vanilla ice cream
1 large egg
2 ounces grape juice
Shaved ice
Seltzer water

Blend first four ingredients until smooth.
Pour into a tall glass and fill with seltzer water.

War & Military
The Chain Is In the Mail

❖ ❖ ❖ ❖

Sticks and stones may break bones, but in the Middle Ages,
an infected wound was the real scare. Chain mail armor
was a warrior's only line of defense on the battlefield.

When you think of knights, you probably picture suits of highly polished armor. This is a common misconception. Throughout much of the Medieval era, a different type of armor—chain mail—was far more common.

Constructed of interconnected metal rings linked together to form a type of flexible mesh, chain mail was effective against blades and even arrows. In an age where broken bones could be set but even the slightest of cuts could result in deadly infections, chain mail armor no doubt saved many lives on the battlefield.

The actual process of creating mail armor, or in the French *maille,* began much earlier than the Middle Ages, likely in the first millennium B.C. when Celtic tribesman in Gaul (what is modern-day France, Belgium, and Northern Italy) invented a crude form of mail by interconnecting loops of iron to form flexible defensive clothing.

It's likely that the Roman Legions of the Republic first came into contact with this form of mail in Gaul and adopted it as their own. Refined versions were used throughout the Imperial Roman era, and mail survived even the Empire's fall. It lasted until the Renaissance, when gunpowder weapons finally rendered it obsolete.

A similar type of mail armor developed independently in the Far East and was used to a limited degree in China and more notably by the Samurai armies of Japan. Instead of serving as full shirts or even suits of armor, the mail of Japan was used to connect plates of armor and provide protection at key joints.

Interestingly enough, the term *chain mail* is actually fairly modern, dating to the 17th century—after its use had already become obsolete.

Fads & Fashion
Great Moments in Kitsch History

❖ ❖ ❖ ❖

Kitsch is a term used to describe objects of bad taste and poor quality. But despite its bad rap, plenty of people go to great lengths to collect kitsch and keep its "charms" alive.

Pink Flamingos

In 1957, Union Products of Leominster, Massachusetts, introduced the ultimate in tacky lawn ornaments: the plastic pink flamingo. Designed by artist Don Featherstone, they were sold in the Sears mail-order catalog for $2.76 a pair with the instructions, "Place in garden, lawn, to beautify landscape." Authentic pink flamingos—which are sold only in pairs and bear Featherstone's signature under their tails—are no longer on the market (Union Products shuttered its factory in 2006), but knockoffs ensure the bird's survival.

Troll Dolls

Danish sculptor Thomas Damm created the popular troll doll as a handmade wooden gift for his daughter. After it caught the eye of the owner of a toy shop, Dammit Dolls were born, and plastic versions with trademark oversize hairdos hit the mass market. The dolls swept the United States in the early 1960s and were lugged around as good-luck charms by people of all ages and walks of life, including Lady Bird Johnson.

Lava Lites

In the early 1960s, Englishman Edward Craven-Walker invented the Lava Lite, and Chicago entrepreneur Adolf Wertheimer bought the American distribution rights after seeing it at a trade show. Within five years, two million Lava Lites had been sold in the United States.

Language
Miltary Jargon Gets Mustered Out

❖ ❖ ❖ ❖

*These interesting military phrases have seeped into
civilian life so successfully that many people don't
realize they started out as soldier slang.*

Blockbuster
Today the word refers to a wildly successful movie, but during World
War II it was a nickname used by the Royal Air Force for large
bombs that could "bust" an entire city block. "Blockbuster" retired
from the military in the 1950s when advertisers started using it as a
synonym for *gigantic*.

Bought the Farm/Gone for a Burton
Because they face death daily, most soldiers try to avoid talking
about it. During World War I, U.S. soldiers often said that someone
missing or killed had "bought the farm"—which is what what many
families did with their loved one's death benefits. Heavy-hearted
British soldiers in World War II would raise a glass—in this case a
British beer called Burton—to a departed brother, saying he'd "gone
for a Burton."

Push the Envelope
If you're tired of your boss urging you to "push the envelope," blame
World War II test pilots. They listed a plane's abilities—speed,
engine power, maneuverability—on its flight envelope and then did
their best to get the plane to outperform its predetermined limits.

Bite the Bullet
During the Civil War, the "anesthetic" often used on wounded
soldiers was a bullet or block of wood on which to bite down. The
patient, with no alternative, was forced to endure the procedure and
excruciating pain so he could get on with the process of healing.

Show Your True Colors/With Flying Colors

Military regiments would end a victorious battle "with flying colors," or with their flag ("colors") held high. To "show your true colors," which has come to mean revealing your intentions, derives from early warships that would temporarily fly another nation's flag to deceive an enemy into feeling safe.

Over the Top

Nobody wanted to go over the top during World War I—that is, to charge over the parapets toward the enemy, a maneuver that resulted in high casualties. Soldiers who went over the top were considered incredibly—even excessively—brave.

Boondocks

In the early 1900s, U.S. troops in the Philippines fought guerillas hiding in the remote *bandok*—Tagalog (the primary language of the Philippines) for *mountains.* Soldiers translated the word as boondocks.

Grapevine

Civil War soldiers likened telegraph wires to grapevines, the latter having a gnarled appearance. News that arrived by "grapevine telegraph" (or simply "grapevine") was eventually considered to be "twisted" or dubious.

Rank and File

Military officers lined up marching soldiers in "ranks," rows from side to side, and "files," rows from front to back. When the soldiers returned to their offices and factories after military service, "rank and file" came to represent the ordinary members of society.

Education
Poisoned Puddings and Puritanism: Harvard's Early Days

❖ ❖ ❖ ❖

*Today, Harvard is famed for a vast endowment, but its
early days were marked by a struggle to get by with
quarter-bushels of wheat donated by local farmers.*

The School's Scandalous First Leader

In 1640, the tiny college of Harvard was in crisis. Founded four
years before by the Massachusetts Bay Colony, Harvard had a student body of nine, a "yard" liberated from cows; and a single, hated
instructor.

Harvard's 30-year-old schoolmaster, Nathaniel Eaton, was known
to beat wayward students. Other students charged Eaton's wife,
Elizabeth, of putting goat dung into their cornmeal porridge, or
"hasty pudding." (Harvard's theatrical society is named for the dish.)
Finally, Master Eaton went too far and was hauled into court after
clubbing a scholar with a walnut-tree cudgel. He was also accused of
embezzling 100 pounds (then an ample sum).

In 1639, Eaton and his wife were sent packing. Master Eaton
returned to England, was made a vicar, then died in debtor's prison.
Following the Eaton affair, Harvard's reputation lay in tatters; its
operations were suspended, and its students were scattered.

The Roots of Learning

The money and work Massachusetts had put into the school seemed
for naught. The colony's General Court had allotted 400 pounds
for a college in what became known as Cambridge, Massachusetts,
across the Charles River from Boston. The school was named for
John Harvard, a clergyman from England's Cambridge University,
which at the time was known to be a hotbed of Puritanism, the
severe, idealistic faith opposed to the dominant Church of England.

John Harvard was a scholar whose family had known William
Shakespeare. When the plague felled his brothers and his father,
John inherited a considerable estate, including the Queen's Head

Tavern. After immigrating to the Boston region, he became a preacher in Charleston, but his career was short. In 1638, at the age of 31, he died of consumption, having bequeathed money and his personal library to the planned college.

Comeback Under the First President

In 1640, the colony's founders were desperate for educational cachet. They offered the post of Harvard president to Henry Dunster, a new arrival from England and another graduate of Cambridge University.

The energetic Dunster tapped into the colony's inherent educational edge. Many of the new Puritan arrivals had studied at the Oxford and Cambridge academes: Some 130 alumni of the two schools were in New England by 1646. Dunster himself was a leading scholar in "Oriental" languages, that is, biblical tongues such as Hebrew.

Led primarily by a Protestant culture that stressed reading the Bible, Boston set up the first free grammar school in 1635; within 12 years, every town in Massachusetts was required by law to have one. Harvard's new president mandated a four-year graduation requirement and rode out angry students who protested over a commencement fee. Dunster obtained Harvard's charter and authored the school's "Rules and Precepts." He bankrolled the facilities through donations of livestock and, over the course of 13 years, some 250 pounds of wheat. He took a modest salary, being underpaid through 14 years of service, and piled up personal debts. Fortunately, his wife, Elizabeth Glover, kept a printing press in their home. It was the American colonies' first press, and its profits underwrote her husband's work. Dunster managed to turn the school around. Harvard's reputation soared, and students from throughout the colonies, the Caribbean, and the mother country flocked to newly built dorms.

Religious Schisms and a President's Heresies

Yet Dunster tripped up on one of the many religious disputes roiling the Puritan colony. In 1648, it was a criminal offense to engage in "Blasphemy, Heresie, open contempt of the Word preached, Profanation of the Lord's Day"; separation of church and state was unknown.

A source of controversy was infant baptism, which the Puritan fathers required by law. Drawing on his biblical knowledge, Dunster noted that John the Baptist had baptized the adult Jesus, but he could find no biblical examples of children being baptized.

In 1653, he refused to have his son Jonathan baptized. At Cambridge's Congregational Church, Dunster preached against "corruptions stealing into the Church, which every faithful Christian ought to [bear] witness against."

This put the Puritans of Boston and Cambridge in a quandary. Dunster's views made him a heretic, yet he was much liked for his work at the college. Early the next year, the colony's officers wrote that Dunster "hath by his practice and opinions rendered himself offensive to this government." They assembled a conference of 11 ministers and elders to interrogate him. Egged on by this assembly, in May 1654 the General Court forbade schools to employ those "that have manifested themselves unsound in the faith, or scandalous in their lives." Dunster resigned from Harvard.

The ex-president then petitioned the court to let him stay in the colony until he could repay the many debts he'd accumulated from his work. Court authorities coldly responded that "they did not know of [such] extraordinary labor or sacrifices. For the space of 14 years we know of none." Dunster, with Elizabeth and their youngest child ill, then beseeched the court to at least let his family stay the winter. The magistrates agreed grudgingly, but the following spring they banished the Dunster family to the backwater town of Scituate. Harvard's first president died there four years later, at the age of 47.

"It might be said now that I have the best of both worlds. A Harvard education and a Yale degree."

—John F. Kennedy

Mythology & Folklore
The Story of Uncle Sam

❖ ❖ ❖ ❖

*Uncle Sam may be one of the most familiar icons to people
in the United States, but no one is sure of the origins of this
goateed and flag-theme-attired image. Was he an actual person,
or just snippets of people and images from popular culture?*

- During the War of 1812, the U.S. Army needed provisions and sup-
plies—especially protein. Samuel Wilson, a meatpacker in Troy, New
York, provided the troops with barrels of preserved meat stamped
"US," likely as a stipulation of his procurement contract. "Uncle
Sam" was clean-shaven, short, and pudgy, the picture of a respectable
merchant of his time, and he likely did not dress up for fun.

- The Uncle Sam character we know today was born in the influential images of Thomas Nast, a prominent 19th-century political
cartoonist who depicted several similar flag-themed figures.

- The most enduring Uncle Sam image—which depicts him pointing a finger and saying "I Want You"—comes from World War I
recruiting posters drawn by James Montgomery Flagg, who also
modeled the famous stern, craggy visage.

- Uncle Sam is actually a national personification: an image that
sums up a national identity. Other countries' examples include
John Bull of England—a stout, thick-necked, top-hatted guy—and
Moder Svea (Mother Sweden), a sword-bearing woman in chain
mail and a flowing skirt.

- It wasn't until 1961 that Congress recognized Samuel Wilson as
the original Uncle Sam. This didn't do Wilson much good, coming more than a century after his death, but it was a good deal for
Troy, New York. The city began to pitch itself as the "Home of
Uncle Sam" and continues to do so today.

- One popular beneficiary of the Uncle Sam concept was the band
Grateful Dead, who used Sam's hat liberally in their imagery. Another is the New York Yankees, whose logo features Sam's top hat.

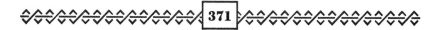

Television
I Want My MTV!

❖ ❖ ❖ ❖

*Screaming out of about a half-million televisions on August 1,
1981, was something most people hadn't seen before: an entire
cable channel dedicated to broadcasting music videos. The
channel was named, aptly, Music Television, or MTV.*

Using a montage of images from the *Apollo 11* moon landing, MTV
kicked off its birthday at 12:01 A.M. with the introduction, "Ladies
and gentlemen, rock and roll." The first video played? "Video Killed
the Radio Star" by The Buggles. During its early days, MTV's format
was similar to that of Top 40 radio at the time—hosts introduced
song after song, but instead of playing a song on the radio, the hosts
played a video on cable. The first hosts, called VJs for video jockeys,
were Nina Blackwood, Mark Goodman, Alan Hunter, J. J. Jackson,
and Martha Quinn.

The Evolution

Early programming on MTV consisted almost entirely of videos
made for cheap or cut together from other sources, such as concerts.
As MTV started to stake its claim in popular culture, however, videos
started to become more slick and developed. Record companies
soon realized the marketing potential that came with having a video
on MTV, so they began to finance the creation of individual artists'
videos. Videos became more elaborate and highly stylized, often
including story lines and character development. Many directors
who would later find success directing feature films started their
careers directing music videos. Many rock groups who were just
starting out hit it big with videos that ultimately gained a huge
following among the MTV audience. Eventually, programming at
MTV branched out into award shows, animated shows, and reality
shows, gradually moving away from music videos.

In the mid-1980s, Viacom bought MTV (among other channels) and created MTV Networks. Shows hosted by VJs slowly lost
airtime in lieu of more conventionally formatted programs. Fea-

tures such as *MTV News* and *MTV Unplugged,* which showcased acoustic performances, were worked into the lineup. In the early 1990s, more animated shows, including *Beavis and Butthead* and *Celebrity Deathmatch,* were introduced. By 2001, reality programming, such as *MTV's Fear* and *The Osbournes*, was placed on the schedule. Almost all of MTV's music programming had been moved to other channels. In addition, the network had launched channels around the globe, taking over airwaves in Europe, Japan, India, and Australia.

The Youth

MTV's audience has always been a young group—people between 12 and 24 years old. *MTV Generation* became a term to define those growing up in the 1980s. But as that generation aged, the channel continued to change its programming and identity to match the interests of the next group of 12- to 24-year-olds. As a result, videos were gradually replaced with reality shows. Series such as *The Real World* and *Road Rules* became staples in MTV's rotation. But as MTV continued to gain popularity and became a huge dictator of taste for the youth generation, it also came under fire for its influence on culture.

Groups such as the Parents Television Council and the American Family Association have criticized MTV frequently, arguing that the channel advocates inappropriate behavior and lacks moral responsibility for its careless programming targeted at kids. Of course, MTV hasn't always been its own best advocate, as seen in controversies such as the 2004 MTV-produced Super Bowl halftime show, in which Justin Timberlake tore off part of Janet Jackson's wardrobe and exposed her (pierced) breast; as well as MTV's problematic coverage in July 2005 of the Live 8 benefit concert, when the network cut to commercials during live performances and MTV's hosts repeatedly referred to the show by anything but its actual name. Given that they were broadcasting the show to the very fans who wanted to see the Live 8 bands they were interrupting, this may have marked a milestone in cultural politics, where the typically liberal youth culture was just as annoyed with the channel as the conservative groups were.

Social Activism

While full recovery from such snafus is probably unlikely, MTV has
tried to respond to criticism about its programming. The network
has a long history of promoting social, political, and environmental
activism in young people. During election years, the network has
invited presidential candidates to discuss their platforms. MTV
has also initiated annual campaigns addressing a variety of issues
affecting the youth culture, including hate crimes, drug use, and
violence. In addition, MTV started branching out into various social
activities, illustrated most notably by the Rock the Vote campaign,
which encouraged young people to vote.

The Meaning

MTV's effect on popular culture has been enormous. Some believe
MTV is a reflection of what's happening in the youth culture today,
but others say it dictates what is happening now and what will
happen in the future. Still, for all its bravado regarding its youth and
flexibility, MTV has stayed the course like any solid corporation. Its
mission has always been to appeal to youth culture. So, while the
gradual decline in the airing of music videos may be bemoaned by
older viewers who enjoyed them during MTV's infancy, the young
people in the 21st century prefer reality shows about rich people
who live in Southern California. The target demographic has stayed
the same, but the people in that demographic have changed.

One critique the network can't seem to dodge, though, is its
effect on the music industry itself. First, MTV has a tendency to
remember only its own history as opposed to musical history in general. Older artists influential in the creation of genres and styles are
oddly left out of the MTV world, despite the fact that so many artists
on MTV are quite obviously in debt to them. Second, by playing only
those artists who fit into a prescribed image and are backed by big
money from music companies, the network has had the net effect
of aiding the consolidation of the music industry and narrowing the
choices to which consumers are exposed. As it was in 1981, MTV
is still screaming out from televisions around the world. But now,
the network is doing so in a highly stylized, profit-making way—and
doing so from *billions* of television sets around the world.

Inventions
From Poland and Iraq to a Car Near You: The Wheel's Origins

✦ ✦ ✦ ✦

It's not difficult to see how important the wheel is to human civilization. The hard part is figuring out who got there first.

The wheel is such a simple tool—and yet, determining when it was invented and who did it earliest is anything but simple. Many accounts assert that it was invented in Asia around 8000 B.C. but fail to elaborate. The Bronocice Pot, found in Polish digs from the Funnel/Beaker culture, dates to 3500 B.C. and seems to depict a wheeled wagon. If so, these ancient late Stone Age people may have beaten the Sumerians to the punch; after all, the fact that the Bronocice included the image on a pot suggests that they actually used the wheel.

One of Earth's most ancient civilizations was Sumer, in southern Iraq, stretching from about 5300 B.C. to just after 2000 B.C. (Its relevance died out, not its people.) Our most descriptive, solid, early evidence of the wheel comes from the excavations at Ur, dated to about 3500 B.C. By Mesopotamian standards, Ur was a great city, though it never reached 100,000 people. Some believe its famous ziggurat was the biblical Tower of Babel.

We have no idea who invented Sumer's wheel, but we know its function: pottery, not transportation. While transportation was valuable to ancient cultures, pottery was more so. One key to civilization is the production of agricultural excess that can be bartered for other goods and services. Without good storage for that excess, varmints will infest it. Whether the first wheel came about by accident or design, it was an industrial tool. The first Sumerian depictions of wheeled donkey carts show up about 300 years later.

Could the Funnel/Beaker people have gotten the wheel from Sumer or vice-versa? It's doubtful. As the bird flies, it's about 1,200 miles from South Poland to Mesopotamia. Each culture probably invented it independently for the inventor's own reasons.

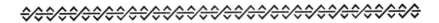

Fads & Fashion
Zoot Suits: 1940s Hip-hop

❖ ❖ ❖ ❖

In their time, zoot suits were more than a clothing fad.
They were the minority cultural statement of their day.

How It Began

There's no way to know for certain who wore the first zoot suit—
the fashion didn't get a name until lots of guys were wearing them.
Reports exist of similar fashions as far back as 1907. To trace the
fashion's early popularity, though, we must go back to Harlem in
the 1930s, where the entertainment was swing or jazz, and young
African American men hitting the nightspots wanted to look sharp.
Like young people of any era, these cats adapted something and
made it theirs.

In the early days, the zoot suit was called a *drape.* It would be
as flashy as the cat could afford: plenty of color, padded shoulders,
accessorized with a long watch chain and a hat. Many young zoot-
suiters topped the look with a "conk," a style in which the hair is
straightened with an agonizing lye treatment. (Please don't put
Drano on your hair; today there are much gentler methods.)

What It Was

For a description, let's consult a zoot-suiter who may be familiar to
you. He was born to a Baptist minister and named Malcolm Little,
but America knows him as African American activist Malcolm X: "I
was measured, and the young salesman picked off a rack a zoot suit
that was just wild: sky blue pants thirty inches in the knee and angle-
narrowed down to twelve inches at the bottom, and a long coat that
pinched my waist and flared out below my knees."

Naming It

Credit for the term "zoot suit" usually goes to Harold C. Fox, a
clothier and musician from Chicago. But how? The language of zoot
suits was a language of rhyme: "reet pleats," "reave sleeves," "ripe
stripes," "stuff cuffs," and "drape shape." Fox claimed that he said

"zoot suit" because in jive, "the end to all ends" was the ultimate praise, so he used the ending letter of the alphabet for a rhyme. The rest of the terminology is well documented, so Fox's claim isn't easy to dismiss. He continued to wear zoot suits for the remainder of his long life, and in 1996 he was buried in one. Now that's old-school.

Branching Out

The zoot suit caught on with young minority males, and more than a few whites, all across the country. In Southern California, the zoot suit became a cultural statement for stylish young Hispanic cats called *pachucos*. This was long before Hispanic America found a national political voice, so the *pachuco* culture was an early regional and cultural identity statement, and its drape was the zoot suit. Nor was it just for men. *Pachucas* wore short-skirted variants of the zoot suit, lots of makeup, and big hair.

Some claim that the term "zoot suit" came from street Spanish (called *caló* in reference to old Spanish gypsy slang), but Fox's Chicago version has clearer roots.

Pedroing Out

As the United States entered World War II, the zoot suit represented frivolity when the nation was in an austere, buckle-down mood. In June 1943, tension boiled over in L.A.'s Zoot Suit Race Riots, with civilians and servicemen attacking any zoot-suiter—typically Hispanic, Filipino, or African American.

By 1950, the fashion was in decline. Now it's part of history.

"You got to be tricking yourself out like the dude... look like a zoot, walk like a zoot, talk like a zoot."
—Thomas Sanchez, from his book *Zoot Suit Murders*

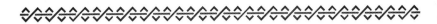

Food & Drink
Baby Ruth's Truth?

❖ ❖ ❖ ❖

Many people believe that the Baby Ruth candy bar was named for baseball great Babe Ruth. Others contend that the honor belongs to President Grover Cleveland's daughter Ruth.

German immigrant Otto Schnering founded the Curtiss Candy Company in Chicago in 1916. With World War I raging in Europe, Schnering decided to avoid using his Germanic surname and chose his mother's maiden name for the business. His first product was a snack called Kandy Kake, a pastry center covered with peanuts and chocolate. But the candy bar was only a marginal success, and it was renamed Baby Ruth in 1921 in an effort to boost sales. Whenever pressed for details on the confection's name, Curtiss explained that the appellation honored Ruth Cleveland, the late and beloved daughter of President Grover Cleveland. But the company may have been trying to sneak a fastball past everybody.

Cleveland's daughter had died of diphtheria in 1904—a dozen years before the candy company was even started. One questions the logic in naming a candy bar after someone who had passed away so many years earlier. The gesture may have been appropriate for a president, but a president's relatively unknown daughter?

The more plausible origin of the name might be tied to the biggest sports star in the world at the time—George Herman "Babe" Ruth. Originally a star pitcher for the Boston Red Sox, Ruth became a fearsome hitter for the New York Yankees, slamming 59 home runs in the same year the candy bar was renamed Baby Ruth. Curtiss may have found a way to cash in on the slugger's fame—and name—without paying a dime in royalties. In fact, when Ruth gave the okay to use his name on a competitor's candy—the Babe Ruth Home Run Bar—Curtiss successfully blocked it, claiming infringement on its own "baby."

BAND NAMES

Whether derived from pop culture references or just a random pick from a book, a band's name is often as important as its music. But even a great sound can't save bands such as The Busiest Bankruptcy Lawyers in Minnesota. Here are the stories behind some interesting band names.

The Cranberries
The band was originally known as "The Cranberry Saw Us," a pun on "cranberry sauce." Members soon shortened the name for simplicity.

R.E.M.
The "rapid eye movement" period in the sleep cycle is the most intense and restful. But the members of R.E.M. didn't choose the name for its symbolic connection to their aesthetic. Instead, they found it while flipping through the dictionary.

Five for Fighting
The stage name for John Ondrasik came from his love of hockey. Players who fight in the National Hockey League get five minutes in the penalty box, or "five for fighting."

Three Dog Night
The name is derived from an Australian Aboriginal custom of sleeping with a dog for warmth during cold nights. The colder the night, the more dogs.

No Doubt
This funky, California-based "third wave" ska band was named after a favorite expression of its founder, John Spence, who ultimately committed suicide.

Toad the Wet Sprocket
Members of this alt-rock band drew their name from a monologue delivered by Eric Idle on a Monty Python album from 1980.

Science
Lunar Legacy: The Big Whack?

❖ ❖ ❖ ❖

*Here's one thing we know for certain about the moon: It isn't
made of cheese. Most everything else, including its origins,
is a matter of scientific reasoning and speculation.*

Mooning Over the Moon
Our planet's moon, our only true natural satellite, has stimulated
romance, mystery, and scientific curiosity. And no wonder—besides
the sun, the moon is the most noticeable member of our solar
system, measuring about one-quarter the size of Earth. Only
one side faces our planet, and every month, because of its orbit
around us, we watch the moon change phases, from full to quarter
to gibbous to new and back again. The moon is also the subject
of various origin theories, which alternately laud it as a deity or
discount it as a flying chunk of rock, depending on the culture.

Blinded by Science
The list of scientific theories concerning the moon's origin is a bit
smaller. One theory suggests that the moon was "captured" by
Earth's gravity as it traveled by our planet; another theory posits that
our planet and its satellite formed side by side as the solar system
developed some 4.56 billion years ago. The moon has simply tagged
along with us ever since.

The most recently accepted theory has its origins in the 19th
century. In 1879, the son of British astronomer George Darwin (son
of Charles Darwin) suggested that a rapidly spinning Earth threw off
material from the Pacific Ocean, creating the moon. The idea drew
criticism on and off for decades. But thanks to the advent of modern
computers, scientists have created a similar theoretical scenario that
makes parts of Darwin's suggestion more reasonable. The data suggests that while Earth was still in a semimolten state, it was hit by
a space body—a protoplanet, or planetesimal—almost the size of
Mars, or about half the size of Earth. The massive collision would
have sent a huge chunk of broken material into orbit around Earth;

over time, those larger pieces could have gathered together—thanks to gravity—creating our moon.

It's All Relative?

Why do scientists now agree with the "Moon, daughter of Earth" theory? One of the main reasons is the Apollo program, the U.S. moon missions. Astronauts gathered and delivered more than 800 pounds of lunar material back to Earth. The dates of those rocks—ranging from 3.2 to 4.2 billion years old for material gathered from the flat, dark maria (lava seas) and 4.3 to 4.5 billion years old for rocks from the highlands—along with their composition, have led scientists to believe that the moon is definitely related to Earth.

The evidence is in the fact that the rocks are similar to Earth's mantle material—the moving, molten layer of our planet just under the crust. If a huge planetary body struck our planet, it would make sense that the resulting material would be similar to rock deep below Earth's surface. In addition, moon rocks have exactly the same oxygen isotope composition as Earth's rocks. Materials from other parts of the solar system have different oxygen isotope compositions, which means that the moon probably formed around Earth's neighborhood.

Is the moon our only satellite? Scientists know there are other space bodies circling our planet, but none of the objects can be considered a moon. They are more likely asteroids caught in the Earth's and moon's gravitation. For example, the asteroid 3753 Cruithne looks like it's following Earth in the orbit around the sun; the asteroid 2002 AA29 follows a horseshoe path near Earth. Neither is a moon, and so far neither rock has been in danger of striking our planet. Another object once caught scientists' eyes: Nearby J002E3 was considered a possible new moon of Earth until it was determined to be the third stage of the *Apollo 12* Saturn V rocket.

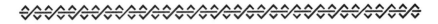

Inventions

Taser: From Children's Book Concept to Riot Policing Tool

❖ ❖ ❖ ❖

Like a .357 Magnum, the Taser makes troublesome suspects less troublesome. Unlike the .357, the tased suspect generally survives to stand trial, and the police save a bundle on coroner costs.

Tom Swift

You've probably heard of the Hardy Boys and Nancy Drew. But unless you're a baby boomer or older, you may never have heard of Tom Swift books, which belonged to the same "teen adventure" genre. Tom, the precocious protagonist, is a young inventor who resolves crises and foils wickedness. One book in the series, called *Tom Swift and His Electric Rifle* (1911), has quite a stimulating legacy.

In 1967, NASA researcher Jack Cover, who grew up on Tom Swift, realized that he could actually make some of the gee-whiz gadgetry from the series. In 1974, he finished designing an electricity weapon he named the "Thomas A. Swift Electric Rifle," or TASER. (In so doing, he departed from canon. Tom Swift never had a middle initial, but Cover inserted the "A" to make the acronym easier on the tongue.)

How It Worked

Cover's first "electric rifle," the Taser TF-76, used a small gunpowder charge to fire two barbed darts up to 15 feet. Thin wires conducted electricity from the weapon's battery to the target, causing great pain and brief paralysis with little risk of death—except in the young, elderly, or frail. That was okay, since the police rarely felt compelled to take down children or senior citizens.

The police saw potential in the Taser. The TF-76 showed great promise as a nonlethal wingnut takedown tool.

Federal Shocker

Never underestimate the creativity-squelching power of government. The Bureau of Alcohol, Tobacco, and Firearms (BATF)

wondered: *How do we classify this thing? It's not really a pistol or a rifle. It uses gunpowder.... Aha!* The BATF grouped the TF-76 with sawed-off shotguns: illegal for most to acquire or possess. A .44 Magnum? Carry it on your hip if you like. An electric stunner that took neither blood nor life? A felony to possess, much less use.

This BATF ruling zapped Taser Systems (Cover's new company) right out of business.

Second and Third Volleys

Taser Systems resurfaced as Tasertron, limping along on sales to police. In the 1990s, a creative idealist named Rick Smith wanted to popularize nonlethal weapons. He licensed the Taser technology from Cover, and they began changing the weapon. To deal with the BATF's gunpowder buzzkill, Smith and Cover designed a Taser dart propelled by compressed air. They also loaded each cartridge with paper and Mylar confetti bearing a serial number. If the bad guys misused a Taser, they wouldn't be able to eradicate the evidence.

To Tase or Not to Tase: That Is the Question...

Modern Tasers reflect the benefits of experience. In 1991, an LAPD Taser failed to subdue a violent, defiant motorist named Rodney King. The events that followed (including the cops beating King with billy clubs) put the Taser on the public's radar as something unreliable. This was not offset (on the contrary, it was compounded) by occasional deaths from tasing. The public might justly ask: "Does this thing really work? Does it work too darn well?"

One fact isn't in question. A nightstick blow to the head or a 9mm police bullet are both deadlier than a Taser. As a result, the debate revolves more around police officers' over-willingness to tase rather than whether or not police should carry Tasers in the first place.

In 2007, the United Nations ruled that a Taser could be considered an instrument of torture.

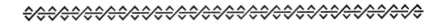

Clubs & Organizations
The Inspirational Origin
of the NAACP

❖ ❖ ❖ ❖

*At the beginning of the 20th century, those who sought equal rights
for African Americans lacked a powerful national organization
to unite them. It took the initiative of one tenacious reformer,
Mary White Ovington, to make the National Association for
the Advancement of Colored People (NAACP) a reality.*

By the turn of the 20th century, African Americans had been free
from the bonds of slavery for almost 40 years, but they still faced a
culture, economy, and political process that made true equality seem
like a distant dream. It was difficult for African Americans to vote,
hold public office, or buy property; segregation laws made quality
education impossible; lynching and violence stood in place of justice.
In 1901 alone, more than 100 African Americans were murdered
by public lynching. Race riots spread like wildfire throughout the
United States.

The Niagara Movement
Organizations that sought to improve this situation were in existence
but lacked money and political influence—not surprising given the
rarity of highly educated African Americans in positions of power.
Nevertheless, in 1905, illustrious scholar and political activist W.E.B.
Du Bois called for a national meeting of black leaders. The result
was the short-lived yet legendary Niagara Movement during which
black leaders and activists delineated their goals of equal economic
opportunity, an end to disenfranchisement for blacks and women, an
end to segregation and discrimination, and the abolition of injustice
in legislation and judicial processes.

Meanwhile, Mary White Ovington, a white journalist and activist from New York City, was putting together a group of her own. In
1906, the *New York Evening Post* sent Ovington to cover the second
annual meeting of the Niagara Movement, where she met and was
inspired by many of the movement's leaders. Then, in 1908, Oving-

ton read a harrowing newspaper article about the violent race riots in Springfield, Illinois, during which several blacks were lynched at random for no reason. Ovington responded by writing a letter to the author of the article, journalist William English Walling. Ovington suggested that she and Walling meet in New York City to discuss their common concern for the plight of African Americans in the United States.

And so in the first week of January 1909 the initial meeting of the fledgling NAACP met in a tiny New York City apartment. Present were Ovington, Walling, and Henry Moskovitz, a Jewish social worker. The three agreed that on Abraham Lincoln's birthday, February 12, they would circulate an open call for a conference about the "Negro situation," as it was called at the time. They managed to get the resulting document signed by 60 prominent activists, black and white, including members of the Niagara Movement.

The National Negro Committee

The first conference convened on May 30, 1909. After three meetings, the participants began calling themselves the "National Negro Committee." Meanwhile, in 1910, conflict within the Niagara Movement caused the group to disband. Many ex-members sought to solidify and strengthen the young National Negro Committee, and they adopted the now renowned title, National Association for the Advancement of Colored People.

This new organization was potent for several reasons. It was biracial, so the power of black leaders was coupled with the legal and political powers that were largely confined to whites. Further, the fundamental principle of the NAACP was to seek radical change through legal—never violent—means. By 1913, the NAACP had opened 24 branch offices in the United States. Over the years, they supported legal battles that advanced equality, most notably the *Brown* v. *Board of Education* decision, which favored desegregation in schools.

Today, the NAACP continues to employ its peaceful means to advance freedom and equality for all. And it all began with a small group of leaders who would not sit back and ignore violence and injustice.

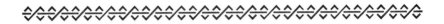

Places & Landmarks
Shenzhen, China: The Birth of the World's Fastest Growing City

◆ ◆ ◆ ◆

Three decades ago, Shenzhen was sparsely populated farmland. Today it's a city of more than ten million.

The year is 1978, and the small area in southern China, soon to be known as Shenzhen, is thinly populated with farmers and fishermen. The inhabitants of this rural enclave don't know it yet, but something's astir in Chinese politics that will change their lives forever. Their small rural land, a place that for centuries had been just a minor producer of crops, also has some features that can't be found anywhere else. Shenzhen is located amid the Pearl River Delta, making it a prime spot for an export economy. It also happens to be just north of Hong Kong, the world's busiest port city.

The change began in the closed chamber rooms of the Chinese government. In the late 1970s, the economy of the People's Republic of China underwent a radical transformation. The new leader of the Republic, Deng Xiaoping (1904–1997), sought to modernize and globalize the country's economy. He appreciated the vast productive potential of China's massive land and population size and the necessity of international trade. Yet in order to be a global player, China needed something it didn't yet have: the West's technology and industrial management skills.

Xiaoping encouraged industries throughout China to open up to foreign partnerships, and he relaxed government restrictions on trade and financial institutions. As part of this plan, Xiaoping established four Special Economic Zones in China. These were based on the duty-free international zones imposed on third-world countries after the end of colonialism. Different areas throughout Africa, Asia, and South America enjoy lower taxes and fewer commercial restrictions in order to encourage an export-based economy. These specialized trade laws enable the developing world to supply the Western world's consumption. The Chinese government took many of the

strategies of these duty-free international zones and applied them to their own economy.

China's State Council officially declared Shenzhen a Special Economic Zone in 1980. Shenzhen quickly proved to be the fastest growing and most influential of all the zones. Migrant workers from across China flocked to the area like moths to a lightbulb. In 1979, the population of the Shenzhen area was, at most, 300,000. Today it is at least ten million—making it more populous than New York City. The Chinese government supplied some of the funds for infrastructure development, but this rapid transformation was mostly the result of joint ventures with foreign companies. Chinese companies supplied the cheap land, labor, and materials; the foreign investors supplied the technology and management.

Within ten years, Shenzhen was a full-fledged modern city, complete with skyscrapers, fancy hotels, and petty crime. Yet unlike other cities, Shenzhen was populated with such haste that it developed some unique characteristics. Shenzhen's population of migrant workers is unusually high. In 2006, poor migrant workers accounted for more than three-quarters of the population. Complex residency restrictions make it difficult for these laborers, who decades ago lived in small villages throughout China, to settle into Shenzhen for the long haul. A sense of rootless restlessness permeates the populace. Surrounding the concentration of wealth and glitz in Shenzhen's downtown area is a high density of gang warfare, prostitution, petty crime, and general desolation. These problems, like the city itself, sprang up overnight, and it's hard to tell what lies ahead in this short story of Shenzhen's sudden growth and development.

"A great city is not to be confounded with a populous one."
—ARISTOTLE

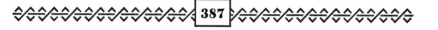

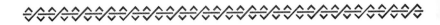

BIRTHPLACES OF THE RICH AND FAMOUS

Was someone famous born in your hometown?

Illinois gave birth to some of the most influential writers of the 20th century, including sci-fi author Ray Bradbury of Waukegan, novelist John Dos Passos and hard-boiled scribe Raymond Chandler of Chicago, legendary expatriate Ernest Hemingway of Oak Park, pioneering feminist Betty Friedan of Peoria, novelist James Jones of Robinson, poet Carl Sandburg of Galesburg, and playwright Sam Shepard of Fort Sheridan.

Having a good sense of humor may be a prerequisite to surviving the cold winters of Illinois. Jack Benny and Bob Newhart were born in Chicago; Bill Murray hails from Wilmette; and Richard Pryor came from Peoria.

America's most famous movie rebel—James Dean—hailed from the farmlands of Marion, Indiana.

No one knows where Teamsters leader Jimmy Hoffa is now, but he was born in Brazil, Indiana.

Though John Wayne and Buffalo Bill Cody are symbols of the Wild West, both were born in Iowa; the Duke was born in Winterset, and Buffalo Bill was born in Scott County.

New Orleans gave birth to jazz, as evidenced by native sons Louis Armstrong, Fats Domino, Al Hirt, Wynton Marsalis, and Jelly Roll Morton.

Avant-garde composer Philip Glass, ragtime pianist Eubie Blake, jazz stylist Billie Holiday, and rock innovator Frank Zappa were all born in Maryland's capital. Who would have thought that Baltimore was such a musical city?

What do singers Bob Dylan and Judy Garland have in common? Both are Minnesotans; Dylan hails from Duluth, and Garland was born in Grand Rapids.

Actress Winona Ryder was born in Winona, Minnesota. Good thing she wasn't born in Bemidji like Golden Age movie star Jane Russell.

Elvis Presley put his hometown, Tupelo, Mississippi, on the map.

Mississippi is also the birthplace of several bluesmen, including Robert Johnson of Hazlehurst, B. B. King of Itta Bena, Muddy Waters of Rolling Fork, and Bo Diddley of McComb. A number of country artists are also from Mississippi, including Charley Pride of Sledge, Conway Twitty of Friars Point, Faith Hill of Ridgeland, Tammy Wynette of Itawamba County, and LeAnn Rimes of Pearl.

Gary Cooper often played the ultimate cowboy hero in Westerns. A real Westerner, Cooper hailed from Helena, Montana.

Golden Age movie star Lana Turner is among the most glamorous natives of Wallace, Idaho.

John Henry Holliday left his comfortable home in the Deep South of Griffin, Georgia, to become Doc Holliday, the most tragic figure to ever walk the Old West.

Most assume Nicole Kidman and Mel Gibson are Aussies through and through, but Kidman was born in Honolulu, Hawaii, and Gibson was born in Peekskill, New York.

Detroit used to be known as the automaker of America, but it is also the hometown of singers Della Reese, Diana Ross, Bob Seger, and Stevie Wonder, comediennes Gilda Radner and Lily Tomlin, and director Francis Ford Coppola.

"If I wasn't Bob Dylan, I'd probably think that Bob Dylan has a lot of answers myself."

—Bob Dylan

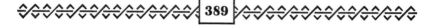

Toys & Games
From Bingo to Uno: The Origins of Popular Pastimes

Life isn't all fun and games. But we sure wish it could be!
Here's a look at the origins of some popular games.

Bingo

Bingo started sometime around 1929 as "Beano." A smart entrepreneur named Edwin Lowe spotted a crowd playing Beano at a fair and ran with the idea. As the story goes, he was hosting a Beano game at his house, and a woman playing the game got her tang all tongueled up. Upon winning, she couldn't blurt "Beano" correctly, and instead said "B-b-ingo!" Lowe jumped on it and started marketing the game as Bingo.

Stratego

The first boxed Stratego set in the United States came out in 1961, but the game's origin is much older than that. An ancient Chinese game called Jungle or Animal Chess very much resembles Stratego. A Frenchwoman patented its modern incarnation as *L'attaque* in 1910.

Scrabble

Would you believe that Scrabble was invented by a guy whose parents named him "Alfred Mosher Butts"? (Arrest them for that!) Al first invented a similar game called Lexiko in 1931, revising it into the equivalent of Scrabble in 1938. The name change came ten years later.

Go

This classic territorial-capture board game originated in China some 4,000 years ago. Legend has it that an emperor invented it to sharpen his dumb son's thinking. Played with black and white stones

on a grid, Go has a following in Asia similar to that of chess in the West.

Twister

The Milton Bradley Company released this unique game in 1966, and it was the first one in history to use the human body as an actual playing piece. Worldwide, approximately 65 million people have entwined in a game of Twister.

Playing Cards

Playing cards have been a tradition in China for millennia, but their present markings date back to 14th-century France. The four suits represent the major classes of society at that time. Hearts are taken from the shield, translating to nobility and the church; the spear-tip shape of spades stands in for the military; clubs are clover, meant to represent rural peasantry; and diamonds are similar to the tiles then associated with retail shops and were therefore intended to signify the middle class.

Uno

Is Uno ancient? Only if 1969 seems ancient to you, since that's when a barber from Ohio invented the popular all-ages card game. Creator Merle Robbins sold Uno to a game company in 1972 for $50,000 plus royalties.

"Life, like all other games, becomes fun when one realizes that it's just a game."

—Nerijus Stasiulis

Sports
League of Dreams

❖ ❖ ❖ ❖

Little League baseball has produced a parade of stars,
but it's the everyday heroes that make it a success.

For Nolan Ryan, Little League was the first stop on his way to the
Hall of Fame and an important one on the journey through father-
hood. The latter, its founders might say, is precisely what Little
League baseball was engineered to be.

Youth baseball leagues were formed in the United States as early
as the 1880s. In 1938, Carl E. Stotz started a league for children in
Williamsport, Pennsylvania, and devised rules and field dimensions
for what would become, officially, Little League baseball. The next
year, the first three teams—Lycoming Dairy, Lundy Lumber, and
Jumbo Pretzel—took the field, with the parents who organized them
forming the first Little League board of directors.

By 1946, there were 12 similar leagues, all in Pennsylvania. Three
years later, there were more than 300 such leagues throughout
the United States, and in 1951 Little League took hold in Canada.
The league has now spread worldwide. Little League baseball is
the world's largest organized youth sports program, with nearly
200,000 teams in more than 80 countries. Williamsport, though, has
remained central. The Little League World Series (LLWS)—a truly
international event—is played there each year, and its final hit the
national television airwaves as early as 1963.

Of these hundreds of thousands of teams, only 16 compete for
the title of Little League World Series champion. To make it to the
finals in Williamsport, teams of 11- and 12-year-olds must advance
through the International Tournament—a process that requires
more games worldwide than six full major-league seasons!

Eight teams from the United States battle for the U.S. championship as eight teams from other countries fight for the international
crown in a ten-day tournament that culminates with the top international team and the winning U.S. squad battling for the LLWS title.
Fans from all over the world pack hotels throughout central Pennsyl-

vania each summer for the event. In 2004, the 32-game World Series drew 349,379 fans.

The format of the event has been tweaked through the years. As the young players have gotten better, the dimensions of the park have grown. From 1947 through '58, the final was played at Original Field, where the outfield fences were all less than 200 feet from home plate. Beginning in '96, a 205-foot blast was required to clear the fences in all fields. As of 2006, those fences stood at 225 feet.

Through all its growth, some things have remained pleasantly constant. For example, the World Series champions get invited to the White House. And Little League's founding goal remains this: to teach children the fundamental principles of sportsmanship, fair play, and teamwork, just as Stotz envisioned more than 70 years ago.

That those principles can help talented young players advance their baseball careers is a bonus Stotz may or may not have foreseen. Nolan Ryan's first organized sports experience was in Little League. "The first field in Alvin [Texas] was cleared and built by my dad and the other fathers of the kids in the program. I played Little League from the time I was nine years old until I was 13. Some of my fondest memories of baseball come from those years."

Little League remains a big deal in towns all over America. Ryan knows. Not only did he pitch a Little League no-hitter long before he threw seven of them in the majors, but he also helped coach his own sons' Little League teams. Less famous mothers and fathers do the same for their less famous sons and daughters on diamonds around the world.

Ryan, of course, graduated from Little League ball to the Hall of Fame, as did George Brett, Steve Carlton, Rollie Fingers, Catfish Hunter, Jim Palmer, Mike Schmidt, Tom Seaver, Don Sutton, Carl Yastrzemski, and Robin Yount. None of those greats ever played in the famed Little League World Series, but all were boosted by their organized baseball experience as youngsters, as were countless other major-league stars.

Only a small fraction of Little League players go on to the ranks of professional baseball, of course. But where would one be without dreams? And Little League baseball is about so much more than reaching the majors.

Inventions
Learning to Fly
♦ ♦ ♦ ♦

*Back in the 18th century, all you needed to reach the
sky was a silk bag, hot air, and a lot of guts.*

The Heat Is On
As the name implies, hot-air balloons rely on heat: As heat is
produced and ultimately rises, it gets caught within the lightweight
balloon. Since the heated air is less dense, it causes the balloon to
rise. Winds push it along, but the balloon operator can also control
the device manually by increasing or decreasing the heat to raise and
lower the balloon. A seemingly simple concept—but one that wasn't
discovered until the late 1700s.

When Sheep Fly...
The first balloon considered fit for flight was invented by French
papermakers Joseph-Michel and Jacques-Étienne Montgolfier.
In 1782, the brothers discovered that a silk bag would float to the
ceiling of their home when filled with hot air. On April 25, 1783,
they successfully launched a hot-air-filled silk balloon. Later that

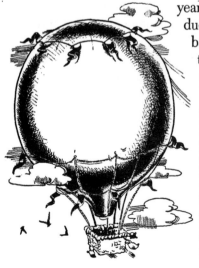

year, their balloon carried a sheep,
duck, and rooster into the air. The
balloon landed safely, and none of
the animals were the worse for the
experience.

All animals aside, October 15 of
the same year marked another
landmark for hot-air-balloon flight
in France. The "Aerostat Reveil-
lion" balloon carried scientist Jean
François Pilâtre de Rozier 250 feet
into the air, though it remained
tethered to the ground by a rope. It
floated for around 15 minutes and
safely landed in a nearby clearing.

But the true prize came on November 21, 1783, in the Bois de Boulogne in Paris: A 70-foot silk and paper balloon made by the Montgolfier brothers was launched without a tether, carrying its first human passengers: de Rozier and Francois Laurent, the Marquis d'Arlandes. The balloon rose to around 500 feet and flew a distance of 5½ miles, remaining aloft for 25 minutes before the straw used to stoke the hot-air pit set fire to the balloon. Although legend tells of the lofty gentlemen handing bottles of champagne to startled farmers upon landing, the real story is that they landed in a deserted farming area just outside of Paris—with no spectators nearby.

History's Great Escapes

Up, Up, and Away, Over the Iron Curtain

On September 16, 1979, Peter Strelzyk, Günter Wetzel, their wives, and four children dropped from the night sky onto a field in West Germany, flying a homemade hot-air balloon. Strelzyk, an electrician, and Wetzel, a bricklayer, built the balloon's platform and burners in one of their basements. Their wives sewed together curtains, bed sheets, shower liners, and whatever other fabric was on hand to make the 75-foot-high balloon. A bid to escape communist East Germany during the days of the Berlin Wall, their famous flight was two years in the making, spanned 15 miles, and took 28 minutes to complete. Unsure whether they had reached freedom, the two families spent the next morning hiding in a barn, until they saw an Audi driving down a nearby road and realized they were in the West.

Clubs & Organizations
Men's Societies

❖ ❖ ❖ ❖

A fraternal organization is a group of men who bond through rituals, handshakes, and sometimes uniforms. They usually have overlapping missions, whether emphasizing fellowship, patriotism, religion, or philanthropy, and most are particularly active in community service. Here are some of the most recognizable, along with notable members past and present.

Moose International, Inc.: Founded in 1913, the Family Fraternity, often called the Loyal Order of Moose (and Women of the Moose), is a nonsectarian and nonpolitical organization. Moose International headquarters, in Mooseheart, Illinois, oversees 2,000 lodges, 1,600 chapters, and approximately 1.5 million members throughout the United States, Canada, Great Britain, and Bermuda. According to the group's mission statement, the moose was selected as the namesake animal because "it is a large, powerful animal, but one which is a protector, not a predator." Moose members are active in their communities, contributing nearly $90 million worth of service every year to charities and social causes in their hometowns.

Famous Moose members: presidents Franklin D. Roosevelt and Harry S. Truman, actor Jimmy Stewart, athletes Arnold Palmer and Cal Ripken Sr., and U.S. Supreme Court Chief Justice Earl Warren.

The Benevolent and Protective Order of Elks of the United States of America: This organization was founded in 1868, making it one of the oldest fraternal organizations in the country. The order has more than 1 million members working in some 2,100 communities, with headquarters in Chicago. The Elks' mission is to promote the principles of charity, justice, brotherly love, and fidelity; encourage belief in God; support members' welfare and enhance their happiness; bolster patriotism; cultivate good fellowship; and actively support community charities and

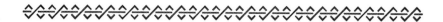

activities. A major component of the Elks' mission is working with and mentoring youngsters.

Famous Elks: presidents John F. Kennedy and Gerald Ford, actor Clint Eastwood, football coach Vince Lombardi, and baseball greats Casey Stengel and Mickey Mantle.

Lions Clubs International: The world's largest service organization, Lions Clubs International includes some 45,000 clubs and 1.3 million members in 200 countries around the world. The international headquarters is in Oak Brook, Illinois. The organization was founded in 1917 in the United States and became international in 1920 when the first Canadian club was established in Windsor, Ontario. All funds raised from the general public are used for charitable purposes, and members pay all administrative costs. Since the Lions Clubs International Foundation began in 1968, it has awarded nearly 8,000 grants (totaling $566 million) to assist victims of natural disasters, fight physical and mental disabilities, and serve youth causes.

Famous Lions: President Jimmy Carter, racecar driver Johnny Ruterford, explorer Admiral Richard Byrd, and basketball star Larry Byrd.

Masons: The Freemasons belong to the oldest fraternal organization in the world. Today, there are more than 2 million Freemasons in North America. Freemasonry, or Masonry, is dedicated to the "Brotherhood of Man under the Fatherhood of God." Masonry's principal purpose is "to make good men better." No one knows exactly how old the movement is, but many historians believe it arose from the powerful guilds of stonemasons of the Middle Ages. In 1717, Masonry became a formal organization when four lodges in London formed England's first Grand Lodge. The oldest jurisdiction on the European continent is the Grand Orient de France, founded in 1728.

Famous Masons: presidents George Washington and James Monroe, composer Wolfgang A. Mozart, astronaut John Glenn, actor John Wayne, and escape artist Harry Houdini.

Prolific Producers

These "movers and shakers" are responsible for more than their fair share of the world's greatest accomplishments.

If asked which country hosts the largest diamond mine, many will guess South Africa. They will, in fact, be wrong. With an average annual production (since 1994) of more than 35 million carats, Australia's **Argyle Diamond Mine** is the world's largest single producer of diamonds.

If fruitful production can be traced to its very roots, **Mrs. Feodor Vassilyev** has no equal. Between 1725 and 1765, the peasant from Shuya, Russia, gave birth to a whopping 69 children. Her pregnancies included 16 sets of twins, 7 sets of triplets, and 4 sets of quadruplets—but interestingly, no single births.

World War I ace **Baron von Richthofen** (the infamous Red Baron) has nothing at all on World War II super-ace **Erich Hartmann**. The German pilot, dubbed the "Black Devil" by his enemies, is credited with 352 "kills," making him the all-time "ace of aces."

Unlike the textbook definition of a prolific inventor, **Johannes Gutenberg's** gift to the world was singular, but it kept giving and giving and giving, much like a philanthropic Energizer Bunny. Fact is you wouldn't be reading this right now had Gutenberg not first invented a practical means with which to duplicate print. That breakthrough came in 1440 with the metal "movable type" printing press, a device that made the laborious handwritten manuscript obsolete and consequently made modern book publishing possible. For his amazing invention that begat immeasurable offspring, Gutenberg is credited with bringing the Middle Ages into the Renaissance.

With more than 300 inventions to his credit, **George Westinghouse** (best known for his Westinghouse brand of home appliances) helped take our world from a quaint, low-tech environment into an anything-is-possible wonderland brimming with modernity. Breakthroughs such as the air brake and rotary steam engine owe their existence to the visionary from Central Bridge, New York, and alternating current (AC) underscores Westinghouse's genius each and every time a light switch is flicked on. "If someday they say of me that in my work I have contributed something to the welfare and happiness of my fellow men, I shall be satisfied," exclaimed the prolific inventor when asked of his legacy.

Visual Art
More Than You Ever Wanted to Know About Mimes

❖ ❖ ❖ ❖

Mimes—you know them as the silent, white-faced, black-clad street performers who pretend to be trapped in boxes or walk against the wind. In case you want to know a little more...

Greco-Roman Tradition

• *Pantomime* means "an imitator of nature"—derived from Pan, the Greek god of nature, and *mimos,* meaning "an imitator."

• The first record of pantomime performed as entertainment comes from Ancient Greece, where mimes performed at religious festivals honoring Greek gods. As early as 581 B.C., Aristotle wrote of seeing mimes perform.

• From religious festivals, Greek mime made its way to the stage: Actors performed pantomimic scenes as "overtures" to the tragedies that depicted the moral lesson of the play to follow.

• Greek settlers brought mime to Italy, where it flourished during the Roman Empire and spread throughout Europe as the empire expanded.

• Today, "pantomime" and "mime" are used interchangeably to refer to a mute performer, but the Ancient Romans distinguished between the two: Pantomimes were tragic actors who performed in complete silence, while mimes were comedic and often used speech in their acts.

The Rebirth of European Mime

• The Roman Empire brought pantomime and mime to England around 52 B.C., but with the fall of the Empire in the fifth century and the progress of Christianity, both were banished as forms of paganism.

• Pantomime and mime weren't really gone, though: The sacred religious dramas of the Middle Ages were acted as "dumb shows"

(no words were used), and historians believe that comedic mime was used by court jesters, who included humorous imitations in their acts.

- After the Middle Ages, mime resurged during the Renaissance and swept through Europe as part of the Italian theater called the Commedia dell'arte, in which comedic characters performed in masks and incorporated mime, pantomime, music, and dance.

- The first silent mime appeared on the English stage in 1702, in John Weaver's *Tavern Bilkers* at the Drury Lane Theatre. It was really more of a "silent ballet" than silent acting.

- British actor John Rich is credited with adapting pantomime as an acting style for the English stage in 1717. His "Italian Mimic Scenes" combined elements of both Commedia dell'arte and John Weaver's ballet.

- Meanwhile, mime flourished as a silent art in 18th-century France, when Napoleon forbade the use of dialogue in stage performance for fear something slanderous might be said.

- The classic white-faced/black-dressed mime was introduced and popularized in the 19th-century French circus by Jean-Gaspard Deburau, who was deemed too clumsy to participate in his family's aerial and acrobatics act.

Mime in the 20th Century

- Mime started to fade in popularity at the beginning of the 1900s but was revitalized with the birth of silent films, in which stars such as Charlie Chaplin and Buster Keaton relied on elements of pantomime.

- In the 1920s, French performer Etienne Decroux declared mime an independent art form—different from the circus form introduced by Deburau—and launched the era of modern mime.

- In 1952, French-trained American mime Paul Curtis founded the American Mime Theatre in New York.

- In 1957, Etienne Decroux traveled to New York to teach a workshop at the Actors Studio, which inspired him to open a mime school in the city.

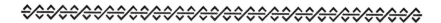

- Decroux's most famous student, Marcel Marceau, expanded modern mime's influence in the 1960s by touring the United States and inviting mimes to train with him.

- When he was growing up, Marcel Marceau had been greatly influenced by the actor Charlie Chaplin. In fact, Marceau's alter ego, "Bip" the clown, was inspired by Chaplin's own "Little Tramp" character.

- The San Francisco Mime Troupe (SFMT), one of the most powerful political theaters in the United States, began as a silent mime company in 1959. It was founded by Ronnie Davis, who had previously performed with the American Mime Theatre.

- Future concert promoter Bill Graham was so moved by an SFMT performance in 1965 that he left his corporate job to manage the group. That led to his career as the legendary promoter of the Rolling Stones, Grateful Dead, and Janis Joplin, among others, in the 1960s and 1970s.

- Robert Shields, a former student of Marceau's, developed the "street mime" form in the 1970s. He performed in San Francisco's Union Square, where he occasionally received traffic citations, landed in jail, and was beaten up by people for imitating them!

- Shields and his wife, fellow mime Lorene Yarnell (they married in a mime wedding in Union Square), brought Marceau's mime technique to TV in the late 1970s with the Emmy Award–winning show *Shields and Yarnell.*

- Though the popularity of mime in the United States declined after the 1970s, it still influences aspects of current culture. Urban street dances, including break dancing, incorporate aspects of mime. Most notable is the evolution of the moonwalk, universalized by Michael Jackson, who was inspired by Marcel Marceau.

Religion
The Oneida Community

◆ ◆ ◆ ◆

*You think the 1960s were a wacky time for religious
cults in America? The mid-1800s has a surprise for the
boomers. Perhaps the most successful "utopian community"
was the Oneida Community of upstate New York.*

John H. Noyes
A Vermonter, Noyes was born in 1811. In the 1830s, while studying
divinity at Yale, he decided a Christian could transcend sin. He
called this philosophy *Perfectionism*. When Noyes pronounced
himself without sin, Yale cast the first stone by revoking his ministry
license and kicking him out.

Putney
Noyes yearned to build a Perfectionist community. After a spiritual
crisis (or perhaps a bout of psychological self-torment), which he
considered a desperate Satanic assault, he moved back to Putney,
Vermont, where his family lived. Converting his siblings and some
locals, he insisted Christ's second coming had already occurred
in A.D. 70. According to Noyes, marriage and monogamy were
nonexistent in Heaven—but sex wasn't. (Noyes himself got married,
notwithstanding.)

For the next nine years, he gathered and taught his flock. Members spent their time farming, studying Scripture, and publishing a
Perfectionist magazine. Women shared ownership and benefits with
relative equality. As for sex, Noyes taught a doctrine called "complex
marriage" (all males are married to all females). Men, he taught,
should practice "male continence"—refraining from ejaculation
unless children were desired. It was the best sexual deal American
women would see until the 1960s.

Here began Noyes's concept of "Bible Communism": commu-
nally held property, focused on biblical teachings (as interpreted by
Noyes). Group criticism sessions were a social norm. But remember: Sino-Soviet Communism hadn't been invented, nor had Lenin,

gulags, Mao, etc. Marx only wrote the *Communist Manifesto* in 1848, just as Noyes's community was moving to New York. Noyes would have considered Marx proof of Satan's ability to pervert Scripture.

The Putney situation imploded in 1847, when the local sheriff arrested Noyes for adultery. Compelled to flee Vermont, in 1848 Noyes found his people's Zion: 40 acres and a sawmill owned by some Perfectionists near Oneida, New York. By year-end, the Oneida Community was 87 strong and busy as beavers: buying and clearing land, planting, building.

Many new arrivals brought useful skills. Noyes believed people should change jobs often to ward off drudgery. Complex marriage meant that postmenopausal women initiated boys into sex after puberty, until the males learned control. Older men (often Noyes himself) initiated girls into sex shortly after menarche. In practice, Noyes decided who should have sex, prioritizing his own very healthy appetites in this regard. Since God advised Noyes, disagreeing with Noyes equaled disagreement with God. Those who disagreed with God/Noyes were welcome to hit the bricks.

The community built, invested, and thrived, growing to about 300 members. Oneida women invented bloomeresque pantaloons two years before Amelia Bloomer. Diverse industries arose: canning, silk, animal traps, furniture, and eventually silverware. Oneida hired outside employees, treating them well.

Downfall

By 1879, the Oneida experiment was a great commercial success but socially beleaguered. Noyes's attempt to install his son as his successor hadn't set well. Dissidents wanted to abandon complex marriage. When Noyes learned of his impending arrest for statutory rape, he bailed to Canada.

The dissident faction soon moved to California. The remaining members reorganized Oneida as a joint stock company and kept up the business. The firm sold off all but the silverware business by 1916. In 2005, Oneida Limited finally outsourced silverware manufacture overseas.

Holidays & Traditions
Seeing Shadows

❖ ❖ ❖ ❖

Will he or won't he? It's a question we all ask ourselves on Groundhog Day as we wait to see whether the furry creature will see his shadow, dooming everyone to six more weeks of winter. But perhaps better questions to ask are these: How did Groundhog Day originate? And how accurate is the little bugger?

The practice of watching a creature's reaction to its shadow to determine whether there will be six more weeks of winter began with German farmers in the 16th century, although they didn't use a groundhog, but a badger. When German immigrants settled in the area of Punxsutawney, Pennsylvania, 300 years later, they couldn't find any badgers, but there were plenty of local groundhogs to act as stand-ins. German folklore had it that if the day was sunny and the creature was frightened enough by its shadow to dart back into the ground, there would be six more weeks of cold weather. That meant that the farmers shouldn't plant their crops yet.

In more recent times, scientific studies have proven that the groundhog's accuracy in prediction over a 60-year period is only 28 percent. In other words, for every year the groundhog is correct, there are almost three years in which it is incorrect. And in truth, the only things determining a groundhog's behavior when it emerges from hibernation are how hungry and how sexually aroused it is. If the groundhog is in the mood to mate—and starving, as well—chances are it'll stick around to see if it can get either or both of those cravings satisfied. The weather, at that moment or for the next six weeks, is the least of the groundhog's worries. Still, we continue to celebrate Groundhog Day. In fact, Punxsutawney draws crowds of 40,000 to its annual Groundhog Day festivities.

Food & Drink
Winging It

❖ ❖ ❖ ❖

Buffalo wings aren't made from buffalo.
But they did come from Buffalo.

Wing aficionados, be sure to mark your calendars for July 29. The city of Buffalo, New York, has dubbed this date "Buffalo Wings Day" in a celebration that dates to 1977. Buffalo wings are actually made from chicken wings that are deep-fried and covered in sauce. Butter and a vinegar-based hot pepper sauce are key ingredients—though just how much hot pepper sauce is a matter of personal taste. Most wings connoisseurs do agree, however, that the savory appetizers taste best when paired with celery and blue cheese or ranch dressing. The dish has become a favorite at bars, restaurants, pizza chains, and sundry weekend BBQs across the country—and even around the world.

But this wildly popular fare is not without controversy. Spicy debates rage over who can take credit for this culinary dynamo. Some folks claim that buffalo wings originated with a man named John Young, who started the wing-fling with a special "mambo sauce" at his Buffalo, New York, restaurant in the mid-1960s. Young went so far as to name his restaurant after the dish, calling it John Young's Wings 'n Things (he even registered said name with the county!). However, another legend credits Anchor Bar on Main Street (also in Buffalo, New York) for the fiery dish. According to one story, Teressa Bellissimo, who owned the bar with her husband Frank, came up with the idea of broiling chicken wings (deep-frying came later) and adding a cayenne hot sauce in 1964. But Frank told a different story, insisting that when he received chicken wings instead of his usual supply order of chicken backs and necks—for use in his spaghetti sauce—he asked Teressa to do something with them. She did, and a gastronomic tradition was born.

Of course, recipes have changed over time, with every person coming up with their own special sauces and preparation methods. But one thing remains constant: Wings are hot stuff!

Science
Sudden Impact

❖ ❖ ❖ ❖

We've all seen movies where an Earth-bound mass of rock from space is set to cause some major havoc. Complete fiction, right? Maybe not. Earth has been invaded by asteroids and comets in the past.

Impact craters are found on most of the planets, satellites, and even asteroids in our solar system—at least those with a surface hard enough to bear a mark. Impact craters are most often caused by one of two culprits: asteroids, which are space bodies that usually reside between the orbits of Jupiter and Mars, or comets, which are masses of gas, dust, and debris. Asteroids and comets are not always well behaved, and wayward ones can—and have—struck Earth.

Time to Duck and Cover?

An impact on Earth isn't as likely as it may sound. For starters, the comet or asteroid has to come close enough to Earth—all the way from Jupiter—to be affected by our planet's gravitational pull. And the body has to be large enough to go through our atmosphere and not burn up before it strikes the surface.

However, in our planet's history, some very large impacting bodies *have* managed to get through. More than 150 impact craters have been identified on Earth, some on the surface and some hidden below the surface. The oldest—at around two billion years old—and largest is the approximately 186-mile-wide Vredefort Dome in South Africa; four other craterlike features on Earth may be older, but they are too eroded to verify dates. The 1.8-billion-year-old, 18-mile-wide Sudbury crater in Ontario, Canada, ranks as another biggie. It's also one of the most profitable—the metals from the 6- to 12-mile-wide

asteroid that caused the crater brought a mother lode of nickel, copper, and platinum, making Sudbury a metal haven.

Where Have All the Dinos Gone?

One of the more interesting terrestrial impact craters is believed to have precipitated the demise of the dinosaurs some 65 million years ago. The 105-mile-wide Chicxulub crater in Yucatán Peninsula, Mexico—an impact crater identified by geologists in 1992—is thought to be associated, or at least partially associated, with the extinction of the dinosaurs. A 6- to 12-mile-wide asteroid fell approximately 64.98 million years ago, throwing enough material into the atmosphere to create climate changes around the world. And it may not have been the only one—but for now, it's the only identified impact crater that is close enough in size and age to have created such chaos.

That Was a Close One!

More recently, we've had some near-misses. On June 30, 1908, a huge explosion was recorded in the northern Siberian region of Tunguska, with theories ranging from a crashing UFO to a mini-black hole. Eventually, scientists realized a stony asteroid had vaporized just above Earth's surface; the shock wave affected a 320-square-mile area. There was no crater, but trees were stripped of their branches and knocked down like toothpicks. More than half the area was incinerated from the blast.

Even more recently, after the U.S. government allowed some of their classified military satellite data to be released, many explosions were identified in the upper atmosphere. These bursts may have been smaller asteroids or comets that actually made it to Earth and burned up in the atmosphere. Either that, or they were larger ones that, luckily, dropped harmlessly into the oceans.

Film
Hooray for Hollywood

❖ ❖ ❖ ❖

Today, Hollywood is almost synonymous with the
film industry. But that wasn't always the case.

The word "Hollywood" not only implies the hub of the American
film industry but also the arbiter of popular tastes and the heart of
America's collective dreams and fantasies. Hollywood is so enmeshed
with the production and romance of "the movies" that it is difficult
to believe that it was not always the center of the industry.

In the early 20th century, the great film centers were New York
City and Chicago. In New York, the most powerful production
companies had formed a cartel, or trust, called the Motion Picture
Patents Company to control film production, distribution, and exhibition; set prices for equipment; and keep independent companies
outside the trust from becoming successful. Chicago was home to
several independents hoping to escape interference by the Patents
Company. The problem with both New York and Chicago was the
winter weather, especially for those who did not have studio spaces.
Bad weather and short daylight hours hampered shooting schedules,
which reduced output.

Hooray for…Jacksonville?

Around 1908, several film companies began sending members of
their crews to other parts of the country to shoot movies. Called
stock companies, some of these groups were part of the Patents
Company and some were independent of it, but all were looking for
picturesque locations, warmer climates, and more daylight hours.

In 1908, Broncho Billy Anderson of Essanay traveled to Colorado
looking for authentic locations for his Westerns, while the Kalem
Company sent a troupe to Jacksonville, Florida, to start production
during the winter months. Other companies quickly followed Kalem
to Jacksonville, earning the city the nickname "the World's Winter
Film Capital." For a while, Jacksonville rivaled Chicago and New
York as a major film center, but in 1917, the city's movie-promoting

mayor lost his bid for reelection and the decline of support by local financial institutions triggered an exodus of production companies to the West Coast.

Among the other locations that attracted production companies were San Antonio, New Orleans, Cuba, Bermuda, Mexico, and Southern California. In 1908, Francis Boggs of Selig Studios shot the exteriors for *The Count of Monte Cristo* in Los Angeles. This may have been the earliest film shot by a major company in the Los Angeles area. Boggs returned the following year to set up permanent facilities on Olive Street. In 1910, Selig established a studio in Edendale, while American Mutoscope and Biograph—one of the major production companies in the Patents group—arrived in Los Angeles to shoot a few films. By 1911, almost 20 production companies had studios in Los Angeles and its suburbs, including Hollywood, where the Nestor Company had bought property at Gower and Sunset.

Why Hollywood?

As the decade progressed, the Hollywood and Los Angeles areas became a permanent film center, primarily because of the stability of the warm climate and sunshine. Another important factor was the variety of landscape—from desert to beaches to mountains—which gave moviemakers a range of scenic choices for picturesque settings. The production companies that relocated to the West Coast found real estate to be inexpensive, which encouraged them to buy large tracts of land to establish studios with huge staging areas, labs, offices, and backlots. Realizing the benefits of this fast-growing industry, the financial and political infrastructures of Los Angeles and its suburbs were supportive of the studios. Another advantage to Southern California was that it was far from the Patents Company, which frequently stirred up trouble for independents. However, as more and more production companies settled in the West, the Patents Company lost its bite and its relevance.

By 1920, weather, landscape, cheap land prices, and cooperative city fathers combined to make Hollywood and the surrounding area the undisputed film capital of America—a title the City of Dreams still holds to this day.

Inventions
Breaking Morse Code

❖ ❖ ❖ ❖

In these high-tech times, most people are glued to their cell phones 24/7. We have Antonio Meucci, an Italian American inventor, to thank for this. If it weren't for him, we'd have to listen to dashes and dots—the basis for Morse code—when we call our significant other to find out if we're running low on coffee.

The transition from Pony Express to transcontinental telegraph lines took years. The first telegraph was invented by Charles Wheatstone and William Fothergill Cooke in 1831. That same year, Joseph Henry would develop the basic principles of enabling an electric current to travel long distances.

American inventor and painter Samuel Finley Breese Morse found a practical use for Henry's principles. With technical assistance from chemistry professor Leonard Gale and financial support from Alfred Vail, Morse invented the Morse Code. In 1837, he unveiled his new way of interpreting communications over telegraph wires to the public in New York, Philadelphia, and Washington, D.C. He received a patent for his code in 1840, and by 1843, the U.S. Congress had approved an experimental line.

In a watershed moment for telecommunications, Morse sent his first message via Morse Code on May 24, 1844: "What hath God wrought?" The communication traveled from Washington to Baltimore.

By 1861, most major cities were connected by lines that transmitted electrical signals, and each dash and dot was translated by operators at telegraph stations. This was a boon to communications (and often the bane when the enemy cut lines) during the Civil War. The short signals were called *dits* (seen as dots), and the long signals were called *dahs* (seen as dashes); in combination, the signals represented the letters of the alphabet and ten numerals. For example, the most well-known use of the Morse code is the SOS signal—or dit, dit, dit, dah, dah, dah, dit, dit, dit.

What Do You Mean by That?

Blue Bloods

In the Middle Ages, the veins of the fair-complexioned people of Spain appeared blue. To distinguish them as untainted by the Moors, they referred to themselves as blue-blooded.

Rob Peter to Pay Paul

In the mid-1550s, estates in St. Peter's, Westminster, were appropriated to pay for the new St. Paul's Cathedral. This process revived a phrase that preacher John Wycliffe had used 170 years before in *Select English Works*.

Humble Pie

While medieval lords and ladies dined on the finest foods, servants had to utilize leftovers (the "'umbles," or offal) when preparing their meals. To eat humble pie means to exercise humility or self-effacement.

Men of Straw

In medieval times, men would hang around English courts of law, eager to be hired as false witnesses. They identified themselves with a straw in their shoe.

White Elephant

Once upon a time in Siam, rare albino elephants were to receive nothing but the best from their owners. Therefore, no one wanted to own one.

Touch and Go

English ships in the 18th century would often hit bottom in shallow water, only to be released with the next wave. The phrase indicated that they had narrowly averted danger.

By Hook or by Crook

This phrase describes a feudal custom that allowed tenants to gather as much wood from their lord's land as they could rake from the undergrowth or pull down from the trees with a crook.

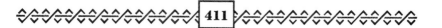

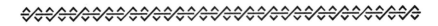

Media & Communication
New York News Before
The New York Times

❖ ❖ ❖ ❖

*In the once-budding metropolis of New York City, no newspaper
was unbiased enough to cross the myriad political and ethnic
lines that were drawn everywhere. And then came* The New York
Times, *which published only the news that was fit to print.*

"Extra! Extra!"—Not Everyone Wanted to Read All About It

In order to understand the founding of *The New York Times,* one
has to envision New York City in 1851, the year the newspaper was
founded. The population stood at half a million, and new people
came every day. The city's rapid development created gaping power
vacuums, and corrupt groups vied for control and influence.

There were many types of printed news sources. Some were
frivolous and suited to popular culture; others were highbrow and
political. Unlike today, newspapers made little attempt to appear
"objective." They explicitly linked with political parties, and sensa-
tionalist editorials lampooned some groups while revering others.
The two founders of *The New York Times,* Henry Jarvis Raymond
and George Jones, met in the office of New York's most popular
newspaper in the 1840s: *The New York Tribune.* Jones was working
in business management, whereas Raymond was an editorial assistant. *The New York Tribune* was masterminded by Horace Greeley,
who imbued his paper with politics; Greeley was a Whig (the forerunner of the Republican Party) with socialist leanings, and one
needn't read between the lines too much to figure the rest out.

The Herald was another popular paper of the time; it was the first
to focus on hard news coverage of the urban underbelly: stories of
crime, drugs, and prostitution were common, which was not appreciated by those who held to the Victorian ideals of the time. On the
opposite end of the spectrum, pretentious newspapers with smaller
circulations, intended for an elite readership, were still preferred

among the upper classes. No single paper transcended these complex class lines.

One Paper for a Mass Readership

What journalism needed was a new approach that would appeal to academics and laypeople alike: a paper that focused on news without sensationalizing sex and violence; a paper that was political but nonpartisan; a paper that was intelligent, yet accessible to the growing literacy of the lower and middle classes. Raymond and Jones were aware of this need, and for years they tossed around the idea of starting a paper together.

The moment finally came in 1851. Jones was a businessman at heart, so he'd moved to Albany to redeem bank notes—a profitable venture in the days before standardized bank practices. In 1851, legislation was in the works that would regulate bank note redemption. One day, Jones and Raymond were walking along the Hudson, and Raymond mentioned that in the previous year, *The Herald* had brought in a profit of $60,000. By the end of that fateful stroll, Jones and Raymond made an agreement: If the bank note legislation passed, the two would start a paper together.

The bill passed. With the help of additional investments from mutual friend E. B. Wesley, the paper was officially established in September as *The New-York Daily Times* (the name was changed in 1857). The founders committed to objectivity and temperance in opinion; the paper was to be "the best and the cheapest daily family newspaper in the United States," and it was "not established for the advancement of any party, sect, or person." The first issue was published on September 18, 1851, with the prophetic pronouncement that "we publish today the first issue of *The New-York Daily Times,* and we intend to issue it every morning (Sundays excepted) for an indefinite number of years to come."

Computers & Cyberspace
ARPANET: Grandfather of the Internet

◆ ◆ ◆ ◆

Rumors abound that ARPANET was designed as a communications network that would withstand nuclear attacks. That simply isn't true. The creators of ARPANET weren't seeking invulnerability, but reliability—in order to fulfill one man's vision of an "inter-galactic" computer network.

On October 4, 1957, the Soviet Union launched the world's first artificial satellite, *Sputnik I,* into space. It was a clear message that Russian technology was more advanced than American technology. To amend this oversight, the Advanced Research Projects Agency (ARPA) was formed to fund technical research. The United States already had a substantial financial investment in computer tech—the initial purpose of ARPA was to figure out the best way to put that to use. Though it fell under the auspices of the U.S. Department of Defense (and was renamed DARPA), the research was never intended to be used solely for military purposes. Instead, the agency's purpose was to develop technology that would benefit civilization and the world in general.

Not Connected to Other Galaxies—Yet
The expert chosen to head ARPA's initial effort was Joseph "Lick" Licklider, a leading computer scientist. Lick had a vision of a worldwide communications network connected by computers, which he referred to as the "inter-galactic computer network." Lick departed ARPA in 1965, before his plan could be implemented, but he left a lasting impression on his successor, Bob Taylor.

Taylor selected a new leader for the system design team that would make Lick's vision a reality: Dr. Lawrence "Larry" G. Roberts, an MIT researcher. He became one of the four people most closely associated with the birth of the Internet. (The other three are Vinton Cerf, Leonard Kleinrock, and Robert Kahn.) Roberts had gained experience in computer linking while at MIT, having linked comput-

ers using the old-fashioned telephone method of circuit switching. The concept of packet switching was at first controversial, but it proved to be one of the key factors in linking multiple computers to form a network. The other important technical achievement was the use of small computers, known as interface message processors (IMPs), to store and handle the data packets.

By 1968, the concept for ARPANET was in place, and invitations to bid on the project were sent to 140 institutions; only 12 actually replied. The others apparently believed the concept to be impractical, even bizarre, and never bothered to bid. In the end, BBN Technologies—Licklider's former employer—got the nod.

A Hesitant Start

The first piece went to UCLA, thanks to the reputation of Professor Kleinrock, an expert in computer statistical analysis and measurement. The first IMP link was with Stanford Research Institute (SRI). The first message was sent on October 29, 1969, and was supervised by Kleinrock—it was an omen of things to come. The message was supposed to be "login," but after two letters, the system crashed, and only "lo" was sent. About an hour later, the system was up and running again, and the full message was transmitted. By December 5, 1969, four IMPs were linked: UCLA, SRI, University of California at Santa Barbara, and the University of Utah. These IMP sites were chosen on the basis of their ability to research and implement the protocol that would allow for the continued growth of ARPANET.

ARPANET was no longer just a vision—it was a reality. The growth of ARPANET during the 1970s was phenomenal, as newer and better protocols were designed. In 1971, e-mail was born; in 1972, telnet was developed; and in 1973, file transfer protocol came into play.

By 1986, ARPANET had serious competition from the National Science Foundation Network (NSFNET), which became the true backbone of the Internet. ARPANET closed up shop in 1990. In 1991, NSFNET opened to the public, introducing the Internet we know today. Within four years, more than 50 million people had traveled the information superhighway. As of March 2008, worldwide Internet usage stood at 1.4 billion—and that's only the beginning.

Museums
The Smithsonian:
A Nation's Inheritance

❖ ❖ ❖ ❖

Perhaps no American museum is as well-known, and as beloved, as the Smithsonian Institution's complex of art, science, history, and zoological museums in Washington, D.C.

In 1835, an unknown, illegitimate Englishman named James Smithson died, childless but not penniless. He had inherited a substantial estate from his parents—one of royal blood and the other a duke—and in death he left the world a magnificent gift: an endowment for an American institution "for the increase and diffusion of knowledge among men"—the Smithsonian Institution.

Smithson's motives behind his unusual bequest remain a mystery. He never visited the United States, and there is little evidence that he ever even wrote to any American. The bastard son of the Duke of Northumberland, he may have felt slighted by a British society that deprived him of the privileges of a "legitimate" ducal heir. Or he may have taken a far-off interest in the bustling new democracy in which ideas and industry appeared to rule the day.

Whatever his motives, Smithson's offer of 100,000 gold sovereigns was too enticing for the young republic to refuse. U.S. President Andrew Jackson urged Congress to accept Smithson's gift, and upon congressional approval, the British gold was recast into 508,318 Yankee dollars.

Now What?
Having accepted the money, the nation faced an important question: "What do we do with it?"

Initially, Congress leaned toward using Smithson's gold to establish a national university. Plans for an institution specializing in the classics, science, or teaching skills were all proposed and rejected in turn. Other ideas—a national observatory, a laboratory, a museum, or a library—drew both support and opposition from the divided legislature. So the deadlocked Congress settled the matter by avoid-

ing the issue entirely, leaving it to the Smithsonian's board of directors to determine the direction of the new institution.

America's Attic

The first proceeds were used for a building that would house the many tasks assigned to the new institution—teaching, experimenting, and exhibitions for the public. The building, located on the National Mall and now known as "the Castle," was designed in the medieval revival style, reminiscent of the ancient universities of Smithson's homeland.

While the research and scientific functions of the Smithsonian grew steadily after the 1855 completion of the Castle, it was the national collection of odds and ends that captured the public's mind and earned the Smithsonian its reputation as "America's attic." Fueled by the great American explorations of the Arctic, Antarctic, and interior regions of the United States, the Smithsonian's holdings grew from a small collection of pressed flora and preserved animal specimens to an assemblage that required the construction of a new building, the United States National Museum, in 1881.

Today, more than 170 years after Smithson died, the institute that bears his name comprises 19 museums, 4 research centers, a zoo, and a library research system. It is the largest single museum complex on the globe. From the fabled Hope Diamond to the historic Wright Flyer, from George Washington's dress sword to the original Kermit the Frog, the Smithsonian Institution pulls together the best of America's history and many relics of the world in which we live. Its collection, an astounding 136.9 million objects, and its museums are graced by 23 million visitors per year. With assets worth $2.2 billion today, James Smithson's bequest has grown into the world's biggest museum.

"Most convicted felons are just people who were not taken to museums or Broadway musicals as children."
—LIBBY GELMAN-WAXNER

Places & Landmarks
The World in Wax

◆ ◆ ◆ ◆

Madame Tussaud's waxworks might seem like a fun place for a "celebrity" encounter, but there is a dark side to the origins of wax portraiture with which few are familiar.

Madame Tussaud's of London exhibits wax portraits of historical persons and contemporary celebrities, tableaux of significant events, and a Chamber of Horrors. It remains the most well-known collection of wax figures in the world.

Born Marie Grosholtz in 1761 in Strasbourg, France, Madame Tussaud learned her craft from an uncle, Dr. Philippe Curtius of Bern, Switzerland. Dr. Curtius made wax models of human limbs and organs as medical teaching tools because cadavers were so difficult to obtain. A talented modeler, Dr. Curtius extended his business to include miniature portraits in wax.

Around 1770, Dr. Curtius moved to Paris to open a wax studio and an exhibition of life-size figures of prominent people of the era, including royalty. A few years later, Marie became his apprentice at the studio, which was visited by such notables as Benjamin Franklin. At age 17, young Marie made a portrait of Voltaire, which still survives.

Madame Tussaud's Exhibitions

Marie inherited her uncle's talent for wax portraiture, and she began teaching wax modeling to the royal court at Versailles. Soon the young artist was caught up in the winds of political change when the French Revolution swept the country with a fury. Marie was arrested for having royalist sympathies, but the revolutionaries spared her life in order to put her skills to use. She produced death masks of some of the most famous royal heads ever to be severed by the bloody guillotine, including Louis XVI and Marie Antoinette. She also modeled the head and body of revolutionary Marat, who was stabbed to death in his bath by Charlotte Corday.

Marie married engineer Francois Tussaud in 1795, and the couple had two sons. Unfortunately, the marriage failed, and in 1802, Madame Tussaud and her children moved to London, taking 70 wax exhibits with them. For 33 years, Marie toured the United Kingdom with her wax figures and tableaux, generating a loyal following for her exhibition of history come to life.

At age 74, she acquired a permanent home for her waxworks on Baker Square in London. Among Marie's most famous wax figures was a self-portrait modeled by her own hand when she was 81. Marie died on April 6, 1850, but her waxworks continued to expand. In 1884, the museum and studio were moved to their present site on Marylebone Road, and descendants of Madame Tussaud continued her craft until the death of great-great-grandson Bernard Tussaud in 1967. Wax figures are still produced by Madame Tussaud's for their museums in London and Amsterdam.

The Legacy of Madame Tussaud

A living witness to some of the most important events in history, Madame Tussaud excelled at re-creating important historical figures and events. Though waxworks today tend to focus on movie stars and celebrities, many of them are still dedicated to re-creating history—offering children a chance to experience that history in a colorful, unpretentious venue.

Marie was also party to another side of history—a darker, more notorious side not found in schoolbooks. Who can say what effect making death masks of guillotine victims had on the young woman caught in the middle of a revolution? One of the most famous rooms in Madame Tussaud's is the Chamber of Horrors, where murderers and tyrants executing their brutal, bloody deeds are captured for all eternity. Also featured are instruments of torture and tools of murder. Later wax museums followed Madame Tussaud's lead and included their own chambers of horrors, making this type of exhibit standard. Yet, few had first-hand knowledge of the dark side of history like Marie Grosholtz Tussaud. For decades, the centerpiece of Madame Tussaud's Chamber of Horrors was a working model of a guillotine, which she displayed in the "Separate Room."

Clubs & Organizations
The House of David

❖ ❖ ❖ ❖

The only thing more startling than seeing men with waist-length hair and long beards playing baseball in the early 1900s might have been knowing every player on this early barnstorming team was a member of a highly controversial religious sect known as the House of David.

From Kentucky to the Second Coming

Based in Benton Harbor, Michigan, this religious sect centered around its charismatic leader, Benjamin Franklin Purnell, and his wife, Mary. The couple believed that they were God's appointed messengers for the Second Coming of Christ, and that the human body could have eternal life on Earth. They also believed that both men and women should imitate Jesus by never cutting their hair. Purnell based his teachings on those of an 18th-century English group called the Philadelphians, which were developed from the prophecies of a woman named Joanna Southcott who claimed she was the first of seven messengers to proclaim the Second Coming. Purnell somehow deduced that he was also one of those seven.

Growing Hair, Religion, and Crowds

Born in Kentucky in March 1861, Purnell and Mary traveled around the country for several years while polishing their doctrine. After being booted out of a small town in Ohio, possibly because Benjamin was accused of adultery with a local farmer's wife, they landed in Benton Harbor in March 1903. Members of a sect related to the Philadelphians called the Jezreelites lived in nearby Grand Rapids, and Purnell had been in touch with the Bauschke brothers of Benton Harbor, who were sympathetic to his cause.

With the backing of the Bauschkes and other prominent local citizens, Purnell soon attracted a crowd of believers and called his group the Israelite House of David. The 700 or so members lived chaste, commune-style lives on a cluster of farms and land, served vegetarian meals, and started successful cottage industries, such as a toy factory, greenhouse, and canning facility.

As word spread of the long-haired, oddly dressed members and their colony, the curious began making Sunday trips to observe them. Purnell turned this into a cash opportunity by opening an aviary, a small zoo, a vegetarian restaurant, an ice-cream parlor, and, ironically, a barber shop. The crowds grew, and, in 1908, he started work on his own amusement park, which included an expanded zoo and a miniature, steam-powered railway whose trains ran throughout the grounds.

Entertainment Evangelism

In the meantime, some members of the group had formed a baseball team that also drew crowds, so Purnell added a large stadium next to the amusement park. The team traveled as well, and added to their popularity with comical routines, such as hiding the ball under their beards. Building on the sports theme, the colony also featured exhibition basketball, and later, miniature car racing.

The colony also boasted a popular brass band, whose members capitalized on their showy long tresses by starting each concert facing away from the audience, hair covering half of their snazzy uniforms. They often played jazzy, crowd-pleasing numbers rather than the expected somber religious tunes.

Religious activities continued, too. Adopting the title "The Prince of Peace," Purnell often held teaching sessions, including one in which he was photographed allegedly changing water into wine.

Problems in Paradise

As happens with any large social enterprise, some members became disgruntled and left. Purnell referred to them as "scorpions." Rumors flew concerning improper relations between Purnell and young females in the group, especially when the colony purchased an island in northern Michigan where they ran a prosperous lumber business. Newspaper reports alleged that rebellious group members were killed and buried there and that Purnell kept a group of young girls as sex slaves. The public was also suspicious of mass weddings he conducted. Lawsuits had begun against Purnell in Ohio and continued to mount even as the Michigan colony progressed.

In 1926, Purnell was finally arrested on charges that included religious fraud and statutory rape. He endured a lengthy trial, but he was ill for most of it, and much of his testimony was deemed incoherent. Most charges were eventually dismissed.

Purnell died in Benton Harbor on December 16, 1927, at age 66. But shortly before passing, he told his followers that, like Jesus, he would be back in three days. As far as anyone knows, he wasn't. His preserved remains were kept in a glass-covered coffin on the colony grounds for decades, although at one time Mary's brother reportedly insisted that the body was not Purnell's but that of another colony member.

Remains of the Day

After his death, some of the believers switched their allegiance to Purnell's widow, Mary, who lived until 1953 and started a new colony called Mary's City of David, which still plays baseball and runs a museum in Benton Harbor. The grounds and businesses were split between the two groups, and only a handful of members remain in either. The zoo closed in 1945, with the animals given to Chicago's Lincoln Park Zoo, and the amusement park, remembered fondly by many local residents, closed in the early 1970s. The original area east of Benton Harbor's city limits still serves as the headquarters for the two groups. And many credit Benjamin Purnell as the forerunner of later, high-style evangelical leaders such as Jim Bakker and Oral Roberts.

"Whiskers! Whiskers! Whiskers!
Strangest of all baseball attractions
Weird and Eccentric!"
—1930 POSTER PROMOTING A GAME BETWEEN THE HOUSE OF DAVID BASEBALL TEAM AND THE BUFFALO BISONS OF THE INTERNATIONAL LEAGUE

The House of David team played in the first professional night baseball game, in Independence, Kansas, in 1930.

Law & Politics
The First War on Drugs: Prohibition

❖ ❖ ❖ ❖

It's hard to conceive of today: Ban the sale and manufacture of alcohol! Sure, Prohibition didn't work, but a study of its roots shows why people thought an alcohol ban was feasible enough to etch it into history by the indelible (if repealable) mechanism of a constitutional amendment.

But First...
Did you bring your ax? Let's shatter a kegful of mythology! Did you know that...

... *the Prohibition movement actually began before the Civil War?* The temperance movement registered local victories as early as the 1850s.

... *one-third of the federal budget ran on ethanol?* This was before federal income tax became the main source of revenue.

... *Prohibition didn't ban alcohol consumption?* Clubs that stocked up on liquor before Prohibition legally served it throughout.

... *women's suffrage didn't affect the passage of Prohibition?* The Eighteenth Amendment enacted Prohibition. The Nineteenth Amendment gave women the vote.

... *Prohibition didn't create gangs?* The gangs were already there. They just took advantage of a golden opportunity.

... *Eliot Ness's "Untouchables" really existed?* They were agents of the Bureau of Prohibition.

Temperance
Strictly speaking, *temperance* means moderation, not abstinence. By the early 1800s, most people realized that drunkenness wasn't particularly healthy. As the industrial age gathered steam,

working while intoxicated went from "bad behavior" to "asking for an industrial maiming by enormous machinery." Immigration also factored, for nativist sentiment ran high in the 1800s. Many Americans didn't like immigrants with foreign accents (many of whom saw nothing wrong with tying one on) and made alcohol an "us versus them" issue.

The XX (Chromosome) Factor

Women, logically, formed the backbone of the temperance movement. Just because you can't vote doesn't mean your brain is disconnected. With a woman's social role limited to home and family, whatever disabled the home's primary wage-earner threatened home economics. Worse still, alcohol abuse has always gone fist-in-mouth with domestic violence.

Organizations and Advances

In 1869, the Prohibition Party was formed to run antialcohol candidates. It typically polled 200,000+ popular presidential votes from 1888 to 1920 but never greatly influenced national politics in and of itself. The compressed political energy and intellect of American women—denied access to congressional seats and judgeships—found its outlet in 1873: the Woman's Christian Temperance Union (WCTU), which still exists today. By 1890, the WCTU counted 150,000 members.

Meanwhile, the male-dominated Anti-Saloon League (ASL) was founded in 1893 and achieved rapid successes due to smart campaigning. By appealing to churches and campaigning against Demon Rum's local bad guys, it drew in nonprohibitionists who disapproved of the entire saloon/bar/tavern culture. While the ASL would later hog the credit for the Eighteenth Amendment, the WCTU laid the foundation for credible temperance activism.

Only three states were "dry" before 1893. In 1913, the ASL began advocating Prohibition via constitutional amendment. By 1914, there were 14 dry states, encompassing nearly half the population; by 1917 another 12 had dried up. In that same year, the Supreme Court ruled that Americans didn't have a constitutional right to keep alcohol at home. Prohibition's ax, long in forging, now had a sturdy handle.

Eighteenth Amendment

By January 29, 1919, the necessary 36 states had ratified this amendment. In October of that year, Congress passed the Volstead Act to enforce the amendment. One year later, it would be illegal to manufacture, sell, or transport intoxicating liquors. Of course, everyone stopped drinking.

Okay, that's enough laughter.

What we got was the Roaring Twenties. Alcohol went underground, corrupting police departments and providing limitless opportunity for lawbreakers. The understaffed, oft-bought-and-paid-for Bureau of Prohibition couldn't possibly keep up. America's War on Alcohol worked no better than the later War on Drugs, which would so casually ignore history's lessons.

Enough Already

On December 5, 1933, the Twenty-first Amendment repealed the Eighteenth—the only such repeal in U.S. history. Prohibition was over.

Everyone had a few beers, and then got busy worrying about marijuana.

12 Countries with Highest Beer Consumption

Country	Gallons per Person per Year
1. Ireland	41.0
2. Germany	32.0
3. Austria	28.0
4. Belgium (tied)	26.0
5. Denmark (tied)	26.0
6. United Kingdom	25.5
7. Australia	23.5
8. United States	22.4
9. Netherlands (tied)	21.0
10. Finland (tied)	21.0
11. New Zealand	20.5
12. Canada	18.5

Personal Hygiene
Potty Talk

❖ ❖ ❖ ❖

Our bathrooms are some of the most important
rooms in our homes, and they provide privacy and
sanctuary—in addition to their primary function.

A Bathroom by Any Other Name
There are quite a few names for this little space—pick your favorite:
restroom, powder room, crapper, loo, little boys' room, little girls'
room, water closet, WC, porcelain god, lavatory, commode, latrine,
the facilities, the necessary room, the john, washroom.

A Toilet Before Its Time
In 1596, an inventor named John Harrington, godson to Queen
Elizabeth I, tried to create a more advanced chamber pot. The
queen and her godson both used the flush model he came up with,
but Harrington was ridiculed by his peers for fooling around with
such a ridiculous idea, thus ending his career as an inventor.

Toilet Paper Beginnings
In 1857, New Yorker Joseph C. Gayetty produced the first packaged
bathroom tissue in the United States. It was called "The Therapeutic
Paper" and contained aloe for added comfort. The company sold the
paper in packs of 500 sheets at 50 cents apiece, and Gayetty's name
was printed on every sheet.

Germs, Germs, Germs
A lot of people think a public toilet seat is the filthiest place on
Earth, but that may not be true. According to experts, the floor of a
public bathroom is much dirtier, with around 2 million bacteria per
square inch—that's 200 times higher than what's considered sanitary.

Washroom Attendants
Not so long ago, unless you were wealthy and enjoyed eating at
expensive restaurants, washroom attendants were not people you'd

come into much contact with. Now, in both the United States and United Kingdom, washroom attendants are becoming regular public bathroom "fixtures." An individual stands in the bathroom and hands out towels, dispenses soap, and usually offers gum, candy, mints, and any number of other accoutrements to patrons—for a tip, of course.

Don't Go Left

In places like India and in many parts of Asia, bathrooms provide a little cup of water—but no toilet paper. When you're done doing your business, it's customary to use your left hand to wash your bum of any leftover fecal matter and then wash your hand with the cup of water. This is precisely why it's rude to shake hands with your left hand in most of Asia and the Middle East.

Locate-a-Loo

Thanks to the magic of the Internet, you never again have to search blindly for a bathroom in your hour of need. If you've got a handheld device that connects to the Web, just go to www.thebathroomdiaries. com for info. The Bathroom Diaries site is "the world's largest database of bathroom locations" and lists by state everywhere you can relieve yourself.

Protect Your Seat

What started as a fad for germophobes are now available in bathroom stalls almost everywhere—but do paper toilet seat guards work? Well, sure, but only if the seat is dry to begin with. If the seat guard is placed on a seat that's already wet or dirty, it actually sucks the bacteria and viruses up from the toilet seat onto your bare skin even more quickly.

American Restroom Association

Hey, somebody has to be a watchdog for public restrooms, right? Even though they garner more than a few snickers when they appear in the news (every year the World Toilet Summit is held in a different city), the ARA has a clear mission statement: "The American Restroom Association advocates for the availability of clean, safe, well-designed public restrooms." And no one who's ever had to use a gross public bathroom is going to snicker at that.

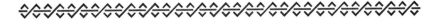

Places & Landmarks
The Washington Monument: George in Roman Drag?

❖ ❖ ❖ ❖

We cannot tell a lie: The Washington Monument definitely wasn't built in a day. In fact, it wasn't built in a century. From concept to completion, the narcoleptic project spanned 102 years. You might mention that the next time someone claims that today's Congress is inefficient!

George's Lifetime

The Revolutionary War concluded in 1783. The colonies were now the United States of America, and General George Washington was their greatest war hero. A veteran proposed a statue of the great man on horseback (as was typical for statues of generals). Congress approved the project but initiated no planning or building. Washington passed away in 1799 without seeing a single stone laid. In any case, Washington's passing stirred public opinion: There should be at least one memorial or sepulcher somewhere in the capital city. Of course, Congress got right on that.

Cornerstone

Just kidding. It wasn't until 1833 that someone finally got around to founding a Washington Monument Society, but this time the plan bore fruit. In 1836, architect Robert Mills's design won the Society's approval. The Monument was to be a 600-foot, flat-topped obelisk with a circular colonnade at the base. Atop the colonnade would stand a heroic statue of Washington in a Roman toga, driving...a chariot. Thirty other Revolutionary heroes would also get statues. The work was finally under way.

Well, not really. The project stalled until 1848 when—amid great fanfare—workers laid the obelisk's cornerstone. Progress continued until 1854, when funds ran low. Then a bigoted political party found a creative way to compound the existing fiasco.

Knowing Nothing

In the mid-19th century, a nativist party and quasi-secret society known as the Know-Nothings became a player in U.S. politics. (Their name, while intellectually honest, wasn't meant as such. It came from their response to queries: "I know nothing.") The first huge wave of Catholic immigrants had arrived in the United States, many fleeing the Irish potato famines for the land of religious freedom (and some lunch). As conspiracy theorists and haters of Catholicism and immigration (especially Catholic immigration), the Know-Nothings considered the immigrants a papal plot to Catholicize the United States.

We wouldn't care, except in 1854 the Know-Nothings gained control of the Washington Monument Society. Annoyed, Congress chopped the funding. The Know-Nothings knew little about masonry; what little construction they achieved had to be ripped out later due to crummy workmanship. In 1858, the Know-Nothings finally did something beneficial for the Monument: They quit the Society. By 1860, the monument was just an ugly vertical rectangular stub about 152 feet high—barely one-fourth complete and going nowhere.

Civil War

In 1861, of course, the Confederate States of America seceded from the Union. This, at least, was a legitimate reason to suspend work. During the Civil War, the sacred site served various hallowed purposes: cattle grazing, beef slaughtering, troop encampments, and drill training. The Confederacy surrendered in 1865, so the construction immediately resumed.

At Last!

Ha! Surely you're wise to this by now. Congress goofed around until 1876, when the Centennial reminded everyone that it was about time to finish memorializing the first president and

commander in chief of the Continental Army. By now, Robert Mills was no longer living, so the new guard edited his design. There would be no colonnade, no George Ben-Hur; also, to allay the concerns of the Corps of Engineers about how much weight the ground could sustain, the obelisk would taper off at 555 feet.

The change in color you see on the modern Monument is where construction resumed—a slightly different type of marble was used to finish the project where the Know-Nothings left off. Construction was completed in 1885, and the government opened the interior to the public in October 1888.

George Washington would have turned 156 that February.

❧❧❧❧❧❧❧

The Washington Monument consists of 36,491 marble, granite, and sandstone blocks and weighs approximately 90,854 tons.

At the time of its completion, the Monument was the world's tallest structure, a title it held only until 1889, when the Eiffel Tower was completed in Paris. Today, it holds a place in the record books as the world's tallest freestanding stone structure not created from a single block of stone.

You'll have to climb 897 steps to reach the top of the Washington Monument. That's a lot of steps! Fortunately, you can also make the trip by elevator if you so choose. If you take the elevator, it will take you 70 seconds to reach the top. We can't tell you how long it will take if you choose to climb the stairs!

War & Military
The Ancient Pedigree of Biological and Chemical Warfare

❖ ❖ ❖ ❖

Considered the pinnacle of military know-how, biological and chemical warfare has actually been around for millennia.

China's Deadly Fog

Inventors of gunpowder and rockets, the Chinese were also among the first to use biological and chemical agents. Fumigation used to purge homes of vermin in the seventh century B.C. likely inspired the employment of poisonous smoke during war. Ancient Chinese military writings contain hundreds of recipes for such things as "soul-hunting fog," containing arsenic, and "five-league fog," which was laced with wolf dung. When a besieging army burrowed under a city's walls, defenders struck back. They burned piles of mustard in ovens, then operated bellows to blow the noxious gas at the subterranean attackers. In the second century A.D., authorities dispersed hordes of rebellious peasants with a kind of tear gas made from chopped bits of lime.

Ancient Greek Poisons

The ancient Greeks were also experienced with biological and chemical weapons. Herodotus wrote in the fifth century B.C. about the Scythian archers, who were barbarian warriors dwelling near Greek colonies along the Black Sea. By his account, Scythian bowmen could accurately fire an arrow 500 yards every three seconds. Their arrows were dipped in a mixture of dung, human blood, and the venom of adders. These ingredients were mixed and buried in jars until they reached the desired state of putrefaction. The poison arrows paralyzed the lungs, inducing asphyxiation.

Another bioweapon figured prominently in the First Sacred War. Around 590 B.C., fighters from the city of Kirrha attacked travelers on their way to the Oracle of Delphi and seized Delphic territories. Enraged at the sacrilege, several Greek city-states formed the League of Delphi and laid siege to Kirrha. For a time, the town's

stout defenses stymied the attackers. However, according to the ancient writer Thessalos, a horse stepped through a piece of a buried pipe that brought water into the city. A medicine man named Nebros convinced the Greeks to ply the water with the plant hellebore, a strong purgative. The defenders, devastated by diarrhea, were rendered too weak to fight, and the Greeks captured the town and killed every inhabitant.

Flying Corpses Spread the Black Plague

In 1340, during the siege of a French town during the Hundred Years War, catapults were used to throw the diseased bodies of dead animals, including horses, at the castle of Thun L'Eveque. Reports indicate that "...the ayre was hote as in the myddes of somer: the stynke and ayre was so abominable." Vlad the Impaler, the 15th-century Romanian warlord and real-life model for Dracula, used a similar method against his Turkish foes.

Scholars believe that this ghastly biological warfare tactic played a big role in spreading the worst plague in human history, the bubonic plague, better known as the Black Death. In 1346, merchants from Genoa set up a trading outpost in Crimea, which was attacked by Tartars, a warlike horde of Muslim Turks. However, during the siege, the attacking forces were decimated by the plague. To even the score, the Tartars catapulted the corpses of plague victims over the walls of the Genoan fortress.

Horrified, the Genoan merchants set sail for home. In October 1347, their galleys, carrying rats and fleas infested with the Black Death, pulled into Genoa's harbor. Within several years, the plague would spread from Italy to the rest of Europe, felling more than a third of its population.

A Pox on All Their Houses

In America, biological warfare darkened the French and Indian War. In 1763, during the vast rebellion of Native Americans under Chief Pontiac, the Delaware tribe allied with the French and attacked the British at Fort Pitt. Following the deaths of 400 soldiers and 2,000 settlers, the fort's defenders turned to desperate means.

William Trent, the commander of Fort Pitt's militia, knew that a smallpox epidemic had been ravaging the area, and he concocted

a plan. He then made a sinister "peace offering" to the attackers. Trent wrote in his journal, "We gave them two Blankets and an Handkerchief out of the Small Pox Hospital. I hope it will have the desired effect." It did. Afflicted with the disease, the Delaware died in droves, and the fort held.

Trent's idea caught on. Soon after the Fort Pitt incident, Lord Jeffrey Amherst, the British military commander in North America, wrote to Colonel Henry Bouquet, "Could it not be contrived to send the Small Pox among those disaffected tribes of Indians? We must on this occasion use every stratagem in our power to reduce them." Amherst, for whom Amherst, Massachusetts, is named, added, "Try every other method that can serve to Extirpate this Execrable Race."

The Da Vinci Formula

Even one of history's best and brightest minds, Leonardo da Vinci, dabbled with chemical weapons. The artist and sometime inventor of war machines proposed to "throw poison in the form of powder upon galleys." He stated, "Chalk, fine sulfide of arsenic, and powdered verdigris [toxic copper acetate] may be thrown among enemy ships by means of small mangonels [single-arm catapults], and all those who, as they breathe, inhale the powder into their lungs will become asphyxiated." Ever ahead of his time, the inveterate inventor even sketched out a diagram for a simple gas mask.

"Just as courage imperils life, fear protects it."
—LEONARDO DA VINCI

"War will disappear only when men shall take no part whatever in violence and shall be ready to suffer every persecution that their abstention will bring them. It is the only way to abolish war."
— ANATOLE FRANCE, FRENCH WRITER

Science
Tracking Tektite Truths

❖ ❖ ❖ ❖

The origin of strangely shaped bits of glass called
tektites *has been debated for decades—do they come*
from the moon? From somewhere else in outer space?
It seems the answer is more down-to-earth.

The first tektites were found in 1787 in the Moldau River in the
Czech Republic, giving them their original name, "Moldavites."
They come in many shapes (button, teardrop, dumbbell, and blobs),
have little or no water content, and range from dark green to black
to colorless.

Originally, many geologists believed tektites were extraterrestrial
in origin, specifically from the moon. They theorized that impacts
from comets and asteroids—or even volcanic eruptions—on the
moon ejected huge amounts of material. As the moon circled in its
orbit around our planet, the material eventually worked its way to
Earth, through the atmosphere, and onto the surface.

One of the first scientists to debate the tektite-lunar origin idea
was Texas geologist Virgil E. Barnes, who contended that tektites
were actually created from Earth-bound soil and rock. Many scientists now agree with Barnes, theorizing that when a comet or
asteroid collided with the earth, it sent massive amounts of material
high into the atmosphere at hypervelocities. The energy from such a
strike easily melted the terrestrial rock and burned off much of the
material's water. And because of the earth's gravitational pull, what
goes up must come down—causing the melted material to rain down
on the planet in specific locations. Most of the resulting tektites have
been exposed to the elements for millions of years, causing many to
be etched and/or eroded over time.

Unlike most extraterrestrial rocks—such as meteorites and
micrometeorites, which are found everywhere on Earth—tektites
are generally found in four major regions of the world called *strewn*
(or splash) fields. The almost 15-million-year-old Moldavites are
mainly found in the Czech Republic, but the strewn field extends

into Austria; these tektites are derived from the Nordlinger Ries impact crater in southern Germany. The *Australites, Indochinites,* and *Chinites* of the huge Australasian strewn field extend around Australia, Indochina, and the Philippines; so far, no one has agreed on its source crater. The *Georgiaites* (Georgia) and *Bediasites* (Texas) are North American tektites formed by the asteroid impact that created the Chesapeake Crater around 35 million years ago. And finally, the 1.3-million-year-old *Ivorites* of the Ivory Coast strewn field originate from the Bosumtwi crater in neighboring Ghana. Other tektites have been discovered in various places around the world but in very limited quantities compared to the major strewn fields.

❖❖❖❖❖❖

Depending on its composition, glass will melt at between 2,600°F and 2,900°F.

You'll need to travel at 6.96 miles per second in order to escape Earth's gravity. You'd have an easier time leaving the Moon—its escape velocity is only 1.5 miles per second.

Chicxulub Crater in the Yucatán Peninsula is the largest confirmed impact crater on Earth. The asteroid that formed this 105-mile-diameter crater is widely credited with killing off the dinosaurs.

The deepest place on Earth is Challenger Deep in the Marianas Trench, with a depth of 35,840 feet below sea level. If you put Mt. Everest into the Deep, there would still be a mile of water between its peak and the surface.

Sports
Abner Strikes Out

❖ ❖ ❖ ❖

Generations of baseball fans have been led to believe that the game was invented by Civil War hero Abner Doubleday in Cooperstown, New York, in 1839. Historians tell a different story.

The Doubleday myth can be traced to the Mills Commission, which was appointed in 1905 by baseball promoter Albert Spalding to determine the true origins of the game. Henry Chadwick, one of Spalding's contemporaries, contended that the sport had its beginnings in a British game called *rounders,* in which a batter hits a ball and runs around the bases. Spalding, on the other hand, insisted that baseball was as American as apple pie.

Can We Get a Witness?

The seven-member Mills Commission placed ads in several newspapers soliciting testimony from anyone who had knowledge of the beginnings of the game. A 71-year-old gent named Abner Graves of Denver, Colorado, saw the ad and wrote a detailed response, saying that he'd been present when Doubleday outlined the basics of modern baseball in bucolic Cooperstown, New York, where the two had gone to school together. In his account, which was published by the *Beacon Journal* in Akron, Ohio, under the headline "Abner Doubleday Invented Baseball," Graves alleged to have seen crude drawings of a baseball diamond produced by Doubleday both in the dirt and on paper.

The members of the Mills Commission took Graves at his word and closed their investigation, confident that they had finally solved the mystery of how baseball was invented. The commission released its final report in December 1907, never mentioning Graves by name, and a great American legend was born.

Sadly, Graves's story was more whimsy than fact. For one thing, he was only five years old in 1839, when he claimed to have seen Doubleday's drawings. But even more important, Doubleday wasn't even in Cooperstown in 1839—he was a cadet attending the military

academy at West Point. In addition, Doubleday, a renowned diarist, never once mentioned baseball in any of his writings, nor did he ever claim to have invented the game.

Nonetheless, the Doubleday myth received a boost in 1934 when a moldy old baseball was discovered in an attic in Fly Creek, New York, just outside Cooperstown. It was believed to have been owned by Graves and as such was also believed to have been used by Abner Doubleday. The "historic" ball was purchased for five dollars by a wealthy Cooperstown businessman named Stephen Clark, who intended to display it with a variety of other baseball memorabilia. Five years later, Cooperstown became the official home of the Baseball Hall of Fame.

Who Was Baseball's Daddy?

If anyone can lay claim to being the father of American baseball, it's Alexander Cartwright. He organized the first official baseball club in New York in 1845, called the Knickerbocker Base Ball Club, and published a set of 20 rules for the game. These rules, which included the designation of a nine-player team and a playing field with a home plate and three additional bases at specific distances, formed the basis for baseball as we know the sport today. Cartwright's Hall of Fame plaque in Cooperstown honors him as the "Father of Modern Base Ball," and in 1953, Congress officially credited him with inventing the game.

Notable Nonetheless

Abner Doubleday may not have invented baseball, but he was still a man of historical significance. He was at Fort Sumter when it was attacked in 1861 (initiating the Civil War), and he aimed the first Union gun that was fired in the fort's defense. Doubleday also participated in some of the most important battles of the Civil War, including Antietam, Fredericksburg, Chancellorsville, and Gettysburg.

Inventions
The Teenager Who Invented Television

✦ ✦ ✦ ✦

Responsible for what may have been the most influential invention of the 20th century, this farm boy never received the recognition he was due.

Philo T. Farnsworth's brilliance was obvious from an early age. In 1919, when he was only 12, he amazed his parents and older siblings by fixing a balky electrical generator on their Idaho farm. By age 14, he had built an electrical laboratory in the family attic and was setting his alarm for 4 A.M. so he could get up and read science journals for an hour before doing chores.

Farnsworth hated the drudgery of farming. He often daydreamed solutions to scientific problems as he worked. During the summer of 1921, he was particularly preoccupied with the possibility of transmitting moving pictures through the air.

Around the same time, big corporations like RCA were spending millions of research dollars trying to find a practical way to do just that. As it turned out, most of their work was focused on a theoretical dead-end. Back in 1884, German scientist Paul Nipkow had patented a device called the Nipkow disc. By rotating the disc rapidly while passing light through tiny holes, an illusion of movement could be created. In essence, the Nipkow disc was a primitive way to scan images. Farnsworth doubted that this mechanical method of scanning could ever work fast enough to send images worth watching. He was determined to find a better way.

His "Eureka!" moment came as he cultivated a field with a team of horses. Swinging the horses around to plow another row, Farnsworth glanced back at the furrows behind him. Suddenly, he realized that scanning could be done electronically, line-by-line. Light could be converted into streams of electrons and then back again with such rapidity that the eye would be fooled. He immediately set about designing what would one day be called the cathode ray tube. Seven

years would pass, however, before he was able to display a working model of his mental breakthrough.

Upon graduating from high school, Farnsworth enrolled at Brigham Young University but dropped out after a year because he could no longer afford the tuition. Almost immediately, though, he found financial backers and moved to San Francisco to continue his research. The cathode ray tube he developed there became the basis for all television. In 1930, a researcher from RCA named Vladimir Zworykin visited Farnsworth's California laboratory and copied his invention. When Farnsworth refused to sell his patent to RCA for $100,000, the company sued him. The legal wrangling continued for many years and though Farnsworth eventually earned royalties from his invention, he never did get wealthy from it.

By the time Farnsworth died in 1971, there were more homes on Earth with televisions than with indoor plumbing. Ironically, the man most responsible for television appeared on the small screen only once. It was a 1957 appearance on the game show *I've Got a Secret*. Farnsworth's secret was, "I invented electric television at the age of 15." When none of the panelists guessed Farnsworth's secret, he left the studio with his winnings—$80 and a carton of Winston cigarettes.

❖❖❖❖❖❖

"I find television very educating. Every time somebody turns on the set, I go into the other room and read a book."
— GROUCHO MARX

"If everyone demanded peace instead of another television set, then there'd be peace."
— JOHN LENNON

░░

Law & Politics
Counting On You Since 1790: The U.S. Census

❖ ❖ ❖ ❖

The U.S. Census builds on a governmental question dating back to ancient Mesopotamia: "How many people do we have?" Of course, the original U.S. Census had a few...well, inequities.

Ever since ancient Sumer, governments have desired to estimate military-capable manpower, facilitate urban and transportation planning, provide some idea of economic status, and (most importantly) aid taxation.

After full independence (1783), it took the young United States some years to do the things real nations did: mint coins, lean on bootleggers, build a real navy, enact shortsighted public policy, storm out of diplomatic summits over petty slights, oppress minorities, and tell the citizenry "no" once in awhile. Real nations had censuses; plus, the Constitution mandated one to determine congressional representation. Congress decreed August 2, 1790, Census Day.

The First Census
Remember that time when you didn't answer the door for the Census people? Good luck with that; U.S. Marshals took the first census. If you lied or didn't cooperate, the fine was $200 ($4,680 in 2007 dollars, following the Consumer Price Index). The cops wanted to enumerate (census-ese for "count") everyone living in each dwelling, specifically:

• Who's the head of household?

• How many free white males age 16+ live here? Under 16?

• Free white females (age irrelevant)?

• Nonwhite free persons (specify gender and color; age irrelevant)?

• Slaves (gender and age irrelevant)?

Sexist, surely; racist, terribly—but it revealed the country's military and industrial potential. In a pattern Native Americans would

soon recognize, the census didn't count them. For tax and legislative purposes, a slave counted as three-fifths of a person, thus clarifying where they stood in the Land of Liberty's pecking order.

The first census revealed 3.93 million people, including nearly 700,000 slaves (actual number before the three-fifths coefficient was applied). Thomas Jefferson and George Washington figured the police had botched it somehow, that the numbers should have been higher.

The First Century

Congress decided to take a decennial census (census-ese for "once a decade"). Some changes as they occurred:

1800: More age categories, and women's ages now mattered. Native Americans now counted.

1810: First attempt to gather economic data. Data reveals that marshals are lousy at collecting economic data.

1820: First occupational questions. Results indicate that marshals are also sloppy and inconsistent at collecting occupational data.

1830: First use of standard questionnaires; age data now collected by decade of life. Government gives up on economic data for the time being, since cops keep bungling that one. First questions about blindness, deaf/muteness.

1840: Nosiest census yet with questions about education, literacy, occupation, and resources.

1850: The Census begins taking its modern shape. Every free person is listed by name (even females!). Slaves are assigned numbers. "Mulatto" is now an official racial category. In addition to deaf, blind, and "dumb," a person of any race can be described as "insane," "idiotic," "pauper," or "convict." Slaves cannot be described as paupers or convicts (which makes a certain tragic sense) but can still be "insane" or "idiotic." The number of escaped slaves must be

described, as must the number manumitted (released from slavery) in the past year. Clearly, equality is on the march.

1860: Marshals are out of the census business. Much rejoicing among marshals.

1870: With slavery abolished, slave questionnaire no longer necessary. First census to include racial categories "Chinese" (all east Asians) and "Indian" (Native American).

1880: Enumerators first ask about crippling disabilities (other than blindness, deafness, idiocy, or insanity).

1890: First use of an electric tabulating system. No one realizes it at the time, but this system is an ancestor of 1900s computing monolith IBM.

And, finally:

1903: U.S. Government celebrates Census's 113rd anniversary by finally establishing the U.S. Census Bureau.

"I just want to know how people with multiple personalities fill out their census papers."

—ANONYMOUS

" 'Tis pedantry to estimate nations by the census, or by square miles of land, or other than by their importance to the mind of the time."

— RALPH WALDO EMERSON

Travel
My Folks Went to Athens and All I Got Was This Lousy Peplos

❖ ❖ ❖ ❖

Tourism works like this: You go to a place, and the people in charge of the place take all your money. And you're okay with that. It's a peculiar setup, with roots that trace back to the ancient world.

"On Your Left, the Hanging Gardens ..."

What did the very earliest tourists—if there were any at all—enjoy? Cuddly saber-toothed kittens at the petting zoo? Tar-pit paddle boat rides? Well, that was prehistory, and tourism wasn't yet an industry, but with the passing of many centuries, city-states and empires became sophisticated enough that tourism was feasible. Visitors couldn't enjoy Six Flags over Carthage, but that's only because it hadn't been invented. There were other places to go and things to see, but travel beyond one's own borders was nevertheless a risky proposition.

By the first millennium B.C., Near Eastern empires had developed waterways, roads, lodging, and systems of commerce sufficient to encourage tourism. Even better, there was a mass of potential tourists to make added investment in infrastructure worthwhile. Then with the rise of the Persian Empire in mid-millennium (around 500 B.C.), two additional key elements—peace and effective government—made tourism not just possible but relatively pleasant.

The earliest tourist destinations evident in the Western historical record are Babylon (present-day Iraq) and Egypt. Both destinations had neat things to see: the Hanging Gardens, pyramids, temples, festivals, and street markets. The ancient world also had museums, lighthouses, religious celebrations, and a lively system of commerce to lure well-heeled visitors.

Going Greek

When Greece caught the attention of curious travelers around 500 B.C., visitors favored the sea route rather than brave the wilds of Asia Minor (modern Turkey). At about the same time, the Levantine

ports of what are now Syria, Lebanon, and Israel flourished. In the 400s B.C., Greeks wrote travel guides that evaluated locations and facilities—a little like *Lonely Planet,* but at that time the known limits of the planet were much smaller.

Greek and Levantine destinations attracted visitors, but tourists still had to remain on guard. In those days, people carried cash (no credit cards, right?), which attracted the attention of swindlers, pickpockets, and cutthroats. Seas around favored ports were controlled well enough to allow local and regional commerce to thrive, but a ship full of people wearing the ancient equivalent of Bermuda shorts was easy prey for pirates. Until things became safer and easier, tourism couldn't grow.

Roamin' Romans

With its seafaring rival Carthage put out of the way by 202 B.C., Republican Rome began its rise to undisputed dominance of the Mediterranean Sea. By the time Rome had a bona fide empire (about 27 B.C.), well-laid Roman roads encircled *Mare Nostrum* ("our sea"), with inns spaced just a day's travel apart. Armed patrols ensured the security of land routes. The Roman fleet aggressively hunted down pirates, making sea travel safer than ever before. Roman maps told travelers where they might go; chroniclers offered details about the sites.

Many would-be travelers had the hardy soul that was required, but then as today, serious travel was for the affluent. Most Romans were too poor to enjoy the diversions of new places. And even for those who could afford visits to Athens, Judea, and Egypt, the land route meant overpriced food of unpredictable quality and uncomfortable lodging.

The Mediterranean's sea lanes may have been swept of pirates, but nothing could be done about storms and other nautical hazards. Mindful of this risk, Romans struck bargains with the gods before travel, promising to do this or that in return for a safe voyage. Of course, even the most attentive Roman gods couldn't guarantee a *pleasant* trip.

Fun and Games for Grownups

So what was there to see and do around *Mare Nostrum?* For the simple pleasures of gluttony and sin, one might try the western

Italian coast. Although Sparta was some 300 years into decline by A.D. 1, travelers were drawn there by the echoes of its martial past and by the quaint Spartan notion of equality between the sexes.

Athens had reached its Classical-era peak around the fifth century B.C., and was in decline by the first century A.D., but was swarmed with visitors drawn by the city's architecture and sculpture. In Egypt, the Pyramids remained a major attraction, and Alexandria had the fabulous library that dedicated itself to collecting all of the world's knowledge. Then there was *Novum Ilium* (New Troy), also known as Troy IX, as the site had been destroyed or abandoned, and subsequently rebuilt, many times over the centuries. In 85 B.C., the Romans put it back together as a living memorial to their supposed Trojan heritage, with enough Greek and Persian touches tacked on to further intrigue travelers.

Other Mediterranean destinations and diversions included zoos, freak shows, prostitutes, exotic foods—and above all, bragging rights for having undertaken a pleasure trip in the first place. The ancient traveler was considered nothing if not cosmopolitan.

Two-way

Because "Rome" signified a still-vast empire by the first century A.D., the city not only provided a class of tourists who traveled from the city, but hosted countless citizens who came to Rome from the empire's farther reaches. These visitors were inevitably impressed, and not a little intimidated, by the city's sprawl, grime, and confusion. More than a million people lived in Rome, and the effect of the city upon visitors from quieter realms must have been breathtaking—and not always in a pleasant way. Still, any provincial who returned from *Roma Eterna* was hailed back home as a sophisticate, just as a Roman who could speak gracefully about the ancient route of the Greek poet Homer enjoyed an elevated social status.

As Rome declined, so did tourism, but pleasure travel never died out completely. Although today's Mediterranean tour guides, bus drivers, trinket sellers, and desk clerks may not realize it, they are practitioners of a popular art that is ancient and perhaps even noble.

Sports
The Thrill of the Joust

❖ ❖ ❖ ❖

The medieval competition that became known as jousting
brought together horsemanship, battle-honed knights,
and the brutal competitiveness of feudal Europe.

You spur your horse, and in an instant you're charging forward. The track is 80 yards long. There is a marker at 20 yards, and when you reach it you had better be in full gallop. You sit high in the saddle, slightly tippy with the weight of your armor and the 15-pound heft of your lance. Your fighting hand is cosseted by a heavy gauntlet, and the bell-like vamplate just forward of your grip gives some additional protection. You need it because another rider, very much like you, urged his own mount onward at the moment you spurred yours, and now he's coming at you, ceremonial plumes pushed horizontal by the power of his charge, clods of earth leaping from the impacts of his horse's hooves. You present virtually the same picture to him. Each of you grips the lance in your right hand, which means that the weapon must be angled across the crest of your horse's neck, toward your opponent. When it comes, the impact will not be as powerful as if struck dead-on, but angled lance or not, the force gener-ated by the weight of the speeding horses will be crushing. The 80 yards have disap-peared in what seems like a heartbeat. Lances lowered, now, you and the man you face are mir-ror images. In another instant, you'll feel the shock of impact, and half an instant after that you'll still be in your saddle—or on your back in the dirt, the wind pushed from your lungs, defeated.

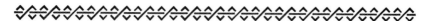

This is jousting (sometimes called *tilting*), which may have originated with the gladiators of ancient Rome, but has more recognizable roots in Europe of the tenth century. It was then that mounted knights emerged as a potent and much-feared fighting force. The joust began as a way for these warriors to hone their horsemanship and refine their use of the lance, the weapon favored by armored aggressors during the Middle Ages.

In 1066—the year William the Conqueror invaded England and introduced the "feudal" system of land division—a French knight named Godfrey de Preuilly combined the necessity of practice with the art of formal competition. A mounted knight sized up his opponent "between the limbs," the area protected by armor. The winning knight was the one who unseated or severely stunned the other.

Today, dozens of jousting clubs operate in the United States and Canada. The Jousting Hall of Fame in Mount Solon, Virginia, has hosted an annual tournament since 1821. And in 1962, jousting became the official sport of the State of Maryland.

"A true knight is fuller of bravery in the midst, than in the beginning of danger."
—SIR PHILIP SIDNEY

"No lance have I, in joust or fight, To splinter in my lady's sight; But, at her feet, how blest were I For any need of hers to die!"
— JOHN GREENLEAF WHITTIER

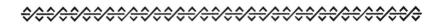

Film
And the Award of Merit Goes to . . .

❖ ❖ ❖ ❖

*The Academy Awards were almost an afterthought for
the Academy of Motion Picture Arts and Sciences.*

When the Academy of Motion Picture Arts and Sciences (AMPAS)
was created, bestowing "awards of merit" for distinctive achievement
was not their first priority. The Academy was the brainchild of director Fred Niblo, actor Conrad Nagel, and producers Louis B. Mayer
and Fred Beetson, who were concerned that the film industry had
no official voice to counter criticism that it was a bad influence on
society. In addition, Mayer hoped to prevent the various craft groups
(directors, writers, actors, etc.) from unionizing by forming one large
professional organization for all. Thus, AMPAS, which received
its official charter on May 4, 1927, was intended to encourage the
improvement and advancement of the film industry, promote a har-
monious working relationship among the different groups, counter
criticism, and sponsor technical research.

The Academy is made up of five branches representing different
creative groups—producers, directors, writers, actors, and technicians—with each group receiving equal representation. At a banquet
to recruit additional members on May 11, 1927, newly elected president Douglas Fairbanks mentioned in passing that the Academy
might also bestow "awards of merit."

The Committee for the Award of Merits was formed shortly after
to develop the voting process. In the meantime, Mayer asked MGM
art director Cedric Gibbons to come up with an award statue.
Gibbons designed the familiar figure, nicknamed Oscar, which holds
a sword while standing on a film reel with five spokes, each of which
represents one of the five branches of the Academy.

The First Academy Awards
In July 1928, the Committee announced a voting system for the
awards. The original system allowed each Academy member to
nominate a film for his/her branch. Then a Board of Judges counted

the votes to determine the nominations, turning over the results to a Central Board of Judges. The Central Board, consisting of one representative from each branch, selected the winners. The films eligible for the first Academy Awards were released between August 1, 1927, and July 31, 1928. The Central Board met to decide the final winners on February 15, 1929. Part of the reason for the long, drawn-out nomination process was that many Academy members either forgot or ignored the eligibility dates and nominated films from as far back as 1925, so the voting had to be done all over again. Nominations were made in 12 categories, including two "best production" categories, one called Production and the other Artistic Quality of Production.

Winners were announced on February 18, 1929, with the awards banquet scheduled for May 16. Since the winners had already been announced, there was no sense of anticipation at the banquet. Consequently, few of the losing nominees, such as Gloria Swanson and Charlie Chaplin, attended. Because three months lapsed between the announcement of the winners and the banquet, excitement had waned, and several of the winners, including Best Actor Emil Jannings, did not show up either. *Wings* won for Production and *Sunrise* for Artistic Quality of Production, but the distinction between the two categories was never clear.

The following year, the Artistic Quality of Production category was dropped, as was Comedy Direction, Title Writing, and Engineering Effects. Also, the winners were announced at the banquet, which made the ceremony a more highly anticipated event. Over the years, more changes were made in the categories and the voting rules as the awards process and ceremony evolved into their now-familiar forms. Currently, members of each branch nominate films in their field, while the entire Academy votes for the winner in each major category. The exception is Best Picture, for which every member is eligible to select the nominees and then vote for the winner.

Eventually, the Academy Awards became the most visible function of AMPAS, with few moviegoers realizing that the organization has other responsibilities.

Food & Drink
Setting Sake Straight

❖ ❖ ❖ ❖

*Most Americans consider sake a Japanese rice wine, but it is
actually more akin to beer. Furthermore, a look back in time
suggests that sake may have originated in China, not Japan.*

What Is Sake?

The Japanese word for sake, *nihonshu*, literally means "Japanese
alcoholic beverage" and does not necessarily refer to the specific
rice-based beverage that foreigners exclusively call *sake*. What dif-
ferentiates sake from other alcoholic beverages is its unique fermentation process. Although all wines are the result of a single-step
fermentation of plant juices, sake requires a multiple-step fermentation process, as does beer. The requisite ingredients are rice, water,
yeast, and an additional substance that will convert the starch in
the rice to sugar. People have always found ways to make alcohol
with whatever ingredients are available, so it is likely that beverages
similar to sake emerged soon after rice cultivation began. The most
popular theory holds that the brewing of rice into alcohol began
around 4000 B.C. along the Yangtze River in China, and the process
was later exported to Japan.

The Many Ways to Ferment Rice

The sake of yore was different from the sake that's popular today. At
one time it was fermented with human saliva, which reliably converts
starch to sugar. Early sake devotees chewed a combination of rice,
chestnuts, millet, and acorns, then spit the mixture into a container
to ferment. This "chew and spit" approach to alcohol production has
been seen the world over in tribal societies. Subsequent discoveries and technological developments allowed for more innovative
approaches to fermentation. Sometime in the early centuries A.D.,
a type of mold called *koji-kin* was discovered to be efficient in fer-
menting rice. In the 1300s, mass sake production began in Japan,
and it soon became the most popular national beverage.

Holidays & Traditions
The Cola Claus

❖ ❖ ❖ ❖

Although the Coca-Cola Company helped popularize Santa Claus,
it cannot take credit for creating the ubiquitous Christmas image.

Nothing says "Christmas" like the image of a white-whiskered fat man in a red suit squeezing down a chimney with a sack full of toys. But Santa Claus hasn't always looked that way. When the Coca-Cola Company used the red-robed figure in the 1930s to promote its soft drinks, the classic image of Santa was cemented in the public consciousness.

Sorting Out the Santas

Santa Claus evolved from two religious figures, St. Nicholas and Christkindlein. St. Nicholas was a real person, a monk who became a bishop in the early fourth century and was renowned as a generous gift-giver. Christkindlein (meaning "Christ child") was assisted by elfin helpers and would leave gifts for children while they slept.

Santa Claus originated from a Dutch poem, *"Sinterklaas,"* and the legend was added to over time by different writers. Until the early 20th century, though, Santa Claus was portrayed in many different ways. He could be tall and clad in long robes like St. Nicholas, or small with whiskers like the elves who helped Christkindlein.

In 1881, Thomas Nast, a caricaturist for *Harper's Weekly*, first drew Santa as a merry figure in red with flowing whiskers—an image close to the one we know today. Printer Louis Prang used a similar image in 1885 when he introduced Christmas cards to America. In 1931, the Coca-Cola Company first employed Haddon Sundblom to illustrate its annual advertisements, choosing a Santa dressed in red and white to match the corporate colors. By then, however, this was already the most popular image of Santa Claus, one that was described in detail in a *New York Times* article in 1927. If Coca-Cola had really invented Santa Claus, children would likely be saving the milk and leaving him soda and cookies on Christmas Eve.

Inventions
The Beta Wars

*When videotape recorders entered the consumer market,
formatting differences between Betamax and VHS didn't exactly
spark a shooting war, but in some quarters they could have.*

On first hearing about high-definition television, comedian Paula
Poundstone said that she wasn't buying into another system until she
was certain that it was the *last* system. It was a complaint that most
Americans understood.

The question of media formatting goes back at least to the days
when the printing press replaced hand-lettered manuscripts, but it
became a matter of open, partisan warfare in 1975 when videotape
was introduced as a mass medium. Sony introduced the Betamax
video system, which was followed a year later by JVC's totally incom-
patible VHS. It was eight-tracks and cassette tapes all over again.

Quality Versus Price and Convenience

There is little disagreement that Sony's Betamax was a technically
superior system, but JVC's VHS (which stood for Video Helical
Scan) was marketed intensively. Its players were cheaper and easier
to make, and other manufacturers started to adopt the VHS format.
Additionally, Beta featured only one-hour tapes—not long enough to
record a movie—while VHS had two-hour tapes. By the time Beta
developed B-II (two-hour) and B-III (three-hour) formats, VHS had
a four-hour format. Eventually, Beta achieved five hours, and VHS
reached 10.6 hours.

In 1985, Sony introduced SuperBeta; JVC countered with Super-
VHS. As the systems tried to outdo each other, Beta was never quite
able to catch up. Major studios released fewer movies on Beta.
Then, in a 1989 episode of *Married...with Children,* the Bundys
were described as "the last family on earth with Beta." That offhand
comment was the kiss of death.

VHS ruled the roost. At least, that is, until DVDs came along.

Places & Landmarks
The True Pyramid Scheme

❖ ❖ ❖ ❖

*The Egyptians built three big pyramids at Giza, Egypt, to bury
King Tut and so forth, right? There's actually much more to it.
They built many more than three, and you didn't have to be a
monarch; you just needed enough money. Had Donald Trump
been an ancient Egyptian, he'd have built himself a pyramid.*

Mastabas

One might call mastabas proto-pyramids. The oldest examples date
to 3500 B.C., and most resemble large pyramid bases made of mud,
brick, and/or stone. A typical mastaba contained artwork, images
of the deceased, the usual Egyptian grave goods, and of course,
mummified Uncle Kahotep (or whomever).

Throughout and after the pyramid era, mastabas remained the
budget mausoleum alternative for moderately affluent Egyptians.
Builders clustered mastabas in funerary complexes, as they would
later do with pyramids, so we often see them together.

Let's Stack These . . .

Our best information dates the earliest step pyramid to around
2630 B.C. at Saqqara, Egypt. The architect Imhotep built mastaba
upon mastaba, fashioning a 200-foot-high pyramid as a mausoleum
for Pharaoh Djoser. With its original white limestone facing, Djoser's
tomb must have been quite a spectacle when the rising sun's light
struck it.

The new tomb style secured Imhotep's immortality—literally, for
the Egyptians deified him, and the Greeks identified him with their
healing-god Asklepios. Even today, some consider him a patron saint
of civil engineers and architects.

I Want One Too!

Pyramid mania began. Over the next thousand years or so, Egyptian
engineers built several large pyramid complexes along the Nile's
west bank. The most famous and popular today are those at Giza,

but dozens of others survive. Some are majestic and well preserved; many are just mounds, either unfinished or ruined by time—enough to inspire valid doubt as to whether they qualify for the label.
We used to think pyramids were built under the lash. Modern scholarship doubts this, but they were definitely huge projects. Some took decades to finish.

Much later, during Roman times, Egypt's southern neighbor Nubia also had a pyramid-building phase. Most Nubian pyramids were steeper than Egyptian ones—obelisks rather than pyramids in some cases—and their workmanship and beauty impress visitors to this day. Sadly, in A.D. 1800s, a greedy looter named Giuseppe Ferlini opened about 40 Nubian pyramids like beer bottles (by removing the caps) in search of plunder. They'd be even lovelier today but for this mutilation.

What's Inside a Pyramid?
Stone, mostly. They aren't hollow. Long ramplike walkways angle down and up to burial chambers. Narrow shafts extend from these chambers and walkways to vent air out the upper exterior. Most contain painting and writing that has taught us much about Egyptian life, history, and belief; those that were not looted in antiquity have yielded fabulous artifacts. The burial chambers housed the mummified deceased, of course, with his or her guts nearby in jars.

Why Build Them?
The Egyptians didn't have a separate word for religion; it touched all aspects of their daily lives. A massive Pharaonic tomb represented an act of immense popular faith and devotion, for the Pharaoh was a semidivine figure. The tomb was supposed to protect the sacred remains and grave goods because, in antiquity as now, many cared far more for gold than for the sanctity deceased.

The pyramid shape's spiritual significance remains a bit uncertain. Egyptians

considered a mound of earth to symbolize new life, so the mastaba shape may have indicated the deceased's rebirth. The nearest thing to a scholarly consensus is that the structure's upward steps represented the decedent's ascension into the heavens.

Why Stop?

Well, building pyramids required a lot of human and material resources. Worse yet, looters still looted them. All that expense and effort, and some jerk breaks in anyway? Some people have no respect!

After about 1800 B.C., the Egyptian art of pyramid construction declined in step with Egypt's own gradual eclipse in the ancient world.

The Great Pyramid of Giza

Located on the west bank of the Nile River near Cairo, Egypt, this is the largest of ten pyramids built between 2600 and 2500 B.C. Built for King Khufu, the Great Pyramid was constructed by thousands of workers toiling over the span of decades (2609–2584 B.C.).

The structure consists of more than two million 2.5-ton stones. If the stones were piled on top of each other, the resulting tower would be close to 50 stories high. The base covers an astonishing 13 acres. It's not known exactly how the blocks were lifted. Theories include mud- and water-coated ramps or an intricate system of levers. Not only did the blocks have to be lifted, but they also had to be transported from the quarries. Even the experts can't say exactly how that was done.

The pyramid originally stood 481 feet high but has been weathered down to about 450 feet. It was considered the tallest structure on the planet for 43 centuries. The Great Pyramid is the only Wonder of the Ancient World still standing—a testament to one of the mightiest civilizations in history.

Written Word
A Literary Archaeology of *MAD*

❖ ❖ ❖ ❖

For those who know it only by reputation, MAD *is a satire magazine that makes fun (of the PG–13 variety) of anyone or anything, from Saddam Hussein to pop culture to the British royal family. It's a thick-skinned reader's hoot and a touchy reader's cerebral hemorrhage.*

Pre-*MAD*

MAD has been *MAD* since the early 1950s, but its prehistory extends back to the darkest days of the Great Depression. Its emblem, Alfred E. Neuman, dates back even further.

Contrary to popular belief, iconic publisher William "Bill" Gaines didn't invent *MAD*. His father, Max Gaines, pioneered newsstand comic books in the mid-1930s as cheap, commercially viable amusement for children. Son Bill was an eccentric prankster, the type of kid peers might label "Most Likely to Publish an Iconoclastic Satire Mag." Upon his father's tragic death in 1947, Bill inherited the family comic book business, Educational Comics (EC). He steered EC to stand for Entertaining Comics: a publisher of garish horror comics veering into sardonic social commentary.

In 1952, Bill's early collaborator Harvey Kurtzman proposed a new comic called *MAD,* which would poke fun at just about anything. Kurtzman's brainchild was a success, and in 1955 Bill allowed Kurtzman to convert *MAD* from comic book to magazine. Kurtzman left EC shortly thereafter, but their creation still thrives more than a half century later.

MAD Under Fire

The assaults on *MAD* came early and often from two predictable directions: 1) *MAD* corrupted America's youth. (Horrors!); 2) *MAD* violated some copyright. (Uh-oh.)

In *MAD*'s natal McCarthy era, mocking traditional American anything meant painting a target on one's own back; it could even suggest Communist leanings. *MAD*'s shameless irreverence, gory

imagery, and refusal to kowtow sent Bill Gaines before a Senate sub-committee. An interrogator would show Gaines a gross image from an EC comic like *MAD* and ask, "Surely you think this is too disgusting for children?" "Nah," Gaines would reply, reveling in the indignant sputters. Gaines didn't back down, and *MAD* didn't ease up.

The intellectual property issues generally came from heavy hitters like National Periodical Publications (*Superman*) and composer Irving Berlin. The core question was *MAD*'s legal right to poke fun at pop culture: songs, cartoon characters, ads. *MAD* won most such challenges. Its dopey mascot, Alfred E. Neuman, came to symbolize the right to parody.

What, Us Worry?

MAD first depicted its wing-eared, asymmetrical, fictitious emblem and soul as "The What, Me Worry? Kid" and "Melvin Coznowski" in 1954. The image reportedly came from an old postcard. In 1955, the staff began calling him "Alfred E. Neuman," a name evidently nicked on a lark from successful film composer Alfred Newman. *MAD*'s bright, talented staff never fatigues of telling the reader how stupid and mediocre the magazine is, and Alfred's vacant gaze appears to bear them out. But *MAD* didn't invent him. We don't know who did, but *MAD* had to go to court to keep him.

In 1965, *MAD*'s use of Alfred withstood two serious legal challenges from plaintiffs alleging previous copyrights. In the end, *MAD*'s lawyer located advertising and artistic images of proto-Alfred dating back to 1895, undermining both claims. Alfred still grins his vacuous smile on most *MAD* covers.

MAD's Evolution

Like any publication that celebrates a 50th birthday, *MAD* has seen change. By the late 1950s, it had abandoned horror motifs in favor of increased contemporary political satire.

MAD's content has grown saltier and more risqué but is now far less sexist and homophobic. Fear not, though: *MAD*'s still as stupid as ever—as its circulation staff advises every subscriber with each subscription renewal offer. As for us, we show that we don't learn from our mistakes: We keep renewing!

Education
The Montessori Movement

❖ ❖ ❖ ❖

You may have heard of Montessori schools,
but what of the woman behind them?

In the Beginning...

When Maria Montessori was a schoolgirl, a teacher asked if she'd like to become famous. "Oh, no," she answered, "I shall never be that. I care too much for the children of the future to add yet another biography to the list."

By any standard, Montessori cared for the children. She was born on August 31, 1870, at Chiaravalle, near Ancona, Kingdom of Italy. An excellent pupil, she went to technical school in 1886. After her graduation in 1890, she chose to study medicine—a strictly male field. At first, her father objected, and the medical school vetoed her desires—rather bluntly. Montessori persisted, though, until they finally let her in.

The Inspiration

As Montessori later explained, her movement really began on the street. She had just walked away from a dissection task, fed up with med school. As she moped down the street, a female beggar accosted her for money. The beggar woman's two-year-old sat on the sidewalk, her entire attention locked into play with a piece of colored paper. Seeing this child, oblivious to her poverty—silent, serenely happy—sent Montessori straight back to her grisly assignment with a new will. She soon earned a title then unique for an Italian woman: *La dottoressa* Montessori, of medicine.

In 1896, Drsa. Montessori went to work with special-needs children. The status quo appalled her. Contemporary thinking classed them as "idiots" or "lunatics" and placed them in schools that were more like jail than education. They were denied dignity, freedom, even anything to manipulate with their little hands. Drsa. Montessori felt she knew what they needed. She believed she could help them through education.

Early Success

Her chance came in 1899. Italy's educational bigwigs established Drsa. Montessori in a small school composed of children rejected from mainstream schools. Most couldn't read. After two years, she sent her kids to take standardized tests. Not only did many pass, some did better than the mainstream students. It was nothing short of miraculous. Now Drsa. Montessori had people's attention.

She spent the next few years traveling, studying, thinking, experiencing, and doctoring. Then in 1906 Drsa. Montessori was invited to take over an out-of-control preschool/daycare for the rowdiest preschoolers Rome had seen since Alaric the Visigoth. She was elated at the possibility: Given what happened with slower kids, what might children with normal intelligence manage?

Answer: Wonders. She found that preschoolers had phenomenal powers of concentration. They loved repetition. They liked order better than disorder; left to their own devices, they would put things away. They responded very well to free choice of activity; work—not play— was their natural preference. They had a strong sense of personal dignity and flourished when that dignity was respected; they thrived on adult attention. And perhaps most shockingly: They taught themselves to write, a phenomenon called "explosion into writing." Reading soon followed. Unruliness gave way to great self-discipline and strong respect for others. They were now "great kids."

They always had been. Drsa. Montessori had just found a way to let them show it.

Full Speed Ahead

From there, the Montessori movement gathered momentum. As she refined her methods, Montessori influenced educators all over the world, and her celebrity grew. By her death in 1952, a fair percentage of young adults in the child-development field were products of her approach. Fifty years and change since her passing, that approach remains popular.

Drsa. Maria Montessori didn't trademark her philosophy. You can use it without worrying about royalties, intellectual property lawyers, or cease-and-desist letters. Her life's work was her gift to humanity.

Places & Landmarks
America's First Skyscraper

❖ ❖ ❖ ❖

Chicago's Home Insurance Building certainly earned the grandiose nickname "the father of the skyscraper"—its creation set off the trend toward today's array of sky-climbing constructs.

Completed in 1885, William LeBaron Jenney's architectural innovation was the first building ever to feature a structural steel frame. It was initially erected at what is today a diminutive ten stories tall, or about 138 feet. Even with two additional stories tacked on five years later, the structure known as "America's First Skyscraper" would, at 180 feet, still be tiny when compared to Chicago's current skyscraper giant, the Sears Tower, which boasts a rooftop height of approximately 1,450 feet. Stack up eight Home Insurance Buildings, and the Sears Tower would still soar overhead.

Vertical Construction
Modeled in classic Chicago School architectural styling, the Home Insurance Building led the burgeoning trend toward the upward urban sprawl that now defines major U.S. cities. Prior to its creation, architects had only plotted building growth in a horizontal fashion. But with this new breed of building, the future of architecture was all upward. After all, why rely on mere land when the sky's the limit?

Torn down in 1931—fewer than 50 years after its construction—the Home Insurance Building was replaced just three years later by the still-standing, 45-story LaSalle National Bank Building, which was originally called the Field Building. The Home Insurance Building had served its purpose, and the city was ready to ring in the next round of architectural advancements. And just as the Home Insurance Building initiated a new era in architecture, the replacement structure was significant for its own gateway effect: It capitalized on the architectural trend of the time by capturing the magniloquence of the Art Deco movement. But as significant as the Field Building may have been, it didn't break new ground in the same way as the Home Insurance Building had.

Clubs & Organizations
Good Knights and Good Luck

◆ ◆ ◆ ◆

*Don't believe everything you see in the movies. Hollywood might
have you believe that the Knights Templar were the guardians
of hidden treasures and spectacular secrets. But whether the
Christian military order ever really found the Holy Grail, knew
the location of the Ark of the Covenant, or had the inside track on
whether Jesus Christ survived his crucifixion is lost to the ages.*

The truth is, the Templars had a power that rivaled the kingdoms of
Europe. For two centuries, they were an extremely powerful order,
both militarily and economically. Today, the Templars are remembered as crusader knights of the Christian cause, but the Knights
Templar also acted as medieval bankers with official Papal sanction—
at a time when the lending of money was generally considered a sin.

Defending the Faithful
It was the Crusades in the Holy Land that led to the rise—and,
ironically, the eventual fall—of the Knights Templar. On July 15,
1099, the First Crusade stormed Jerusalem and slaughtered everyone
in sight—Jews, Muslims, Christians—didn't matter. This unleashed a
wave of pilgrimage, as European Christians flocked to now-accessible
Palestine and its holy sites. Though Jerusalem's loss was a blow to
Islam, it was a bonanza for the region's thieves, from Saracens to
lapsed Crusaders: a steady stream of naive pilgrims to rob.

French knight Hugues de Payen, with eight chivalrous comrades,
swore to guard the travelers. In 1119, they gathered at the Church
of the Holy Sepulchre and pledged their lives to poverty, chastity,
and obedience before King Baldwin II of Jerusalem. The Order of
Poor Knights of the Temple of Solomon took up headquarters in said
Temple.

Going Mainstream
The Templars did their work well, and in 1127 Baldwin sent a
Templar embassy to Europe to secure a marriage that would ensure

the royal succession in Jerusalem. Not only did they succeed, they became rock stars of sorts. Influential nobles showered the Order with money and real estate, the foundation of its future wealth. With this growth came a formal code of rules. Some highlights include:

- Templars could not desert the battlefield or leave a castle by stealth.
- They had to wear white habits, except for sergeants and squires who could wear black.
- They had to tonsure (shave) their crowns and wear beards.
- They had to dine in communal silence, broken only by Scriptural readings.
- They had to be chaste, except for married men joining with their wives' consent.

A Law Unto Themselves—and Never Mind That Pesky "Poverty" Part

Now with offices in Europe to manage the Order's growing assets, the Templars returned to Palestine to join in the Kingdom's ongoing defense. In 1139, Pope Innocent II decreed the Order answerable only to the Holy See. Now exempt from the tithe, the Order was entitled to accept tithes! The Knights Templar had come far.

By the mid-1100s, the Templars had become a church within a church, a nation within a nation, and a major banking concern. Templar keeps were well-defended depositories, and the Order became financiers to the crowned heads of Europe—even to the Papacy. Their reputation for meticulous bookkeeping and secure transactions underpinned Europe's financial markets, even as their soldiers kept fighting for the faith in the Holy Land.

Downfall

Templar prowess notwithstanding, the Crusaders couldn't hold the Holy Land. In 1187, Saladin the Kurd retook Jerusalem, martyring 230 captured Templars. Factional fighting between Christians sped the collapse as the 1200s wore on. In 1291, the last Crusader outpost at Acre fell to the Mamelukes of Egypt. Though the Templars had taken a hosing along with the other Christian forces, their troubles had just begun.

King Philip IV of France owed the Order a lot of money, and they made him more nervous at home than they did fighting in Palestine. In 1307, Philip ordered the arrest of all Templars in France. They stood accused of apostasy, devil worship, sodomy, desecration, and greed. Hideous torture produced piles of confessions, much like those of the later Inquisition. The Order was looted, shattered, and officially dissolved. In March 1314, Jacques de Molay, the last Grand Master of the Knights Templar, was burned at the stake.

Whither the Templars?

Many Templar assets passed to the Knights Hospitallers. The Order survived in Portugal as the Order of Christ, where it exists to this day in form similar to British knightly orders. A Templar fleet escaped from La Rochelle and vanished; it may have reached Scotland. Swiss folktales suggest that some Templars took their loot and expertise to Switzerland, possibly laying the groundwork for what would one day become the Swiss banking industry.

Shroud of Turin: Real or Fake?

Measuring roughly 14 feet long by 3 feet wide, the Shroud of Turin features the front and back image of a man who was 5 feet, 9 inches tall. The man was bearded and had shoulder-length hair parted down the middle. Dark stains on the Shroud are consistent with blood from a crucifixion.

First publicly displayed in 1357, the Shroud of Turin has apparent ties to the Knights of Templar. At the time of its first showing, the Shroud was in the hands of of the family of Geoffrey de Charney, a Templar who had been burned at the stake in 1314 along with Jacques de Molay. Some accounts say it was the Knights who removed the cloth from Constantinople, where it was kept in the 13th century.

Some believe the Shroud of Turin is the cloth that Jesus was wrapped in after his death. All four gospels mention that the body of Jesus was covered in a linen cloth prior to the resurrection.

Others assert that the cloth shrouded Jacques de Molay after he was tortured by being nailed to a door.

Is the Shroud of Turin authentic? In 1988, scientists using carbon-dating concluded that the material in the Shroud was from around A.D. 1260 to 1390, which seems to exclude the possibility that the Shroud bears the image of Jesus.

Toys & Games
A Toy So Fun It's Silly

❖ ❖ ❖ ❖

Is Silly Putty a toy or an industrial compound? Both, actually.

What's not to like about Silly Putty? It bounces, it stretches, it breaks. It's good, clean fun. But surprisingly enough, Silly Putty didn't begin its career as a toy. It's actually a by-product of war.

During World War II, the Japanese military began a series of conquests in southeast Asia with the intention of cutting off the Allies' supply of rubber. In response, the United States began to look for ways to develop synthetic rubber products. Because, after all, it's hard to fight an effective war without rubber.

Enter James Wright. While working at General Electric in 1943, Wright combined boric acid with silicone oil. The result was a polymerized substance that could bounce and stretch and had a high melting temperature. Unfortunately, it couldn't replace rubber and thus served no purpose for the military.

General Electric was determined to find a use for Wright's invention. The company bounced the putty across the country, hoping to drum up interest. In 1949, the putty landed in the hands of a New Haven, Connecticut, toy-store owner named Ruth Fallgatter. Fallgatter teamed up with marketing guru Peter Hodgson to sell the product through her toy catalog as a bouncing putty called Nutty Putty. It was an instant hit.

In 1950, Hodgson christened the new toy "Silly Putty" and went on to sell the product in the now-famous egg-shape containers. Originally marketed to adults, the product ultimately found success with kids ages 6 to 12—especially after 1957 when a commercial for Silly Putty debuted on the *Howdy Doody* show.

Silly Putty has done a brisk business over the years, with more than 300 million eggs sold since 1950. Silly Putty also has practical uses—it is useful in stress reduction, physical therapy, and in medical and scientific simulations. It was even used by the crew of *Apollo 8* to secure tools in zero gravity. Because there's nothing silly about being hit in the head with a wrench when you're in space.

Sports
The Seventh-inning Stretch

❖ ❖ ❖ ❖

In a time-honored tradition, baseball fans rise from their seats between the top and bottom of the seventh inning to sing a hearty rendition of "Take Me Out to the Ball Game." Was this custom really started as a nod of respect to President William Howard Taft?

Rather than being remembered for his one-term residency in the White House and for being the only man to serve as both president and chief justice of the Supreme Court, Taft is probably best known as the fattest man ever to serve as commander in chief. Indeed, Taft's girth was impressive, and it sometimes restricted his movements, especially when he attended Washington Senators baseball games (a pursuit that was his preferred method of relaxation). After sitting through a few innings of action, Taft would extract himself from the compressed confines of his chair, stand, stretch, and waddle off to the men's room. The denizens sitting near him would also rise, showing a measure of respect for their honored guest. This presidential pause for the cause was rumored to have occurred in the seventh-inning break.

However, there's no proof that the president was responsible for instituting or influencing the tradition. Taft attended many ball games, but he rarely stayed as late as the seventh inning. It's been said he had more pressing matters on his home plate—running the country, for instance.

Presidents Who Pitch

On April 14, 1910, Taft became the first president to toss the first pitch on opening day of the season, a convention that has since been followed by every chief executive, with the exception of Jimmy Carter.

Religion
Roots of the Kabbalistic Tree

❖ ❖ ❖ ❖

Judaism's mystic tradition extends so far back it's
hard to see its exact origins, but we can identify
some transformational teachers and phases.

Scattered Seeds

Kabbalah (pronounced "ka-ba-LAH" in Hebrew) may predate the
rise of Christianity, with influence from various pre-Christian Near
Eastern spiritual systems. Jewish tradition dates it as far back as
Judaism itself. Only scattered writings from this era hint at the subject;
perhaps there were as many Kabbalot (plural) as there were mystics.
You couldn't sign up for Kabbalah night classes at your synagogue; an
adept would have to train you, likely through oral tradition and Torah
study. In any case, no written text survives from this era. Most adepts
had probably heard of a few others and had actually met fewer still.
That's vague, but so is Kabbalah's early history.

Sapling

The oldest surviving manuscripts with clear reference to Kabbalah
date to about A.D. 100–200. Kabbalah has never been a monolith, but
by the end of the first millennium A.D., it acquired a sort of broad
consensus orthodoxy. Jews call this era the *Diaspora,* or dispersion: a
time when their ancestors did a lot of migrating to avoid persecution,
mostly away from Palestine but in some cases back to it. This phase
paid a dividend for Kabbalah. With diverse subgroups of Jews
meeting up here and there, scholars shared Kabbalistic views—and,
for the first enduring time, wrote them down. A difficult period, but
one of intellectual ferment born in adversity.

Bearing Leaves

The Kabbalah known to modern scholars came together in the
high to late Middle Ages (A.D. 1100–1400). Several Kabbalistic texts
from this phase formed the basis for the *Zohar,* compiled in the
late 1200s by Spanish rabbi Moshe ben Shem-Tov. The *Zohar* was

the first widely read mystical Torah commentary, taken by modern Kabbalistic scholars as its fundamental text. In this phase, too, came the first known use of the actual term *Kabbalah* (a transliteration, though often spelled "Qabalah").

Kabbalah's next major influence was Rabbi Yitzhak Luria (1534–72). In Tsfat, Palestine, Luria taught (what we now call) the Lurianic Kabbalah as a structured system of Jewish mysticism. Luria clearly defined the ten *s'firot* ("spheres"), which compose the Tree of Life, Kabbalah's central mandala and depiction. Much of today's written material is based on Lurianic teaching.

Branching

As early as the 1600s, non-Jews were adapting Kabbalistic notions to their own views of the cosmos. Come the 1800s, a group of Masonic mystics in England formed a society called the Golden Dawn, a magical/religious stew of tarot, Egyptian, Masonic, Kabbalistic, Hermetic, and astrological thought. One of its members, Aleister Crowley, made quite a Beast of himself.

Some modern Kabbalists orient themselves toward the Golden Dawn's descendant beliefs; others follow the Jewish tradition. Thanks to a recent fad among celebrities, many modern Americans have heard of Kabbalah. The fad will one day fade, but Kabbalah won't; after all, it hasn't faded in two millennia.

A Little More About Kabbalah

- Famed *Golden Dawn* author Dion Fortune calls Kabbalah "the Yoga of the West." It's hard to improve upon her concise summary.

- *Kabbalah*, or *Qabalah*, comes from the Hebrew letters *quph, bet,* and *lamed,* representing the concept of receiving something (in this case, teachings). Modern shorthand for Qabalah is "QBL," representing these root letters.

- The flipside of the *s'firot* (spheres) are the *qliphoth* (shells). As each *s'firah* represents an angel, each *qliphah* represents a demon or demoness. Traditional Kabbalists don't go there.

- The goal of traditional Kabbalah is to perfect one's understanding of the Torah, and by extension Hashem (Elohim, or God).

Old-school Olympics

❖ ❖ ❖ ❖

Imagine attending a sporting event where blood and broken limbs
are the norm. It's hot out but water is scarce; the food is overpriced
and lousy. Motels are few, pricey, and crummy. Almost everyone has
to camp out. Your bleacher seat feels like freshly heated limestone.
Forty thousand drunken, screaming savages surround you.

No, you aren't at a modern Division I-A college football game hosted
by an eastern Washington agricultural university. You're at the
ancient Greek Olympic Games! Millennia later, nations will suspend
the Games in wartime; for these Olympics, Greek nations will (for
the most part) suspend wartime.

What, When, Where, Why

Olympia was a remote, scenic religious sanctuary in the western
Greek boonies. The nearest town was little Elis, 40 miles away.

According to chroniclers, the ancient Olympic Games started in
776 B.C. That's about a century after Elijah and Jezebel's biblical difference of opinion. Rome wasn't yet founded; the Assyrian Empire
ruled the Near East. Greece's fractious city-states waged constant
political and military struggle. In 776, with disease and strife even
worse than usual in Greece, King Iphitos of Elis consulted the Delphic Oracle. She said, roughly translated: "Greece is cursed. Hold
athletics at Olympia, like you guys used to do, to lift the curse."

"Done deal," said the king. Greek legend spoke of games of old
held at Olympia in honor of Zeus, occurring perhaps every four
or five years, so Iphitos cleared some land at Olympia and put on
a footrace. The plague soon petered out. "Wish it was always that
easy," Iphitos probably said.

Play It Again, Iphitos

It's uncertain why the Eleans decided to repeat the Olympics every
four years; that was probably the most prevalent version of the
ancient tradition. Likely, they lacked the resources to do it more

often. Whatever the reason, the Games became Elis's reason for being. Its people spent the intervening years preparing for the next Olympiad. Given the amount of feasting and drinking that happened at the Games, the first year was likely spent recuperating.

Over the centuries, the event program extended to five days. The Eleans added equestrian and combat events. Any male Greek athlete could try out for the Games. Winners became rock stars, with egos and fringe benefits to match. There were no silver or bronze medals; losers slunk away in shame.

Temples and facilities sprang up at Olympia over the years: a great arena, shrines, and training facilities. In their lengthy heyday, historians believe 40,000-plus people would converge on Olympia to see a sport program ranging from chariot racing to track-and-field events to hand-to-hand combat.

Except for the boxers, wrestlers, charioteers, and *pankratists* (freestyle fighters)—who were frequently maimed or killed—the athletes had it easy compared to the attendees. The climate was hot and sticky, without even a permanent water source for most of the ancient Olympic era (a rich guy finally built an aqueduct). Deaths from sunstroke weren't rare. Sanitation? Most people had no way to bathe, so everyone stank, and disease ran rampant.

Married women couldn't attend, except female racing-chariot owners. The only other exception was a priestess of Demeter, who had her own special seat. Unmarried girls and women, especially prostitutes, were welcome. According to historians and pottery depictions, athletes competed nude, so there was no chance a woman could infiltrate as a competitor.

An Endurance Event for All

For five days every four years, Olympia combined the features of church, carnival, track meet, martial arts, banquet, racing, bachelor party, brothel, and tourist trap into a Woodstock-like scene of organized bedlam. The Olympics weren't merely to be watched or even experienced. They were to be endured and survived.

In A.D. 393, Roman Emperor Theodosius I, a first-rank killjoy, banned all pagan ceremonies. Since the Games' central ritual was a big sacrifice to Zeus, this huge heathen debauch clearly had to go.

The party was over. It wouldn't start again until 1859.

Mythology & Folklore
Muse of the Nursery

❖ ❖ ❖ ❖

There was an old lady,
With the name Mother Goose.
She told children stories,
Could she just be a ruse?
Did she really exist?
That legend of old,
The elderly storyteller,
Of whom we were told?
You'll have to read on,
To discover the truth.
To tell you right here,
Would be rather uncouth.

Whether it's the Muffin Man, the Farmer in the Dell, or Humpty Dumpty, Mother Goose has rhymes for them all. While collections of these nursery rhymes bear the name Mother Goose and the illustration of an old peasant woman, most of the so-called Mother Goose tales originated centuries ago as folktales and legends handed down from generation to generation. Mothers would comfort their young children by singing rhyming verses to the tunes of ballads and folk songs.

Many have tried to track down the identity of the real Mother Goose, but she is, in fact, a mythical character. The earliest written reference to Mother Goose appeared in a poem titled *La Muse Historique* in a 1660s issue of French critic Jean Loret's monthly periodical. Loret wrote, *"... comme un conte de la Mère Oye,"* which translated means "...like a Mother Goose story."

Charles Perrault, who served on the staff of King Louis XIV, was the first author to use the name Mother Goose in the title of a

book. In 1697, Perrault published a collection of children's stories titled *Histoires ou Contes du temps passe* ("Histories or Tales from the Past with Morals"). The frontispiece carried the subtitle, *Contes de ma mère l'Oye* ("Tales from My Mother Goose"). On the book's cover was an illustration of an old woman telling stories to a group of children. The book contained a compilation of eight folktales, including Sleeping Beauty, Cinderella, Little Red Riding Hood, and Puss in Boots.

It took more than 30 years for Mother Goose to make her debut in English. In 1729, writer Robert Samber translated Perrault's book into English under the title, *Histories or Tales of Past Times, Told by Mother Goose.*

London bookseller John Newbery had published a collection of nursery rhymes in 1744. In 1765, he incorporated the name Mother Goose when he published *Mother Goose's Melody, or Sonnets for the Cradle.* Newbery's book contained more than 50 rhymes and songs and marked a shift in the subject of children's books from fairy tales to nursery rhymes.

Mother Goose made her first appearance in America in 1786, when Massachusetts printer Isaiah Thomas reprinted Robert Samber's book using the same title. Over the course of 14 years, Thomas's version of the book was reprinted three times.

It was in America that Mother Goose would take hold as the keeper of nursery rhymes. In the early 19th century, she became even more popular when Boston-based Munroe & Francis began printing inexpensive and lavish Mother Goose editions. Since then, numerous collections and editions of Mother Goose stories have been published.

Regardless of whether the original Mother Goose was an actual person, she is real in the minds of many infants and young children. The rhythms, alliteration, and silly stories found in the Mother Goose tales have entranced children for centuries; and as long as there are babies to sing to, they will no doubt continue to do so. As the old storyteller said in the preface of the 1843 edition of the book *The Only True Mother Goose Melodies:*

"My Melodies will never die,
While nurses sing, or babies cry."

Places & Landmarks
Forget Getting In: Studio 54

❖ ❖ ❖ ❖

*It was the ultimate disco pleasure palace, though its heyday
lasted only a few years. If you want to understand disco, then
you first need to understand the nightclub called "Studio."*

Pre-function

It began with an odd couple: Steve Rubell and Ian Schrager, New
Yorkers and friends from college. Rubell was loud and outgoing,
Schrager quiet and businesslike. They ran steakhouses in the NYC
metro area, but they wanted to operate at the top of the Big Apple's
food chain: Manhattan. They teamed with young Peruvian party
promoter Carmen d'Alessio, who would handle PR.

At 254 W 54th St., Manhattan, stood an old CBS TV studio.
Rubell and Schrager leased it and started costly, rococo renovations,
complete with a huge man-in-the-moon that had a hanging spoon
rising up to his nose. One could hardly find a more obvious way to
say "Inhale Cocaine Here." From the address and the building's history came the logical if unimaginative name: Studio 54. It was a big
place, larger than a football field. It would need to be.

Party On

Opening Night was April 26, 1977. In those days, New York normally
reacted to new discos like husbands react to their wives' new shoes:
That's nice, hon; is there any pizza left? But hundreds could smell
the hedonism in the Manhattan air. For most commoners, that was
as much of Studio 54 as they would snort that night.

A young employee, Joanne Horowitz, had convinced Rubell she
could lure some glitterati. Note to world: Joanne can deliver. The
early opening hours were slow, but soon a platoon of celebrities
came: Margaux Hemingway, Mick and Bianca Jagger, Salvador Dali,
Donald and Ivana Trump, Brooke Shields, Cher, and more. Frank
Sinatra, Henry Winkler, and Warren Beatty didn't get in—nor did
most of the throng waiting outside. The doorman, 19-year-old Marc
Benecke, was the most envied college kid in town.

Studio became *the* place—to which you could only hope to gain entrance. Rubell decided who got in, using criteria only he comprehended. Unless you were a major celebrity, or lucky, you didn't. Behind the doors, nearly anything went. Studio served alcohol, naturally, but others inside dished cocaine, Quaaludes (Rubell's favorite appetizer), and similarly illicit party favors. Nudity and open sexual activity—straight, bi, or gay—were common.

Hungover and Throwing Up

Incredibly, Rubell was operating on one-day caterers' permits rather than a liquor license. Three weeks after opening, the liquor authorities simply denied the daily permit and sent a police raid. (*They* got in.) Studio spent five months as a disco juice bar until the license affair was straightened out, but the club didn't lose its mojo.

Rubell should have left the PR to d'Alessio. In late 1978, he bragged to the papers that Studio had made about $7 million the previous year, asserting that only the Mafia made more. Might as well rename Studio "Audit 54." On December 14, 1978, the IRS showed up. The very walls were stuffed with cash, and the safe yielded detailed incriminating records. As for drugs, any investigator incapable of finding those in Studio would have been hopeless.

After a lengthy investigation, Rubell and Schrager were charged with tax evasion, skimming, and more in June 1979. Studio threw one last wingding on February 4, 1980, before their jail time began.

Rehab

From jail, the partners sold Studio. At this writing:

Studio 54 is a sometime theater and nightclub.

Joanne Horowitz manages actor Kevin Spacey.

Carmen d'Alessio runs a club in Lima, Peru.

Marc Benecke is a real estate broker.

Released after 13 months in the lockup, Schrager and Rubell went into the hotel business together. Ian Schrager remains a very successful hotelier, though as of April 2009, he was facing financial troubles at at least one of his establishments.

In 1985, Rubell tested HIV positive but didn't take care of himself. He died July 25, 1989, with the official cause listed as hepatitis. He was 45.

Inventions
Who Invented the Printing Press?

❖ ❖ ❖ ❖

*Sure, Johannes Gutenberg's development of the printing press
in 15th-century Germany led to mass-market publishing.
But innovations in printing technology were around
long before Gutenberg revolutionized the industry.*

The Stamp of Uniformity

Although printing is usually associated with reading materials, the original impetus behind printing technology was the need to create identical copies of the same thing. Printing actually began with coining, when centralized states branded their coins with uniform numbers and symbols. In those days, written manuscripts were copied the old-fashioned way, letter by letter, by hand. Only the upper echelons of society were literate, books were costly, and the laborious and artistic method of copying matched the rarity of books.

The first major innovation in printing came with the Chinese invention of block printing by the eighth century A.D. Block printing involved carving letters or images into a surface, inking that surface, and pressing it on to paper, parchment, or cloth. The method was used for a variety of purposes, from decorating clothes to copying religious scrolls. The blocks were usually made of wood, which posed a problem as the wood eventually decayed or cracked. Oftentimes entire pages of a manuscript, complete with illustrations, were carved into a single block that could be used again and again.

The Chinese also invented movable type, which would prove to be the prerequisite to efficient printing presses. Movable type is faster than block printing because individual characters, usually letters or punctuation, are created by being cast into molds. Once this grab bag of individual characters is made, they can then be reused and rearranged in infinite combinations by changing the typeset. Movable type characters are also more uniform than the carved letters of block printing. Pi-Sheng invented this method in 1045 using clay molds. The method spread to Korea and Japan, and metal movable type was created in Korea by 1230.

Supply and Demand

The Chinese didn't use movable type extensively because their language consists of thousands of characters, and movable type makes printing efficient only in a language with fewer letters, like the English alphabet's 26. Meanwhile, Europeans used the imported concept of block printing to make popular objects like playing cards or illustrated children's books. During the Middle Ages, serious secular scholarship had all but disappeared in Europe, and the reproduction of new and classical texts was mostly confined to the Asian and Arab worlds.

That is, until literacy began to spread among the middle classes, and lay people, especially in Germany, showed an interest in reading religious texts for themselves. Thus, German entrepreneur Johannes Gutenberg, the son of a coin minter, began to experiment with metal movable type pieces. It's believed Gutenberg was unfamiliar with the previously invented Chinese method, but at any rate, several other Europeans were experimenting with similar methods at the same time as Gutenberg.

By the 1440s, Gutenberg had set up a printing shop in Mainz, Germany, and in 1450, he set out to produce a Bible. Gutenberg perfected several printing methods, such as right justification, and preferred alloys in the production of metal types. By 1455, Gutenberg's press had produced 200 copies of his Bible—quite the feat at the time, considering one Bible could take years to copy by hand. These Bibles were sold for less than hand-copied ones yet were still expensive enough for profit margins equivalent to modern-day millions.

Presses soon popped up all across Europe. By 1499, an estimated 15 million books had been produced by at least 1,000 printing presses, mostly in Germany and then throughout Italy. For the first time ever, ideas were not only dreamed up and written down—they were efficiently reproduced and spread over long distances. The proliferation of these first German printing presses is commonly credited with the end of the Middle Ages and the dawn of the Renaissance.

Holidays & Traditions
Where Did the U.S. Flag Salute Begin?

❖ ❖ ❖ ❖

The Salute began along with the Pledge of Allegiance.
Was it developed by the D.A.R. to make patriotic hearts
swell with pride? Nah. Truth being stranger than fiction,
it started as a magazine's marketing gimmick.

The Youth's Companion

From 1827 through 1929 (yes, 102 years), a magazine called *The Youth's Companion (TYC)* saw print. Somewhat similar to today's *Reader's Digest, TYC* meant to reinforce wholesome values like conformity, patriotism, and Christianity.

TYC used premium incentives to build its subscriber base. Here's how: Suppose your daughter sold subscriptions. If she sold a few, she could earn a watch; if she sold more, she could get a sewing machine, maybe even a piano. This brilliant scheme turned young customers into energetic salespeople and helps explain why half a million U.S. households took *TYC*—thus putting them squarely in the path of any new marketing pitch the magazine might try.

Francis Bellamy

Reverend Francis Bellamy, the Salute's actual author, was an interesting fellow: a Freemason, a Baptist minister, and a Christian Socialist. A lot of modern Masons, Baptists, ministers, Christians, and socialists might find the combination odd, but Bellamy didn't. Even Masonic Baptist Christian Socialists have to make a living, and in the 1890s, Bellamy got a job in *TYC's* premium department. That department's boss, James Upham, would play a key role in how the rest of the story played out.

His Salute

TYC advanced the view that all schools should fly the U.S. flag. Naturally, the magazine sold flags. The premium department hit on the idea of sending schoolchildren flag cards, each to be sold for a

dime apiece and representing 1 percent of a school flag. Sell a hundred cards, get your school a flag! Then Upham thought: *What if we came up with something for kids to actually do with the flag besides just fly it—perhaps say a daily salute and loyalty oath?* He tasked Bellamy with inventing a pledge and salute.

The Bellamy Salute, as historians now call it, began with a military salute: right hand touching forehead, palm down. Where they said ". . . to my Flag," the kids extended the arm gracefully toward the Colors. Of course, careful readers have noticed an oddity in that wording. In 1923, to thwart immigrants from the verbal equivalent of crossing their fingers during the Pledge, the National Flag Conference changed ". . . to my Flag" (which might as well refer to Denmark's or Italy's) to ". . . to the Flag of the United States of America . . ." The hand now began over the heart but still extended at the correct time. Bellamy complained but to no avail.

There were, of course, local variations on the Salute. Not everyone adopted the 1923 changes or even had a flag salute or flag. Some never extended the arm to begin with.

Achtung!

TYC merged with another youth magazine in 1929. Bellamy died in 1931, never living to see Germany dominated by fascist racists usurping his salute. The Nazi-sympathizing German-American Bund quickly noticed that they could salute the U.S. flag and that of Adolf's Third Reich with the same motion. As early as 1935, Americans—having seen newsreel footage of vast Nazi rallies—expressed discomfort with the similarity. In 1939, Hitler went to war with Poland, France, and Britain; the United States remained neutral.

By 1942, the United States was at war with Germany. Even though the U.S. usage of the Salute predated Hitler's by 30 years, it still looked lousy for American schoolkids to start class each day looking like a Reichstag session. That year, Congress formally enacted the Salute we know today: hand over the heart.

Museums
Treasures of an Empire

❖ ❖ ❖ ❖

A product of the Age of Enlightenment, London's British Museum carved a new path in the diffusion of human knowledge when it opened to the public in 1759.

It took the death of an obscure British physician, Sir Henry Sloane, to launch the world's first public museum. In his will, Sloane left a collection of some 71,000 natural and historical objects to the United Kingdom in return for a £20,000 stipend for his heirs.

Britain's King George II expressed little interest in the purchase of oddities and miscellanea, but far-sighted members of Parliament moved to accept Sloane's posthumous deal. An Act of Parliament dated June 7, 1753, accepted the bequest and established a lottery to raise funds for the purchase and maintenance of the Sloane collection, as well as other items left to the king and country by wealthy collectors.

The collection originally consisted of three groups: Printed Books, Manuscripts (including medals), and "Natural and Artificial Productions," which included everything else. It slowly grew as George II contributed the Old Royal Library—rare works owned by Britannia's sovereigns. But the British Museum's place in world history was secured on January 15, 1759, when the museum opened its doors to "all studious and curious Persons" free of charge. Great Britain had founded the world's first public museum.

As the sun rose over the British Empire, the museum naturally benefited from exotic artifacts acquired from other lands by explorers, merchants, and generals. Classical sculptures from long-gone civilizations became a central feature of the growing museum, and before long, the 17th-century mansion in which the collection was housed had to make way for a larger building. Between 1823 and 1857, the space around the old museum was rebuilt to accommodate a growing collection, as well as the throngs of ordinary citizens who came to see what the empire had collected.

In the early 19th century, the British Museum's curators embarked on a project that today would be called "public outreach."

They scheduled public lectures, improved displays for visitors, and published a Synopsis, or museum guidebook, that ran to 60 editions before the end of the century. The museum also sponsored excavation projects abroad, and many treasures uncovered in these digs were sent to the museum.

The August 1939 Nazi-Soviet pact shook up British authorities, who decided to disperse much of the museum's collection among safer locations. Their precautions were warranted, as the museum was damaged by German incendiary bombs during the 1940–41 Blitz of London. Fortunately, Britain's most important treasures remained untouched and were repatriated when the war ended.

The postwar years marked a renewed effort to make the museum's holdings accessible and enjoyable to the public. The 1972 exhibition "Treasures of Tutankhamun" drew more than 1.6 million visitors to the museum and became the museum's most successful exhibit of all time. Since then, the museum has promoted temporary exhibits as well as traveling exhibitions spanning the globe.

Today, some five million visitors a year tour the astonishingly varied collection of art and artifacts, which totals some 13 million objects. At the British Museum, tourists can find highlights of the collection, such as the Rosetta Stone; the Elgin Marbles, ancient statues that graced the pediments of the Athenian Parthenon; Michelangelo's sketch *The Fall of Phaeton;* the earliest surviving copy of *Beowulf;* and a colossal bust of Egyptian Pharaoh Ramses II. The world's first public museum is a fitting capstone to the empire that built it.

Clubs & Organizations
Mailing It In Since 1775: The U.S. Postal Service

❖ ❖ ❖ ❖

*Endemic griping aside, the U.S. mail system has
long been one of the best of its kind. Here is where
it came from, and what it's gotten up to.*

Pre-Revolution

The first organized postal service between Britain and its American colonies began in 1639. Over the next 135 years, the colonials
cemented core American traditions: taking the P.O. for granted,
complaining about its pricing, and underrating its efficiency. By
1774, though, slow mail was the least of the Colonials' beefs with the
British. Not even an ultra-cheap tea offer had placated them; the
audacious rascals had gotten drunk and turned Boston Harbor into
the Sea of Tea in 1773. The British were flummoxed.

Much to the annoyance of Philadelphia publisher William Goddard, that year the British post office halted delivery of his newspaper, which advocated rebellion against British rule. Goddard was
out of business for the moment, but he got back at King George III
in good time. He began designing a colonial postal service and presented it to the Continental Congress on October 5, 1774.

In the finest American political tradition, Congress took no
immediate action.

Stirrings of War

It soon became evident that the Colonies might tell King George to
go pound crumpets. His Majesty would probably not comply; more
likely it would mean war, in which case the Continentals would need
messengers to coordinate struggle from Florida to Maine. If the
rebellion won independence, that messenger service would give the
citizenry a way to continue the postal whining tradition. Win-win-
win. Congress: "Maybe the time for Goddard's ideas has come."

On July 26, 1775, the Second Continental Congress formed the
Constitutional Post, appointing Benjamin Franklin postmaster-

general. His salary was $1,000 per year. (If you calculate that today using the unskilled wage index method, it's just shy of $500,000, so wise Ben wasn't working on charity.) The appointment made sense. Due to Franklin's seditious activities, the Crown had recently canned him as its colonial postmaster—a post he had held nearly 40 years, so he was highly qualified (and looking for work).

Heard 'Round the World

The war raged from 1775 to 1783. Franklin's couriers assisted the war effort from start to finish. Without them, the Continentals might have lost.

In 1792, the Postal Act turned the Constitutional Post into the Post Office Department (POD). It would keep that name for 179 years. (The organization didn't gain its current name, The United States Postal Service, until 1971.) The Act laid down some principles we now take for granted. Printed matter, necessary to the exchange of ideas, would qualify for cheaper postage. And the POD was forbidden to open any deliverable mail item—no snooping!

Modernization

As the nation expanded, the POD would proactively extend its reach to far-flung areas. In 1847, it issued the first U.S. postage stamps, making it easier for the sender to prepay. Lights sparkled in the eyes of future junk-mailers. By 1855, prepayment was required. The famed Pony Express was a brief but essential phase between 1860 and 1861, speeding delivery to the far West before railroads antiquated riders. Parcel Post came in 1913, Airmail in 1918.

Through it all, Americans were fortunate to have one of the better postal systems on Earth. But the indomitable American spirit has never been deterred by facts. The people clung tenaciously to cherished freedoms: cussing the post office and kvetching about postage rates. We're proud to confirm that these ancient rituals thrive well into America's third century.

Interesting fact: The USPS has tried nearly every imaginable conveyance, including mail missiles (which bombed, so to speak). The oddest USPS delivery today must surely be the mule train that delivers life's necessities five days a week to Havasupai Native Americans in Supai, Arizona, under the Grand Canyon's south rim.

BIRTHPLACES OF THE RICH AND FAMOUS

Was someone famous born in your hometown?

Two influential actors from the 1950s, Marlon Brando and Montgomery Clift, were famous for their intensity. Both were born in Omaha, Nebraska. Nick Nolte, an intense and serious actor from a later generation, was also born in Omaha.

Singer-songwriter John Denver wrote lyrics about West Virginia and Colorado, but he was born in alien-infested Roswell, New Mexico.

Newark, New Jersey, is the birthplace of several famous writers, including novelists Philip Roth and Stephen Crane, poet Allen Ginsberg, and journalist Albert Payson Terhune.

Jon Bon Jovi rocked his hometown of Perth Amboy, New Jersey, while Bruce Springsteen raised the roof in nearby Freehold.

Many important screen actors have hailed from the heartland of Ohio. Cowboy hero Hopalong Cassidy was born in Cambridge, and pioneering African American actresses Dorothy Dandridge and Ruby Dee were born in Cleveland, as was movie star Paul Newman. The actress who helped develop acting for the big screen, Lillian Gish, was born in Springfield. Glamorous Golden Age stars Tyrone Power and Clark Gable were born in Cincinnati and Cadiz, respectively.

Beloved Golden Age movie star Jimmy Stewart was born in Indiana, Pennsylvania.

Vanna White learned her alphabet in North Myrtle Beach, South Carolina.

Several Native Americans who gave the U.S. Army a run for its money during the Indian Wars of the Old West were born in South Dakota. But when it was their land, Sioux chiefs Crazy Horse, Rain-in-the-Face, Red Cloud, and Sitting Bull had other names for it.

Tennessee has given birth to many creative people, including actors Morgan Freeman and Cybil Shepherd from Memphis. However, Tennessee hosts two music capitals, Memphis and Nashville, so most artists who hailed from this state have been singers and musicians, including

Aretha Franklin of Memphis, Eddy Arnold from Henderson, Chet Atkins from Lutrell, Isaac Hayes from Covington, Dolly Parton from Sevier County, Minnie Pearl from Centerville, Dinah Shore from Winchester, and Tina Turner from Brownsville.

From deep in the heart of Texas come bluesman Stevie Ray Vaughn of Dallas, choreographer Alvin Ailey of Rogers, cowboy singer Gene Autry of Tioga, comedienne Carol Burnett and movie star Joan Crawford of San Antonio, multimillionaire Howard Hughes of Houston, movie star Cyd Charisse of Amarillo, country singer George Jones of Saratoga, rocker Janis Joplin of Port Arthur, actor Tommy Lee Jones of San Saba, country rebel Willie Nelson of Abbot, and journalist Dan Rather of Wharton.

The proliferating Osmond family, including Donny and Marie, hails from Ogden, Utah.

Brother and sister Warren Beatty and Shirley MacLaine were born in Richmond, Virginia.

Legendary grunge-rock guitarist and singer Kurt Cobain was from Aberdeen, Washington.

What do magician Harry Houdini and actor Willem Dafoe have in common? Both were born in tiny Appleton, Wisconsin.

Flashy Liberace, the king of Las Vegas glitter and glamour, was born in low-key West Allis, Wisconsin.

The stars of the blockbuster *Pirates of the Caribbean* series come from both sides of the world: Johnny Depp calls Owensboro, Kentucky, his hometown; Orlando Jonathan Blanchard Bloom was born in Canterbury, England; and Keira Knightley is from London, England.

"A celebrity is a person who works hard all his life to become well known, then wears dark glasses to avoid being recognized."
—FRED ALLEN, COMEDIAN

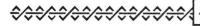 

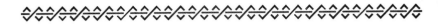

Food & Drink
The Green Fairy

✦ ✦ ✦ ✦

*Few alcoholic beverages have the mythic cache of absinthe, a
notorious liqueur associated with Bohemian Paris during the
Belle Époque. Legendary for its supposed hallucinogenic and
addictive effects, absinthe was blamed for making strong men
sterile, turning good girls bad, and leading nice people to murder.*

Absinthe was an aperitif made from alcohol and distilled herbs, particularly grand wormwood, green anise, petite wormwood, fennel,
and hyssop. It was the wormwood that supposedly gave absinthe its
narcotic and addictive properties, though some claim that the high
alcohol content (at 140 to 160 proof) was partially to blame. Gentle
heating of the herbs during the production process caused the tell-
tale green color. The coloring combined with the liqueur's seductive,
intoxicating power gave absinthe its nickname, the Green Fairy.

Because absinthe is bitter to the taste, the accepted method of
consumption was to place a lump of sugar on a perforated flat spoon
and rest it on the rim of the glass filled with alcohol. Iced water was
slowly poured over the lump of the sugar, and the sweet water was
allowed to drip into the drink. The weakening of the alcohol via the
sugar water turned the drink a milky opaque color.

Dr. Pierre Ordinaire
The origins of absinthe can be traced to the region near Couvet
in Switzerland and to the Doubs region of France. Supposedly
Dr. Pierre Ordinaire developed the drink around 1792 to use
for medicinal purposes, and his original formula ended up in the
hands of the Henriod sisters. Major Henri Dubied purchased the
formula from the sisters in the early 1800s to manufacture absinthe
as an aperitif: a drink designed to stimulate the taste buds and the
stomach before a meal. But, the origins of the story have been
embellished over the years into an offbeat tale of an eccentric doctor
and his peculiar elixir. Evidence indicates that an absinthelike drink
was made in the Neuchatel region during the 1750s, which means

Ordinaire did not invent it. It is likely the doctor simply picked up the method of making the drink and then sold it as a cure-all to make some extra money.

Production began in earnest in 1805 when the Pernod Fils distillery was established in Pontarlier in Doubs by the Major's son-in-law, Henri-Louis Pernod. By the time Pernod's grandsons were running the company, it was one of the largest and most successful businesses in France. The popularity of absinthe increased after the French troops used it as a fever preventative while fighting in Algeria. By the time the soldiers returned home, they had developed a taste for the Green Fairy.

During the reign of Napoleon III (1852–1870), absinthe was the preferred drink of the bourgeoisie, who used it as an aperitif. When licensing laws were relaxed during the 1860s, thousand of bars and restaurants opened, launching a café culture that defined Paris for decades. Absinthe was so popular that each café hosted a daily "l'Heure Verte," or Green Hour, at 5:00 P.M.

La Vie Bohème

The cafés of Montmartre attracted a highly creative and unconventional literary and artistic crowd; they romanticized the Green Fairy in their poems, novels, and paintings. From Edgar Degas's painting *L'Absinthe* to Marcel Pagnol's poem "The Time of Secrets" to Pablo Picasso's *Woman Drinking Absinthe,* the liqueur became legendary as a symbol of *la vie bohème* ("the bohemian life").

Absinthe use peaked in Europe from 1880 to 1910, and it became popular in America during the 1890s. However, a series of high-profile murders among the middle class in Europe were blamed on absinthe drinking, leading several countries to ban it. In 1905, Swiss family man Jean Lanfray drank two absinthes and then killed his pregnant wife and two children. Three years later, a man named Saliaz binged on absinthe and then chopped his wife into bits. Absinthe was outlawed in Belgium, Switzerland, the United States, and finally in 1915, it was banned in France. But no worries—many countries have since lifted their bans. The Green Fairy dances again.

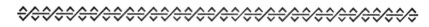

Music
Six Strings of Electricity

❖ ❖ ❖ ❖

What if Chuck Berry's "Johnny B. Goode" hadn't been so good?
Or if David Bowie's "Ziggy Stardust" actually played violin? For
that matter, what if Stardust inspiration Jimi Hendrix had to play
an acoustic set at Woodstock? Certainly, life would have been
different had it not been for the advent of the electric guitar.

Rock 'n' roll may never have evolved had it not been for early jazz
guitarists in the 1930s who began to "mic" their hollow-bodied
instruments to get a louder sound while playing in larger bands.
Eventually, instead of merely placing a microphone next to the
guitar, the musicians would place smaller microphones, called *pick-*
ups, within the guitar. And this is how traditional "acoustic" instruments got electrified.

The earliest electric guitars were designed by a variety of musical
instrument manufacturers, musicians, and even electricians. Several
major guitar makers that exist today were born of the same innovation. Adolph Rickenbacker and George Beauchamp helped devise
the first Rickenbacker guitars, which were essentially hollow-bodied
acoustic instruments.

One of the first solid guitars was a cast aluminum electric steel
guitar that was nicknamed the "Frying Pan" or the "Pancake Guitar,"
but the sound it created was far from ideal. A better substance was
needed to create a better sound, and thus, the solid wood guitar was
born.

Jazz guitarist and musical innovator Les Paul successfully
invented a solid-body electric guitar in the early 1940s, but it was
Leo Fender who can take credit for introducing the first commercially successful guitar in 1946. Originally known as the Broadcaster,
the guitar would become legendary as the Fender Telecaster. Les
Paul's legend lives on in the form of the Gibson Les Paul, a solid-
body guitar designed by Ted McCarty but endorsed and used by
Paul. Today, these are among the most popular guitars in rock music.

Holidays & Traditions
Don't Sing Too Loudly!

❖ ❖ ❖ ❖

Many people believe that "Happy Birthday to You"—the most
frequently sung song in the English language—is a traditional
folk melody that rests comfortably in the public domain.
In fact, the song is protected by strict copyright laws.

That four-line ditty is as synonymous with birthday celebrations as
a cake full of candles. According to the *Guinness Book of World
Records,* the most popular song in the English language is "Happy
Birthday to You." What is less well known, however, is that it is not
a simple tune in the public domain, free for the singing by anyone
who chooses. It's actually protected by a stringent copyright that is
owned and actively enforced by the media conglomerate AOL Time
Warner. You are legally safe to sing the song at home, but doing so in
public is technically a breach of copyright, unless you have obtained
a license from the copyright holder or the American Society of Composers, Authors, and Publishers.

The popular seven-note melody was penned in 1893 by two
sisters, Mildred J. Hill and Patty Smith Hill, as a song titled "Good
Morning to All." It remains unclear who revised the words, but a
third Hill sister, Jessica, secured copyright to the song in 1935. This
copyright should have expired in 1991, but through a number of
revisions to copyright law, it has been extended until at least 2030
and now lies in the hands of AOL Time Warner. The company earns
more than $2 million a year from the song, primarily for its use in
movies and TV shows. Because licensing the rights to the song is
a costly endeavor, low-budget movies have to cut around birthday
scenes, and many popular chain restaurants insist that their employees sing alternate songs to celebrate their customers' birthdays.

Unless you license the rights, singing the song in public could
result in something decidedly unhappy. And if you're going to be
arrested on your birthday, don't you want it to be for something
more exciting than copyright infringement?

Index

❖ ❖ ❖ ❖

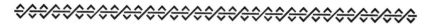

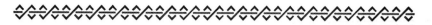

I

J

K

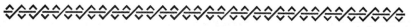

Verlaine, Tom, 235
Very Frightful Life of the Grand Gargantua, The (Rabelais), 82
Viagra *(sildenafil)*, 116
Video games, 238–39
Videotape, 452
Vinci-Heldt, Margaret, 182
"Vision of Piers Plowman, The" (Langland), 98
Visual art, 37, 68–69, 336–37, 399–01
Voight, Angelina Jolie, 117
Voight, Jon, 117
Vonnegut, Kurt, 122
Vyse, Stuart, 131

W

Waffles, 346
Wait, Pearl B., 196
Wakefield, Ruth, 291
Wakefield, Tim, 167
Walling, William English, 385
Wang, An, 287
War and military
 Area 51, 137
 biological and chemical warfare, 431–33
 chain mail armor, 364
 military slang, 366–67
 Molotov cocktails, 41
 Pearl Harbor attack, 221
 thumbs-up gesture, 64
Warner, Ezra, 20
Warren, Earl, 149
Washing machines, 279
Washington, George, 247
Washington Monument, 428–30
Watch Night (New Year's Eve), 78–79
Waterbeds, 130
Waterman, Lewis, 200
Watson, Thomas Jr., 259
Watson, Thomas J. Sr., 258–59
Wax museums, 418–19
Wedding rings, 124–25
Wegener, Alfred, 162–63
Weishaupt, Adam, 276–78
Wertheimer, Adolf, 365
Wesley, John, 78

Westinghouse, George, 113, 398
Wham-O, 165
Wharton, John, 83
Wheels, 375
Whittier, John Greenleaf, 447
Wicca, 132–33
Williams, Hank, 109
Williams, T. L., 36
Wilson, Samuel, 371
Wilson, Woodrow, 95, 247, 320–21
Winthrop, John, 63
Wolfe, Thomas, 255
Woman's Christian Temperance Union (WCTU), 424
Wonder Woman, 141
Woodward, Orator Frank, 196
World War II, 64, 398
Wright, James, 464
Wright brothers, 295
Written word
 comic books, 140–41
 "dark and stormy night," 272
 epitaphs, 108–09
 Mad magazine, 33, 456–57
 Oxford English Dictionary, 232–33
Wynne, Arthur, 112

Y

Yamazaki, Shunpei, 357
Yarborough, Cale, 81
Yarnell, Harry, 221
Young, Brigham, 208–209
Young, John, 405
Yo-yos, 303
Yuppie (word), 120
Yuppie Handbook, The, 120

Z

Zamboni, Frank Joseph Jr., 101
Zamboni machines, 101
Zamenhof, Ludwik L., 299–300
Zero, 328–329
Zoot suits, 376–377
Zugsmith, Albert, 49

Contributing Writers

Jeff Bahr: From laboratory technician to motorcycle journalist and author, a long, strange road led this "hired pen" to the *Armchair Reader™* series. *Origins of Everything* showed the unlikely author that he wasn't the first "earth object" to follow a divinely convoluted path.

Patricia Barnes-Svarney's origins go back to the Big Bang; thus, in a convoluted way, she is a distant cousin to Alexander the Great and maybe even Donald Trump. She prides herself on the fact that she can't be pigeonholed: Her more than 30 published books (some award-winning) and hundreds of magazine articles cover science, science fiction and fantasy, and humor—for adults and middle readers.

Susan Doll teaches cinema and pop culture studies at Oakton Community College in addition to writing and consulting on projects related to film, art, and history. She is also the author of several books, including *Elvis for Dummies, Florida on Film, Elvis: Forever in the Groove, Understanding Elvis,* and *Marilyn: Her Life and Legend.*

Katherine Don is a freelance writer who hails from a Chicago suburb and currently lives in New York City. When not typing away on her trusty Macbook, she volunteers for nonprofit organizations that deal with health-care and penal-system reform, and researches for her book-in-progress. She is currently a graduate student at New York University's program in literary journalism.

James Duplacey is an author and sports historian who has written more than 60 books on sports, culture, and entertainment. An avid fan of baseball, literature, film, and all things jazz, he originated in Moncton, New Brunswick, and is currently residing in the home of the Calgary Stampede on the vast prairie flatlands of Alberta, Canada.

J. K. Kelley has a B.A. in history from the University of Washington in Seattle. Thus far he has contributed to seven *Armchair Reader™* books. He resides in the desiccated sagebrush of eastern Washington with his wife Deb, his parrot Alex, Fabius the Labrador Retriever, and Leonidas the miniature Schnauzer. His love of writing originated with a mom who had him reading the whole encyclopedia—for fun—before he went to kindergarten.

David Morrow is an accomplished writer and editor who has worked in the publishing industry for more than 20 years. His recent work includes co-authoring *Florida on Film* and contributing to the reference guide *Disasters, Accidents, and Crises in American History.*

Donald Vaughan originated on January 11, 1958. Since then, he has worked as a staff writer and editor and also as a freelance writer for an eclectic array of publications, including *MAD* magazine, *The Weekly World News, Military Officer Magazine,* and *Nursing Spectrum.* Donald is also the founder of Triangle Area Freelancers. He lives in Raleigh, North Carolina, with his wife, Nanette, and their very spoiled cat, Rhianna.